"In *Dangerously Bound*, Eden Bra... tale of second chances and dark ye... love's shadowed edges. Mick is a hero to inspire wicked dreams, while Allie is a strong woman who is not afraid to admit to a fascination for dominance and submission. I enjoyed every luscious word!"
—Angela Knight, *New York Times* bestselling author

PRAISE FOR THE NOVELS OF EDEN BRADLEY

"Intelligent, haunting and sexy as hell . . . for you people who like story and heart with your erotica, I'd definitely recommend any of Eden's books."
—Maya Banks, #1 *New York Times* bestselling author

"Honest, tender and totally sexy—a feast for the senses and the heart."　　　　—Shayla Black, *USA Today* bestselling author

"Brilliant, seductive and dangerous. All of my favorite things."
—R. G. Alexander, author of *Tempt Me*

"A hot and steamy ride to the climactic end . . . This story will steam up your glasses."　　　　—*Library Journal*

"An exciting, erotic page-turner that does not disappoint . . . Ms. Bradley's wonderful storytelling ability and knack for description transport you right into the story and hold you there until the very last page."　　　　—*Night Owl Reviews*

continued . . .

"Graphic, loving and incredibly well written, the sex scenes ratchet up the drama with unbelievable intensity . . . Sexual desire intertwines with emotional intensity, resulting in a book you won't want to put down."   —*Romance Junkies*

"Bradley delivers the goods. There is intense intimacy and heart-wrenching emotions . . . This is delicious and delightful from the first page until the conclusion."   —*RT Book Reviews*

"Eden Bradley is an incredible author who writes scorching-hot love scenes with characters who are very memorable and so very well written."   —*Fallen Angel Reviews*

"Eden Bradley knows how to heat up the pages in a hurry. She creates sexual tension and love scenes that will get your heart racing. But she also creates characters that are realistic and fun to read."   —*Fiction Vixen*

"Eden Bradley has a knack for penning extraordinary erotic romances."   —*Wild on Books*

"Dark and seductive; it left me breathless and eager for more. I loved it!"   —*My Secret Romance Book Reviews*

"Highly erotic and sensual."   —*Under the Covers*

Titles by Eden Bradley

DANGEROUSLY BOUND

Writing as Eve Berlin

PLEASURE'S EDGE
DESIRE'S EDGE
TEMPTATION'S EDGE

Anthologies

EXCLUSIVE
(with Jaci Burton and Lisa Renee Jones)

DANGEROUSLY
Bound

EDEN BRADLEY

BERKLEY BOOKS, NEW YORK

THE BERKLEY PUBLISHING GROUP
Published by the Penguin Group
Penguin Group (USA) LLC
375 Hudson Street, New York, New York 10014

USA • Canada • UK • Ireland • Australia • New Zealand • India • South Africa • China

penguin.com

A Penguin Random House Company

This book is an original publication of The Berkley Publishing Group.

Library of Congress Cataloging-in-Publication Data

Bradley, Eden.
Dangerously Bound / Eden Bradley.
pages cm. — (A dangerous romance ; 1)
ISBN 978-0-425-26962-6 (paperback)
1. Sadomasochism—Fiction.   2. Bondage (Sexual behavior)—Fiction.   3. Erotic fiction.   I. Title.
PS3602.R34266D34 2014
813'.6—dc23   2013051060

PUBLISHING HISTORY
Berkley trade paperback edition / April 2014

PRINTED IN THE UNITED STATES OF AMERICA

10 9 8 7 6 5 4 3 2 1

Cover photo of Rope by Phil Cawley/Alamy; Wrought Iron by Purestock/Getty.
Cover design by Judith Lagerman.
Interior text design by Tiffany Estreicher.

ACKNOWLEDGMENTS

To Dawn, for being the most amazing beta reader ever, and brainstorming this story with me!

To Sidney Bristol, for cheerfully getting down on the floor to demonstrate the viability of a certain hog-tie. The first dungeon scene in this book only happened the way it did because you were such a willing coconspirator!

And always, to R. G. Alexander, for being my unending support; for being the person I can take any crazy idea to and talk it out as many times as I need to; for helping me to build depth into my characters and cleverness into my dialogue—but most of all, for being my friend.

A note to those of you who know rope: Thank you to the many people who have been directly or indirectly involved in my research, through hands-on experience as well as observation. My intention here was to present rope bondage in a way readers who may never have seen it could understand, so I have left out the more technical terms for the beautiful knots, materials and suspensions.

DANGEROUSLY
Bound

CHAPTER

One

THERE WAS SOMETHING about New Orleans—something about the air itself—a certain sultriness found nowhere else, that silky touch of humidity on skin, like fingertips dragged slowly over your flesh. Or maybe it was only that this was Mick's town. Every side street and café thick with memories of him, each corner she turned leaving her breathless with the possibility of running into him, seeing him again.

She couldn't come back without thinking of him. Without the hard yearning that had never gone away, running like honey in her veins.

Mick . . .

Damn it.

But it was her town, too—her hometown. Allie had been gone for the better part of the last twelve years, away at college in San Francisco, then at culinary school in Europe, then back to San Francisco to practice her pastry arts. She'd returned to

New Orleans on occasion to visit family and friends, but Mick had always managed to avoid her. Except for that one summer when she was twenty years old. The summer Mick had finally—finally!—come to his senses and *had* her.

One night. One night that had left her shattered. And more unable to forget him than ever.

She stepped off the running board of the trolley car that ran the length of Chartres Street and moved toward the small French café that was her destination. Patrons sat at white-clothed tables in front of the old brick structure. Like so many in New Orleans it was a little decayed by the tropical moisture, the bricks literally crumbling at the corners. Yet it was covered in the yellow and pink lantana that lent a spicy perfume to the air all over the old city.

She paused, catching her reflection in a shop window, and ran a hand through her long, dark hair.

He'd always loved her hair.

She could see his face in her mind, the face she'd known since those very first moments when her body had awakened to desire and come to know what it was to be *female*.

He had hard features, but he was beautiful in the most masculine way. So tall, towering over her. She loved that about him—that he could intimidate with his height, with that well-earned air of bad boy. She loved the way his black hair fell into his face. And those soft gray eyes that always melted her . . .

A woman bumped into her, apologizing, and the noise of the passing cars and the crowds on the sidewalk came to her as she shook her head, shook herself out of the memories that tried to come flooding back. If she was going to be in New Orleans, live here again, she'd better get a hold of herself. It wasn't as if she'd come back specifically *for* Mick, although he was definitely on her radar.

Which was why she was meeting Jamie for lunch today, only

a few days after she'd returned to the city. He was one of her oldest friends—and Mick's best friend. Not that she didn't want to see Jamie—she did, of course. She'd missed him. But the struggle she fought against every day, between the part of her that wanted to forget Mick and the part that yearned to know every detail of his life, was impossible in New Orleans. *Their* town, where everything had happened. She couldn't resist asking Jamie about him. And if Mick was still available—and since her best friend was married to Mick's brother she had some insider information that told her he was—well, she had a plan. Jamie was the one person who could help her execute it.

Feeling like she was involved in some espionage plot, and a little silly, as well, she settled her purse on her shoulder and squeezed between the outdoor tables and into the cozy bistro where they were having lunch.

She spotted Jamie at a table by the window, all six feet of his long legs sprawled out in front of him, but he rose as soon as he saw her, a wide grin on his gorgeous face.

"Allie."

He pulled her into a long hug, and she stood on her toes to wrap her arms around him. It felt lovely, familiar, and she realized with a sudden pang how much she'd missed New Orleans and all the people in it. But she was done missing everyone. She may have let Mick Reid chase her away all those years ago, but she was back. And she was determined that everything would be different this time.

Pulling back, she took a good look at Jamie. "You've shaved your hair almost completely off!" She ran a hand over the brown buzz cut. "Ooh—it's soft. And it suits you. I like the eyebrow piercing, too."

He laughed and pulled out a chair for her, held it while she settled into it before seating himself across the small table from her. "I'm glad you approve. You can give me all the style advice you want. I'm just glad you're back."

"I am, too. It's so good to see you. What have you been up to?"

"The usual. Working on cars. Trying to stay out of trouble."

"How's the shop doing?" she asked. Jamie's business was restoring vintage muscle cars, work he'd loved since high school.

"It's doing great. We're finally recovering, along with the rest of the city. Business is good. In fact, my cousin Duff is coming in from Scotland in a few months. We'll be expanding the shop to include his specialty—he restores vintage motorcycles. We just gutted the space next door and are about to start the build-out. What about you? Are you settling into the house?"

"The house" was a small cottage in the Garden District left to her by her great-aunt Joséphine, her father's aunt—the reason she'd initially decided to return to the city and make it her home once more.

"The house is a bit of a mess, actually. The kitchen needs to be completely redone, and it needs to be painted—a few other things. I wanted to ask if your brother Allister is available to take on the job."

"Of course. He runs several crews these days. I'll talk to him, have him give you a call."

"Thanks." She smiled at him over her menu.

The waitress brought water to the table, and they ordered.

"So . . ." Allie started, wanting and not wanting to ask about Mick.

Jamie raised an eyebrow. "So?"

"So . . . I ran into Summer yesterday."

"Summer Grace?"

"Yes. It was nice to see her. We ended up sitting down and talking over coffee. You know she still has the hots for you."

He groaned. "Jesus, do people still say 'has the hots'?"

Allie couldn't help but grin at his discomfort. Summer Grace Rae—Brandon's sister—had been after Jamie since they were all kids. "She's a total sex kitten, that girl. You could do worse."

"Worse than hitting on my best friend's little sister? The one who he asked me on his deathbed to look after?"

"That could be one way of doing it," she teased.

He blew out a breath, his hand rubbing the stubble on his head. "Why do I have the feeling you're using this to avoid the conversation you came here to have with me?"

"Am I that obvious?"

"Yes," he answered simply.

She bit her lip, her fingers tightening around the white cotton napkin she held. What the hell—she was going to ask sooner or later.

"Okay. So, I was wondering . . . How's Mick? Is he in town?"

"Mick's fine. And yeah, he's here in town. What's the rest of the question?"

Allie tried to laugh, but it came out short and sharp. "You know me too well."

"I know you both too well."

"Just tell me, Jamie. What's going on with him? Is he . . . is he single? And God, did I really just ask you that?"

Jamie laughed. "You did, sweetheart. And it's Mick. Of course he's still single."

Allie folded her napkin, laid it carefully across her lap, avoiding her friend's gaze.

"Is he still playing at the club? The Bastille?"

"We both are." He narrowed his gaze at her. "What do you know about The Bastille?"

She looked up then, met his gaze. "Everything. I know about your kink, about Mick's. Maybe it's time we talked about mine."

He raised his brows. "Yours? Your kink? What are you saying, Allie?"

She took a deep breath. "I should have told you sooner. I don't know why I didn't, especially since I've always known you would never judge me." She paused. "I learned a lot while I was away. In Berlin. Amsterdam. I went to my first club when I went to culinary school in Paris. It was . . . eye-opening. Life changing, really. I belong to two of the top clubs in San Francisco—I'm sure you know their names. Sanctuary. The Ring. Everywhere I went to learn pastry, I went to the clubs. I've probably had as much experience with kink as you. Maybe more."

"More, huh?" He nodded thoughtfully, and she could see he was trying to absorb everything she'd just revealed to him. "I do know of those places in San Francisco. Good clubs. Solid reputations."

"I joined The Bastille a few months ago when I knew I was coming back here. I've seen your online profile. And Mick's. You've admitted to some of this stuff over the years so it was no surprise. And Mick . . . well, I've known about him for a long time. And I understand that's why he never thought he could be with me."

"You know that's only part of it, Allie. You know Mick. All that lone-wolf bullshit."

She caught his gaze. "Exactly. It's bullshit."

Jamie let out a long breath. "I imagine you'll be coming to The Bastille, then, now that you're living here. That could be . . . awkward, where Mick is concerned."

"Are you saying you don't think I should come?"

He held up his hands. "Of course not. You know me well enough to know I'd never say that."

"I do know. And I get it. I'd really rather it weren't awkward."

She leaned across the table, grabbed one of his hands. "Jamie, will you help me?"

"Help you? With what?"

"With Mick. With this whole . . . situation. It's more than awkward. It could be untenable. I've been thinking about this, and I only see one solution. I want you to help me see him. Not just *see* him. I want you to negotiate a scene at the club—one between Mick and me."

"Allie, you're crazy if you think he'll agree to that. You know how he feels. He still sees you as you were at sixteen."

"What if I told him—if you helped me tell him—about where I've been, the things I've done? That I'm an experienced bottom."

"He'd always doubt it. He'd doubt himself."

She sighed. "Why? I don't get it. I'm almost thirty years old. This is ridiculous. Are you saying you think he doesn't want me?"

"We all know damn well he does. Always has. Always will. That's the problem. You're the one he wants. The one he can't allow himself to have."

"Jamie, please. I need you to do this for me." She knew he was her only chance. "Mick will refuse to see me if I just ask him myself, won't he?"

"Jesus, Allie," he groaned, pulling his hand back.

"Don't let me leave here today not knowing how things are going to be when I walk into that club and see him there. This is the only way. You have to get him to sit down with me and talk this out. All you have to do is set it up."

He blew out another long breath. "If I set it up—and I am *not* promising anything—then I sit through the detailed negotiations between you two. Not just the initial conversation in which I get him—*maybe*—to agree to do this. It'll be my responsibility as the Dominant introducing the negotiations, despite your history together. It's proper protocol. No arguing about it."

She nodded. "Of course. I understand that." She paused, bit her lip. "Not sure if Mick will understand," she muttered.

He scrubbed a hand over his head. "Two minutes back in town and already causing trouble. What am I going to do with you, girl?"

She smiled at him. "You're going to help me give Mick Reid what we've both always wanted. Each other."

ALLIE PUSHED OPEN the screen door and stepped onto her porch. The old wood boards creaked under her bare feet—she'd have Allister look at that.

It was an unseasonably warm and humid night for May, and she hadn't had time yet to replace the old cottage's air-conditioning. It was cooler out there, with a small breeze picking up the damp tendrils of hair that had escaped from her ponytail. She pressed her glass of iced tea against her hot neck— not the traditional New Orleans sweet tea—she'd broken herself of that habit in her years living in Europe.

She moved to the edge of the screened-in porch, searching the sky for the moon. It was a small crescent in the inky sky, the stars glimmering from between the clouds. Hard to believe Mick shared this same sky with her somewhere in the city. That he was that close.

It always came back to him. Especially now. Especially here, with the warm, sultry air soft on her skin, making her remember.

He wasn't the first boy she'd kissed, but kissing him had changed everything. It was a mad rush of heat and need. Startling at first. Then something she looked forward to, craved.

They'd made out like crazy in high school. Mick would pull

her aside every chance he got in the hall at school, into a dark doorway when they were walking down the street. His kisses were demanding, even in those days.

A small, soft breath escaped her lips as she remembered, as she closed her eyes and imagined the warm press of his mouth against hers. Desire was a low, steady hum in her system, heat blossoming between her thighs.

Oh, yes, Mick Reid could kiss like the devil himself.

He was every bit as wicked. She'd known it then. Loved it. Wanted more than he'd ever been willing to give her. But things were different now. She was all grown up. She knew how to get what she wanted. And she would find a way.

But back to the kissing . . .

She sat down in one of the wicker chairs on the porch, set her tea on the floor next to her, leaned back, and closed her eyes once more.

There had been those moments when he looked at her—watched her—and she knew he was about to kiss her. He'd pause, making her wait. Make her breathe in her desire, and his. Pure torture, but she'd loved it. Then he'd pull her in hard and crush her body to his, his lips to hers, and oh . . .

She pressed down on her aching sex through the thin cotton of her dress.

His tongue would push into her mouth, sweet and silky and full of need. She'd loved the way he *needed* her, as if he'd die if he couldn't touch her, kiss her.

She was dying right now.

She opened her eyes for a moment. The porch was dark—she hadn't turned on the lights. The street was quiet, empty. She closed her eyes and pictured his face once more, those lovely moments of anticipation before he took her mouth.

She slid her hand beneath the hem of her dress, slipped her

fingers under the lacy edge of her panties and found her sex slick with need. She took in a breath, let her fingers slide through her damp heat, over the already-swollen folds.

God, the first time he'd gone down on her she thought she would die of pleasure. It was the one thing he'd given in on—he refused to take her virginity. But that plush, clever mouth kissing her there, licking, sucking . . .

"Oh . . ."

She pressed a finger into her body, moaned quietly. Added another.

He'd push his tongue inside her, then draw it out, pause endlessly, making her wait before he dove in once more, all wet tongue and soft lips, then he'd push his fingers into her.

She pumped her fingers a few times, need swarming her, her hips arching. Then she slid her fingers out to rub at her hard clitoris.

Mick . . .

God, she needed him. Needed to feel him again. Needed him to spank her, like he had that one night. His big hand coming down on her flesh, making her sore. Making her wet. Making her pant with need. Until, his fingers buried inside her, she'd come. Come apart. Screamed his name.

"Yes . . ."

She pressed into her needy sex once more, the heel of her hand pressing onto her mound. She shivered, remembered the sting of his palm on her flesh, his fingers working her mercilessly, milking her climax from her as she shivered in his arms.

"Oh!"

She came, hard, her body jerking, her sex tightening over and over around her plunging fingers.

"Mick . . ."

She gasped his name over and over until, finally, her body calmed, and she moved her hand from beneath her dress.

All around her was the sound of cicadas, a car driving by. She felt enveloped by the dark sky. By the pleasure still simmering in her system.

She needed to do it again, properly this time, with her vibrator, her legs spread.

Desire rose once more, her nipples pulling tight.

Yes, she needed it. Needed to come again and again tonight. Probably every night until she saw him. Until he touched her. And then *Mick* would make her come.

She groaned, got up and went into the house, letting the screen slam shut behind her, her glass of tea forgotten. It didn't matter. All that mattered was this driving need.

She moved through the dark living room, past the old furniture and the boxes of her belongings, and into the bedroom. She pulled her toy bag from beneath the high four-poster bed and yanked on the zipper. It was dark in the room, the moon casting a pale silver light, but it only took her a few moments to find what she was looking for.

Impatiently, she stripped her sundress off over her head and flung it onto the floor. She climbed up on the bed and lay down next to the items she'd lined up on the white cotton coverlet: her big vibrator and a smaller one, a string of anal beads, a bottle of lube, some clamps, their metal chain glinting in the sliver of moon and starlight that hit the bed.

She got on her hands and knees and grabbed the big, phallus-shaped vibrator, switched it on and touched it to her clit. It was almost too much, she was so hot already. She bit her lip, rode it out, shivering all over, then spread her knees wider and plunged it inside her.

"Oh, God."

She surged back onto the big vibrator, loving the way it filled her. The way Mick had filled her with his big, lovely cock.

His cock was thick and long, a heavy shaft of velvet-covered iron. She'd gotten to touch it, to wrap her hand, her mouth around it, to get him off. But he'd never been willing to fuck her until that night . . .

He'd held himself over her, heat coming off his big, finely muscled body in waves. She'd been writhing beneath him, waiting for him. He'd made her wait, as he always did, until she'd sobbed his name. Begged for him.

"Please, Mick," she whispered, pressing the vibrating phallus deeper.

It wasn't enough.

She sat up on her heels, the vibe still deep in her sex, and picked up the clamps. She felt the weight of them in her hands for a moment, the cool metal chain running between them, pressed it to her aching breasts.

"For you, Mick," she whispered as she drew one nipple between her fingers, pinched it tight.

She pulled in a breath, loving the spark of pain. She slipped her fingers over the hardened tip, caressing, then tugging, drawing the sensitive flesh out, did it again before closing one of the metal clamps around it.

She gasped at the sharp pinch, breathed it in, rode the pain out as she'd been taught to do.

She let the weight of the chain hang for a moment while she prepared her other nipple, caressing, pinching, pulling, then attaching the other clamp.

She drew in a hissing breath, let it out, let the pain carry her away for a moment, smiling as pleasure washed over her. Picking up the bottle of lube and the beads, she coated them, leaned forward, spread her thighs wider. She contracted her sex to keep the big vibrator inside her as she pressed the tip of the beads to her ass, took in a breath and slowly blew it out as she pushed the first bead in.

There was the familiar burning sensation as it reached the first ring of muscle. She forced her body to relax past the burn, past the keen pleasure shimmering through her from the vibrator and the clamps. She pushed it in a little more, adding the second, larger bead. Again there was the slight burn as it moved past the muscle, but pleasure surged just as deep inside her.

Her breath hitched as she pushed it in farther, and she had to bite back her orgasm. She needed to come. But she wanted it all. Wanted him.

Mick . . .

He'd never taken her ass. She'd wanted him to. Wanted it to be his big, beautiful cock pressing into her from behind. He'd wrap an arm around her waist, holding her tight. Making her feel *owned*.

She pushed another bead in, moved her hand to pull the big vibe from her sex, pushed it back in hard.

"Ah! Yes, Mick, please."

She started pumping, the motion causing her breasts to sway, the heavy chain of the clamps pulling on her nipples. Pain and pleasure danced through her, from between her thighs, deep inside her. The sensations merged, began to blur, and she stabbed into her body over and over, the big vibrator pressing against her G-spot.

Her whole body was pulsing with the need to come. But she knew he'd want her to hold it back.

"For you, Mick."

She went down, her shoulders supporting her body, her ass high in the air, her breasts pressed into the soft coverlet. She gasped when her clamped nipples came into contact with the bed, pain a sharp, lancing spark making everything more intense. She had to stop the motion of her hand, let the vibrator rest inside her. Had to take in a breath.

He would want more from her.

She reached back, imaging it was his big hands pulling the beads out of her, pushing them back in, using the motion to rub against the vibe, touching off shivers of sensation in the core of her body.

It was too much. She panted, then keened her pleasure as her climax ripped through her, making her shake all over, blinding her. Making her sob his name.

"Mick!"

When it was over she collapsed on the bed, drew the beads out and laid them on the small towel she'd spread next to her, withdrew the vibrator and turned it off, laid it beside the beads. Finally she turned onto her back and slowly released one clamp. She hissed as the blood rushed back into her deprived flesh, bringing a fresh surge of pain, a fresh surge of pleasure. She took a moment before she did the same to the other.

Groaning, she pushed her hair from her face. Her skin, her hair, was damp with sweat. It was several long minutes before she caught her breath.

Goddamn Mick. It was him every time. It had been for years. No matter the wonderful lovers she'd had in Paris, in Copenhagen. The Dominants she'd played with in Berlin, Amsterdam, San Francisco. It was always him she fantasized about. It was always his face, his hands, his body in her mind when she was coming.

This was why she had to see him. Had to have that one last chance to make him see her for who she was. For it to either work out, or finally be over. Because this had to stop—this obsession with a man who wouldn't admit that he wanted her, needed her.

Now was the time. She would either get Mick to admit they belonged together or finally say good-bye. Forever.

MICK PACED THE living room floor of his French Quarter flat, the wood warm beneath his bare feet. His fingers flexed. He shook them out.

What the fuck was with him? Just because he'd heard Allie was back in town . . . Hell, she'd been in New Orleans at least a dozen times over the years, visiting her family in the summers or during holidays. He'd always tried his best to be gone when she was in the city, scheduling work gigs whenever he could. He hated to admit that he fucking hid from her, but he couldn't lie to himself.

He couldn't hide now.

He flopped down on the big brown leather sofa, grabbed the TV remote, rubbed his thumb over the buttons.

She was back to stay. Or so Jamie had told him. Inherited some old house in the lower Garden District.

If only he didn't have such an efficient staff, he could use work as a reason to get away for a while.

An *excuse.*

Jesus Christ.

He tossed the remote down onto the table he'd built himself years ago from old reclaimed barn wood, and got up to pace some more, ending up in front of the windows that overlooked the street below. A couple moved under the streetlamp at the corner, stopped to wrap their arms around each other. He watched as they kissed, as the kiss went on. As they made out like teenagers. Maybe they were—he couldn't tell.

He'd made out like that with Allie when they were teenagers. Kissed her until he almost had enough of her. But it was never enough. Not even that one night they'd spent together three years after the breakup, when he'd finally done with her a few of the things he'd always wanted to. *Needed* to. That had been nothing more than the most excruciating taste of something he'd never have again.

His mind wandered back, as it had so many times over the years, to the night when he'd had to tell her—*had* to—that they couldn't be together. Fucking excruciating to see her cry.

"I don't understand, Mick."

She rubbed at her damp cheeks. His hands ached with the need to wipe her tears. To take her in his arms and tell her it was a mistake, that he was taking it all back. But he knew what he had to do before he ruined her.

"I'm leaving for college in Baton Rouge—"

"It's not that far away!"

"I'll be busy with classes . . . and you need to enjoy your senior year, time with your family before you go off to college yourself."

"Mick, that's just . . . stupid. We love each other." When he didn't answer she blinked at him, her eyes welling with new tears. *"Don't we?"* she whispered.

His gut was churning with the lie he didn't dare say aloud. "You'll understand someday that this is the right move, Allie."

She shook her head, her dark eyes flashing. "You're wrong, Mick. I'll never understand. Never."

Why was he thinking about this now? Allie was the past. But the truth was, he'd never stopped thinking of her. Never stopped remembering what they'd had.

He ran a hand over his jaw. He had to shift gears.

Allie in his bed. At twenty she'd been more beautiful than ever. Her body had filled out in the best way possible, still lean but with the curves of a woman. And Christ, her lush breasts had filled his hands, the nipples going hard the moment he'd touched her bare flesh.

Jesus, her bare flesh . . . the taste of her skin, the feel of her body under his . . .

The sex had been amazing. The kink had been lightweight stuff, but he'd never forget it. He'd never forgive himself.

That had really been the end. And that monkey had ridden his back ever since. Nearly ten years and he still felt like shit for having led her down that dark path. And just as much for having turned his back on her without nearly enough of an apology.

You are a Goddamn coward.

It was true. Allesandra LeClair was the one thing in life he was afraid of.

Not her, exactly. She was the sweetest girl ever born. It was the way he felt about her. Even now, after all these years.

Crazy that he'd never gotten over her. He'd traveled all over for work, almost as often to visit the BDSM clubs all over the country, giving rope bondage demonstrations, lecturing. He'd been with some of the most gorgeous women in the world. But it was always Allie in his head.

Allie and her long, silky hair, her big, brown eyes. Eyes like a doe—wasn't that what they called it? There had always been something about the length of her neck, the way she moved . . . pure graceful innocence and pure sex all rolled up into one beautiful package.

And totally off-limits.

Which meant he'd have to find some way to stay away, even with her right there. New Orleans could be a small world sometimes.

He stepped back from the windows and went to the console table where he kept his favorite bottle of rum, poured his two-finger limit into a glass and tossed it back, set the glass down.

It was good rum, but he still felt the burn going down. Enjoyed it. Needed it.

Because his damn head was spinning a million miles an hour with thoughts of Allie. Her face. Her sleek golden skin. Her scent like a summer evening—that wicked combination of purity with an edge of sinful promise.

He pulled in a breath, held it, tried to get his shoulders to loosen as he let it out. But it was no good. He was knotted as tight as piano wire, and that knot wasn't just in his shoulders. His groin was pulled tight with desire. For her.

Her face. Her skin. Her scent . . .

He grew hard. The room grew warm.

He yanked his shirt off over his head, ran a hand over his jaw. Muttered, "Fuck it," and moved his hand lower, over the bulge pressing against his jeans.

He was hard as stone just picturing her. How much harder would he be if he got his hands on her again?

It would be different than last time. He'd do all the things he'd been wanting to do. Tie her up, using his ropes to subdue her. To subdue his own raging need. Control them both. Then he'd use his hands on her—no toys, just his bare hands on her bare flesh. Just touch her. Pinch her. Scrape his nails over her naked skin.

Plunge his fingers into her.

He groaned, gripping the hard ridge of his erection through the denim.

"Fuck it," he said again before he unzipped and pulled his cock out.

He leaned his back into the wall, not wanting to take the time to get in the shower or on the bed or even sit down. He was too desperate to get this driving need out of his system.

He closed his eyes and began to stroke.

He remembered when he'd taught her to give him head. She'd wanted to—had practically begged for it, which was hot as hell. He remembered her wet mouth, those plush lips swallowing him, her tongue . . .

"Christ."

His hips arched into his fisted hand, pleasure stabbing into him. He stroked faster. And remembered the lush curve of her breast in his hand, the tight, succulent flesh of her nipple as he drew it into his mouth.

He groaned, gripped his hard shaft tighter as he pumped.

Allie.

"Fuck!"

Pleasure slammed into him like a wall, hard and fast. He came into his fist, hips surging, breath panting, her name echoing in his dazed brain.

It was several moments before he opened his eyes and turned to stare out the window. The moon was a small crescent in the inky sky. The stars hid behind a drifting veil of clouds. And somewhere out there in New Orleans was Allie.

My girl.

He'd never been able to think of her any other way. His girl that he would never—could never—have.

ALLIE'S STOMACH WAS fluttering as if a thousand butterflies were trapped inside as she went to sit down with Jamie at the outdoor table at Pâtissier, the small neighborhood café where they'd set up their meeting with Mick.

Jamie stood and hugged her briefly before pulling out her chair.

"You okay?" he asked.

She sat down and sipped at the sharp-tasting chicory coffee he'd ordered for her. "Sure. Yes. I'm just . . . well, as much as I want to do this, I don't know how it'll turn out."

"He's going to be mad as hell."

She tried to smile. "That much I knew."

Jamie shrugged. "Don't worry. Mostly he'll be mad at me. I can handle him."

"I'm sure you can. I'm just not sure *I* can," she muttered.

"Too late now, sweetheart."

She looked up. And saw him.

He was as imposing as ever: tall, dark, his goatee making him look every bit the wicked Dom she was sure he was. And his gray eyes went absolutely stormy when he spotted her.

"*Allie?* What are you—what the hell, Jamie!"

"Come on now, Mick. Sit down. You two were going to run into each other sooner or later. Don't be rude to the lady."

Mick nodded, just a brief tilt of his strong chin. She saw that he had a scar down the side of his nose that hadn't been there before. Which looked . . . rakish. Charming.

God, had the word *rakish* just gone through her head?

There was a tattoo on the inside of his left forearm she hadn't seen before—something in Latin, the bold script highlighting the corded muscles.

Yes . . . charming and rakish.

"Hello, Allie."

Her breath stuttered in her throat. That low, smoky voice, a little bit gravel, a little bit velvet. She shivered and cleared her throat.

"Hi, Mick."

He stared at her. She stared back, transfixed by him. She felt stunned. Had he looked this good the last time she'd seen him?

The years had made him more rugged. Sexier, if that were even possible. But the warm pit heating to a slow simmer in her body was telling her it was true.

Mick.

Finally.

"Either of you going to tell me what this is about?" Mick demanded.

"As soon as you sit down, buddy," Jamie said, carefully keeping his tone even.

She could see Mick was ready to bolt by the way he held his broad shoulders, by the hard set of his mouth.

"Please, Mick," she found herself saying, her voice a breathy whisper.

That seemed to catch his attention. He raised one eyebrow, watching her for several moments while she held her breath. Then he pulled out the chair next to her and slowly settled his big frame into it.

God, he was close enough that she could smell the earthy scent of leather that was always attached to him, whether he was wearing one of his motorcycle jackets or not. That and the citrus-scented soap he'd always used, which made him feel a little exotic to her. But what was Jamie saying?

"You look like you got knocked around, Mick. What happened?"

It was then she noticed the bruise darkening his left cheek.

Mick shrugged. "Nothing. Fought this morning."

"Fought?" She sat up in her chair. "You're seriously still doing that ridiculous bare-knuckled boxing?"

He answered slowly, his gaze challenging her. "Yeah, I am."

"That's just . . ." she sputtered, ". . . stupid."

"It's nice to see you, too, Allie."

"She's right and you know it, Mick," Jamie interrupted.

"Although now isn't really the time for that discussion, *Allie*," he said pointedly.

"Change of subject, both of you. I'm sitting. Jamie, you going to start? Or do I ask her?"

"Can't old friends have some coffee together?" Jamie asked, his expression challenging his friend.

"Theoretically. When that's all it is." Mick spoke to Jamie, but his gaze hadn't left her face.

He was studying her. Looking for answers, maybe. She shifted in her chair.

"Mick," she finally said, forcing the words out, "I'm sure you know I've moved back to New Orleans."

"I've heard."

"Don't you think after all these years it's about time you and I faced each other? It's not that big a town. Especially when you consider our common . . . the friends we share."

"Maybe so. I still don't appreciate being ambushed. Or you using Jamie to do it."

"Would you have agreed to see me any other way?" she asked, knowing what the answer was. Unable to prevent herself from baiting him just a little. Why did he have to be so stern with her? *She* hadn't done anything wrong.

"Don't give me those puppy dog eyes, Allie."

"Don't be so damn grumpy with me, Mick. After all this time, is that really necessary?"

His shoulders dropped a little. "I guess not. No. I'm sorry."

His eyes softened as he spoke, and it melted the anger she'd been carrying around. A bit, anyway.

He turned to Jamie. "Since you set this meeting up, I figure you have an agenda, *buddy*."

Jamie nodded. "Do you want a coffee first?"

"I want answers first."

"Fair enough."

"Please don't be mad at Jamie," Allie said. "I made him do it."

"And I'm sure a delicate thing like you twisted his arm real hard."

She reached out to lay her hand over his. "Please. Just listen."

He yanked his hand back as if he'd been burned, and she blinked away the hurt she knew would be shining in her eyes.

"Shit, Mick," Jamie said quietly. "You don't have to be such an asshole."

Allie heard that faint touch of Scottish accent come through, which usually only happened when he was angry or drinking, even though he and his family had been in the US since Jamie was seven.

"Okay. Okay." Mick raised his hands, palms outward, and leaned back in his chair. "I know I'm being a bit of a bastard. You two go ahead and explain. I'll try to mind my manners."

"About time," Jamie muttered. "You want to start, Allie, or should I?"

"I guess I should." She turned to Mick. It was hard to look at him, to see the stark male beauty of his face, the storm still raging in his eyes. To see him and not touch him.

"So, Mick . . . look, I'm here, and we were going to see each other sooner or later. Probably sooner. That's why I pushed for this meeting. Because you and I have a few things to get straight, but we can't do that until I come totally clean with you."

"About what?"

"About kink."

"About *what*, now? Are you serious?" His voice was pure gravel. "We're having this conversation right here, right now, with Jamie?"

"Yes. Because I need his help in explaining a few things to you. Because I think you won't quite believe me."

He'd gone eerily still. "What wouldn't I believe?"

"I'm in the lifestyle, Mick. I have been for years. And I know you don't want to hear those words come out of my mouth."

She could see from the shock on his face she was right.

"Mick, Allie's been to BDSM clubs all over the world," Jamie put in, filling up the tense silence. "She's an experienced bottom. She's been under a collar of protection to a well-known Dom in San Francisco for three years. She knows about you and me, our involvement in the lifestyle. She's done her homework. And I checked out her story—she's told me the truth."

She turned to Jamie in surprise. "You checked me out? I already told you everything. Jesus, Jamie—"

Their friend didn't flinch. "I had to make sure, Allie. It's my responsibility, given that you asked me to speak on your behalf. I had to know you were as experienced as you claimed to be before agreeing to do all this. Before bringing you into The Bastille."

"Now wait one damn minute," Mick exploded. "You are *not* taking Allie to The Bastille! Over my dead and bloody stump of a body. Are you out of your fucking mind?"

"I'm going with or without your approval," Allie said, her tone low but firm.

Mick turned on her. "I don't know what game you think you're playing at, Allesandra, but this is not happening."

"Oh, but it is." Anger simmered, flooding her veins. "I live in this city again, too, Mick. And you can't deny me access to the kink community that I have as much a right to as you do. That I *need*. Why would you want to make me feel isolated in my own hometown?"

"If your family ever found out what you were doing—"

"They'd be just as shocked as most of yours would. By the way, I know your brother Neal knows about you. Marie Dawn told me. She knows all about me, of course. I don't think she's told your brother . . ."

"Jesus Christ." Mick huffed out a breath, ran both hands through his dark, moppy curls. "That's what I get for letting my brother marry your best friend," Mick huffed, dropping his hands into his lap. "Okay. I guess you're right, damn it. We just have to find a way to deal with this. Schedules or something, so I don't have to . . . see you there. Fuck," he muttered.

"That's why we're here, buddy," Jamie chimed in. "Allie has a solution, and I think it's a good one or I wouldn't be here supporting it."

"Why do I have a feeling I'm not going to like this?" Mick asked.

"Probably because you're not," Jamie said, his tone almost cheerful.

Allie had to suppress a smile. He really was a little bit of a sadist.

"All right. Give it to me."

Jamie leaned forward, his expression sobering. "Mick, I'm here not only as your friend and Allie's, but to act as formal mediator."

"Formal . . . for what?"

Allie put her hand on his arm. He didn't pull away this time. His skin was warm, just the way she remembered. She suppressed a shudder as the heat zinged through her system. "For negotiations, Mick. Jamie is going to help you and I negotiate play."

His pupils widened, his nostrils flared. Then his jaw ground so tight she could see the tick in his cheek. He rose to his feet so fast his chair tipped over behind him.

"Fuck no."

I T HAD BEEN thrown at him so fast he could hardly wrap his heads around the words. Him play Allie? The one person in the world he'd sworn to protect from that side of himself? Insane. Beyond insane.

"Mick." He heard a small threat in Jamie's tone. He didn't give a damn. Rage was simmering in his system. Rage and a wild, fierce protectiveness when it came to Allie he couldn't find a damn *place* for in this mess.

"I was right the first time—you are out of your fucking minds. Both of you."

Jamie stood, not quite as tall as Mick was, but he had his Dom on. "Mick, sit down and shut up for a minute."

"Not a chance."

"Let her have her say."

"You've both said more than enough."

Jamie stared him down. "I don't think so."

"Goddamn it, Jamie—"

Allie shot to her feet. "You two stop it. You're making a scene. And Mick, I'm telling you right now, if you don't have this conversation with me, I'll have it with someone else."

She grabbed his arm again, and her touch scorched his skin. He had to grit his teeth not to pull away. Not to grab her and pull her in for a long, hard kiss. She moved in closer.

Yep. She still smelled like summer. Damn it.

He started to shake his head.

"Mick, sit down. You, too, Jamie," she demanded, dropping down into her chair.

He looked down at her. She was so beautiful it almost broke his heart to see the urgency in her big brown eyes. Jamie sat but Mick stayed on his feet, leaning on the edge of the table.

"This is the Goddamn craziest thing I've ever heard."

"This is reality, buddy," Jamie put in. "Oh, go ahead and shoot me that dirty look. But you're going to hear us out."

"I don't know how the hell you did it, but it looks like I don't have much choice."

"Sure you do. You can walk away knowing Allie means it—if you aren't the one to bring her into the club, there'll be a dozen men lined up for the privilege, and we both know it. She can handle the trolls, I'm pretty damn certain. I just wasn't sure she could handle *you* on her own. And I wouldn't have let her. She came to me about this, which makes her my responsibility."

"Christ, Jamie."

"You know I'm right. That's part of the code we live by. She's under my protection now. Until someone else takes over that role. It could be you. Or it could be some other Dom."

Mick straightened up and rubbed both hands over his face, dropped them. "Never." He heard the danger in his own voice. "And that's what you were counting on, wasn't it?"

"I was counting on you," Allie said, her voice soft.

His laugh was ragged. "I don't know why. You've never been able to before."

"That's true. And maybe it's crazy, but I want to give you one last chance to redeem yourself."

So did he. That was all he'd ever wanted. For what he'd done to her. For what he'd done to his life by being an idiot at eighteen with that damn motorcycle.

A flash of that day—the flashes he had too Goddamn often. The green and gray of the trees shading the wide street whirring by, becoming a watercolor blur as the bike started to go down. The strain in his muscles as he struggled to right himself. Then the world exploding as he hit . . .

Fuck.

But that wasn't the only reason he needed redemption.

He'd done without Allie—and the motorcycle—since he'd screwed up so badly. Screwed up his life, his future. He'd given up Allie before the accident even happened, but that had been the nail in the coffin of the life he'd once wanted with her. He still felt with utter certainty he'd done the right thing.

But he had to focus on what was happening right now. Such serious expressions on both their faces—his best friend and the woman he'd loved since he was seventeen. Both of them offering him something he'd always wanted. Tempting him with things he could never have.

They had to be fucking kidding. Except they weren't.

He could not play Allie at The Bastille—or anywhere.

"Jamie, I can't believe you'd be a party to this . . . this insanity."

"Someone had to facilitate a conversation between you two."

"Not *this* conversation," Mick ground out.

"Yeah, exactly this conversation. Because you know damn well, if you just calm your ass down and think for a minute, that our Allie is not going to give up kink just because the great Mick Reid is too stubborn to play her. She could have her pick. Hell, I'm her friend—I'd fucking play her. At least then I'd know she'd be in good hands."

Mick's hands curled into fists. "You fucking *will not*."

Allie tugged on his hand, then released it and crossed her arms over her chest. "All right, I may be the submissive at the table, but you are not going to tell me what I can and cannot do, Mick. I've had enough of that to last me a lifetime."

He couldn't help the grin that crooked the corner of his mouth. There was definitely evil intent behind it. "Isn't that exactly what you're asking me to do, sweetheart?"

She huffed out a breath. "You're impossible. You know what I mean."

He shook his head. He liked to see her all riled up, her cheeks pink, her eyes blazing. He couldn't help himself. But he was damn well not going to play her. Even if the idea made him hard all over.

Control.

"The fact is, you're both impossible," Jamie said. "But since you're both my friends and Allie asked me to present the terms, I'm going to do this right. As with any submissive new to our club it's my duty to see that it's done correctly, so you'd better settle down, Mick, and let us get started."

"Christ, Allie. You'd really go and play with some other Dom? Just to irritate me?"

"I'd play with some other Dom to get my *needs* met. Surely that's something you understand? But I'd rather it was you." Her eyes were shining—he wasn't sure if it was a sheen of tears or the way the café was lit. "How long are you going to think of me as a child, Mick? I'm no innocent kid anymore, not by a long shot. Do you need my references? I can have three trainers contact you by tomorrow. More Doms that I've played with in the next few days. I can get you a dozen references that will testify to my experience and my fitness as a bottom, including lists of toys I've experienced and the clubs where I've played."

He didn't want to hear it. Didn't want to know about the things she'd done with other men. The idea of some other Dom putting a collar around her neck . . .

His fingers flexed.

Control.

He took in a deep breath.

"Stop glowering at me, Mick. Jesus."

"What? I'm not glowering, Allie. I'm thinking."

She sighed. "Can you please think sitting down? People are starting to stare."

He picked up his fallen chair and sat. "Are you saying exhibitionism isn't on your list of likes?"

"As a matter of fact, it is," she said calmly.

Oh, she'd be perfect, tied up in his bonds, her naked flesh crossed with rope and shadows from the dungeon lights.

He had to stop thinking like that.

Fuck it. Maybe he'd better start. Because no one else was going to have her.

"I never believed this was you, Allie. You know I never thought—"

"Maybe what you believe is wrong," she interrupted. "Maybe it's time you gave me a chance to show you how wrong you are about me, Mick."

"So?" Jamie asked him.

Goddamn this girl. But she was no girl anymore—he could see that much. But what was she going to be after he took her to The Bastille and let loose the beast that lived within him on her all-too-willing flesh?

That was what the ropes were all about. Restraining her. Containing the fire that burned inside him, the animal snarling to get out. Was it possible *this* was what he needed? Or was that some excuse he was making to get his hands on her?

He dragged a hand through his hair, blew out a long breath. "Fuck. Fine. Let's talk terms."

"That's better, buddy." Jamie leaned forward in his chair. "Let's start with any health complaints. Allie?"

"Just one—I sprained my right ankle last year, and it still gives me some trouble from time to time, so I can't do any inverted suspension."

"Jesus, Allie, where did you learn about inverted suspension?" She just glared at him. "Next question, Jamie?"

"Hard limits?"

"No face-slapping, no gags, no age play, no watersports or scat, no humiliation or degradation, no rape play, no pony or puppy play, no heavy canes. Oh, and no blindfolds."

"That's it?" Mick asked, incredulous. "That's your *entire* list of hard limits?"

She nodded, watching him. "Other than the usual non-consensual stuff.

"And sex?" Jamie asked.

"Fuck, Jamie, you can't ask her that!"

Jamie shrugged. "It's a standard aspect of negotiations. You know that, Mick."

"She and I will talk about that later," he growled. "Move on."

Jamie stared at him for several moments, challenging him, but no one was going to win this power struggle but *him*. Not when it came to Allie.

"Okay. I'll trust that you won't try to skip that part."

"You know me better than to believe I'd shirk my duties, *buddy*."

Jamie nodded, ceding the point. "I do." He pulled a piece of paper out from somewhere. "Here's a list of her kinks. Her preferences, if you will."

He slid it across the table toward him. Mick picked it up, folded it and tucked it into his back pocket.

"Aren't you going to look at it?" Allie asked.

"I'll study it later, then we'll talk more."

She looked surprised. But it had had exactly the effect on her he wanted—to allow him to take back control of the situation.

"Tell me how I contact you, Allie. Email."

He caught the slightest flaring of her nostrils. She was a little mad. Maybe more than a little. Okay, he could allow her that. He knew he had it coming. And he'd find a way to work the anger out of her in his ropes.

Jesus Christ. He was going to have Allie—Allie!—in his ropes. Under his hands. His body . . . his mind . . . both were in some sort of slowly building turmoil. That and a hard buzz of desire like a pulsebeat beneath his flesh.

"Mick, don't you want to go over your limits as a Top?" Jamie prompted.

"That's easy enough. Don't fail to use your safe words if you need to. Total honesty with me about what you need, what you want, what you don't. Total honesty after a scene if something didn't work for you. Don't ever try to play if you're sick—I don't want you pushing yourself too hard. And I won't draw blood on purpose, so if that's something you're looking for—"

"It's not." Allie's brown gaze was on his, smoldering with heat. A heat that went through him like a small electric shock. Jesus—she wanted him. *Wanted* in the same way he wanted her.

Despite his arguments, this was about to get interesting.

"But you intend to push me," she said. It wasn't a question.

He smiled. "If you've done your research, then you know I'm a sadist, Allesandra."

She smiled. "That's why I'm here."

WAS IT? ALLIE knew in her heart that was only partly true. She was there for Mick, kink or not. Although the fact that there was going to be kink, well . . . it was a big part of what had led her back to him. That and knowing she had something to prove in this arena. To him. Maybe to herself when it came to him. That she could be the woman he'd never believed she was. The woman who was exactly right for him, if he'd drop the damn savior complex and let her show him.

If this didn't work, nothing would.

"So?" Jamie asked before she had a chance to. "Are you both in?"

Allie nodded. "Yes."

"Mick?"

"Goddamn it, Jamie. Yes, I'm fucking in. Okay?"

He ran a hand through his hair, something she knew he'd always done when he was agitated. Apparently, Jamie recognized it, too.

"Buddy, you and I will talk more before this happens."

"Damn right we will."

"And you and Allie need to talk more, too."

"When are we doing this?" she asked.

"Give me your email and I'll contact you tonight," Mick said.

"But I—"

"Allie. If we're going to do this, we're going to do it my way. I'm still the Dom. And you're about to find out to what degree I mean that. I suggest you start with some level of compliance to show me you know how to be a proper submissive."

She could almost feel steam coming out of her ears.

"I am submissive, but there's nothing proper about me. And I suppose you're about to find out to what degree I mean *that*."

They stared each other down, and she never blinked. But the intensity of his gray eyes was making her legs go weak. Mick Reid was going to be one wicked Dom. She looked forward to it, even if he was pissing her off. She knew she'd go down with a struggle. But the fact was, she was going down. For Mick. It was everything she'd ever wanted. She wasn't going to ruin it by allowing him to be an ass—Dom or not.

She grabbed a pen from her purse and scribbled her email on a napkin, pushed it toward Mick.

"Good girl," he said quietly, and despite the cocky smirk on his face, those words went through her like a magic wand dusting her with pure pleasure. He hadn't taken his eyes off her for a moment.

"So," Jamie asked, "is there anything else you two need me here for?"

"No," they said simultaneously.

"Okay, then." Jamie rubbed his hands together. "Looks like my job here is done—for the moment. You are still under my protection, Allie. Tell me if you need anything. *Anything*." He stood up. "I'll leave you two lovebirds to get to know each other again. Don't stay out too late, kids."

Mick glanced up at him with a growl. Jamie ignored him and leaned down to plant a soft kiss on Allie's head.

"Thank you, Jamie."

"You're welcome, sweetheart. See you, Mick."

Once he'd left and it was just the two of them, the space between them suddenly seemed too small. Allie shifted in her chair.

"I can't believe you set me up like this, Allie," Mick said, his tone low and smoky. A little threatening. "I didn't know you had it in you."

"There's a lot you don't know about me, Mick. Partly because I've been gone for so long and I've been through changes, grown up. And partly because you refuse to see me for who I am. You always have."

He watched her for several long moments. "You know this is not going to end any differently than it did before," he said finally, his tone low.

"Meaning you think *you* haven't grown or changed in all these years, Mick?"

"Sure I have. But I can't change history—*my* history. At the core I'm still who I've always been. Oh, I'm not the troublemaker I was in my teens, but I'm not any better for you now than I was when we were in high school, or when we were in college. Not any better for a girl like you than I've been this whole time. Some things I can't do anything about, Allie."

"That's a cop-out. And what do you mean by *a girl like me?*"

"It's the simple truth. And you know what I mean."

"It's crap, Mick—a story you tell yourself. One you've told me too many times. And I don't agree."

"Then we'll have to agree to disagree, unless you want this to stop now."

She bit her lip. "I still disagree," she said stubbornly.

"One thing that's come with the years is that I know exactly who I am, Allie," he insisted.

"And who's that?" she asked, really wanting to know with a sudden urgency that made her stomach knot up. "Because maybe it's about time you told me, since you seem to think I'm so delusional when it comes to you."

"That's a pretty big question."

"Then I'll expect a big answer."

He stared at her for several seconds. "At some point you'll have it, maybe. Maybe."

"Ah, you want to remain the enigmatic Dominant. A man of mystery."

He shrugged, his massive shoulders a ripple of muscle beneath his T-shirt. "Maybe I don't feel like talking about it here."

"We can go back to your place and talk," she said, angling her chin.

"Allesandra LeClair, you just flirted with me."

"Maybe I did." She blinked, bit her lip.

"You're doing it again."

"Am I?"

He laughed. "Your 'coy' isn't very good—you might need some practice, princess."

Princess.

He hadn't called her that since high school. A warm shiver went through her.

"Then maybe I'll practice on you."

"You've developed a bratty side, you know that?"

She nodded, grinning. "I think you like it."

"And I think it's nothing throwing you over my knee and spanking the hell out of you won't cure."

"Yes, please," she said quietly.

He stared at her for several moments, his gray eyes going dark. "Touché."

They sat quietly staring each other down again, but some of the ice had melted.

Allie leaned toward him, her elbows resting on the table. "So, you'll email me?"

"I will. And I'll look over your list, shoot you over any questions I have, send you my list. Then, because you and Jamie are crazy and apparently so am I for agreeing to this, we'll start the real negotiations. Check your email tonight." He stood, towering over her. "Don't think because we're all old friends that I'll go easy on you, Allie. That's not who I am."

"That's good. Because asking a Dom to go easy on me is not who I am, either."

"We'll see about that." He paused, his gaze raking her face, her upper body, before coming back to meet hers. "Meanwhile, learn to drop the attitude. Don't make me show you how."

She nodded without a word. He cracked the edge of a smile, tossed a ten-dollar bill onto the table, turned and headed for the door.

Allie watched him walk out of the café—actually, saunter was more like it—his shoulders so broad, the way his muscles in his back worked beneath the thin cotton T-shirt. His superb ass.

She realized she was trembling all over, just a small shiver beneath the surface of her skin. Mick was one fine-looking man—all sharp angles and rough exterior, with those glossy eyes, his lush mouth made even more enticing by his evil-looking goatee. And his hair—those wild, loose black curls.

She remembered the way his hair felt in her hands . . .

She let out a small groan.

She was turning into a small puddle right there in the café. If she'd been at home, she would have already dug out her toys.

"God . . ." she murmured under her breath, the heat of desire scorching her system, lighting her up with need.

She had to get home. Had to get into bed with every damn toy she owned and try to work a little of Mick out of her body. Not that it *would* work, of course. But she had to do something until she got the email from him that would tell her what he wanted her to do.

Hell, she simply had to do *something*.

She dropped another five on the table, grabbed her purse and left, walking out on shaky legs. She wasn't sure she could wait until she got home to ease the insistent ache between her thighs.

She waved down a cab as soon as she reached the street. She couldn't wait for the ambling streetcar today—she was in a hurry. Because if she didn't get home, get into bed with her vibrator as soon as possible, she was going to explode.

That's what he did to her. Always had. Probably always would. She had no idea how much more intense, how out of control her desire would be when he was touching her in the way she'd been craving for years. Mick—with his hands rough on her, tying her up, spanking her, paddling her . . . *touching* her.

She put a hand over her mouth to quiet the moan that escaped. What had she just gotten herself into? This could be her fondest fantasy come to life. Or it could be that Mick Reid was the one man who was going to push her past her limits, make her—for once—truly lose control.

She was very much afraid of the outcome. She could barely stand the wait before they could begin.

SHE WAS EXHAUSTED by the workout she'd given herself with her toys. Four orgasms later Allie got up, wrapped herself in her pink cotton robe and made herself a cup of coffee in the cottage's small kitchen. Her legs felt like rubber, and she knew she couldn't take anymore. But somehow her need was still left unsatisfied.

Somehow . . . because it's not with Mick.

She'd always known that was an issue for her, no matter her toys, her lovers, the men who dominated her at the clubs. But after seeing him that whole thing had shifted into high gear.

The sun was starting to go down, the light turning misty,

touched with shades of pink and orange as it filtered through the sheer curtains above the sink.

Tonight.

Time to check her email.

She sat at the round kitchen table, her heart starting to pound as she opened her laptop. His message was the first one to pop up. She clicked it, saw the words *It begins here* in the subject line . . . and somehow her elbow hit her coffee mug, spilling the hot liquid onto the table.

"Shit!"

She managed to snatch her laptop and whisk it out of harm's way before she grabbed the paper towels and wiped up the mess.

"Just breathe, Allie," she muttered.

She slowly inhaled the soft New Orleans air, then let it out. She moved the laptop back onto the table, sat down and started to read Mick's email.

Allie—

You and I have known each other a long time. But you're right—we don't really know each other anymore, and maybe what we thought we knew was all wrong. It starts here, then— us getting to know each other so we can play safely together, and in a way that satisfies our needs.

I've seen your list of kinks and desires, your limits, your maybes. Here is mine. I am of the mind that I don't need to have every one of my kinks met with any one given playmate. This list is a fairly complete itemization of what interests me. If there is something on it you haven't considered before but that is a limit for you, let me know. I've already told you what I absolutely require—that you always use your safe words if you

feel you need to. That you're honest with me about what's
working for you and what isn't. That you are completely
transparent about any health issues or anything that might act
as a negative emotional trigger. Standard stuff for those of us
who operate in the Safe, Sane and Consensual community,
which it seems you know.

My kinks:

Flogging, paddling, spanking, abrasion play, hot wax, clips/
clamps/clothespins, handcuffs, seeing a woman in high heels
and lingerie, tearing the lingerie to shreds as I take it off you—
probably with my teeth. Did I mention I love biting? Then there's
mind-fuck, pinching, posture collars, corsets, canes, vampire
gloves, tickling, vibrators, hair pulling, ice cubes, single-tail
whips, and maybe most of all, rope bondage/kinbaku/shibari.

There are some variations, of course, and new kinks that
develop along the way, but this is my basic list.

Allie took a deep breath, trying to calm her racing pulse, the
heat spreading like wildfire through her system. Her sex was a
hot pool of desire. She crossed her legs, found that only made
it worse, and uncrossed them.

"Jesus," she murmured.

It was everything she loved or wanted to try. With Mick
attached.

"Tearing the lingerie to shreds as I take it off you . . ."

She might have to climax again right there!

She shook her head.

Pull it together, girl.

She focused once more on her computer screen.

Tell me now if you're still in this. You are welcome at any time
to withdraw, of course, but I want to hear from you now that we

are on the same page about the things we want to do together.
That having seen my list (which I noticed is very similar to
yours), you're still interested.

You know I have my doubts about this. Not that you're
dragging me kicking and screaming into playing you (not that
anyone could, something you would do well to remember), but
I have to tell you up front that this is a bit of a mind-fuck for me,
and I am damn well not used to it.

I am always in control when I play. I can promise you I will
maintain that control with you. Glory in it or fight it, it doesn't
matter. I'm simply telling you how it will be.

I want you to take a little time before you reply. Think it
through. Then write back and tell me what your answer is. And
again, contact me with any questions or concerns.

Mick

She knew exactly what her answer was. Her body was already
screaming it. She typed one word. *Yes.*

She tapped her nails against the keyboard, waiting to see if
he was online. If he would email her back. Several moments
passed. She picked up the new cup of coffee she'd poured herself,
and sipped. It was cold. How long had she sat there reading and
rereading his email?

"Okay," she said to the empty kitchen, "I can't sit here all
night waiting for his answer."

She stood and pulled her X-Acto knife from a drawer and
moved into the dimly lit living room. There were boxes everywhere and the scent of old furniture, tinged with a bit of lilac
that was her aunt Joséphine's favorite scent, apparently—it was
everywhere in the house. She chose a cardboard box marked
kitchen, sliced it open and started to pull something wrapped

in white paper out of it. Her laptop pinged. She barely remembered to retract the blade of the knife as she hurried back into the kitchen.

Her laptop sat like some glowing temptress on the table. She set the knife down and flexed her fingers before sitting down again and clicking the email open.

> *A brief but succinct reply. Which, under other circumstances, I might approve of. Here, however, you and I need to communicate.*
>
> *When we play I will instruct you to answer any questions in the briefest way possible so I don't inadvertently pull you out of subspace (and trust me, I will take you there). Right now I view this as part of the fight in you. I don't mind the struggle because I have absolute confidence that I will win. Keep in mind, though, that even though we both see pain as pleasure, it can also be punishment.*
>
> *We meet this Friday at 8:00 in the evening for your debut at The Bastille. I will pick you up. I will email you again with instructions as to how you should dress for me.*
>
> *Mick*

Dress. For *him*.

She exhaled a long, hot breath, full of a wild wanting and the innate stubbornness that yearned to argue the point. But this was Mick. How much could she really argue? She'd wanted him—only him—since she was sixteen years old. The only question was, was she truly ready for him?

She pushed her hair from her face, too hot suddenly. Even her robe seemed like too much weight on her shoulders. And the same heat danced almost viciously between her thighs.

She stood, loosening her robe as she moved down the hallway and back into the bedroom. She arrived there naked, tossing the robe onto the end of the bed.

Her toys were still lined up on the smooth sheets. The comforter lay in a pile on the floor at the foot of the bed. She bit her lip, chose two items and moved into the bathroom.

She reached into the shower and turned it on, made sure the temperature was cool before she stepped in, her toys in hand.

She gasped a little as the cold water hit her heated skin, then let her body melt into it. She closed her eyes, leaned against the pink tiles, enjoying the flow of water over her body. And thought about Mick.

God, the things he'd written in his emails. The list of kinks. His attitude—cocky to the point of arrogance, but the level of command there was staggering. Maybe because it was him. Maybe because he simply *was* that commanding. Either way, her body was responding like crazy. And despite her earlier orgasms, she needed to come again. Badly.

Mick.

She could imagine him binding her in his ropes, her arms behind her back while he built a harness around her breasts.

"Oh . . ."

She switched on the small bullet vibe and pressed it between the slick folds of her aching pussy. Paused for several moments, enjoying the buzzing vibrations before she pushed it inside.

"Oh!"

It felt so good, pleasure coiling tight, waiting to be sprung free.

He would pinch her nipples once he had her breasts bound. His fingers would be hard and punishing.

"Please, Mick," she whispered as she turned the other vibrator on—this one a small pink textured vibe. It was long, narrow, but had a powerful buzz she loved.

Squeezing her sex so the bullet would stay put, she touched a fingertip to one hard nipple, squeezed her breast, kneaded it, finally drew out her nipple between her fingers. Then, pinching hard at the base, she touched the tip of the vibrator to her sensitive flesh.

She moaned, did it again, just brushing her taut nipple, the electric shivers running through her body joining with the vibrations deep inside her sex.

Her climax hovered, but she bit it back. For him.

She breathed in, held the air in her lungs, held on as long as she could. But in moments Mick's face, his words, the shivering vibrators, did their job. She pinched her nipple hard as she came, pleasure exploding in her body, in her head. Stars whirled behind her closed eyelids. Mick's face was there, his big hands. His deep voice commanding her to come harder.

She did, her hips jerking until she had to press her fingers to her clenching pussy to keep the bullet inside her.

"Oh, God . . . Mick . . ."

Even his name was hot on her lips. And before her climax could fade away, another began, shaking her, making her sob his name.

"Mick!"

The long vibrator slipped from her hand, but it didn't matter. It was knowing she was going to him, and oh, God, the things he was going to do to her. That alone was enough to make her come.

Finally her body calmed and she pulled the bullet from her sex, switched it off. She sank to her knees on the hard porcelain, trying to catch her breath as the cool water poured over her.

It was never going to be enough. Because it was Mick. Even once they were playing together, when the fantasies in her head were finally brought to life, would that be enough for her?

She didn't know. He was intoxicating. Dangerous. She hadn't

known the truth of it until she'd seen him again. She hadn't known exactly what that man could do to her body simply by talking to her, by just being *himself*. And how much more powerful would his effect on her be when she was naked beneath his hands? When she was vulnerable in subspace?

For the first time she had to question the viability of her plan. Maybe she was crazy to think she could be with Mick. Be with him, if he was not going to . . . what?

"If he's not going to love me," she admitted, her voice a breathless whisper.

The water fell, echoing around her. She let the cold calm her.

No. She could do this. If Mick wouldn't give her his heart, then at least she could finally give him her body. All of it, with everything out on the table between them.

Except that she was still in love with him. That secret she would keep to herself.

CHAPTER

Three

M ICK LOCKED THE door to his flat and went downstairs.
Moving out onto the quiet New Orleans street, he jogged
down the sidewalk. Nothing too fast, keeping an easy, even
pace, warming up for the workout he'd do once he reached the
gym ten blocks away.

He needed the workout. Not only to keep in shape for his fights,
but after seeing Allie, his blood had been humming too damn fast.
Too damn hot.

He needed to work her out of his system before she was in
his hands.

A part of him could hardly believe he was going to have Allie
at The Bastille. Under his command. In his ropes. He was a bastard
for agreeing to her crazy plan. But she had the references. She
obviously knew what she was getting into from the BDSM side of
things. She sure as hell didn't know what she was getting into with
him, no matter how many years they'd known each other.

He took a right down Esplanade Avenue, free of traffic and crowds this early in the morning, heading toward the Faubourg Marigny. He picked up his pace, reveling in the way his lungs opened up.

How did you warn someone of your own bitterness? He didn't like to admit it to himself. But it was there, like a serpent hiding in the shadows. Bitterness about his own foolish mistakes. About what he'd had to deny himself because of it—being a firefighter, like his father, his brothers, his grandfather. That anger burned through him to this day, but he kept it banked through the fights, and through the control he exerted as a Dominant.

Except that Allie challenged his control too damn much. But he was going to play her anyway.

Maintain control.

Words to live by. And he did, damn it. He *would*.

He passed the old iron gates of Washington Square, the trees bent, their leaves nearly touching the ground. A few homeless, regular residents of the park, still lay sleeping under their blankets on the grass, where later in the day the local musicians would jam.

He and Allie had spent some time on that grass, listening to music, talking, kissing . . .

The old plaid blanket he kept in a roll on the back of his bike. Allie lying on it, her hair spread in long, silky strands, her eyes glinting golden in the sunlight.

"Mick, kiss me again." A small smile on her lovely face, her hands coming up to push his hair out of his eyes, then skimming down to grab the lapels of his leather jacket and pulling him closer. She laughed. *"Come on, Mick. You know I can never get enough. Kissing is my favorite thing."*

"You're my favorite thing, Allie girl."

"Oh, now you really have to kiss me."

He leaned in to press his lips to hers. Lips like plush velvet, tasting of summer. Tasting of her. Their skin, their hair, smelling of the sunshine in the park. Kissing until their lips hurt, then laughing about it. His heart hammering simply because he held his girl so close, because her eyes were so damn pretty, shining with love when he pulled back to look at her. Love for him. Pretty heady stuff. But she was his girl, and this was exactly how it should be.

Except for the dark beast he kept hidden away from her. The one side of him he could never show her.

Damn it.

He pushed himself harder, starting to break a sweat in the humid morning air.

He needed to stop thinking of her for one damn minute. That was how he'd let his sparring partner's fist through yesterday morning.

No point in thinking about it now. He forced his mind to empty, to focus on his breathing, on his feet pounding the pavement as he ran the last few blocks.

He slowed as he reached the gym and swung open the door. It was already crowded, but he spotted his sparring partner, Antoine Duke, working out with the double-end bag, his dark skin gleaming with sweat. He'd see if Antoine would have time to work the heavy bag with him when he was done. He'd be meeting his Muay Thai instructor later for a more thorough MMA workout. Meanwhile, he'd start on the speed bag. It'd be good for him. Help him burn off some of this energy raging through his system.

He would be in the gym every morning until he saw Allie. And maybe every night. He hated to admit how much he needed it right now, but seeing her had dragged memories to the surface, things he'd rather forget.

Sometimes he thought he'd rather forget her—not that it was possible. Especially now that she was in New Orleans.

And he was going to play her at the club.

He took a quick jab at the bag, let his fist plow a lot harder into it than he should since he hadn't warmed up his hands yet. Fuck it. He would do whatever it took to calm the hell down. Had to. Because these same hands would be touching her bare flesh all too soon.

He slammed the bag again, focusing on the pain in his knuckles. Welcomed it. Deserved it.

Allie. Naked. Under his command.

Oh, yeah. He was definitely going to hell. He was pretty sure it'd be worth it.

MORNING CAME TOO early, the sky a still blanket of fog outside her windows when Allie realized she wasn't going to be able to get back to sleep. She'd tossed and turned all night, waking up as often as every hour. Always thinking of Mick.

She sat up, stretched, threw back the covers and picked up her robe, slipped it on. She made her way into the kitchen, pausing to open up her laptop as she passed the table before she started coffee brewing. She'd need it this morning. She sat down and browsed through email while she waited for the coffeepot to finish.

She'd always loved the scent of coffee. It reminded her of her father. He'd always been the first one up in the morning, making coffee for her mother before she left to go to Dolcetti, the family bakery, at four a.m. It was her father who was there to help her get ready for school, who made her breakfast, packed her lunch, even braided her hair. Except when he was on tour—then her mother and her aunts would take turns staying with her until it was time for school. But it was those mornings with her father she had loved best.

Bertrand LeClair had been a brilliant concert pianist. She remembered music in the house, always, whether it was him playing the old grand piano in his study she wasn't allowed into without his permission, or the symphonies and operas he'd listened to.

Her mother hadn't been to the opera since her father died. She couldn't bear it. But Allie still adored the opera her father had taught her to love.

She got up when the coffeepot beeped and poured herself a cup, took it back to the table and clicked into her music library, opened her favorite recording of *Lakmé*. It was a sad opera about ill-fated lovers. She'd often thought of herself and Mick as Lakmé and Gérald. Not that she planned to kill herself, like the poor, grieving Lakmé. It was simply that sense of impossibility that had haunted her for so long.

She'd accepted it all these years. But no more. Mick Reid was going to give her one more chance whether he liked it or not. She would do her best to see that he did.

It was in her, that need to please. It always had been. She'd never understood what it was when Mick whispered the words *good girl* in her ear, all those years ago. She'd only known it had made her shiver.

God, to hear him say that to her again . . .

A small shudder went through her, leaving goose bumps all over her skin.

She shook herself. She couldn't sit there mooning over him all day. She had work to do.

She fired off an email to Jamie reminding him to ask his brother to call her about doing the repairs on the house, then opened up the business plan she'd spent months putting together to expand the family business. Her mother and aunts would be hard cases, she knew, but she'd always had so many ideas, and now she had the training and experience in the field to back it up. Maybe this time they wouldn't turn her down.

Two cups of coffee and two hours later, her cell phone rang. She got up and picked it up off the counter, smiling when she saw her best friend's name on the screen.

"Marie Dawn, you're up early."

"Neal had an early shift at the firehouse—I've been up since five. I didn't want to wake you, but I'm dying to know how things went yesterday. I got your message but I couldn't call you back. I was taking care of *grand-mère* until late last night."

She poured herself another cup of coffee and stood at the counter with it. "It's no problem, hon. And I've been up since six myself. I couldn't sleep. Too much on my mind."

"Let me guess what that might be."

"You don't exactly have to be a mind reader."

"So, tell me everything," Marie Dawn prompted.

"Well . . ." She paused, sipped her coffee. ". . . He was pissed."

"As we expected him to be. *Continue.*"

"I'm really glad Jamie was there. It helped, even if it was mostly to give us both something else to focus on. And why in the world didn't you tell me Mick is still fighting, Marie Dawn?"

"Because I knew you'd worry, and I didn't want to do that to you. If he was ever seriously injured I would have let you know."

"He hasn't been?"

"Nothing more than a few broken fingers, and that badly broken nose, but that was years ago, when you were still in Europe. There would have been no point in telling you then."

"I noticed the scar yesterday. And a bruise on his face. I don't like it."

"He's not about to stop, *mon amie.*"

"I know." Allie blew out a long breath. "No one has ever been able to tell Mick anything."

"Does that mean he didn't agree to your plan?"

"Actually, he did. I'm a little surprised, to be honest." In truth, she was shocked. As brazen as she'd been going into it, she'd always doubted he would agree. "I just had to try, you know, Marie Dawn? Even if he'd walked away, at least I'd have given it one last shot. That was what was really in my mind. I had to be determined."

"Why are you being so fatalistic?" her friend asked. "Especially now that he's going to do this?"

"You know our history better than anyone but Jamie. And I don't even know if he knows that Mick and I slept together that time."

"I do know the history. But I also know how Mick feels about you," Marie Dawn said. "It's obvious any time your name is mentioned. He loves you, Allie."

"So everyone keeps telling me. And . . . I think he does, too. Or maybe I just like to think so." She sighed. She couldn't help it. Hope was a tight knot in her chest. "Maybe I'm delusional."

"You're not."

"We'll see. He's taking me to the club Friday night."

"We're finally giving up the details! More, *s'il vous plaît.* How did you accomplish this feat?"

Allie couldn't help but smile at the glee in her friend's voice. "Jamie and I managed to corner him into it by telling him if he didn't play me, I'd find someone who would."

"Very clever."

"I almost feel bad about it. It was manipulative."

"How do you think I got Neal to marry me?"

Allie snorted. "You did not. Everyone knew he was going to marry you the day you two met."

"Still, men sometimes need a little push. Or a big one in Mick's case. But the bigger they come, the harder they fall. I almost wish I shared this kink of yours so I could be there to see it."

"You're married to his brother. Mick would freak if you showed up at the club."

"And I don't have any real desire to go, but I *do* want to know every detail. Can we have lunch on Saturday?"

"That would be great."

"Okay, good. I need to go run a few errands, but call me this week if you want to talk."

"I will. And I'll see you on Saturday."

They hung up and Allie poured the rest of her coffee down the sink. She was jittery enough—she didn't need the caffeine. Instead, she'd go for a run, then head to Dolcetti to gauge her family's mood before she launched her plan to convince them to let her into the business.

She felt a bit better after talking to Marie Dawn. If nothing else, it was nice to know she and Jamie were on her side. Now that left only Mick.

She was nervous about Friday night. And incredibly, almost unbearably excited. Physically. Emotionally. She was also a little afraid. Or maybe a lot.

What if she and Mick didn't gel when it came to the kink? Their physical chemistry had always been mind-blowing, but she knew that didn't always translate to a good kink match. On the other hand, what if their kink compatibility was as amazing as their sexual chemistry, but Mick still turned away from her after they'd played? She wasn't sure she could bear it. But there was always the possibility that she wasn't what he was looking for in a submissive. That she might not please him. And in this realm, within the D/s and S/M dynamic, that was a crucial element. She could be very submissive in the BDSM realm, which was the polar opposite of who she was in her everyday life, but she was no service sub. What if he wanted more of a slave mentality, ultimately? She'd never be able to go there, not even for Mick.

And . . . she had to accept that she simply wasn't going to know until they were together at The Bastille on Friday night.

Friday couldn't come soon enough.

She busied herself with eating a bowl of oatmeal with honey and raisins while shopping for curtains and new bathroom fixtures online for another hour, then she decided it was time to go for her run, and got up to get changed. Her laptop pinged. Without sitting down again, she leaned over and glanced at her email. Her heart was a sudden hammer in her chest when she saw it was from Mick. She clicked it open.

Allie,

You are to do exactly as I instruct. Be ready for me at 8:00 on Friday night, as we discussed. You are to wear a dress, no stockings, high black heels—shoes, not boots. I don't care for boots on a sub—they're for Dominants, in my opinion. Your lingerie should be black or red. I enjoy the symbolism of the darker colors. I am certain you understand what I mean by that. Wear only a thong and a bra. Expect that they will be removed. No jewelry, which only gets in the way of play.

Before I pick you up, I want you to concentrate on the ritual of preparing yourself for me. Take a bath, rather than a shower. Take the time to soak, and while you're there, think about what may lie ahead. Think about being in my hands. Think about what my hands will do to you. They will command you. Pleasure you. Bring you the pain you've asked for. And they are my

hands. Never forget that. In fact, you might spend the rest of
the week thinking about these things.
    8:00. Be prompt.

Mick

God, she was trembling all over, her sex going warm and wet.

"And they are my *hands. Never forget that."*

As if she could!

She almost wished his email had come later in the week, giving her less time to think about it. But she also knew he'd done it on purpose. He was a sadist, after all. Exactly what she wanted. And everything she feared.

It was going to be a very long week.

MICK'S COMPUTER BEEPED at him, and he checked his email. Allie had written three words back. *"Of course, Mick."*

He could almost hear her saying those words to him, her voice low and soft, like a caress on his skin.

He could make her say those words to him. What a wonderfully wicked idea.

His cell phone went off and he picked it up.

"Reid here."

"Mick, it's Jamie."

"Ah, our flesh merchant."

"Ha! Hardly."

"Our negotiator, then. Is that better?"

"Much, actually. And that's what I'm calling to talk to you about."

"If you think you're going to lecture me about how to handle

Allie, keep it. You're the one who set this thing up. You wouldn't have done it if you didn't know I can be trusted with her."

Jamie said quietly, "Can you, buddy? And I'm not asking because I intend to lecture you. It's because I think maybe you need to talk it out."

"I'm not that much of a talker."

"Yeah. I just need to know your head is in the right place."

"I'll get it there by the end of the week."

"Which is why I'm calling. Look, Mick, we both went through the Dominant's mentor program at The Bastille. Are you now so experienced—or so damn macho—that you've forgotten it's okay to ask for help?"

He ran a hand over his goatee. "Of course not. But I can handle this on my own."

"It's Allie we're talking about, Mick. Which makes this different from any other woman you've played, and you fucking know it."

"I do fucking know it, all right?" he exploded. He pushed his chair back from the old wooden door he'd made into his desk and stood up to pace. "Fuck, Jamie. Sorry. But I *do* know. I understand this will be a challenge. And believe me, I was not too happy with you—or with her—at first. But now . . . I've had some time to mull it over and I'd be lying if I didn't tell you I'm looking forward to it. To playing her. To the challenge of it."

"But you believe you can absolutely maintain with her?"

"I wouldn't go near her if I didn't think so." A small lie—it burned on his tongue. "Yes. Of course I can maintain control, with her or anyone."

There was a long pause on the other end. Then Jamie said, "It's not that I don't have confidence in you as a Dominant, buddy. But this is different."

"Why all the dire warnings about something that was your idea?"

"It was *her* idea. And I'm making a point. If you're in denial about this stuff—"

"I'm not," he interrupted.

"If you were, it could be dangerous," Jamie finished.

"What we do is always dangerous."

"Agreed. And it's exactly why the 'dire warnings' aren't warnings as much as a reality check."

"Duly noted."

He was getting annoyed with Jamie, even though he knew he was right. The things they did at the dungeon—or at home, in some cases—were dangerous. Physically. Sometimes emotionally. He was always careful with the women he played. He would be even more careful with Allie.

"Okay. Since I'm still responsible for her as her mediator, we'll check in again on Thursday or Friday and see how you're doing."

"Yeah. Fine," Mick agreed grudgingly.

"Fine. I'm heading to the gym around seven tomorrow night. Meet for a workout? We don't have to talk about this."

Despite his boxing workout that morning and the martial arts training he had scheduled that evening, he wouldn't mind working with some weights with Jamie. It would calm him down. He hoped. "Sure."

"See you then."

They hung up and Mick tossed his phone onto the desk. His body was flooded with adrenaline, as it was every time he thought about Allie. Which was most of the time since she'd come back to the city. Adrenaline or a hard-on that wouldn't stop no matter how many times he came. In bed, in the shower, at his desk.

He was growing hard even now just thinking about her for three damn seconds.

Allie.

He pressed on his aching cock through his jeans.

Control.

But he couldn't get her face out of his mind. Her beautiful, lithe body.

He remembered what her naked breasts looked like, the hardening nipples a dark, dusky pink. So succulent under his fingertips, his tongue.

His cock grew rigid. He reached for his zipper. His cell went off again.

"God fucking damn it."

He pulled in a quick breath before he picked it up and looked at the screen. A business call. He had to switch gears. Get his focus on work.

"Reid here."

Twenty minutes later he hung up, having negotiated a job for the coming Monday. Which meant he'd be gone soon after playing with Allie, unavailable to do aftercare should she experience a delayed subdrop, those moments—or days, sometimes—when a bottom's brain "dropped" after being high on the endorphins and seratonin that often flooded them during play. They could go through depression, feelings of emptiness, tears. And as the Top who took them there, it was his responsibility to see them through any aftereffects. If Allie was prone to subdrop, if Jamie wasn't around to help out with her while he was out of town, then Friday night would be off.

He didn't fucking want Jamie to do her aftercare.

But since Allie was new to the New Orleans scene, she might not have any other local kink friends yet, so Jamie would be it. Not that he was threatened by his best friend.

Damn it. He'd have to speak with Allie.

He dialed her number. It went to voice mail.

"Hey, it's Mick. Something's come up and we need to talk about Friday. Call me."

He hung up. He hadn't meant to sound so short.

He scrubbed a hand over his jaw.

Almost unbearable even to hear her voice on her outgoing message.

He dropped his phone on his desk once more and began to pace again. But his office—the second bedroom in his flat—was too small to contain the thrumming energy running through his body. He went into the living room and was drawn, as he so often was when he had something to figure out, to the windows overlooking the narrow street.

It was quiet down there, no people, no cars. Just the row of close-set buildings, stucco and brick and softly painted wood, some with the intricate wrought iron balconies and gates New Orleans was known for. He tried to allow the familiar scenery to lull him, but he was crawling out of his skin.

Maybe he should go for another quick run. Either that or get into a scalding hot shower and fist his hand around his throbbing cock until he came again.

"Because twice already this morning apparently wasn't enough," he muttered. Then, when his cell phone went off again in the other room, "Whoever you are, I do not want to talk to you."

He stalked into his office and grabbed the phone.

Allie.

Well, that statement had been bullshit.

"Hey."

"Hey yourself." It was that smooth, purely female voice of hers. More mature now than when they'd met in high school, but still the same Allie he'd always known. Sweet.

Not as sweet as he'd imagined, or they wouldn't be having this conversation.

"Mick? You there?"

"Yeah. Sorry. I was working on something when you called."

When had he turned into such a liar?

"Oh. I'm sorry to interrupt, but your message sounded important."

"Yeah. We need to talk about Friday."

"Don't tell me you're backing out on me," she said, warning in her voice, which he wouldn't have put up with from any other submissive. There was something else beneath the bravado. Disappointment?

"Not necessarily," he said. "I'll run the scenario by you, then we can talk it out."

"Okay."

"I've had a job come up in Atlanta. A small venue concert, but it's for someone I've worked with for years, so I didn't want to turn it down. It means I'll be gone on Monday."

"I . . . don't understand what that has to do with Friday. Do you need to leave that soon?"

"No, I'll leave early Monday. But it means I won't be available again until Thursday. I haven't checked with Jamie to make sure he'll be around—I wanted to talk with you first. In case you need someone here for subdrop. I know we haven't discussed this yet. I'd planned to talk through your aftercare needs later this week."

"My aftercare needs are pretty basic—some water, a snack if my blood sugar is low, a blanket. I'm relaxed and happy after play if the connection is good. I've never felt subdrop, although I've sat with friends through it."

"You're certain?"

"I'm certain. Usually I'm a little giddy and dreamy the night

I play, then the next day I'm a bit tired if I haven't slept enough. Or, those times when I've played a whole weekend with someone, the energy just keeps going until the play is over—the endorphins, the adrenaline. The rush. Then I just sleep it off."

He didn't want to think about her playing with anyone else. He couldn't stand it.

"Tell me what you usually feel like a few days after." He had to ask. It was his responsibility, and responsibility was something he never took lightly.

"A few days after I just feel like myself. Sometimes a little happy and floaty still, but that's a good thing. And sometimes I'm sore, of course. Loving my marks."

Lord, he'd love to be the one to mark her. To welt that fragile-looking skin. To put bruises there. Teeth marks.

He got hard again in such a hot, sudden rush he had to swallow down a gasping breath.

He adjusted himself through his jeans, and his own hand against the iron-hard erection beneath the denim had him shivering.

Control.

"Okay," he said. "But I'm checking in with Jamie anyway to make sure you aren't left alone if you need someone."

"That's fine. I know I can go to Jamie, anyway. And I always have Marie Dawn, of course."

"Do you know anyone else here yet?" he asked. "I don't know that she'd know what to do."

"I've talked with a few people online, but I haven't met anyone in person yet. So, no—no one close. But I'll be fine, Mick."

"Just covering the bases. That's part of my job here, Allie. Or haven't you played with anyone who goes by those standards?"

"Of course I have! Mick, I'm not 'kindergarten playing' at

kink any more than you are. The people I've played with are the real thing. Check my damn references."

Oh, he loved the fire in her. But her sharp-tongued reply was deserved.

He blew out a breath. "That was an asinine thing for me to say."

"It was. But I'm glad to see you can admit it when you're wrong."

"I can. Just know those times are rare."

She laughed. "God, you are such a Dom."

"Am I supposed to be insulted?" But he couldn't help the slow grin that quirked the corners of his mouth.

"Nope. Probably not."

He lowered his tone. "Don't think for a minute that I am anything but dominant, Allie."

"Don't worry. I'm pretty sure you won't let me forget."

"You've got that right."

"Okay, so, Friday night at eight, appropriately dressed and in the appropriate frame of mind," she said, her tone shifting. He could tell by the breathiness in her voice she was switching gears, edging into her submissive role the slightest bit. He liked it.

What would she be like to play? To have her submit to him? Feisty or not, she would submit. He'd see to it that she did. He didn't need a service sub in order to feel that yielding.

His groin tightened.

"We need to discuss sexual contact," he told her.

"Oh. Of course."

"Right now my limit is no sex."

There was a long pause. "No sex?"

It was going to kill him, but if he was going to hang on to any shred of control, there had to be some line drawn in the sand.

"I feel fine with some contact and, frankly, in getting you

off—I wouldn't leave anyone high and dry. But we're not going to get that involved."

There was another pause. "I understand."

"Do you? It's *us*, Allie. The contact has to reflect how complicated this is."

"It doesn't have to be, Mick," she said quietly.

"You know it does. It just *is*, and we can't pretend this is something it's not. We are not two people who've just met or have had nothing more than friendship between them. Safe, Sane and Consensual also means being realistic."

"Okay. I get it. I honestly wouldn't choose to impose those limits, but if that's where you stand . . ."

"It is."

"All right," she agreed.

Thank the Lord. He wasn't sure how long he'd have been able to hold out against any real argument.

"Since I have you, is there anything else you'd like to discuss before we play?" he asked. "Any questions for me?"

"I think we've covered everything for now. I understand some things change, and will expect that we can renegotiate as needed—outside of scene time, of course."

"Yes. As a matter of fact, I'll check in with you that night before we start to see if you feel differently about anything, to see how you're feeling physically."

"You're very thorough," she said.

"I am."

"You've always been a perfectionist, though, haven't you? I remember even in high school you'd polish your motorcycle for hours, making sure every inch of chrome gleamed. I liked hanging out in the garage with you, watching you work. Listening to music."

He didn't want to think about the damn motorcycle. Not now, not ever. He moved back into the living room, stared out the window without really seeing anything.

It wasn't the bike that had ruined his life—it was his own bad judgment. But Allie referencing their past . . . those had been good days, and he couldn't find it in himself to focus on the bad part that had come later—either with the bike or with her. Not now, with her voice soft in his ear.

"The music was great," he admitted, "except for your strange fascination with Nickelback."

"What? I still love them," she defended. "His voice is amazing."

"You'll never convince me of that."

"Do you remember our song, Mick?" she asked, her voice going soft.

He didn't want to answer. Didn't want to think about him and Allie together back then.

After a few silent moments she said, " 'Drive' by Incubus. I . . . still listen to it sometimes."

"Great song," he said gruffly, his breath catching in his throat.

Damn it.

"Allie, if we're going to play at the club, maybe we'd better set some ground rules for this stuff."

"What stuff?"

"Trying to bring back the past. That was a long time ago."

"Okay . . ." She drew the last syllable out, and he could hear the hurt in her voice. But he had to lay down some boundaries or things were going to get messy.

Hell, they already were messy. This whole thing was messy. But he wouldn't go back on his word. Maybe a night of play and they'd both have it out of their systems.

Yeah, right.

And then she'd go on to play with some other Dom at his home club, and he'd fucking want to kill the guy.

"Mick?"

"Yeah."

"You're right. We should stay focused on the present. Not get caught up in history."

"Glad you see it my way."

"You always are," she muttered.

"I heard that."

She laughed, breaking the tension. And knowing Allie, that had been her purpose.

"I'll see you Friday," he told her. "We should both talk to Jamie, just in case."

"I'll do that."

"And give Marie Dawn a heads-up."

"Yes, Sir."

He could hear the capital *S* in the way she said it, that breathiness again. His cock twitched.

"Friday at eight. Don't be late."

"I wouldn't think of it."

"And Allie?"

"Yes?"

"Be prepared for me to smack some of that sass out of you."

"I'll count on it."

They hung up and the view through the window came into focus. He braced himself with one hand on the frame.

She would be perfect. She always had been, always would be. But at The Bastille . . .

He groaned.

He knew he was damn good at what he did. He'd had years of practice, was confident in his abilities. But this one girl just threw him off his game. He'd find a way to overcome it. He'd have to. For his own sake as well as hers. He'd have to really watch himself with her.

Allie was definitely back in town, and was under his skin already.

Friday evening came, and Allie was trying to remind herself of what she'd told Mick—that her needs were simple. But there was nothing simple about the way she couldn't stop thinking about him.

She'd had a long lunch with her mother, catching up on news of family and old friends, local politics and concerns about the bakery's neighborhood, but Mick had been firmly in the back of her mind the entire time. Enough that her mother had asked her several times what she'd been daydreaming about. Allie had thought she'd managed to skirt the question, but by the end of lunch her mother's appraising gaze told her nothing had escaped her, and Allie realized hiding her obsession with Mick—she didn't currently know what else to call it—wasn't going to be simple at all when it came to her family.

She breathed out a sigh as she checked her reflection in the full-length mirror on the closet door for the tenth time, looking for a bit of mussed hair, a smudge in her makeup. She liked the way her simple black knit dress fit her—short and tight across her hips, but blousy on top, with a wide neckline that fell off one shoulder.

There was nothing simple about the way her heart was beating, as if a train were chugging through her chest. There was nothing simple about the way fear had set in the day before, the way it had grown all day until she was nearly bursting with it. But there was one thing that *was* simple.

Her need for him was simple. Primal. Primitive.

The need was like fire in her veins, burning her up inside, making her nipples hard beneath the filmy black mesh of her bra. She was wet simply thinking about the evening ahead, about Mick touching her, finally, after all these years. She could remember the feel of his rough hands on her body . . .

She put her own hand over her chest, trying to calm her racing heartbeat, but she knew nothing would help other than getting to The Bastille, having Mick put her in his ropes, and silencing her fears and need with subspace.

She glanced at the clock on her nightstand. Seven forty-five.

Somehow she could not stand the next fifteen minutes. She dug in her purse and found her cell phone, dialed Marie Dawn's number.

"Hello?"

"It's me."

"Allie, I thought tonight was the big playdate?"

"It is. He'll be here in a few minutes. Just . . . tell me I'm doing the right thing."

"Oh, *chérie*, only you can know what's right. But . . . you've been convinced this was what you had to do until now. What's changed?" her friend asked.

"It's more real. This is when I'll know . . . when *we'll*

know . . . if there's anything there between us. If he'll . . . have me. And God, I hate to sound so pathetic. I felt so strong going into this. I don't know what's wrong with me."

"Allie, we both know I don't really get this BDSM stuff, so feel free to correct me if I'm wrong, but could part of it be that subspace thing you told me about?" Marie Dawn asked. "You did say he specifically asked you to think of him and what'll happen tonight while you were getting ready, and you've explained to me how the getting ready part is like a little ritual . . . Well, do you think you're hitting subspace at all? Could it be making you feel more raw? This evening is important for you. I don't know if you've ever played with anyone where there was this heavy an emotional load going into it. That's got to affect you."

"No. I mean, yes—you're absolutely right."

She was. If Allie took a moment to step back and detach from her nerves, she could see it clearly. She was starting to drop into subspace already, simply knowing it was Mick who would play her tonight. And that meant a certain level of vulnerability, with much more to come.

"It's all the strain of . . . hope, I guess. Hope that's had nearly eleven years to build. Hope that built in the time between him leaving me in high school and that one night we had when I was twenty years old."

"That's a lot for anyone to deal with. Under these circumstances where, from what you've told me, you have to have a large element of trust . . . I can't even imagine what that has to do to your head."

"That's it exactly. Although the psychology of it, the mind-fuck, is also what makes it so damn thrilling."

Marie Dawn laughed. "Better you than me, *chérie*. I'd rather get my thrills in a fast car or skiing down a mountain."

Allie couldn't help but smile. "What can I say? We kinky folks are a strange bunch."

"Yes, you are, but I love you anyway."

"Love you, too. Oh, God, there's the door."

"Lunch tomorrow—don't forget!"

"I won't. Must go!"

"Bye!"

She tucked her phone back into her small black purse and went to answer the door, pausing to check her reflection in the hall mirror. She set her purse down on the narrow table beneath the mirror, freeing her hands to quickly smooth her hair, her dress. She inhaled, murmured to herself, "This is it," and opened the front door.

He looked enormous in the doorway of the old house. Big and handsome and radiating authority. He was dressed in dark jeans, a black dress shirt with the sleeves rolled at the cuffs, a dark undershirt beneath it. Around his neck was a leather thong with a silver cross hanging from it. Simple. Utterly masculine, like everything else about him.

"You letting me in, Allie?"

"Oh. Yes, come in."

She opened the screen door, and he took it from her and swung it wide. Then he charged in—it was more sudden and forceful than merely walking—and he was on her. One hand went to her shoulder and held on just tight enough for her to understand he was taking over already. The other took one of her wrists and pinned it behind her back as he pushed her up against the wall. She could feel the heat of his breath on her face. Could see the glittering gray depths of his eyes, the pupils wide and dark. He leaned in and a lock of his hair tickled her forehead. And all she could do was take in slow, gasping breaths, her body and her mind giving over to his command immediately, her muscles going slack.

"That's it," he said so softly she could barely hear him over the blood pounding in her ears. "You go down nice and easy, like silk under the water. I like it, Allie. I do."

He tightened his hold on her wrist and shoulder, gave her a small, hard jerk. Her heart hammered. Her nipples went tight. Her knees went weak.

"Yeah, just give it over to me, princess. I can feel it, you know. The way your limbs have gone all soft. Weak against me. And if I wanted to I could slip my thigh right between yours. Like this."

He did as he said, the strong muscles of his thighs parting hers. So close to the need blossoming between them, but not touching her.

She moaned.

"I can hear the way you're breathing," he went on. "The small catch in your throat that tells me everything I need to know. You're going down already. Aren't you?"

She did not want to give up all control to him. Not this soon. Not without her having some hold on the situation. To go into it this fast . . . her head was spinning.

"Tell me," he demanded.

She tried to push against him, to push him away, but it only brought her aching mound into contact with his thigh.

"Mick, stop."

He eased back an inch or two.

"*Stop* is not the usual safe word, Allie, you know that. But tell me, are you safe-wording out? If you are, I'll let you go right now."

She drew in a few panting breaths, desire and confusion twining together deep in her body, her mind.

"I . . . no."

"No what?"

"No, I'm not using my safe word."

He drew her in against his body, his hands gripping both wrists behind her back now. She could feel every rock-hard plane and muscle: abs, chest, shoulder, and his thigh pressing between hers, making her hot and wet. The cross he wore around his neck dug into her flesh, but she welcomed it.

He lowered his head, his mouth a hairsbreadth from hers. She tilted her face, needing to be kissed—that need was scorching her. But he only held her there, inhaled her breath, then another, and another, until she sank into the rhythm of it. Her limbs relaxed into his hold on her. Safe. Familiar.

Mick.

This was Mick. Finally. He wouldn't hurt her. Not in any way she didn't want him to.

"Good girl," he whispered against her mouth, and her knees nearly buckled.

He held her tight, just breathing with her—it was the only sound in the room. She raised her gaze to his, found his eyes dark and stormy, but with desire or some other emotion she couldn't tell. All she knew was that his eyes looked right into her, through her, in the way they always had, yet even more intense with all the life he must have lived in the intervening years.

"Tell me what you're feeling," he said. Commanded.

"I . . . I'm warm all over," she answered quietly. "Loose but filled with tension at the same time."

"What's the tension about?"

"Being with you. Knowing we'll play tonight. That we already are. Needing you to kiss me, Mick."

She felt his chest heave as he drew in a long breath. His hold on her didn't change. She waited.

The angle of his chin shifted. His mouth drew closer to hers. Held there. She didn't dare do what she so desperately wanted to—to lift up on her toes, tilt her chin, claim his lips.

His grip on her wrists tightened painfully, his gray eyes going dark. She didn't care. She waited while she measured the sharper cadence in his breath, the gleam of stark desire in his eyes. Felt glad to see it there, to know he needed her in the same way she needed him.

Why wouldn't he kiss her?

Unbearable.

He twisted his crushing grip, twisting the skin until it pinched, and she gasped. She lifted her chin, the need too powerful, but he moved away just enough to avoid her seeking lips.

No!

But she remained silent. Waiting. Just as she'd been taught. She would wait for him. Be good for him. Please him.

"We'll go now," he told her, releasing her so quickly she almost fell. He caught her with an arm around her waist, stood silently while she regained her balance, asked, "You good?" and waited for her affirmative nod before letting her go.

Her mind was emptying already, beginning to float as he put her purse into her hands and led her onto the porch, closed the door behind them.

The change in air brought her back to the surface a bit, but not too much. New Orleans air was always a bit magical, after all. The night was soft and sultry, like scented oil in a warm bath. Like she knew his skin felt at the small of his back.

Mick wrapped his palm around her waist and led her down the stairs, careful of her in her high heels, the black pinup-style stilettos with the peep toe and the small velvet bow she'd worn just for him. He led her to his big black truck parked at the curb, the sleek paint shining in the moonlight. He helped her up onto the high seat, buckled her in with careful hands and closed the door before going around to the driver's side and getting in.

The drive to the club didn't take long from her house in the lower Garden District to the Warehouse District, just south of the French Quarter. There was some jazz playing on the stereo, just loud enough to fill the silence. But it was comfortable that they didn't talk. Natural. Meditative.

They turned onto Magazine Street and passed a few blocks of warehouses—some of them actually used for that purpose, some housing galleries or nightclubs. Mick pulled into a parking lot and came around to help her step down from the truck.

The big warehouse in front of them didn't look any different from the others on the block, except for the red light over the doorway. Mick led her up to it, and they went up the short flight of stairs. He nodded to the doorman, a wall of a man in a leather vest, before opening the door and ushering her inside.

She blinked in the bright light. They were in a small room filled up by a large antique desk. Behind it sat a small woman in her sixties, Allie would guess, who watched them over a pair of blue-framed bifocals worn low on her nose.

"Evening, Mick," she said. "You must be Allesandra. Welcome to The Bastille. I'm Pixie—we chatted online."

"Yes, we did."

"You've already read and agreed to the house rules and sent in your paperwork, including your membership card from your club in San Francisco, so all I need is a copy of your ID and you're good to go."

Allie fumbled in her purse for a moment, found her ID and passed it to Pixie, who disappeared through a door for a few moments, then gave it back to her.

"Enjoy your evening. Cell phones off, dears."

"Of course, Pixie," Mick said, pulling his out of his pocket and smiling at the tiny woman as he shut it off. "Allie, give me yours."

She handed it to him, and he powered it down before returning it to her.

A small part of her mind was screaming at her that she wasn't behaving normally, and another part was reminding her this was the way things happened when a Dom shows up at your house and practically brings you to your knees before taking you to a haven for kinky people who were just like you were, even in all the myriad variety of kinks and personalities. She breathed a long, sweet sigh of relief as Mick took her through a door and into the club.

The lighting was dim, shades of red and purple, with a few spots of soft amber gleaming from the lamps set here and there at the cleaning stations, supplied with bottles of antibacterial spray and paper towels, small first-aid kits and bottled water. But she could see that inside The Bastille looked like anything but a warehouse. The walls were finished in a highly lacquered black, with heavy wooden posts polished to a high sheen every few feet. She could see the eyebolts, some with the occasional lengths of chain attached, set into the wood. Placed around the edges of the room were couches and chairs and ottomans upholstered in red velvet, large tables in carved wood, everything oversized and luxurious and slightly ornate in what she thought of as Bohemian gypsy style. Here and there, high on the walls, were paintings of naked women in seductive and often wanton poses, some bound in rope or chains or leather straps, corseted or cuffed. There were people in the room in the same state of undress, many bound, corseted. Wanton.

She immediately felt a sense of home.

Beside her Mick whispered in her ear, "What do you think of our little club?"

"It's beautiful. And it's not little at all."

"There are private and semiprivate rooms, the themed rooms. The school room. The Victorian boudoir. The medieval torture chamber. The medical room. Do you see the curtained areas off to the sides? Those are aftercare rooms, full of pillows. And in the back there's the kitchen and an outdoor patio. But I'll give you the tour another time. I don't want to break this space inside your head too much. I like where you're at."

She turned to him. "Do you?"

He stroked the underside of her chin with his finger. "I do. I think we're going to play very well together. Come."

He took her hand and led her across the floor of the main room. The music was a low throb of ambient tones as they passed a row of spanking benches: two floating, padded tables suspended from the ceiling by heavy chains. They moved past an enormous wooden frame in the middle of the room. A woman was bound in heavy leather cuffs, her arms stretched over her head and attached to the frame by carabiners clipped to hooks set into the wood. She wondered vaguely where he might be taking her, but that sinking sensation was beginning to ground her in the moment, in her body, and she was content for now to simply follow him.

They reached the back of the room, where long couches and a few overstuffed chairs made cozy conversation areas. He stopped in front of one of the couches, set his play bag down on a table, nodded at her, a sharp lift of his chin that made her focus on the chiseled edges of his features, all pure masculine man.

"Down on the floor, Allie. On your knees. And wait for me." He turned away to unzip his bag.

"I . . . what?"

He turned back to her, his gaze narrowing. "This is standard drill, Allie. I thought you were an experienced submissive," he said, doubt lacing his tone.

"I am."

"Then what's going on?"

"I just . . ." She had to pause, catch her breath. "It's because it's *you*. Well, you and me. I guess I thought . . ." She trailed off, shaking her head.

"You thought what? That because it's us things would happen differently than they would with any other play partners we may have had? That I'd handle you with kid gloves because of our history, despite the things you and Jamie have told me about your experience in the scene? Despite our negotiations?"

There was an edge to his voice she found a little frightening, yet at the same time knowing he was the full-on Dom with her was reassuring—that he wouldn't cut her any slack he shouldn't in these circumstances.

Remember who you're dealing with. Remember this is what you've always wanted.

"No. No. I'm just . . . making a mental adjustment, I guess."

"Well, make it fast, girl, because if you're not down on your knees in about ten seconds I'm putting you there myself."

Really love to have him do just that to me.

She almost groaned aloud. But she wasn't going to give him that. Not yet.

She sank to her knees on the Persian carpet in front of the sofa, her gaze on his as he watched her, trying to assess his response. Was he pleased with her? Or was he still so pissed that she'd forced his hand in the situation that she'd have to really stretch herself to satisfy him? To make him see she could be the perfect submissive for him. That *she* could be perfect for him.

She sank back on her heels and clasped her hands behind her back. Waited.

"Eyes on the floor," he said gruffly before turning back to his big black bag as if nothing had happened, as if their little exchange hadn't left her heart slamming into her ribs.

She tried to breathe as she'd been taught—in, exhaling slowly through her mouth, concentrating on telling her limbs to relax. Soon it was working and she was able to spread her focus to the sounds around her: the dungeon music, the moans and cries of the others being played, a little laughter from somewhere, the lovely sound of a leather flogger hitting flesh.

She'd always loved that sound, the simple knowledge of what it meant. It made her want to feel it herself. To smell the leather. She inhaled, letting the scents of leather and anticipation sit in her lungs—and gasped when his fingers sank into her hair and *pulled*. Pulled her hair back unto she was forced to meet his gaze.

He bent low over her, brought his mouth almost to hers and whispered, "I thought you could do it, Allie. After we talked I had a pretty good idea that you really could submit. But seeing you down on your knees tells me everything I need to know. For the moment, anyway. We'll have to see what else you know, what else you can do. But this trick . . . oh, yeah, you have this one down."

She didn't dare say anything. He was all Dom right then, and she didn't want him to be anything else. His hand gripping her hair, his imposing presence, his whispered threats and words of encouragement, were making her shivery all over. Wet between her thighs.

"Arms up while I get you undressed," he ordered.

She raised her arms high, let him pull the dress over her head, leaving her in her scant black mesh lingerie and her heels.

"Very nice," he murmured, moving behind her and reaching out to sweep her hair aside. "I'm going to start with your hair."

"What? My hair?"

"Is this an argument?"

She swallowed. "I . . . no."

"Then quiet now."

He swept her hair back from her face with both hands, and began to work some slender rope into it. She'd had this done before—had her hair bound into a sort of ponytail of corset lacing. She didn't know what had surprised her into speaking out a moment before. In a few minutes he was done. He swung her bound hair over her shoulder, then drew one finger slowly down the back of her neck, sending a trembling warmth down her spine. She tried to curve into his touch, but he stilled her with a palm flat between her shoulder blades, pressing just enough to make her feel it. Strength. Command.

"Oh no you don't, my girl. You move when I tell you to. Right now you are to be my toy to play with. Mine to move and shift around as I please. And I *will* please. Know that. Know it's coming. That *you* are. Eventually." He moved around her, tracing the line of her jaw, the side of her neck, over her collarbone, down the side of her breast, making her ache. "But now   now I'm going to sit down here on this couch and relax for a few minutes and just watch you. I want you to hold very, very still. Can you do that for me? Don't speak—nod yes if you think you can without me binding you yet."

Oh, Jesus! He was going to make her lose her mind. But she found herself nodding her chin.

"Good girl."

Heat shot through her system.

From the corner of her downturned eye she saw his booted foot as he settled onto the furniture. She swore she could *feel* him watching her, as if his hand were still on her bare skin.

"I think I'd like it better with your hands clasped behind your neck."

"Mick . . ." she whispered, her throat going tight, her body resisting being that vulnerable with him.

"Allie, the correct answer is an immediate agreement to do as I ask you by simply *doing* it. Or the answer is no. I'm not going to play these games, which I believe I've already told you."

She drew in a deep breath. She *wanted* to comply. And she wanted to fight it. But the part that wanted—needed—to be taken over by him was winning as her muscles went loose at the tone of utterly inarguable dominance in his voice.

"I'm sorry, Mick. I can do it. I will."

His voice softened, and she understood why he was such a good Dominant—he knew exactly when to be tough, and when to show tenderness. "Take a breath, then. And try it again. Yeah, that's much better."

She knew being in that position arched her back, made her breasts stand higher. It made her feel as if she were on display. It made her feel more submissive.

She waited. And waited. Until the waiting itself seemed almost unbearable, even more so because it was *him*. Hadn't she already waited for Mick long enough? Tears burned at the back of her eyes, but she swallowed them down. She *would* please him, damn it. Do as he said. Show him she knew what his game was all about, that she could play it, too.

She had to calm down, to still herself for the ropes, his favorite form of play.

She closed her eyes, pulled in a long breath.

The rope slipped around her wrist so fast she wasn't even aware of it until he'd already pulled it tight and started to tie what felt like a quick half-hitch knot. Then another and another, until he'd made a brace of rope that covered her entire forearm. He dropped the end of the rope, and without breaking contact through one hand on her shoulder, he grabbed another piece and started on her other arm, then finished it off by tying her wrists together.

She had a small moment of panic when she realized this was it—he'd effectively rendered her helpless in mere moments.

"Flex your fingers for me," he told her, and she did, knowing he was checking for circulation. "They feel okay? Good blood flow, still? You can answer me."

"Yes."

"Yes what?"

She swallowed. "Yes, Mick."

"That'll do for now. But it might be 'Sir' later. Be ready for it."

He slid a length of rope over her shoulders and let the ends fall down her back.

"You particularly attached to this lingerie?" he asked her. "Shake your head yes or no."

She shook her head no, wondering what he was going to tie her up with that would damage the delicate material. But before she had time to really consider it she felt the cool touch of metal against her skin and glanced down to see him slipping a pair of safety scissors under the front band of her bra. She gasped as in one snip it fell open, and in two more the straps were cut and the remains of the filmy garment fell to the floor.

She knew what was coming, but all the same it made her breath catch when he cut her underwear off her and pulled the fabric away, leaving her in nothing but a few feet of rope and her heels. But she was proud of her body—she only arched her back, raising her bare breasts higher.

She heard a small chuckle from him. "Very good, princess. That's exactly what I want to see. I can tell you like it, being naked, on your knees." He leaned over her and fisted her bound hair in his hand once more, yanking hard, and she pulled in a sharp breath. His face was right next to hers, his cheek pressed against hers. He said quietly, "Now we'll find out just how much you like this."

She closed her eyes as he pressed two fingers right into the damp heat between her thighs, sliding in her juices. Pleasure lanced into her.

"Christ, you're wet, baby. Do you know what that does to me? Entices the beast to come out of its cave. But we can't have that. Not yet, that's for sure. We'll just have to do something about it."

He let her hair go, pulled his fingers from her, leaving her shivering with need and heat, and returned with more rope, which he laid on the floor next to her, coiled into bundles. With quick hands he began to fashion a harness around her breasts, the rope sliding and slinking over her skin like a snake, sending small vibrations through her system. She loved every moment of it—the sensation of being slowly decorated, of being rendered helpless, being in his hands.

His hands.

As he drew the ropes tighter around her breasts, one rope across the top, another beneath them, she felt the pressure, making them even more sensitive, the sinuous slide of the rope across her skin making her nipples hard. Making her shiver. He worked the rope between her breasts, making a series of knots in the center that pressed painfully against her ribs, but she loved it. Wanted it.

He slid his hand under the rope there, pulled hard, pulling her up onto her knees. Ah, this was good, being handled this roughly. She didn't dare look up at him, keeping her gaze on the floor. But oh, how she wanted to. Wanted to see that animal banked and burning in his gray gaze.

"Very good," he murmured. "I like seeing the rope on you, the way it presses into your flesh. What do you feel in them, Allie? Tell me."

"I feel . . ." She had to pause, to take in a breath, which was a bit harder to do with the chest harness in place, just as it was when she wore a corset. "I feel . . . as if I'm being held. Hugged. I feel . . . excited. And safe, somehow."

"You are made for this, Allie girl. Made for my ropes, aren't you? Stay right there."

The ropes were sliding again as he worked them through the chest harness and down around her body—her ribs, her waist, across her back, and finally, between her legs. The rope slipped between her thighs, against her aching sex, and she almost cried out, her thighs shaking.

He was quiet as he worked, but she could hear his breath, almost as heavy as her own, felt the pressure and easing of hands as he moved the rope, tied knots, stopped to pull on the harness for no other purpose than to make her feel commanded. To make them pull hard against her swollen clit, to tighten there until the rope sank painfully between her pussy lips.

Oh, God, she loved it.

When he tipped her over onto her side she didn't protest, she just went down onto the floor, the rug a bit scratchy against her bare skin. He rolled her over onto her stomach with rough hands. She had always loved being manhandled a bit while in scene. But when he pulled her ankles up and she understood he meant to hog-tie her, something in her rebelled, her legs going stiff.

He was on her in a moment, his knee in her back, one hand pulling her torso up off the floor by the ropes crossing between her shoulder blades. She felt utterly helpless, taken over, which was exactly what she wanted, yet was also what was making her panic now.

"Allie, I'm going to give you a chance to tell me what this is about."

"I can't, Mick," she started, but tears lodged in her throat and she had to stop.

"You can't what?"

"I can't be . . . humiliated. Not with you. Please don't."

"This is not humiliation. This is beauty," he said, his tone low, quiet. Reverential in a way she understood. In a way that calmed her instantly. He ran a hand over her spine between the ropes. "The graceful angles of the body. The level of submission it signals. Seeing the flesh bound in my ropes is pure art to me. Your flesh . . . well, I've been waiting a long time to do this, which I believe you already know. That's . . . almost indescribable. So damn beautiful."

She felt her limbs loosen. His grip on her softened, and he let her back down onto the floor, where she turned her cheek, resting it on the wool rug.

"You're ready now," he told her. *Told*, not asked. It didn't matter. It was true.

He drew her ankles up once more, wrapped them in the sensually sliding rope, making her acutely aware of the bones and flesh there, then he tied them off with a few knots. He slipped a length of rope under the knots between her ankles and led it to her body harness, where he worked it through the ropes across her back, and pulled on them until they drew her ankles up a bit more.

She was truly helpless now, except for her safe words, of course. But she didn't need them. Her head was sinking deeply into subspace, which she realized distantly she hadn't quite expected without more pain play. The only pain was the slight throbbing of her bound breasts pressed against the carpet, her nipples grazing the wool, and the rope that pulled hard against her sex. But she was soaking wet.

Mick's big hand wrapped around her bound wrists, which

were clasped behind her head. She heard the soft *snick* of moving rope as he bound the corset tie on her hair to her wrists. Then he pulled up, lifting her chest off the floor, raising her head with it.

"Tell me that you're doing okay, Allie."

"Yes. Yes," she whispered.

"Are the ropes too tight anywhere? Cutting off circulation? Pressing too hard into bone?"

"No. The ropes are . . . good."

She tried to just keep breathing, to keep her body loose. When he slipped some rope between her wrists and tied it to her ankles, drawing her body up, making it bow, shock coursed through her. The discomfort of the position was a part of the power of it all, she understood, but Jesus, she'd never felt so utterly helpless. But it was for *him*.

Him.

Mick.

He began to run his hands over her flesh, so gently she wanted to cry. Her skin was alive, every nerve ending in hyperdrive. She felt his touch like fire. Like nothing she'd ever felt in her life.

"You feel so damn good, Allie girl. Skin like fucking silk. I love the way the ropes press into your body."

He reached down then and slid a hand under the knots at the small of her back, making the rope press harder against her sex.

She moaned.

"Yes, I like that, my girl—to hear how it hurts you, how you love it. Oh, yeah, I understand perfectly well it's both pleasure and pain. And make no mistake—that is my intention. Because as much as I love rope, I am a bit of a sadist. But you already knew that. You wanted it, or you wouldn't be here, would you?"

He moved his hand between her thighs, his fingers sliding in her juices.

"Christ, but you're soaked." His voice had turned to raw gravel, low and full of desire. "Makes me want to just . . . yeah."

He was quiet for several long moments, giving her time to wonder what he might do to her next. To crave it. To fear it. To fear how he would break her down.

But it was Mick. Finally. And she was *his* in this moment. Relief and emotion and an almost unbearable pleasure suffused her. For the moment, that was enough.

M ICK LOOKED DOWN at Allie's body. A part of him could barely believe it was *her* bound in his ropes. The fantasy image raging inside him all these years was nothing compared to the perfection that was this reality. And seeing her here . . . it was some small epiphany. Small, but enough to cause a crack in the glass wall he'd erected around his memory of who and what she was to him, like some fucking fairy princess in a castle. Maybe he was the one who'd put her there, but it had always seemed to make sense. Until now. Now he might have to question his perceptions. Because *this* Allie was real. This moment was real.

Too real.

He flexed his fingers, had to actually take a step back.

Calm the fuck down.

He pulled in a breath, then another, but his heart was beating like a drum and he was hard as steel.

He'd have to find a way to distance himself a little until he regained the control that kept him—that would keep them both—safe from the primal thing inside him, the dark shadows that drove him.

He reached into his bag and found what he was looking for: a small croplike implement that was really more like a slender wire rod with a few inches of black sandpaper at the end—the perfect tool for his intentions.

He stood at Allie's side, leaned in and listened to her breathing. It was slow and regular, and he knew she was slipping deeper into subspace simply from being bound in this way. He paused to check circulation in her hands and feet, found the flesh pink and healthy. Then he bent over her and swatted the bottoms of both bound feet with the sandpaper crop.

"Oh!"

"Shh. Stay quiet, Allie girl. Quiet and as still as you can."

He swatted her feet again, and this time, although he felt a small jerk in her body, she didn't pull too hard against her bonds.

He began a regular cadence, then, smacking the bottom of one foot, then the other, playing over the arches, the balls of her feet, the heels, the tips of her toes. He loved it when her breath began to come harder, loved it when she was quietly squirming in the ropes, her toes curling and uncurling. He could see she was processing the sensation well. He knew it didn't hurt too much—this particular toy used on the feet hit all the acupressure points, and often tickled more than hurt. But he didn't want to play her any harder than this right now. He simply wanted to bring her sensation, sensation that didn't come directly from his own hands. It would be too much to touch her.

He let himself relax into the rhythm, watching her breathing, visually testing the tightness of the ropes. He went on for a good ten minutes while the world around them shrank into the bubble in which it was just the two of them. Mick and Allie. The way it should have always been.

Fuck.

He stopped as his pulse began to race, fast and choppy. He tossed the toy at his bag, being far more careless with his equipment than he ever was. But he *had* to stop. Now.

He was topping out.

He'd heard a Top could drop the same way a bottom did. But he'd never expected it to happen to him—it never had before.

He'd never scened with Allie.

There was a small rage building in his chest. Rage that he hadn't held it more together. That he'd allowed his so-tightly-held control to slip.

He pulled his safety scissors from where he'd tucked them into his belt and snipped the rope holding her hair to her wrists, then the one holding her wrists to her ankles. He caught her across the chest in time to lower her head safely to the floor, and her feet at the same time. Her warm flesh burned into him like fire.

He kept cutting, tearing the ropes from her body, rolling her onto her back to work faster. He caught her confused gaze and cursed himself. It wasn't right, the way he was handling her, taking her down without any explanation.

"Mick, are we . . . I'm sorry for talking but are we ending the scene?"

Hurt in her voice. It cut him to the quick. But he couldn't take this any further. Not tonight.

"Yeah," was all he managed to say.

He pulled her into a sitting position, careful to be more gentle with her, then to her feet so he could finish cutting her out. She swayed, and he caught her with one arm around her waist. Lord, she felt like a china doll in his arms, and he was a bastard for doing this to her.

Soon the ropes lay in tatters on the floor, and he grabbed the small blanket he kept in his bag and wrapped it around her before leading her to the sofa and sitting her down. The panic was roaring in his ears as he settled next to her, needing to keep away from her, but knowing he couldn't do that—that if he couldn't manage an explanation, the least he had to do was offer some aftercare. But instead of leaning into him for comfort, as most bottoms did after play, she sat there woodenly. He didn't blame her.

"Allie . . . fuck, I know the energy is off . . ."

Why the hell couldn't he think straight?

She pulled the blanket tighter around her shoulders. "Off? It's all kinds of fucked up, Mick."

"I know. I'm sorry."

"What?"

"I'm sorry." He paused, shook his head. "Believe it or not I'm able to apologize when I'm wrong."

Her brown eyes welled with tears, and he felt even more like an asshole.

"Mick, what are you talking about? I'm the one who should be sorry. I forced you into this. How could I possibly have expected the dynamic to work? It's my own fault. I just wanted . . ." She paused, sniffed, wiped her cheeks with her palms. "Well, it doesn't matter what I wanted. I was wrong to do this."

"Allie, you are my responsibility right now, and I'm doing a lousy job. This is not your fault. You're just bottoming out."

"Maybe I am a little—I don't know—but I do know that I screwed this all up, or the scene wouldn't have gone wrong. We wouldn't be here doing this at all. I'm sorry, Mick. I really am."

Another tear slid down her cheek and he reached out, brushed it away with his thumb—he couldn't help himself. But when her face just crumpled there was nothing he could do but pull her into his arms and hold her. She was stiff at first, but in moments she was curled against his chest, crying softly, his shirt gripped in her hand.

Her body was all warmth and softness and the scent of summer. His pulse was still racing, hot and hard in his system. His mind was spinning, numb.

This was Allie, *his* Allie. He didn't know how he could think of her any other way.

He couldn't do this to her.

But I can't stay away. Not anymore.

He held her tighter, and she melted into him for a moment, then she started to pull away. He tightened his arms. She pushed at his chest. He let her go.

Fuck.

"Mick, don't. Please just . . . don't. I shouldn't have done this to you."

"You haven't done anything to me," he insisted.

"Oh yes I did. I manipulated you. It was wrong of me, and now you're trying to comfort me. You don't have to do this. Okay? You don't have to. Just . . . take me home."

"We should talk. I don't want you going home alone like this."

"I'll call Marie Dawn. I promise. I know you feel responsible as the Top. I get it. But I'm really the one who put myself here, and I'll see that I'm taken care of. I'll handle this myself. Which is what I should have done all along, instead of trying to pull you back in. You were right. I'm caught up in the past. I'm sorry, Mick."

It tore at him to see the expression on her face. He didn't know how they could resolve things tonight. They were both too raw. And he needed some time to understand what had happened to him.

"All right. Let me get your dress. But Allie . . . I'm sorry for a lot of things. You should know that."

She just shook her head mutely, and he handed the dress to her. She slipped it over her head, let the blanket fall. When he tried to help her into her shoes, she waved him away and did it herself, then sat in silence while he packed up his bag. She remained just as silent as they went back through the club to the front and got their coats. He was grateful that Pixie gauged their mood and kept quiet as they left.

He helped Allie step up into the truck, a hand on her elbow, but she was shut off to him. He went to the driver's side and got in, started the engine.

"Are you not talking to me at all?" he asked her.

"I just can't, Mick. I'm sorry. I don't know what else to say, and if I say anything more, I'm only going to make it worse."

"You need to stop apologizing."

"Because I'm completely blameless? Come on, Mick. We both know that's not true."

He scrubbed at his goatee with one hand, the other firmly on the wheel, when all he wanted was to stop the damn truck and take her in his arms again.

He knew she was right. He had felt manipulated the other day, but he'd accepted the situation as inevitable. But tonight everything had shifted once he had her in his ropes, under his hands. It wasn't the sight of her bare flesh, although that was pretty damn spectacular. It was *her*. Stronger than she used to be. Braver. What had it taken for her to get him to do this?

"I didn't think you'd be able to argue with that," she said quietly.

"No. I mean, I was thinking."

"It's better if we don't think, Mick."

He glanced at her profile, her high cheekbones, the tips of

her long lashes gilded by the streetlights. So damn beautiful. Stubborn as ever. And closed to him.

And not a damn thing he could do about it.

It hurt her heart to shut him out, but she had to do it. The guilt was eating her up inside.

She'd come so close tonight to living out her wildest dreams, only to have them come crashing down around her. She'd handled this horribly.

She bit back the tears as the truck moved through the dark streets, and soon they reached her house. Mick came around to let her out, but when she would have moved past him, he grabbed her arm.

"I'm walking you to the front door like the Southern gentleman I'm supposed to be. Like the responsible Dom, damn it."

Oh, he was mad. She didn't blame him.

She turned and together they moved up the front stairs.

"Hand me your keys."

"Mick, I—"

"Just do it, Allie. Stop arguing with me."

She exhaled on a sigh as she pulled the keys from her purse and handed them to him. His large fingers wrapped around her hand for a long moment, and she looked up to find his gaze on hers, dark and glittering in the pale light of the porch.

"Mick . . ."

"Shh."

"We're not in scene anymore."

"No. We're not. We're just two people saying good night. And this we're going to do right."

He leaned in, and even though she knew what was coming, she couldn't pull away. Her body wouldn't let her. She breathed in his scent mixed with the cool night air, which only made him seem darker, sexier.

His arm wrapped around her waist, pulling her closer. She tilted her chin, blinked hard as he lowered his face toward hers until his breath was warm on her lips.

He moved in closer and the breath just went out of her, her body melting in anticipation. His hand gripped her waist, his fingers digging in. She closed her eyes. Waited.

He gave her one more squeeze before he pulled away.

"You know, everything that happened when we were younger . . . I remember what it was like between us. Don't think I've ever forgotten. Tonight kind of brought it back to me, made it fresh again. Real."

Her chest pulled into a tight, complicated knot. "What are you saying, Mick?"

He shook his head, his eyes shadowed. "I don't know." He paused, repeated, "I don't know. And I don't know exactly what's going on in that pretty head of yours, but I felt like I needed to say something."

"And . . . ?"

He shrugged. "That's it." He was silent for several moments, then he reached out, drew one finger across her cheek, his gaze on her face. He whispered, "Good night, Allie."

"Oh . . ."

His brows drew together and she thought he might say something more, but he only stepped back, let his hand fall from her side. He stuck it in the pocket of his jeans.

Her pulse was fluttering, hot and thready.

"Good night, Mick," she managed to get out.

"I want you to call me tomorrow." His voice was rough and low. "We don't have to talk. Just check in, let me know if you're okay. And call Marie Dawn tonight. Call Jamie. Someone. No arguing."

"I will."

"Promise me you'll do it."

"I promise."

He stood watching her for a moment. Her heart thundered in her chest. Finally he took another step back.

"Okay. Good night, Allie."

"Good night, Mick."

She waited but he didn't budge.

"I'm not leaving until you're safely inside."

"Oh. Oh."

She made a useless fluttering motion with her hand, realized what she was doing and turned away from him, went into the house and shut the door behind her. She leaned her back against it, her gaze on the plaster ceiling as she let out a long, sighing breath.

Jesus, this man! How could he have come so close and then *not* kissed her? Pure torture, and not even the kinky kind, she felt certain. But it was all her own damn fault. Her body was buzzing with need, but her mind was buzzing even harder. With doubt. Guilt. Questions.

She would do as she'd promised—for herself as well as for him. She moved from the entry hall into the living room and emptied her small purse onto the low coffee table, found her cell phone and dialed Marie Dawn.

"Allie? What's up, *chérie*?"

"I'm sorry. I know it's late."

"Never a problem, honey. Talk to me."

"We went to the club, Mick and I. And at first everything was just flowing. It was too perfect being there with him. Knowing it was finally happening. But Marie Dawn, I fucked up."

Her breath caught, and she curled her free hand into a fist, letting the nails bite into her palm. "I shouldn't have tried to con him into this."

"Well, there may have been other ways to go about it, but we both know Mick Reid is one of the most stubborn human beings on the planet, so really, this may have been the only way."

"That was my thought, too. That was how I justified it." She paused, swallowed the tears that burned in her throat. "He was so damn nice about it, apologetic, but the scene was ruined."

"Allie, you can't blame yourself for this. He started it years ago—you're just trying to repair the damage. So, the scene went wrong. So what? That doesn't mean you two never talk again, or maybe even try the club again. Does it?" Marie Dawn asked.

"No. I mean, there's nothing in the kink handbook that says we can't try again, if we want. But . . . this whole thing obviously messed with his head, and I don't think he'll want to."

"I think you're wrong."

"I don't know." She moved to the lace curtains at the window, let the streetlights outside blur into a wash of pale amber against the tears pooling in her eyes. "He told me that being there with me tonight brought up how he used to feel, and I *think* he was talking about our relationship, back when things were good between us. I think. I just don't know."

"Are you okay? Do you need me to come over? Because I can come right now. You just say the word."

"No, I'm okay." She bit her lip. "I'll be okay. I'm confused and . . . I'll be fine. I just need to get some sleep and try to work this out in my head. He did make me promise to call him tomorrow."

"Good. It'll give you a chance to talk. You do want to talk to him?"

"Yes. Of course I do. I just couldn't talk to him tonight. I couldn't stand to face him."

"Go easy on yourself, honey," Marie Dawn said quietly. "Love is always hard enough."

"I do love him," she said, her voice low, a little strangled. "Wow. I haven't said those words out loud since I was a teenager." Awe made goose bumps rise on her flesh.

"Maybe it's about time."

"Maybe. I just don't think . . . I don't think Mick will ever love me back."

"Oh, he loves you. He has for years. Give him a chance to figure it out. And Allie? Personally I think forcing him into facing this is the best way—probably the only way—to get through to him. Don't you give up. You're stronger than that."

Allie smiled. "What would I do without you to mama me?"

"You know I love you, *chérie*."

"I know. Thank you."

"You sure you don't need me? Neal wouldn't even know I was gone. I can slide into my slippers and be there in fifteen minutes."

"I'm okay. Really. You stay home with your husband."

"Check in with me tomorrow."

"I will."

They hung up and she found herself feeling marginally better. Amazing how the support of a good friend could hold her up when she was down. How had she lived so far from Marie Dawn all these years? But she was back in New Orleans—to stay, it seemed. She didn't have to be separated from her best friend anymore. Or her family, whom she loved dearly, even if they could be a little crazy and overwhelming sometimes.

Or from Mick, maybe.

She took in a breath, exhaled and pulled in another. There

was the familiar scent of New Orleans—old wood and plaster, dust on lace curtains, and always the scent of flowers that seemed to come from everywhere.

If she shook her head so that her hair fell against her cheek, she could still smell Mick's scent on her.

Her pulse raced. Her body heated.

No matter how emotional she might be, that primal need for him was always lurking, waiting for one small thought to bloom into sharply burning desire.

His hands had been on her tonight—all over her body.

She had been naked and under his command.

A soft moan escaped her lips. She wiped at her mouth with the back of her hand as if it would erase the need for him.

Mick.

She shook her head as she moved down the hall into the bathroom, stripped out of her clothes as she ran the hot water in the shower, turning the temperature down before she stepped in.

She leaned into the tiles, cool against her back, closed her eyes and remembered.

His dark brows drawn in concentration as he leaned over her. The slide of rope on naked flesh. The scent of him filling her lungs.

She remembered the rope slipping between her thighs, pressing hard between the lips of her sex, and reached down to press there with her fingers.

"Oh . . ."

It wasn't enough. Not nearly enough.

She pulled the shower sprayer down and held it so the water hit her clitoris, groaning at the pressure. Parting her thighs, she moved the hard spray of water closer and imagined it was Mick's mouth on her. Teasing, licking, sucking. Pulling that sensitive nub of flesh into his mouth, running his tongue over the tip.

In moments she was on the edge of climax, her clit pulsing, her legs shaking.

"Mick . . . I'm coming." She gasped as the first shock wave hit her. "For you . . . Oh!"

She shivered as pleasure rolled through her, wave after wave. Behind her closed eyes was his face. His scent. His air of command.

Mick.

Always.

She leaned harder into the tiles, panting, dizzy with a need still unsated.

It would always be Mick that she needed. She didn't know how *not* to need him. She didn't know how to tame the raging desire for him without *him* being the one to tame her.

She shook her head. She had to make a decision: Was she going to pursue Mick, or wasn't she? What was fair to him? Could she live with herself if she didn't push for time with him? Could she live with herself if she did and they failed as miserably as they had tonight?

She rinsed off and stepped out of the shower, quickly dried her skin and her hair with a towel. She needed to climb into bed and not think anymore. She'd turn on one of her travel shows and lose herself in whatever part of the world was being explored. It was how she'd always dealt with stress, for as long as she could remember.

She climbed naked into the big four-poster bed that had been in the house when she'd arrived. It was a beautiful piece, probably French, and the first thing she'd done when she'd arrived in town was to replace the mattress and buy a dusky lilac duvet and piles of pillows in lilac and white. The bed was too New Orleans—she couldn't help but make it romantic and plush.

The sheets were cool against her skin as she settled in, plumping the pillows behind her head. She grabbed the remote from the bedside table, turned off the lamp and flicked on the television.

She found a show exploring Tahiti, and let the beauty of the turquoise water and the narrator's smooth voice soothe her until she was too sleepy to pay attention any longer. She turned the sound off and rolled onto her side to stare unseeing at the night sky through the window. She didn't see the moon, half-obscured by cloud. She didn't see the stars shining with their pale light. All she saw was Mick's face. She slept, and dreamed of him through the night.

MORNING CAME TOO early. Allie stretched, testing her muscles for any stiffness after being bound the night before, but it had been over too fast to cause any lingering effects. Not to her body, anyway.

She sat up and flipped back the covers, got out of bed and slipped her robe over her shoulders, pretending she wasn't already full of anxiety. Was it too early to contact Mick? Did she even know what she wanted to say to him?

A glance at the clock told her it was eight thirty, and if she knew Mick—and she still did—he was probably already up and had been to the gym.

"What the hell," she muttered, finding her phone in the living room and dialing him.

It rang, then went to voice mail.

"Mick, hi, it's me. Allie. Um . . . I was supposed to call, so I'm calling, but maybe you're not up yet. I'm sorry if I woke you. I just . . . I'm checking in. Call me back when you can. Okay. Bye."

She hit the End Call button and swore.

"Way to sound like a complete idiot," she muttered.

She rubbed her eyes. Why hadn't she at least had some coffee first so she could manage to make sense?

Tucking her phone into the pocket of her robe, she moved into the kitchen to get coffee started. Her cell phone rang.

Mick.

Her stomach knotted, her pulse fluttering.

Just breathe.

"Hello?"

"Hey, Allie."

"Oh, hi."

"Sorry I missed you. I was just getting out of the shower."

Mick with hot water pouring over his muscular body . . .

She bit back a moan.

"I'm glad I didn't wake you up."

"Already went out for a run this morning."

She had to smile to herself.

"So, how are you doing?" he asked. "Did you get some sleep?"

"Some, yes. And I feel okay. No sore spots."

"What about the rest? Are you still sorry you got me to play you?"

"I'm only sorry you didn't kiss me," she said before she could stop herself.

There was a long pause. Then he said, "Allie," in a low voice.

She ran her fingers through her hair, catching the tangles. "I know, I know. And that's not entirely true. I'm sorry about the tears. The drama."

"I told you last night that wasn't your fault."

"I don't want to argue with you, Mick."

"Good, then don't. Just do as I say."

"What?"

But the sudden authority in his tone was already making her bones melt.

"I thought about this a lot last night after I took you home, and more this morning. The way I see it, we owe it to each other to move ahead with the plan. *I* owe it to you."

"To move ahead in what way, exactly? To do a scene at the club? You don't owe me anything."

"Don't argue with me, Allie."

She walked across the small kitchen, rested her back against the old pink tile at the edge of the sink. She didn't know what to do, whether to argue or to let him take the lead. She wanted to be with him so badly it hurt. But what was he offering her other than another night of play, the opportunity to set things right in that arena?

"Mick, if this is just you trying to live up to your word as a Dominant, then . . . I don't know if I can do that. Just have one more scene with you, try to make it a good one, then . . . I don't know."

There was a long beat. She could hear him breathing on the other end of the phone. "I don't know, either, to be honest. And I have to tell you I topped out last night for the first time—that's why I had to stop the scene. Don't try to take the blame for it—it happens sometimes. You were doing beautifully. But last night started something, and I think we have to see it through. I don't know where to, ultimately. But it's you and me, Allie. We're not just two people who met at the club and decided to take each other out for a spin. It can't ever be that for us. Last night showed me that. Topping out showed me that. Part of it was the reality of being at the club with you. To be honest, it stunned me a little, which I didn't realize until this morning. To know that you really are a part of the kink world—the sweet

Allie I've known since we were kids. I have to wrap my head around that. But yeah, play for us can never be a casual thing. So if we're going there at all, we have to be aware of that."

"You're right. But Mick . . . do we really try to do this? Because as you said, it's *us*. And I'm still not sure that me pushing things wasn't a huge mistake."

"Maybe. Or maybe it's time we figure out once and for all if *we're* a mistake."

Tears formed behind her closed eyes. Could she take it if they got any closer, only to find out they'd crash and burn?

"Allie?"

"I'm thinking," she said.

"Don't think. That gets us both into trouble every time, doesn't it?"

"Can you tell me this isn't about you having something to prove, Mick? To me? To yourself?"

"It's always about trying to prove something to myself," he said gruffly.

"But if that's all it is—"

"It's not."

She exhaled, bit her lip. "Okay."

"Okay?"

"Yes. Okay."

"You're not going to fight me on this?" he asked.

"I just said okay, Mick."

He let out a small laugh. "Just kind of hard to believe."

She laughed then, too. "I know."

"The minute I get you back in that club I'll find a way to curb your tendency to argue, Allie girl."

A long, sweet shiver trembled through her body.

"That's what I'm counting on," she told him.

Things had shifted somehow from uncertainty and nerves to a hot sensuality in mere moments, it seemed. But that was Mick. Hard with her one minute and soft the next.

Hard with me . . . oh my.

"Now you tell me what your preference is regarding any sexual contact."

"I . . ." She pressed her fingertips to her lips for a moment. "I really don't want to be the first one to say it."

"What if that's an order?"

"Then I'll disobey. Just accept that you're not going to get me to roll over on this one, Mick."

He laughed. "All right, stubborn girl. I'll tell you that I think it's a bad idea to put too many strict limitations on how things go. Again, this is us. We're not strangers. We should give it every chance to allow things to flow naturally."

"I agree. Except . . . actual sex is something else, Mick. It's too intimate. We need to see how play goes, how *we* go, before we can even begin to negotiate that."

"Agreed. But I'll send my clean health papers to you. I get STI checked every twelve weeks. I'll expect you to do the same in the name of transparency whether we're having actual intercourse or not. So, we need to discuss when we do this again," he said. "What's your schedule like?"

"I don't really have much of one yet aside from house renovations, which haven't begun. Lunch with Marie Dawn today—"

"Good."

"See? I can follow instructions sometimes."

"Sometimes," he said wryly. "What else this weekend?"

"That's it."

"Then we're back to The Bastille tonight."

The breath went right out of her. "Oh."

"Is that an argument, Allie?"

"What? No. I just didn't expect things to happen so fast."

"I like fast."

God, she was going wet just hearing the tease in his voice, the authority.

"You always have."

"I'll pick you up at eight. Be ready. Same instructions as last night."

"Yes, Sir."

"Don't be smart, Allie. You'd do well to remember I'm as much a sadist as I am a rope Top."

"And I'm as much a masochist as I am a rope bottom."

They were both silent for several long moments while her system burned with desire.

"Tonight," he said finally.

"Tonight," she repeated.

They hung up and she clasped her cell phone in her hands, pressed it to her chest.

This was either going to be amazing or heartbreaking—again. She wasn't sure she could handle heartbreak. But Mick was right: if they didn't try, how would they ever know? She didn't want to live with a head full of the might-have-beens. She'd been doing that for years, and she'd never gotten over it. But she also couldn't go into this with a heart full of dread. She would need to gather her strength, to not let the fear defeat her. She would do it. For him.

And she would do it for herself. They both deserved, finally, to *know*.

SOMEHOW SHE'D KEPT herself busy all day, talking with Allister about the remodel, which he would start next week after a good look at the place on Monday, then at the hardware store, picking out paint and looking at kitchen cabinets. She'd taken a long bath, let herself sink into the ritual of smoothing lotion onto her body, doing her makeup, brushing out her hair until it shone.

This time she wore red silk lingerie and a black knit tank dress that skimmed the tops of her thighs, and high black sandals with straps that crossed delicately over her instep. By seven forty-five she was ready, heart racing once more, checking her reflection in the mirror, wanting to be perfect for him.

When the doorbell rang at exactly eight o'clock, it startled her, even though she'd been waiting for it.

Calm down.

She shook her head at her own ridiculousness as she went to open the door.

Just like last night, he seemed to dwarf the doorway. And he was so damn sexy, with his devilish goatee. He wore a bit of a smirk.

"Very nice, Allie girl. You ready to go?"

She nodded.

He opened the screen and took her arm, pulling her out. Silently, she handed him the house keys and he locked the front door, handed the keys back to her and kept a hand at the small of her back as he led her to his truck and helped her in.

She was sinking already, her mind emptying of everything but the sense of déjà vu and the overwhelming sense of Mick's presence as he drove them to the club.

"You doing all right?" he asked her.

"Yes. Just getting my head in the right place."

They stopped at a light and he turned to her. "I think you're there already."

She smiled. "Yes. I can't help it."

"I don't want you to. You're exactly where I want you, in fact. Going to The Bastille with me, starting to float your way into subspace. About to be in my hands. Oh, yeah. That's about perfect."

She didn't know what to say as a sense of satisfaction at his pleasure flooded her.

For you, Mick.

They reached the club and he parked, came around and helped her from the truck. Inside, the same woman—Pixie—sat behind the desk.

"Welcome back."

Allie nodded. "Thank you."

She was glad there was no more conversation aimed her way. She didn't want to lose her head space.

And Mick didn't let her. He grabbed her arm hard, his fingers biting a little into her flesh, the command coming through in the small shock of pain, but she welcomed it. Her head sank deeper as she followed him into the club.

He took her to the back of the main room and through a doorway that opened into a long hall.

"We're going to keep things private tonight," he said, his mouth close to her temple as he steered her down the hallway. "I don't want our focus to be interrupted even by the thrill of exhibitionism, the sounds of other people. It's just you and me tonight, Allie."

She shivered at the thought.

He guided her through a door and shut it behind them.

They were in a small room that had several pieces of equipment in it: a padded spanking bench with knee and armrests in one corner, a large bondage frame in another, and in the middle of the room was a hanging "bed" suspended from chains at all four corners and covered in red vinyl. Against one wall was a love seat upholstered in red velvet.

"What do you think, Allie?" he asked her, moving in close and wrapping his fist in her hair. "I'm going to lay you out on that table. I'm going to tie you down and do some wonderful and terrible things to you."

All she could say was, "Yes, please."

CHAPTER

Six

SHE DIDN'T DARE to look at him. Not because he was the Dom, but because she was afraid if she did her legs would shake too hard to hold her up.

He leaned into her and whispered in her ear, "I can sense you, you know. Feel what you're feeling right now. That trembling under your skin. Your pulse racing. I can see it at the base of your throat. I can feel it."

He pressed two gentle fingers to her neck, and she sighed.

"Ah, there it is. That honesty. You can't hide it, can you? But I don't mean that as any sort of judgment. I *want* to hear it. Your sighs, your moans. I want to know your pleasure. Don't hide it from me. Don't try to hide anything from me. You're familiar with this process—you know what we have to do in order for this to work. So tell me now, what are the nerves all about? This hard set to your jaw, your shoulders? Because I feel like if I put my arm around you right now you might break in some way."

"I might," she murmured, having to bite back tears for some reason she didn't understand.

"Allie, I don't want to hurt you. Not in that way."

She swallowed. "I know. But you might, Mick."

She heard him exhale on a long breath. "I'll do my damnedest not to."

She nodded, glanced away, letting her eyes lose focus in the dim, colored light.

"Look at me," he demanded.

She swallowed again, the lump in her throat thickening. She couldn't seem to force herself to do as he said.

"Allie," he said more gently. When she didn't answer he said, "Okay, if this is how you want it."

The next thing she knew, he'd picked her up and placed her sitting on the edge of the hanging bed, parted her thighs and stood between them. A tear plopped onto her cheek.

When he took her chin in his hand, she tried to shake him off, but he held on firmly, forcing her to face him.

"Mick, please."

His brows were drawn over his beautiful gray eyes. Eyes like granite and quartz.

"I don't mind if you cry," he said. "But you *will* talk to me."

She started to shake her head, but he wouldn't let her do it.

"Talk, Allie."

"This just . . . isn't what I expected. I don't know what I did expect. Except I suppose I figured that with all my years of experience to draw on, this would be familiar ground—just you and me getting to know each other again through kink, once we got past you being mad about me dragging you here."

"I'm past that—I don't hold a grudge. Well, I do, which I guess we both know. But I'm not mad at you. And this *is* us getting to know each other through kink. Tell me why it's hard for you."

"Isn't it hard for you, Mick? Jesus, don't tell me I'm the only one who's having a rough time with this."

"Yes, it's hard for me. Remembering what we used to be. Figuring out where the hell we are now. Because this part—the kink—has changed . . . maybe everything. But my job right now is to hold it together. To hold *you* together."

The look in his eyes told her he meant it. That he *would* hold her together.

"Okay. Okay. I'm sorry."

"You don't have to be. Just take a breath and find that place in your head again." He dropped her chin and stroked a hand over her shoulder. "I'll help you find it. Come on, now, stand for me."

He helped her from the table and pulled her dress over her head, paused to smooth her hair from her face.

"The red's a nice touch. Too nice to cut off you."

She watched him as his gaze roved over her body, followed by his hands. He stroked her arms, her stomach, making her draw in a sharp breath. She shivered when he stroked the sides of her thighs, the curve of her hips, the small of her back. He pulled her into his body, and she felt the heat of his skin, the hard muscle beneath her cheek pressed against his chest.

His hands moved over her back in featherlight strokes.

"Breathe with me, Allie."

She knew what he meant to do—take her through the slow yogalike breathing methods meant to relax her. Following his lead, she inhaled deeply, blew it out slowly.

"Again," he ordered.

She closed her eyes and drew in another breath, careful to keep time with him, exhaled. Inhaled once more, and exhaled, let her body fall into the slow cadence, let her weight lean into his strong frame.

She didn't know how much time had passed when he said, "Let's begin."

He lifted her, setting her back on the hanging table. He stroked one shoulder, bringing down her bra strap with his fingers. Her nipples went hard immediately. He caressed her other shoulder, drawing that strap down, ran both hands over her breasts, filling his palms with her silk-covered flesh. She arched into his touch.

"Ah, that's it. Good girl."

That phrase could always make her shiver. Coming from him it was like a small orgasm shuddering across her skin.

He undid the front clasp, and the bra fell off and into his hands. He set it down, then bent to remove her shoes, pausing to caress her calves, her thighs. He dropped her shoes on the floor and laid his hands on her shoulders once more.

"Lie back now," he told her, his voice soft, yet no less commanding.

She did as he asked, lying down on the cool vinyl. He stood over her, dwarfing her more than ever, somehow. Perhaps it was his command, or the sense of vulnerability that was always present when she was submitting, magnified now because it was *him*. Not that she minded. She gloried in it.

"I want you to stay there, to stay still," he told her.

He turned away and she heard him unzip his toy bag, heard some shuffling around as he unpacked what he needed. She kept doing the deep breathing, trying her best to still herself even as desire poured through her system like a rush of heat.

The other rush was a keen need to be perfect for him. Even as her mind began to float, she was acutely aware of it. It was a part of submission for her—to be floating off into subspace, yet feeling the need to please, to be good for her partner. And now it was nearly overwhelming. But the lump in her throat was fading away, being replaced by this familiar role she knew she was capable of fulfilling. She knew that *wanting* it to this degree would only make her better for him.

She felt him approach, watched as he lifted her arm, used his brushing fingertips to spread her palm open, bent and placed a soft kiss on the inside of her wrist before gently drawing it up over her head and sliding a length of rope around it.

She sighed at the tenderness of his touch, at the pure sensuality of the way he was handling her as he looped and knotted the rope, making a cuff around her wrist, leaving a line of rope dangling. He moved around the table and once more he lifted her arm, used his fingertips to stroke her palm open, kissed her wrist, then her palm, sending a shiver of desire through her body. He wrapped the other wrist in the same way, a few loops and knots, leaving a long length of rope trailing.

She felt the tug on one wrist as he slung the rope through a chain link somewhere above her, and her arm drew up and outward. He pulled it a bit tighter before he secured it. She relaxed into the lovely, familiar safety of the rope as he did the same to her other arm. She loved this sensation of calmness mixed with the near frenzy of pleasure and need coursing through her.

Mick.

The rope.

Mick . . .

He moved toward the end of the table and wove more rope around first one ankle, then the other, before he secured them to the chains at the bottom of the hanging table, pulled it tight so that her legs were spread wide.

"So damn beautiful," he said. "And so gorgeously helpless."

She smiled. She couldn't help it. It was exactly what she loved about being bound.

"What shall I do with you now, I wonder?" he mused.

She knew he didn't require an answer—that the remark was designed to get her mind spinning.

What *would* he do?

He trailed a finger up the center of her stomach, over her ribs, between her breasts, and her nipples tightened.

"Ah, here's a good place to start."

He stroked his fingertips over one nipple, and her sex went damp immediately. When he pinched the hardened flesh between his strong fingers, she groaned.

"Good, Allie? But you don't have to answer. Your body answers for you." He kept her nipple pinched firmly between his fingers, making her have to breathe through the pain, eyes closed, as he reached for the other and caressed the tip. Pleasure and pain were a sweet cocktail in her system. Yet the ropes held her safely, giving her something to hold on to.

When he tweaked both nipples hard, she arched up off the table with a gasp, pain lancing into her. But he let go almost right away, stroking and teasing the tender flesh, letting her breath out the pain, take in the pleasure. It was too good. Her pussy was swelling with need.

He pinched again, and she hissed out a breath.

"Inhale," he instructed her.

She did, and he squeezed harder.

"Oh, God," she muttered.

"Shh. You can take it, Allie. Look at me."

She blinked, clearing her vision, and focused on his face, his gaze locking onto hers.

He pinched, twisting cruelly, and she gasped, but his gaze held hers as firmly as his strong fingers held her aching flesh. Pain radiated, brought burning desire in its wake.

"Yeah, there it is," he said, his tone low. "Your cheeks are going pink, and the same flush is on your beautiful breasts. Your eyes are glittering, the pupils wide. I can feel your need in the heat coming off your body. And your nipples are so damn hard."

He eased his grip, and she felt the hot rush of blood there as circulation returned. Still watching her carefully, he caressed her nipples again, and pleasure was even more acute, rippling over her skin, deeper, into her belly, her sex.

"Oh . . ."

"Quiet now, Allie girl. Be good for me." She bit her lip, making him smile. "You know I've always loved to see you do that. As if you're considering your pleasure. Well, I'm considering it, too. Oh, yeah, I am."

He smoothed a hand over her tight stomach, right down under the silk and between her thighs.

She moaned as his fingers slid in her wet heat. Her thighs trembled when he teased her clit, then slid down and slipped inside her.

"Oh, yes . . ."

His other hand clamped hard over her mouth. "Quiet, my girl."

She loved the command in his tone, in his hand across her lips, in the way he suddenly pumped his fingers harder inside her. Faster and faster, his fingers curving to hit her G-spot until she couldn't hold still. She writhed against her bonds, her hips arching into his hand, arms and legs pulling against the rope— she couldn't help it as pleasure poured through her system, hot and iron-hard. Her sex clenched at his thrusting fingers as he worked her roughly, mercilessly, his thumb pressing down on her clit.

"Don't do it," he ordered. "Don't you come until I say you can, princess."

She groaned, flexed her toes, her breath hot against his hand still over her mouth.

He kept at it, his fingers surging into her aching pussy, and she was soaking wet, gushing even though she hadn't come yet. But she was so close she could barely stand it.

"Hold it back. That's it."

He kept fucking her with his fingers, stroking her G-spot hard and fast, his thumb causing an almost unbearable pressure on her clitoris. Pleasure crested, and her body arched again.

"Not yet. Hold it back. *Hold it*," he commanded.

She groaned, a purely animal sound low in her throat, but she held on to that razor-sharp edge, her body poised. She was panting, her breath burning in her lungs.

"Are you ready, Allie?"

He plunged in hard, drew his fingers out slowly. Pure torture.

She watched his face as he watched her. His gray eyes were glossy. The idea that he was probably hard as stone for her right now passed through her mind, and a new shiver of need coursed through her, making her pussy convulse around his fingers.

"Yeah, you are. Come on then, baby. Come for me."

He thrust into her and she bucked into his hand. She started to come, and he paused, making her feel as if her entire body were suspended in midair. Then he started again, his gaze hard on hers as he fucked her in quick, pummeling strokes, his fingers burying to the hilt, pulling roughly out, plunging once more.

Her orgasm was like a flood of heat and need, her hips jerking. She cried out against his hand, her throat going raw as her cries turned into a scream. And still he thrust into her, his fingers milking her for every last drop of pleasure.

She was soaking wet, gasping for air, shivering all over. And she was lost in the intensity on his face, the way he looked at her, at the pleasure she saw there.

For you, Mick . . . always for you.

His hand slid away from her mouth, and she drew in a deep

breath. His fingers still moved inside her in a slow, circular motion, and pleasure built once more, hot and unbelievably fast, yet they moved so slowly it kept her suspended again, moment by moment, hanging on the edge.

"Do you need to come again? You can answer me."

"Yes. Please, yes."

A smile crooked one corner of his lush mouth as he pulled his fingers from her pussy and dragged them up over her belly, leaving a trail of her own juices. "I know you do, baby. But we'll save that one for later."

She almost cried out in frustration, but she bit it back just in time.

For him.

Her body was buzzing, a mind-blowing combination of pleasure spent, need unmet, and that sense of being taken over completely. She watched as he turned his back to her, one hand on her stomach so that he never lost contact with her as he picked something up from a chair he'd pulled close to the hanging bed. When he turned back, she saw he held a small, wiry canelike instrument in his hand.

"Have you seen one of these before, Allie? You can answer by nodding if you have."

She shook her head.

"Good girl. This is called an evil stick, or misery stick. I'll leave you to guess why. It's made from a very narrow rod of carbon fiber, making it strong and flexible. The handle is woven leather, just to make it easy for me to hang on to. This one is only about six inches long, but it can cause some sensation, I promise you that. It stings like hell, and it'll mark you faster than almost anything. But then, I'm guessing you're a girl who loves her marks, am I right?"

She nodded, trying to keep her gaze on his and not on what

she was sure would be a wicked little toy. One she couldn't wait to feel the bite of.

"Then let's give you a taste, baby girl."

Baby girl.

Oh, she loved those southern endearments, had missed it so much. No man she'd ever been with could make her melt with a few words the way Mick could.

He stood over her, held the tiny rod by the handle over her stomach, used his other hand to bend the tip up—then let it go. It slapped down onto her skin, the sudden, sharp pain making her yelp.

Mick laughed. "I told you it was evil, baby."

He did it again, and again and again in such rapid succession she didn't have a chance to catch her breath. But she loved the overload as pain spread through her body, from the skin on her stomach to her limbs, leaving a wake of pleasure behind. Endorphins, those lovely natural opiates the brain produced in response to pain, built just as quickly as his merciless onslaught of sensation, until it all became a blur. Pain and pleasure as she struggled against her bonds, not really wanting to escape, but simply unable to hold still.

Her throat was tight and growing sore from holding back the yell that needed to escape. Her breath was a sharp pant, like fire in her lungs. Just when she thought she couldn't take any more without screaming, he stopped and smoothed his palm over the hurting welts on her stomach. She almost purred, it felt so good. Felt proud that she managed to hold it back, that she'd managed the pain without screaming.

"You mark beautifully," he said, studying her stomach, his gaze focused, his brows drawn. "Lovely little welts on your skin. They almost look like scratches." He scraped his nails over her flesh, and she gasped. He went back to caressing her, murmuring, "Skin like a baby. Just as soft as ever. I always did love the feel of your skin."

He went quiet for several long moments and she lay still, enjoying his lingering touch, the power of his attention being so acutely focused on her.

He was more present than any man she'd ever met, any Dom she'd ever played with. She didn't know if it was their dynamic or if that was simply *him*. But she understood how powerful an aphrodisiac it was for her. She was wet and ready for more already. Still.

Always.

He bent over her until his cheek was right next to hers and whispered, "Time for some more rope, baby girl," and kissed her cheek softly.

She turned her face, wanting him to kiss her, *needing* him to, but he straightened up and began to untie her ankles. She almost wanted to cry. She bit her lip instead, holding the emotion back.

Just be in the moment.

She waited while he got more rope, taking a few cleansing breaths, trying to calm herself.

He pulled her red silk panties down, slipping them off, then took her right leg and bent it at the knee, brought it up to her chest.

"Hold it right here," he instructed.

She did, and he began to wrap the rope around her bent leg, binding her calf to her thigh. He looped the rope around and around, and she concentrated on the lovely slip and slide of the rope, on the way he used his hands, touching her now and then as he tested the tightness of the ropes, as he smoothed them against her skin. He tied his knots, then moved to the other side of the table and did the same thing, then slid his hand under her to pull a new length of rope under her body, over her stomach, then again, and again before he knotted it. He used one more piece of rope to anchor her leg ties to the rope around her waist, holding her legs in place. And as he worked she felt a sense of utterly vulnerable openness in this position, with her knees pulled up high, exposing her. Yet at the same time she felt safe in the ropes, in *his* ropes. Cradled. Cared for.

MICK TOOK A moment to step back and simply look at her. She was pure sex to him. She always had been, but right now, bound in his ropes, with her sleek little pussy peeking out from between her thighs . . . hell, if he'd had any less self-control he'd be coming in his jeans right now.

He ground his jaw tight.

Keep it together.

He could do it. He always had.

Except for that night all those years ago when he'd taken her. When he'd done things to her that should only ever be done after negotiations. But he hadn't known about all that back then—the kink community. The rules that kept everyone safe.

Stop kicking yourself.

And she was waiting for him. And Lord knew he couldn't stand to wait one more second for her.

He pressed against his raging hard-on and cleared his throat. His own needs would have to wait. It was his responsibility to do what *she* needed, damn it.

He smoothed a hand over her calf, stroking slowly over the ropes all the way down to her painted toes, enjoying the length of her gorgeous leg, the graceful arch of her foot, the beauty of her bound like this. He stroked up, swept his hand down to her inner thigh, felt the muscle there clench. His groin tightened in answer.

Better to use the toys. Keep a little distance without losing the necessary connection in rope play.

He drew the evil stick from his pocket and flicked it against the back of one thigh, smiling when she moaned. He did it again, harder this time, watched the pink welt come up on her skin.

"Hurts more in some places than others, doesn't it? Marks more easily, too. But I love that as much as you do. I love to see the pink come up on your skin, to feel the rise of the welts. They'll last a week if I do it hard enough. Like this."

He snapped the evil stick hard against the outside of her thigh, and she pulled in a gasping breath. She could take a lot without yelling, screaming, crying out. He admired that about her. But he couldn't help but take it as a personal challenge, too.

He snapped the wicked little toy against her skin again, crossing over the last welt, but she held her tongue. Oh, she was going to be a hard case. But he could break her down.

He flicked the stick on her inner thigh this time, knowing how much more sensitive an area it was, and she flinched. He did it again and again, hard and fast, listening to her breath catch, watching the way she struggled in her bonds, her back arching, her stomach muscles clenching. He knew she was lost in sensation, and he loved seeing her like this. Lost. Flying. *His.*

He kept at it, moving to the other thigh, then back again, striking her welted skin, watching the marks grow red and angry. She was panting hard, but still she held her tongue. He chose one area of untouched skin and snapped the stick over and over in the same spot, letting the pain build. Finally she cried out, and he stopped.

"Oh, that was good, baby girl. You can really take it. I'm so proud of you. And pleased that you kept silent for me. I want you to know I understand that—that proud struggle."

He stroked her cheek, held her chin and looked into her beautiful brown eyes. They were sheened with tears, and something in his chest went tight.

He bent over her, and she blinked up at him. She was watching him closely, need written all over her face, but for what he wasn't certain. To come again, he knew. But there was more there . . .

He leaned in closer, studied the lush curve of her lips, the fineness of her skin, her long, dark lashes. Her mouth . . .

He swallowed a groan as he bent closer, close enough to breathe in her scent—all sweet woman, innocent somehow, even now. Her lips were the prettiest shade of pink he'd ever seen, almost the same shade as her tempting nipples. His chest tightened. His cock swelled. He knew if he kissed her now he'd be as lost as she was in the throes of pain and pleasure.

He leaned in until his mouth was almost on hers. Moved closer, until his lips just touched hers.

His cock jumped, tight with wanting.

He pulled back an inch. Christ, her lips were velvet-soft. Made him crazy to think about kissing her. Really kissing her, making out with her the way they used to.

Making out leaning against a streetlamp, her breath and his, panting together while he crushed her in his arms. Her soft body felt almost fragile to him, and yet he had to hold her tighter, to run his hands up under her shirt and dig his fingers into the flesh at her sides. And all she'd ever done was sigh and press into him, kiss him harder.

Christ, he hadn't understood! Even then, she'd wanted it. Wanted to feel that sense of *possession*. Even the pain, maybe.

But it was the possession that had always counted most. He'd kissed her as if he owned her.

He could kiss her like that now, and she wouldn't resist. Would welcome it.

No.

He pulled back a few inches.

She bit her lip, watching him, the need clear on her lovely face. So damn lovely . . . Lips like fucking velvet.

God fucking damn it.

Have to . . .

He dove in, grasping her face between his hands, crushing his mouth to hers. She made a keening sound low in her throat. It only made him kiss her harder. Made him open her lips with his tongue and search for hers. And Lord, it was sweet, her tongue. Making him crazy as he kissed her, drove his fingers into her silky hair. Heat and softness. Desire and *her.* Allie. *His* Allie, Goddamn it.

She was kissing him back exactly as he'd known she would, and he breathed her in—he couldn't get enough. He pressed harder with hands and mouth, using his strength to still her, to force her to just take it, rendering her helpless. Yes, that's what he needed—to feel her surrender to him completely. To give herself up to him. Because if he wasn't totally in control of things . . .

Oh, Lord, this was way fucking out of control.

He let her go and pulled away.

She moaned softly.

"Mick . . . ?"

He shook his head, ran a hand over his jaw.

Christ, to feel her lips after all these years. His cock was throbbing, hurting. And his heart was hammering in his chest, thundering like a freight train.

Control.

"Shh, Allie."

"Did I . . . ?"

"It's okay, baby," he said.

Was it? He'd have to figure it out later, when she wasn't naked and bound and giving every inch of herself to him.

"It's okay," he said again, maybe more to himself than to her this time.

He took a step back. She watched him do it. It hurt him to see the look on her face. She looked . . . bereft. He felt exactly the same way. But he could satisfy the needs of her body, at least.

He pulled in a deep breath, made an effort to get his body under control.

"Shh," he soothed as he stroked a hand down her leg once more, slid it over her thigh, smoothed his palm across the raised welts, did it again, pausing to scratch lightly with his nails. It did what he'd intended: shifted her focus. And his.

He looked down at her damp slit, at the swollen tip of her clitoris peeking out at the top of the pink folds. So damn pretty.

He brushed the tender lips with his fingertips, felt her shiver. He teased at the lips with his fingers, stroking, tickling, then prying them apart. He forced the burning physical need for her to sharpen his focus rather than fracturing it, his years of practice lending him strength of will and the absolute control he'd long required of himself. He paused, held his hand still, her sex spread open and waiting. He glanced up at her face, found her eyes tightly closed.

Using his middle finger, he pressed against her opening. She sighed.

"Is this what you need, baby? For me to make you come like this? I know what you'd like even better. For me to use my mouth on you. You used to come so hard when I went down on you. Do you remember? I want you to remember now."

Her body convulsed, a slow, liquid movement that told him everything he needed to know. She was right there with him. His cock was pulsing but he ignored it, concentrated on the beautiful woman under his hands.

He slid his free hand under the ropes on her thigh and pulled her legs up higher, opening her pussy even more. She was soaking wet, the pink flesh glistening. Lord, to be inside her . . .

But no. That wasn't part of the agreement.

He would make her come again, though. He would make her come so damn hard she'd never forget it.

Neither would he.

He let her go and moved up to the head of the table, quickly loosened the ropes so that her arms had more mobility. Then, moving around to the end of the table, he grabbed the ropes on her thighs with both hands and slid her body down to the edge. He pushed her legs up once more, held them there with one hand while with the other he parted her pussy lips, hot and slick under his fingers. When he leaned in, he felt the heat of her against his face. He bent closer and breathed in the rich ocean scent of her desire. And as he moved in to flick his tongue at the tight nub of her clit, his cock hammered with need.

He let himself feel the fire there, let his own desire guide him as he licked her, used his fingers to spread her open and pushed his tongue into her waiting hole. She was making a small mewling noise, but he didn't care—he didn't need her to be quiet any longer. He only needed her to need *this*. To come hard for him. He needed to control her pleasure. To control his own through controlling hers.

Christ, he was out of his head.

But she tasted so damn good, like salt and honey on his tongue. He sucked her clit into his mouth, rasping his tongue back and forth across the tip as he pushed his fingers inside her, loving the clenching, wet velvet of her.

He sucked harder, curved his fingers until he found her G-spot, pressing and rubbing.

Her whole body was quivering, her hips arching against his mouth. He sucked harder, flicked his tongue faster, burying his face in her, his fingers sinking into her over and over. He added another finger, then another, filling her up.

He swore he smelled her come before her pussy began to clench with her orgasm. Then she was growling, panting, yelling his name, her back arching off the table. Her hot pussy spasmed around his fingers. He kept licking, sucking, and before her first climax was over it started again. She screamed his name this time.

"Mick! Oh, Godddddd!"

He didn't stop until he was certain she'd stopped coming. He gave her a few last slow, sensual licks, loving how incredibly wet she was, loving the taste of her pleasure. Finally he pulled back and wiped his mouth on her bound calf, kissed her there, nipped at her flesh, kissed her again.

"Beautiful, baby girl. That was perfect," he murmured.

He stroked her legs again, down to her toes, checked the color of her skin for circulation before moving up to her face. He held her chin in his hand.

"Look at me, Allie."

She opened her eyes. They were gleaming, her pupils wide and dark. She was flying—on her orgasm, on the pain play. Maybe on some of the emotional roller coaster he was on. But she seemed okay. Maybe doing better than he was.

He leaned in and brushed a quick kiss across her lips—he didn't dare allow himself more.

"I'm taking you down now," he told her.

She was quiet as he untied her, pulled the ropes off her body, watched the small shivers running through her as he let them slide across her skin. They fell on the floor, and he helped her to stretch first one leg, then the other, before untying the ropes holding her wrists. He stood at the top of the table and massaged her hands while she lay quietly, her breathing steady. He looked at her lithe body, her muscles loose, her eyes closed, her gorgeous hair all around her. So damn beautiful. She was still the most beautiful woman he'd ever seen. No one had ever come close. No one ever would.

His.

His heart knocked against his ribs.

Have to get her into my arms.

He moved around the table and picked her up, and her arms went around his neck. He carried her to the love seat and sat with her in his lap, pulled the soft, gray blanket he always kept in his toy bag around her. She laid her head against his shoulder. She felt so damn good in his arms. Too good.

He didn't want to feel like this. It was dangerous. He'd been young and shallow when he'd walked away from her before. Now he was old enough to know what he'd be losing when he let her go.

And he would have to let her go again. No matter how much he felt she should belong to him. Because . . .

Because of what? Because of the stupid things he'd done when he was younger? Even though she'd come to him, sought him out, sought *this* out?

"Mick? Can I . . . can we talk now?"

"What? Yeah, baby. We're out of scene. We'll do whatever you need to do. This is what aftercare is for."

"I need you to talk to me."

"Do you need to hear that I'm pleased with you? Because I am." He stroked her hair. "You took it all well."

"I'm glad. But I just need to . . . talk. Like we used to."

"Sure. What do you want to talk about?"

"How about you tell me what the tattoo on your forearm means?"

"*Non Timebo Mala*—it's Latin for 'I will fear no evil.' "

"Ah. So . . . what does that mean to you?"

"I'd rather we shelve that discussion for another day. It's complicated."

"Okay. Then tell me about your work."

He lifted her chin to look into her eyes. They were glassy as hell, and he knew she was still subspaced pretty heavily.

"I'm sure Marie Dawn has told you plenty. Is this really what you want to hear about right now?"

"Yes. And she has told me some. But I want you to tell me."

He knew sometimes it helped a bottom to come down by idly chatting. Why did this feel like something more? But he would do it, anyway.

"I'm sure you already know I have my own business. I do private security for fairly large venue events—concerts, boxing, that kind of thing. The company has grown a lot in the last few years. I have a staff of maybe thirty, including three in the office, although mostly I work from home when I'm in town. I'm trying to talk my friend Finn in Atlanta into coming to work with me here, to handle Internet and firewall security for my clients so I don't have to contract that out. And he could do some of the on-site work, too, so I don't have to travel so much. Currently, I travel a lot. I go to meet promoters, the venue managers, to check out a space if there are special circumstances I don't want to leave up to my security heads. Not that I don't trust them. But I might have a few control issues."

"No kidding." She laughed a little, turning her face into his chest. He loved seeing her like this—relaxed with him. It felt easy. Familiar. "You have the perfect job for a Dom," she said.

He smiled. "Yeah. Maybe. What about you? I heard you were studying all over Europe. That must have been incredible."

"It was. It was also hard. The pastry chefs I studied with were like drill sergeants. It was almost impossible to do anything right in their eyes. But when you did . . . well, you knew you'd really done it perfectly, and that makes it all worth it."

"Sounds like you're in the perfect profession for a submissive."

"Maybe. But I really want to do my own thing now. I'm ready."

"What do you want to do?"

She was quiet for several long moments while she played with a button on his shirt.

"Mick."

"Yeah, baby?"

"All I want right now is to be here like this. With you. Is that okay?"

"Sure. We can stay here as long as you need to."

"No. That's not what I meant. I meant can we . . ." She stopped and he felt her breath hitch.

"Can we what?" he asked.

He thought he knew the answer. "Allie, if you're suggesting what I think you are . . ." he started. "I don't know. I just don't fucking know. Do we even dare try again? Everything went so wrong before, and it was my own damn fault. This—the kink—I can handle. But even this is starting to spiral out of control.

This conversation wouldn't even be taking place if we weren't playing together."

"No, of course not."

She looked crushed. He hated himself a little. But he owed it to her to be honest with her.

Damn it.

He never should have kissed her. One kiss, and it could be the beginning of his undoing.

S HE STRAIGHTENED UP until she could look him in the eye.
He could see she was still flying a bit. Probably emotionally
raw. He would have to be very careful about where this conversation was going. He wished he'd been more careful already.

She twisted her fingers in the loose fabric of his shirtsleeve.
"Mick, tell me what happened. Tell me why we haven't been
together all this time."

"Allie . . ."

"It's okay. I need to hear it, and maybe this is the only time
I'm going to be brave enough to ask."

"Do we need to rehash ancient history?"

"Yes," she answered simply.

He knew she was right. But damn it, he did not want to do this.

He tightened his arms around her. "If this makes you bottom
out, I'm going to feel like shit."

"And if that happens, I know you'll take good care of me. Just tell me," she insisted.

He pushed her long, silky hair from her face, stroked her jaw with his thumb, checked her eyes. It was clear she was still pretty full of endorphins. But it was also clear she knew exactly what she was asking.

"Okay. But you know a big part of why we haven't been together is because I haven't wanted to have this conversation."

"I know," she said softly, her tone laced with hurt.

"And you're asking me now because you know damn well I can't say no to you when you're sitting naked in my lap, and you know how badly I want you."

She smiled a little. "Well, I'm sure it doesn't hurt."

"Oh, it hurts. Princess, you sure know how to get your way."

"Not always, apparently. And you're stalling."

"Yeah." He paused to gather his thoughts. How the hell did he say something to her he'd purposely kept from her for nearly eleven years? Something he'd never fully admitted, not even to Jamie? Where did he begin?

"All right. You know how in high school I always told you how sweet you were? You know that was truly how I felt. You always had this sweetness about you. You were so . . . *fresh* is the only word I can find. And I've always had these demons. This darkness. These urges."

"Do you still see your urges for kink as dark? As demons?"

"As dark, sure. Maybe not as demons anymore. I've worked some of those out of my system." He stopped, shrugged. "Some of them are still there, though, if you want to know the truth. But being a Dominant has helped me to control them. That's how I got into rope. That part of me needed to be kept in check, and the rope . . . it's a symbol to me, maybe. The binding, the restraining, restrains my own darkness. I know it doesn't make much sense."

"No, it does. I get it. Go on."

"It's more than that. It's a sense of connection with the bottom, an extension of my hands, *myself.* There's control in the patterns. In the elegance of the knots."

"Yes, that's one of the things I love about it, too," she agreed.

"But it's the way the rope requires control. It's mathematical, even. It's discipline in itself to bind someone properly. And it's that sense of absolute discipline that keeps me on track. That's not something I discovered until a few years after I last saw you, and it's only been in the last couple of years that I've come to understand it more completely. I'm sure I still have more to learn."

"Don't we all? But tell me how this relates to us. To what happened."

He did not want to go there. His gut was in knots. But he was going to do it. She deserved that much from him.

"Back in high school I told you all the time that you were too good for me."

"Which was crap, Mick. Pardon me for saying so, but it was."

"I felt that darkness, though, Allie. I didn't want to sully you with it. You were so innocent."

"Mick, even in high school we were doing things that weren't entirely innocent, even though you wouldn't help me lose my virginity."

"Help you? You say that like it would have been a good thing."

"Only with you," she said quietly.

He couldn't believe she still thought so. That adulthood hadn't brought her more hindsight, especially knowing what she did about him.

"It would have been a disaster."

"I don't agree. I loved you."

Hearing her say it made his heart twist painfully.

"We were teenagers, Allie. What did we know about love?"

"Maybe not very much. I only knew what I felt."

"So did I. Fuck it—you're right." He stopped, ran a hand over his hair. "And I felt it was wrong to have you follow me down that road. That's why when I left for college, I knew leaving you to find another kind of life—a better life without me in it to screw things up for you—was the only right thing to do."

"That is so . . . all kinds of messed up. Did you never think of me after that, Mick?" she asked, her brown eyes burning with gold fire.

"I thought about you all the damn time."

They were both quiet for several moments.

"But you never came back for me."

"I knew I couldn't do that to you. And then there was the accident."

The fucking motorcycle accident that had ruined his life, ruined his future, ruined his sense of self and his place in his family.

He had a flash of that sick, skidding sensation, the world blurring, no control—no fucking control! Intolerable pain, then blackness. Waking up knowing he had fucked up, but not how badly. No, that had come later, when the doctors told him his leg would never be the same again.

"I'm sorry, Mick. I knew it must have been so awful for you, but you refused to see me when you were in the hospital, and after you got home."

"Because I was ashamed," he admitted. "It was damn stupid of me. I threw away everything that was important to my family. My opportunity to serve my city in the way my father and grandfather had. In the way my brothers do now. I couldn't stand for you to see me like that. Defeated by my own fucking foolishness. It was bad enough things had had to end between us the way they did. I couldn't face you. I couldn't face anyone. I'm still ashamed, if you want to know the truth. It fucking haunts me. And that's not something I say to anyone."

IT HURT HER to hear him say it. To hear the old pain in his voice. To feel his body tense up.

"I'm sure they don't hold it against you," she said.

"I do."

"Oh, Mick."

She stroked the back of her hand down his cheek just to feel it, to let him know how she felt.

"Don't pity me, Allie," he said gruffly.

She pulled her hand back. But she knew him well enough not to feel wounded by his tone. "It's not pity. I *feel* for you, that's all. Does your leg still hurt you?"

"Yeah, it gives me some trouble, but I deal with it."

She knew that was what the bare-knuckle fighting was about, that he felt he had to prove himself. She'd caught a glimpse or two of his limp, but he was still the strongest man she knew. He had nothing to prove to anyone. If only he could see that.

"Change of subject," he suggested.

"Okay. I want to hear about what happened in college, when I came home. When we were together."

"Fuck. Really?"

"That's what this conversation was coming to."

He scrubbed at his closely cut goatee. "That night never should have happened. It was all wrong."

"It never felt that way to me. Other than the part where you left and never turned back."

"Allie, you were twenty years old," he protested. His arm was around her waist, holding her in his lap, and his fingers flexed hard.

"Yes, Mick, I was twenty. I wasn't a child anymore, and I wasn't a virgin by then. I'm even less a child now. And that night was everything I'd ever wanted. Not just the sex, but all of it. Being tied up with your belt. The smell of the leather. The biting. The spanking. The roughness of it all."

"That can't be true. You couldn't have known back then."

"*You* did. From what you've said, you knew in high school. Wasn't that what you were trying to protect me from? But can't you see, Mick? Once you gave me a taste for it, that was *my* fantasy, too. You gave me that tempting little bit, then you took it away. You took yourself away from me, too."

"You cried that night after we had sex," he insisted, his tone going harsh. "I saw the tears."

"I was crying because that night with you was the fulfillment of every fantasy I'd ever had!" She almost wanted to cry now. "Fantasies I'd had when I was practically a child, things I didn't understand until much later. But I loved it. I loved the passion of it, the intensity. The pain."

He shook his head. "No, that's not right. It can't be."

She took his face in her hands and gazed into his eyes. His were dark, shadowed, his brows drawn. He was so damn beautiful it made her ache.

"Mick, I wanted it. I wanted you, and I wanted all those things you did with me that night. You say you feel those desires were some kind of demon. If that's true, then I have demons, too."

He tried to shake his head again, and she tried to hold it firmly, but he took her hands and pulled them down.

"Don't say that, Allie."

"How can I explain this to you? It's as if my being here with you, you knowing my kink history, counts for nothing, even though you said it did, that it's made you think, but here we are again with you protesting my desires, Mick! That's what it comes down to—with you still doubting that you can be with me."

"Look, Allie . . . it isn't only the stuff around the breakup in high school. A lot of it was—and maybe still is—the accident. That was something I couldn't come back from. It only proved what I'd always known about myself. You deserve more than that. And what happened between us later, when we slept together . . . that was a mistake. I know I didn't handle it well. I know I was an asshole. A lot of it was because I *had* demonized myself for wanting the kink, and it was only later that I learned to accept that about myself. But us not being together then was the right thing, Allie. You weren't ready for full-on kink at twenty."

She watched him in frustration. His face was shutting down again, a veil of stubbornness over his handsome features. But she wasn't done with this conversation. "Mick, this is something I've been turning over in my mind for years. I'm going to tell you how I see it. You know that for those who are born to New Orleans, it's in your blood. It lingers there no matter where you go. BDSM is the same sort of thing. If you're born to it—the way you were, the way *I* was, whether or not you want to accept that—you can never shake it. It shapes the way you think, the way you respond to . . . everything. And those who were a part of unleashing those desires . . . you never forget them, either. That's what you did for me, Mick. *For* me, not *to* me."

"Christ, Allie. I can't accept that." He looked like he was fuming inside, color high on his chiseled cheekbones.

"Do you think there's something intrinsically wrong with kink? Do you?" she demanded.

"No, of course not."

"Then why is there something wrong about the combination of kink and *me*? I'm not that sweet teenager anymore. I'm not delicate. Haven't I shown you that? What do I have to do to get past your relentless inflexibility, Mick? I would have thought you'd outgrown it by now."

"I have. Some. I guess we've both changed a lot since high school. I just need some time to absorb it."

"We have changed. And you need to learn to see me for who I am *now*."

He tucked a strand of her hair behind her ear, and some of her anger dissolved under that small gesture.

"And you need to see me for who I am now, too," he said. "You were so driven to play with me. You started to ask about us starting over. But Allie, do we even know each other anymore?"

He had a point. Was it Mick as he was now that she was in love with, or some image she'd carried in her head all these years? The idea made her stomach go tight.

"Some, yes," she said, trying to figure it out even as she spoke. "I believe some parts of us never change. I know you're still loyal to a fault. That you love your family. That you can still be grumpy as hell."

A shadow of a grin quirked his mouth. "Yeah, you're right on all three counts. I'm also more stubborn, maybe. More set in my ways. I'm sure I've developed a few more character defects over the years."

"Probably," she said.

"I should spank you for that."

She batted her lashes. "Yes, please."

"You are one bratty sub."

She smiled. "Yes, I am."

"What am I going to do with you, Allie girl?" he asked, his gaze narrowing. But his features had relaxed. So had his hold on her waist.

She laid a hand on his chest over the silver cross he never took off, felt the steady, reassuring beat of his heart beneath her palm. This was still Mick, wasn't it? "How about getting to know me all over again? Letting me get to know you?"

"You make way too much sense for a woman who was deep in subspace only a half hour ago."

"Then can we?"

His tone dropped until she had to strain to hear him. "When you look at me like that, I can't refuse you."

"Then kiss me, Mick. Please."

He stared at her, that intense gaze seeming to look right through her. Then he bent his head and brushed her lips with his. So soft, at first, then he did it again, his hand coming up to hold her cheek, his thumb slipping under her chin to hold her still. To take control.

He pressed his lips to hers hard, making her moan. Pleasure and heat spiraled in her body, and her heart raced. His arm around her waist pulled her in tighter, the blanket falling away as he crushed her to his chest until the buttons on his shirt dug into her bare breasts, until they were crushed against the hard wall of his chest. Until there was no doubt in her mind that he was claiming her as his tongue slipped into her mouth.

Oh, it was good—his lips pressed to hers, his sweet tongue searching, twining, demanding. She gave him everything he asked for, with her mouth, with her pliant body, with the surrender she felt in every muscle and bone and cell. Desire surged, expanded until she was wet and wanting.

He pulled back and studied her face closely. Her heart was beating wildly.

"Allie?"

"Mick, I need you. *Need* you. Can we just . . . start there?"

He nodded. "Yeah." He leaned in to feather his lips across hers once more.

Somehow they got up and together they got her clothes back on. He bundled her out the door and into his truck. He was gunning the engine and pulling onto the dark street before he asked her, "Your house?"

"It doesn't matter."

He glanced at her, then back at the road. "You're right. It doesn't. It never has."

He reached over and took her hand, kept it in his as they moved through the city, down Magazine Street past the warehouses, under the Pontchartrain Expressway and into Allie's neighborhood in the lower French Quarter. He made a turn onto Orange Street, then they were in front of her house, and he parked.

She waited while he walked around the truck to open her door. He lifted her down, his big hands around her waist, and his touch burned into her, making her need all the more acute. She could barely stand to wait as he led her up the walkway, up the steps, took her keys and opened her front door.

He grabbed her wrist, encircling it with his strong fingers.

"Bedroom," he demanded. "Or it's going to be right here on the hall floor."

She nodded and led him down the narrow hall.

He was on her almost the moment they passed through the doorway, stripping her down until she was naked and barefoot once more. Her pulse was a hot, thready beat in her veins, her chest, between her thighs. Desire was something solid, palpable, nearly unbearable.

She put her hands on his chest, tried to unbutton his shirt.

"Mick . . ."

He took her wrists in his hands and pulled them down to her sides, held them there as he looked into her eyes, and she understood, her mind shifting gears. If they were going to be together right now they would be in role, submissive and Dominant. She understood his need to leash his desires. Understood how dangerous he felt he was to her.

She would show him tonight she could take it. That the full darkness inside him was exactly what she wanted, yearned for.

He moved around her, one hand on her body, sliding over her stomach, her side, her back. He stood behind her, and she waited for whatever would come next, her heart hammering, her body aching for more.

When he wrapped his arm around her neck and tightened just enough to restrict her breathing, she felt his command with an enormous sense of relief.

Oh, yes.

She closed her eyes as he pulled tighter. With his other hand he swept her hair aside and kissed the back of her neck tenderly. She loved the combination of roughness and gentleness. Even trusting him enough to do this bit of breath play with her was erotic. Her body flooded with desire, her legs going weak. Even weaker when he bit into her skin, just hard enough to hurt.

She moaned.

"Yeah, baby girl. I want to hear it now. I want to hear everything you're feeling. Every groan. Every panting breath. Give it to me."

She leaned her head back onto his shoulder, and he slid his hand into her hair, grasped it at the roots and pulled tightly.

"Oh . . ."

"You like this. It makes you feel taken over, doesn't it?"

"Yes."

"I like the way your whole body bows when I pull your hair. The way I can see your yielding in the way you move. It's beautiful. And so, so hot."

He pulled harder, the pain making her gasp.

"You like that, too."

It wasn't a question, but she answered anyway.

"Yes, Mick."

He pulled until her neck bent back as far as it could. He pulled harder and she had to arch her back. And groaned when he bent to kiss her throat right where it met her shoulder—her favorite spot.

"Oh, yeah, I remember, Allie. I remember everything about you," he murmured against her skin before he bit her.

"Oh!"

Her legs nearly went out from under her, but he had a firm hold on her. He licked her skin, then bit again, harder this time, hard enough to make her draw in a long, deep breath as she tried to manage the pain. Then his tongue bathed the sore skin once more, a lovely sensation.

When he lifted her arm and bit into the delicate skin on her inner bicep, she gasped. He followed the bite with a soft, lingering kiss, then helped her straighten up and turned her around to face him.

"Can you stand by yourself?"

She nodded.

When he let her go she swayed on her feet, and he steadied her. "You okay, baby?"

She smiled. "Perfect."

He stroked a finger across her cheek. "Yeah, I think you are. But let's sit you down."

He moved her until she felt the edge of her bed at the back of her knees, and he helped her to sit. He was so caring of her, so protective. It was one of the things she'd always loved about a dominant man. It was one of the things she'd always loved about Mick.

As he took off his shirt, she remembered what else she'd loved about him, but his chest and arms were even more developed now. The tattoo he'd gotten right out of high school, the fleur-de-lis that was the symbol for the city of New Orleans with the words *New Orleans Fire Department* in a bold font arching around it, stood out against his pale golden skin, and she noticed once more the Latin script on his forearm. She'd always loved tattoos on a man.

And his abs . . . they were absolutely flawless, a full six-pack that looked as if they'd been cut from granite. She'd felt those hard planes of muscle when he'd held her close, but seeing his body was another thing altogether. It was all pure male beauty, rough and masculine in the same way his face was. All of him matured in a way that made him seem all the more male.

The lines of his body flexed and rippled as he bent over to unlace his big black boots. When he straightened she saw the jagged scar on his ribs from the old motorcycle accident, and she wanted to reach out and run her fingers over that hurting place. She wanted to run her fingers over every inch of him. But that would have to wait until—if and when—there was going to be sex between them without these roles. He was clearly in charge now. And tonight, their first night together again, it couldn't be any other way. She didn't want it to be.

He kept his gaze locked on hers as he kicked his way out of his boots, then his jeans. He was bare underneath—that hadn't changed since high school. She pulled in a breath at the sight of his cock—strong and masculine and so beautiful she had to lick her lips. She wanted to taste him. She needed him inside her. Her fingers fisted in the soft duvet.

"Good girl. Stay still for me."

He watched her, both of them naked, two feet from each other. Her gaze traveled over his body, and there it was—the two long lines of heavy scarring on his left shin from the surgeries that had repaired the badly broken leg and put the metal rod in. She'd only had a small glimpse of it when they'd been in bed together that one time, but the room had been nearly dark then. Now she could really see what he'd been through. But she didn't let her gaze linger—she didn't want to make him uncomfortable—and his beautiful, naked body was a hell of a distraction.

She looked up at his face, saw his unflinching gray gaze on her, saw the power there, shivered with it.

He stepped closer, until she swore she could smell his desire, feel it running like surges of heat over her skin, making her nipples go hard. Excruciating to have him so close and not be able to reach out and touch him. Even more when he ran a hand down his stomach and brushed his fingers over the head of his cock. She bit her lip but remained unmoving, other than her clenching fingers.

"You are so damn beautiful," he murmured. "I need you so badly it hurts. Are you hurting, too, Allie girl?"

"Please, Mick . . ."

He stroked himself once more, a long, lingering caress up the long shaft. "Is that a yes?"

"Yes."

She thought he smiled at her, but she was too mesmerized by his hand on his cock, stroking with his fingertips, then fisting for a moment before beginning to stroke again.

When he took a step toward her she pulled in a breath, and realized only then she'd been holding it. One more step and he was right in front of her. It took everything she had not to reach out for him, to remind herself that he was still in charge.

He placed his hand between her breasts, and his palm scorched her, sent shivers of desire over her skin, making her nipples harden immediately. He pressed down, and she lay back on the bed. He went with her, one knee bent next to her thigh. She was acutely aware of every inch of him: his hand on her chest, his strong thigh next to hers, the scent of him seeming to drown her senses with every breath she took. And above her, his face, which was beautiful to her despite the scars, the sharp lines of jaw and cheekbones, or maybe even more so.

"Still," he commanded.

She wouldn't have tried to argue right now. And she loved the authority in his tone, her body going warm and weak all over.

He began a slow sort of exploration, his hand caressing, squeezing, pinching: her stomach, her ribs, her sides, and finally, her breasts. He smoothed his palm over the full flesh, along the underside, around the nipple. Her sex was absolutely flooded with heat, soaking wet. She had to force herself not to arch her hips, not to arch her back to bring her aching breasts closer to his touch.

"You need me to touch you, baby? Tell me. Tell me exactly what you want."

"Oh, God. I want . . . everything. I want your hands on me. I want you to pinch my nipples hard enough to hurt. I want your hand between my thighs. I want your mouth everywhere. I want you inside me." She had to pause to draw in a long breath. "But what I *need* . . . is for you to kiss me, Mick. Please."

He smiled, then leaned in, hovering over her until his mouth was an inch from hers. His tongue darted against her lower lip. She moaned quietly. Waited.

He did it again, catching her upper lip with the sleek, warm tip of his tongue. She didn't dare move. When he did it once more, this time one long, slow lick of her lips, she sighed. His tongue felt amazing, but she needed so much more.

"Please," she whispered. Begged.

"Shh. You'll have to wait until I'm ready, baby girl."

Oh, that pet name again! That and being told she'd have to wait for everything she so desperately needed. He was killing her.

He shifted until his knee was between her thighs and his hands were braced on either side of her head. He lowered his face and brushed a kiss on her cheek, his lips soft and almost unbearably tempting. He moved to kiss her other cheek, leaving her mouth empty and wanting. But desire was pouring through her system like liquid fire, fueled by his teasing. Her pussy was drenched. He knew just how to play her, to bring her need to the edge, sharp as a knife blade.

He returned to her mouth, his lips feathering over hers, and she couldn't help but groan her frustration as well as her pleasure.

"Spread your thighs," he whispered, but there was no less command there despite the softness of his tone.

She did as she was told, opening her thighs for him. But he did nothing except kiss the corners of her mouth.

"Oh, God, Mick."

"Is this hard for you, baby?" he asked. "Imagine how hard I am for you. I won't let you look now, but I think you know. I feel like I'm about to explode. Pure torture not to touch you, to fuck you, with your naked body so close to mine. Do you feel the heat passing between us?"

"Yes," she breathed.

"Like a volcano about to erupt, isn't it? That burning hot. That's why I can't kiss you."

"Mick!" she cried, her heart thundering.

A small chuckle from him. "Do you really think I'm not going to kiss you, Allie? Do you really think I can stand not to?"

"You're a fucking sadist," she muttered.

"Yeah." He chuckled again. "A sadist who can't resist you, girl."

He leaned in and kissed her, kissed her so hard she was instantly breathless. His lips pressed against hers, hurting her, but she welcomed it. Welcomed his tongue as he pried her lips apart and plunged into her mouth.

She was panting against him, her tongue finding his, twining and wet. She'd never needed anything so much.

He was still kissing her when he grabbed her wrists and held her arms spread wide, held her down on the bed. He used his legs to kick her thighs even wider apart, and she spread as far as she could. But he didn't touch her, other than his hands on her wrists, weighing her down, rendering her helpless. His demanding kisses rendered her every bit as helpless.

Her body was burning up, and still he kept kissing her—nothing more. She felt a trickle run down her thigh, her sex swollen with need. Her breasts ached, her nipples hard as stones. And his lips and tongue were torturing her in the most delicious way.

She lifted her head off the mattress to kiss him back harder, but he pressed her down again, telling her without words to submit to him—a power struggle she had no real desire to win.

Regardless of her wanting—a wanting she was drowning in—or maybe because of it, she felt a gear shift in her head. It was another level of submission, of giving herself over to him, to whatever he demanded.

He pulled away and whispered against her mouth, "Beautiful, baby. This is exactly what I wanted from you. What I needed to see before I fuck you."

He stroked her hair, her cheek, ran his fingertips down the side of her neck, and at that moment it was as erotic as any other man with his hand between her legs.

When he brushed her nipple, she arched into his touch—she couldn't help it.

He kissed her lips, a few soft, brief kisses, before moving down and grazing her nipple with his lips.

"Oh . . ."

He filled his hands with both breasts, flooding her body with another wave of heat before he bent and took one hard tip into his mouth.

She sighed her pleasure as he sucked, his mouth so hot and wet she thought she might come right then, her pussy clenching hard between her spread thighs.

"God, Mick. Yes."

He sucked harder, eased off and bit into her swollen flesh, and she cried out.

"Ah!"

He pulled back and moved to the other side, pulling her nipple in with his lips, swirling his tongue over the tip, then sucking and biting, biting and sucking, squeezing her breast painfully with his hands. Pleasure was fire and rain and thunder all at once, her body hovering on the edge of release. When he thrust one thigh hard against her mound, her clit pulsed against the strong muscle there. He pressed again, and again and again. Her body exploded, white fire behind her closed eyelids, her legs shaking as she came, her fingers grasping the duvet, her hips thrusting against his thigh.

"God, Mick! Oh . . ."

She was still shaking when he asked roughly, "Condoms?"

"No, I don't . . ."

"Hang on."

She felt bereft as his body left hers for a moment, then he was back, and she blinked up to see him tearing a packet with his teeth. He reared back to sheath himself, and even watching him roll the latex over his rock-hard erection was purely erotic to her.

He leaned over her, took her wrists in his hands once more and drew them up until they were raised over her head. He wrapped them both in one big hand and held them there as he used the other to guide his cock to her opening.

"Yes, please, please," she murmured as the tip of him rested against her.

"Look at me," he demanded, his tone harsh, guttural.

When she raised her gaze to his she saw the need in his glittering gray eyes, in the looseness of his features. He kept his gaze locked on hers as he slid into her.

Her sex clenched around him as his thick shaft stretched her, and pleasure shivered through her like an electric current.

"Oh . . ."

"Baby," he murmured. "Goddamn it, you feel . . . amazing."

He gasped as he thrust, driving to the hilt.

She gasped out a breath as he filled her.

He was big, and it hurt. She didn't care. She wanted all of him, every bit she could get. She arched her hips, taking him in.

"Yeah, that's it," he said. "Come on, baby. Fuck me. Fuck me as I'm fucking you."

She did as he instructed, raising her hips to meet his as he drove into her. She saw every stab of pleasure mirrored in his eyes, heard every moan echoed in his deep groans. Sensation built, pushing deeper inside her even as he did, his cock a thick hammer inside her body.

When she felt his cock begin to pulse, he stopped, breathing hard.

"Don't move," he commanded.

She held her muscles taut, stilling herself as best she could. His scent surrounded her, invaded her head, her body, filtering deep within her system. Dark leather, fresh citrus, the smoky scent of sex.

"Allie, I need to . . ."

He trailed off, then he wrapped his hands around her waist, making her feel as if she weighed no more than a doll as he flipped her over onto her stomach. With his hands grasping her hips, he raised her up on her hands and knees. Before she had time to think about it, to protest that connection of face to face, gaze to gaze, he surged into her from behind, and she cried out in pleasure.

"God, Mick!"

He slung his hips, burying his cock deep inside her. Then he wrapped an arm around her waist and reached between her thighs to press her hard clitoris. She sighed when he began to rub, to pinch, to tug on it.

"I'm going to come," she told him, nearly breathless.

"No you don't, Allie girl. You hold it back for me. Don't you come until I tell you."

She groaned.

He pinched her clit hard, and she would have jumped if his big body hadn't been flush up against hers, holding her in place.

He began to move, surging into her, sliding out, and every stroke was exquisite. She was shivering all over, her body working hard not to climax, to hold the need to come at bay. He bucked harder, his fingers tensing on her clit, and she had to bite her lip, to bite her orgasm back.

He was slamming into her, hard enough to hurt, but she welcomed it, *needed* it. Needed to feel him so deep inside her she would carry the bruises for days.

"Baby . . . Christ, you feel so. Damn. Good. So good . . ."

He wrapped his other arm under her breasts and pulled her up until she was on her knees, his arms holding her tight, his bog cock still ramming into her, over and over.

"Now," he commanded, and bit into her shoulder.

Her pussy clenched hard as stars exploded in her eyes, the world spinning, dark, void of everything but their two bodies joined together, the pleasure and the pain. His strong arms held her together as her body shattered with sensation.

"Oh . . ."

He was groaning, bucking into her still, his fingers on her clit rubbing, pressing, driving her climax on.

When it was over they collapsed together on the bed, both of them covered in sweat. He still held her, spooning her from behind. His fingers still played lazily with her clit, sending small frissons of pleasure through her.

"Baby, baby, baby," he murmured, nibbling on the back of her neck.

"Mmm."

She felt amazing. Raw. Sore. Spent. But there was also that one tiny part of her that wished they'd come looking into each other's eyes, that understood he'd turned her over for a reason that wasn't all about the pleasure itself. And it hurt. But she understood that level of true intimacy would take some time.

She tried to let this be enough.

She snuggled back into him and he held her, his hand coming up to smooth over her thigh, sliding up her stomach, her ribs, to cup her breast. He stroked the skin there with his thumb as his breathing calmed.

She could smell the earthy scent of come in the air. Heard the sound of rain coming down outside, splashing against the wide leaves of the banana plant outside her bedroom window.

Felt the small chill in the air brought by the rain. She shivered, and he held her tighter.

"You okay?" he asked.

"Yes. Wonderful."

It was true. But the small doubt that had invaded her mind as soon as they'd finished was there, too, and just as true.

She caught his hand in hers and twined her fingers through his.

"Mick."

"Yeah?"

"This is . . . we're just beginning, aren't we? To see if we can figure this out?" she asked.

"What, baby? Yes, sure. That's what we talked about. That's exactly what we're doing here. It wouldn't have been more than play at the club otherwise. Is that what you're asking me?"

"I . . . yes, I guess it is."

He was quiet for several moments. She wished he'd turn her over to face him, let her look into his eyes so she would *know*. But maybe neither of them really knew yet, as badly as she wanted to. Maybe that wasn't possible.

"We need to start somewhere," he said. "That's the whole point. We can't go back to where we used to be. That isn't where we want to be anyway, is it?"

"No. Of course not."

"So . . . we start here. And see where it goes."

"Okay. Okay. I know you're right. I'm just . . . we've played and . . ."

"Hey. I'm right here, baby. I'm not going anywhere right now."

He kissed her hair, and it made her heart squeeze. She brought their twined fingers to her lips and kissed his.

"See? It's all good," he said.

But was it? She wanted things between them to be good— what was happening now, what might happen down the road.

She *needed* it to be, which wasn't the smartest thing, perhaps, given the way Mick had run from her in the past. Maybe the "need" part was because they'd just played. Maybe she was bottoming out a bit. But whatever the reason, she couldn't help herself. Logic and emotion didn't always play well together. She just hoped she could get the logical part to even have a place in the game.

CHAPTER

Eight

MICK WALKED INTO Flynn McCool's, a favorite pub of his friends and brothers. They'd all been glad the bar managed to reopen after Katrina.

His bootheels scuffed on the weathered hardwood floor as he moved through the place and found Jamie at the bar. He settled onto a stool next to his friend.

"Hey."

"Hey," Jamie answered with a lift of his chin toward the bartender. "A Guinness for the gentleman."

"Yeah, I'm hardly that."

"True enough."

He could tell Jamie had already finished one beer and started another, even though it was only noon—his deeply buried Scottish accent only came out when he drank, or on those rare occasions when he was really pissed off. He was pretty sure he hadn't done anything to piss Jamie off lately. At least, not this week.

The bartender filled a tall mug and passed it to Mick.

"Thanks." He turned to Jamie. "So, what's up?"

"Just checking in with you about last night," Jamie said. "I've already talked to Allie and she's pretty closemouthed. Tell me what's up with you two."

"You know what I really hate, aside from your tendency to have your nose up everyone's ass?"

"That's not one of my particular fetishes, but go on."

"I hate that I can't fucking tell you to go to hell because you're our damn negotiator."

"And your friend," Jamie reminded him.

"Yeah." Mick paused to take a swig of the dark ale. "So you're doing the responsible thing, is that it?"

"Nice to see you, too, buddy. Want to tell me why you're in such a foul mood?" Jamie asked.

"Me? I'm fine. You're the one drowning your sorrows. What's up? Something at the shop?"

Jamie wrapped a hand around his mug, lifted it and took a long gulp. "May twentieth."

"Yeah? And?"

His friend cast him a sideways glance and Mick remembered—the anniversary of his brother's death. Was he a selfish bastard thinking of himself after all Jamie had lost? He already knew the answer.

"Shit, Jamie. Sorry, man. How many years is it?"

"Twenty-three. I can't even believe it's been that long since I've seen Ian. Although I guess he would look just like me, wouldn't he?"

"I'm sorry," Mick repeated, not sure what else to say.

"Trying not to be too morose. Especially after all these years. But there's that twin thing you hear about, you know? It's true, what people say."

Mick clapped Jamie on the back. "You going to be okay?"

"Yeah. Just need a few drinks today. And I will again in a couple of months when it's the anniversary of Brandon's accident. But by tomorrow I'll be back on track. Everyone's allowed a black day now and then, right?"

"Right. Sure." Mick grimaced, wondering if people were allowed black decades.

"So, distract me with the scandal that is whatever's going on between you and Allie."

"Said like a true reality TV whore."

"*Ice Road Truckers* does not a whore make, my friend," Jamie protested.

"I'm sure there are a few along that road."

"Probably. Quit stalling and spill."

Mick hesitated. "What did Allie tell you?"

"That as your best friend I'd better talk to you first."

He grinned. "Good girl."

Jamie set his beer down with a thud. "Jesus, Mick, just tell me what the hell went on so I can get on with my drinking."

"Okay, fine." He paused to sip his beer. "We went to the club and had some good play. Great, actually. Then we went back to her place. I left this morning only after making sure she wasn't in subdrop. She was fine. She promised me she was fine."

Jamie frowned. "Now tell me what's in between the lines."

He had to blow out a breath. "We're . . . talking about being together. Just trying it out, seeing where we're both at."

"Can you expand on that?"

"I'd rather not."

"No kidding. Do it anyway," Jamie demanded. "Because I need to know if Allie really is all right."

"Do you think I'd be here if she wasn't?" Mick exploded, then reined himself in. "Fuck. Sorry."

"Buddy, you are bent way the hell out of shape."

"It was your idea to bring us back together." Mick knew he was being childish, and he sighed, reaching for his beer. "And yeah, maybe I am bent. I don't know what the hell is going to happen. I'm not sure what I want to happen. I'm just going with it for now."

"That is such crap."

"Fuck you, Jamie," Mick muttered into his beer mug before he took a long gulp.

Jamie only shook his head at him.

"Okay, fine. I don't know where my head is at when it comes to her. It's too damn soon to tell. I don't intend to hurt her if that's what you're worried about—"

"It is."

"I get that. But what am I supposed to do?" he asked. "Back off and never see her again because I don't know where we'll end up? Would that be any better?"

"I don't know. Would it?" Jamie asked.

Mick scrubbed at his chin. "I'm trying to figure it out, okay? Don't ride me about this, Jamie," he warned. "I'm doing the best I can."

"You still have feelings for her," Jamie stated.

"And you still have an uncanny gift for stating the obvious."

Despite all the years of his attempts at denial, he knew he'd never been able to hide how he felt about Allie from his best friend. Hell, he hadn't done a good job of hiding it from himself.

Jamie lowered his voice. "Mick, just don't drag this on too long if you can't carry through. That's all I'm asking. Don't hurt her any more than you have to."

He nodded. "I feel like a bastard already for even being with her. I'd feel like a bastard if I refused her. There's no good way out of this."

Except that despite all his bluster he wasn't sure he wanted out. Being with her felt too damn good to stop. Being with her, playing her, having her submit to him.

He understood his own limitations. He knew he'd had his walls up last night, this morning. He'd *had* to. Was it fair to her that challenging his limits was a sort of experiment for him? That he really didn't have any idea how it would turn out?

"Hell, Jamie, this is all new to me. You two sprang it on me—and I'm not saying that to hit you over the head with it, okay? Just stating a fact. But I wasn't ready for it. Not that I haven't thought of being with Allie again, which I'm sure you know, but that was just fantasy material. Until now. Now it's damn real, and I have Allie to be responsible for, without knowing what I'm even fucking capable of these days, outside of the BDSM arena."

"Yeah, I get it, Mick."

He took another gulp of his beer. "I don't know if I can give her what she wants. But I don't know if I can stop. It's a tug-of-war in my head."

No, he couldn't stop now. Having had this taste of Allie—of Allie as a woman, rather than a girl—was something he couldn't resist.

No, he wasn't about to stop.

ALLIE SWUNG OPEN the back door to Marie Dawn's house and walked into the cozy blue-and-white kitchen.

"Hi, honey, I'm home!" she called out as she let the screen door shut behind her.

Her best friend came in from the dining room and immediately wrapped Allie in a warm hug.

"Allie, *chérie*, I've missed you! I'm so sorry I couldn't make lunch yesterday. If it had been anything other than an emergency with *grand-mère* . . . I feel terrible that it turned out to be nothing more than a little indigestion."

"You had no way of knowing—it's fine. And I've missed you, too." She pulled away and held Marie Dawn at arm's length. "And look how gorgeous your hair is! It's almost to your waist. I love it."

"So does Neal," her friend said, beaming.

Mick's brother Neal and Marie Dawn had eloped when she was still in college, and they were still as crazy about each other as they'd been the day they said their vows.

Must be nice.

"Let me get you some coffee. How hungry are you? I have a nice Niçoise salad ready, but I'm dying to hear everything."

Allie sat down at the painted white kitchen table and let Marie Dawn place a cup of coffee in front of her while she tried to organize the chaos whirling around in her brain. She'd lied to Mick that morning when she'd told him she was fine. And either she'd done a great job of it, or he'd been anxious enough to get away that he'd accepted it. Maybe a little of both.

"Everything is a lot," she said, playing with her coffee mug.

Marie Dawn sat down across from her. "Okay. Pick a place and start."

Allie blew out a breath. "Well . . . Mick came to my place to pick me up, and things started to happen right away. I mean, it was obvious who was in charge from that first moment. And I liked it. I'm not complaining. We had an amazing scene at the club. Everything went really smoothly." She laughed. "Well, not smoothly, maybe. The play was a little too rough for that to be the right word. But I know you don't really want to know that part."

Marie Dawn smiled. "Nope. The sexy stuff with my brother-in-law I don't need to hear. I'll just mentally fill in the blanks. Or not. Go on."

"So, during aftercare we talked . . . and it was good. Honest. More honest than we've ever been, probably. I made him talk to me about what had gone wrong with us. In high school, and after that night we spent together later."

"And?"

Allie bit her lip. "And . . . I asked him if we could start again. I didn't expect to blurt it out the way I did, and I think he was surprised, too. Although neither of us should be, I suppose. I wouldn't have forced this whole thing if that wasn't at least part of my intention. And he wouldn't have accepted—and he certainly wouldn't have come back for a second round after that first night—if that weren't part of his intention, too. At least I think so. Things got a little confusing later, but at the club after the scene we really talked. And he admitted a few things to me—things I'd already suspected, for the most part. About us. About how he felt after his accident. I knew it changed him, but I never really saw how deeply breaking his leg, having the rod surgery, the permanent limp, damaged him, maybe because I only actually saw him once after that."

Marie Dawn nodded pensively. "I knew he never got over not being able to be a firefighter. Neal and I have talked about it. The whole family is aware of it. They've always been careful not to guilt-trip him about it."

"They don't need to—I think he does enough of that himself. He feels so ashamed. Because of the family, and because of that family pride in New Orleans, being a part of it."

"Which is crazy," Marie Dawn said. "I told you how much volunteer work he did after Katrina. For *three years* he worked on rebuilding people's homes with Jamie's brother, Allister. He still volunteers once in a while if a particular project comes up. It's not as if he's never paid his dues to this city. He likes to pretend he's a badass, with all that bare-knuckle boxing stuff and his leather jackets, but he's as good a citizen as any of his brothers."

"I know. But he's obviously never gotten over it. It's really shaped how he feels about himself. And maybe how he feels about me."

"In the past, or now?"

"Both, maybe. Because things were going really beautifully last night and then he just . . . turned away from me. Literally. Everything was amazing and . . . beautiful. And then he wouldn't look at me anymore."

Tears burned in her eyes, and she pressed against them with both hands.

Marie Dawn put a hand on her arm. "Oh, no, *chérie*, my sweet, please don't be so sad. Men can be stupid creatures. Believe me, I know—I've been married to one for ten years."

Allie had to smile. She took her hands away from her face and grasped both of her friend's. "You're right. And Mick's stubborn as hell, too—a combination that scares me. But I know if I turn away we won't have a chance."

"It's often the woman who has to take care of a relationship. And that's my sexist comment for the day. But I think you'll need to if you two are going to have a shot at being together. Because to get Mick to admit he's afraid of anything will be pretty much impossible."

Allie rolled her eyes. "That's for sure. I just have to hang in there and see how this all plays out, I guess."

"You can do it. You're one of the strongest people I know."

"I don't always feel strong. But I'm trying."

"When are you seeing him again?"

Allie shrugged. She'd been wondering the same thing all morning. "I don't know. We didn't actually talk about it. I assumed I'd just wait to hear from him, but now I think I'll send him an email and ask."

"Sweetie, just call him and demand his time." Her friend tapped her temple. "Stupid, remember?"

Allie laughed. "I remember. Okay, I'll call him."

"Good. And when you talk to him, you can tell him I think he's an idiot who's too blind to see what's right in front of his face."

"How about I leave that to you? You're family. And he won't threaten to spank you."

"I thought you liked that?"

She grinned. "Oh, I do."

The banter with her best friend was cheering her up. So was the idea that she could take back some of the control in the situation by initiating her next meeting with Mick. She was going to have to in order to work past his walls, and maybe her own, too. Only time together would tell. If she had to force that time with him, she would. Dom or not, the ball was going to be in her court, and Mick would have to play by her rules for a while.

ALLIE HAD SPENT the rest of the afternoon organizing the Power-Point presentation she was putting together for the Dolcetti expansion. Knowing the stubborn streak that ran in her family, she understood it was a long shot, but it was important to her to try—it was something she'd thought about and wanted to do since she'd first started culinary school. It was why she'd gone to learn the art of pastry to begin with. And putting her business plan together was also an excellent way to distract herself from the circling thoughts about Mick. She was dying to call and talk with him now that she'd made the decision, since he'd encouraged her to press the issue with her family, but she also knew guys usually needed some downtime to process things.

At nine o'clock she stood up from the kitchen table and stretched, poured herself a cup of dark coffee from her new French press and inhaled the rich aroma. Good coffee always felt like a luxury to her, one she'd become used to when living in Europe. Just because she was feeling the need for a little self-indulgence she added a spoonful of sugar before finding her cell phone and going into the bedroom to make the call. She set her coffee mug on the nightstand, sat on the bed and plumped a few pillows behind her. Why was her heart racing?

Calm down.

She did some yoga breathing before dialing Mick's number.

"Reid here."

"Mick, it's me, Allie."

"I'm glad. If it wasn't, I'd know my caller ID was broken."

"Oh. Yeah. Right."

He chuckled and she closed her eyes in embarrassment.

Idiot.

"So," she started, "I just wanted to talk to you. We haven't done any checking in today."

His tone sobered instantly. "You're right. I should have. You okay?"

"Yes, fine. I hung out with Marie Dawn today, which was good. But . . . Mick, in my experience it's always good to check in with my Top for a day or two after play, depending on how hard the play was, or the emotional response . . . if there's another layer going on beneath the actual play. Which there is with us."

"Fuck. You're right and I'm sorry. Totally irresponsible of me not to call. It's not like me. I got a call right after lunch and I've been wrapped up in this project all day. But I shouldn't have let myself get too distracted to follow up."

Follow up? Was that all she was to him—a task on his to-do list? But she knew he was covering for emotions he wasn't ready to deal with. Making excuses. Still, it stung.

"Yes, well . . ." She didn't know what else to say. And she realized she was a little mad, too, at his response. Or lack of response.

After a tense moment of silence, Mick swore under his breath. "Allie, look, I *am* sorry. I leave in the morning for a business trip. I have to go to Atlanta for a couple of days to scout out a new venue, meet with a new client. But I'll be back on Thursday. We can see each other then."

"Okay."

She hadn't meant to draw out the last syllable, hadn't meant to sound so irritated. She was caught between the need to be honest with him and the fear of driving him away. But this wasn't high school, or even college. And they'd both been in the kink community long enough to know how this stuff was supposed to be done. Total transparency was always the best option.

She took a breath. "Mick, if you have even an hour to spare, I could really use seeing you tonight. I can come there if that'll be easier. But I need to see you."

He was silent for a moment, and both the anger and the hurt that had been lingering inside her all day surged in her chest. Was he really going to turn her down?

Finally he said, "Sure, come on over. I'm still packing for this trip so it's better if you come here, if you don't mind."

"I don't mind. Is it okay if I come now?"

"Yeah, sure."

They hung up and she raced around the house looking for the right shade of lip gloss, pulled on a clean tank top, found a belt for her low-slung jeans and put on her new sandals and a pair of silver hoop earrings. At the last moment she shucked her way out of her clothes and put on clean—sexy black lace—lingerie.

We're just talking.

Maybe. But one never knew. And even worse than being caught in an accident wearing shoddy lingerie was being caught in a surprise sexual encounter with less-than-stellar undergarments.

She locked up the house and jumped into her aunt's old Coupe de Ville, fired up the big engine and made her way to Mick's place, trying not to think about how unsatisfying their conversation had been, or the fear that was still simmering low inside her.

Parking was awful in his part of town, but she found a spot only two blocks away. If it had been almost any other city in the world, she would be nervous walking alone at night through the narrow streets, but this was her town.

Hers and Mick's.

She found his place, an old plaster-over-brick painted in a rich terra-cotta. It was covered in flowering vines, as so many of the older buildings in the French Quarter were. She'd always loved how most of the city had the scent of flowers overlaying the mild scents of decay and old plaster, the exotic cooking smells. Even the car exhaust added something to the mix that was the distinct urban perfume of New Orleans.

She looked up and saw lights shining down through the windows on the second floor, where he'd told her his flat was. Her pulse grew warm and thready knowing she was going to see him. That he was going to touch her.

Hell, he'd better touch her. She needed to feel his arms around her. Needed to feel the reassurance of skin against skin even more, maybe.

But if that phone call had been any indication, he was probably still too shut down from the intensity of their night together, their open conversation, to give her what she so desperately needed from him. She didn't want to need it, damn it. But the simple fact was that she did. Because it was Mick. Because when it came to him she was always a little desperate and needy. And maybe she was in a more intense state of subdrop than she realized, because "desperate" and "needy" were not like her at all. She sighed. Not when it came to anyone but Mick.

Tears stung her eyes, and she shook her head, tried to shake them away.

Stop it. Stay in the moment. Don't project.

She inhaled, tucked her car keys into her purse and knocked.

She heard him coming down the stairs, and her heartbeat accelerated. To her horror, the tears burned even hotter behind her eyes.

"Goddamn it," she muttered—just as he opened the door.

"All right. I guess I deserved that," Mick said.

"No, it wasn't you. It was . . . I'm just . . ."

A tear plopped onto her cheek and she started to turn away, but he took her hand in his.

"Hey," he said gently. "Where you going, baby?"

And that did it. The damn tears started and wouldn't stop. She hid her face in her hands.

"Hey, Allie girl. Come here."

He pulled her into his chest, and she buried her face into him, took in his scent, tried to stop crying. It didn't work. She pushed away from his hold on her.

"Don't, Mick. Don't do this if it's all about you being Mr.

Responsible. I'm going to be honest—I can't take it if that's what's going on here. I don't *want* it. Do you understand me?"

She was shaking so hard she dropped her purse. She let it sit there.

Mick looked shocked. Not that she could blame him. She hadn't expected this, either.

"That's not what this is about," he finally ground out, some anger in his voice. "You know better than that."

"Really, Mick? How could I know anything after you abandoned me all day to deal with the fallout from last night on my own? No email. No phone call."

"I admit I should have called you, Allie, but I wasn't abandoning you. You're here now, aren't you?"

"Yes, but only because I called you."

"You're right. And I'm sorry. I'm fucking sorry."

"Don't cuss at me! Jesus, Mick."

He scrubbed a hand over his goatee. "Allie . . . I always cuss like a sailor. I wasn't cussing *at* you, just . . . cussing."

"I know. I know that. I'm just . . . God, I don't know what's wrong with me. Look, I'm just . . . going. I shouldn't have come. I shouldn't have called you. I'm just . . ."

She turned to go once more, but he grasped her wrist even tighter and pulled her close to his big body, his arm sliding around her waist and holding her tight.

"Allie girl, tell me what this is about. I know I didn't call and I should have—you're absolutely right about that, and I'm a total irresponsible dick. I know it. But this seems like there's more going on. Talk to me."

"I can't."

The tears were still coming, rolling down her cheeks. She was absolutely horrified, wiping at them with one hand. What the hell was wrong with her?

"Tell me," he commanded, making her take a breath.

"I don't know. I just wanted to talk. Just talk. And then this happened."

"What happened?"

She shrugged helplessly. "I didn't expect you to bail on me today. Maybe I should have known it was a possibility. But somehow I didn't. And I think I've been crashing a little all day. I didn't realize it. And then I come here and you're *mad* at me, for God's sake, making me feel even more abandoned and . . . like a child, Mick. Like when my dad died."

Oh, God. She hadn't meant to say that.

"Christ, Allie." He pulled her into his body and she couldn't fight him anymore. He stroked her hair, his chin resting on top of her head. "Baby. I didn't mean to set off any of that stuff."

"It's not the first time," she muttered, allowing herself the comfort of his touch.

"Fuck. You'd better come inside. We have shit to talk about."

That didn't sound good. But she let him pick up her purse and lead her up the narrow staircase to his flat anyway.

The place suited him, she saw right away, even through her upset and tears. All neutral colors, big furniture, plenty of wood. He sat her down on the leather couch and left her there for a moment, came back with a glass of water. She accepted it and took a few sips before he took it and set it on the coffee table. He sat down beside her and handed her some tissue. She wiped her eyes and nose while he waited quietly.

"Better?" he asked.

She shook her head. "I don't know."

"I do think you're crashing, Allie. That, and I didn't come through for you today, and for that I apologize. To be honest, I was processing last night. And today. More than I thought I'd be. It's a lot to think about."

"For me, too."

"Yeah, I know. Which probably contributed to your subdrop today."

"Yes," she agreed.

"I wish you'd have come to me earlier. I know I should have been the one to initiate contact, but sometimes I can be pretty dumb when I'm caught up in my own head."

"Marie Dawn sort of said the same thing."

"Yeah, well, she's had to live with my brother for a damn long time, so she's familiar with the inherent stupidity of the Reid men."

She sniffed. "She sort of said that, too."

He pulled back and tilted her chin, watching her face, his dark brows drawn over his smoky gray eyes. "What do you need from me?"

It felt like a loaded question. "I don't know." That was as honest as she could be right now.

"Okay. Then how about this? We get undressed and climb into my bed and just curl up and watch some TV. We can talk when you feel like it. Or not. Come on."

He pulled her to her feet and led her into the bedroom.

The furniture was all sleek, dark wood, the bed on a platform and covered in a charcoal gray duvet. Mick left her standing on the white faux-fur rug at the foot of the bed to pull the duvet down, exposing the smoky lilac sheets, only a few shades darker than the duvet on her own bed.

He came back to her and bent to slide her sandals off, drew her jeans down over her hips while she stood passively, her head spinning, a little numbed by too much emotion.

"Climb in. I'll be right there."

She got onto the bed, drew the sheets up to her waist. It felt a little odd, somehow, being in Mick's bed. Maybe because this wasn't about sex and seduction. It was just . . . *them*.

The sex and seduction was easier. There she knew herself. There she was on solid ground. Right now she wasn't sure what to expect.

Calm down. He invited you here—to his home, to his bed.

She watched as he shucked off his T-shirt, and even in her emotional state she couldn't help but admire his broad shoulders, the bulging biceps, the taut lines of his abs. She couldn't help notice once more the long scar running over his ribs that still looked raw and angry, even after all these years. It still hurt her to see it, to know the anguish the accident had caused him. But somehow it just made him sexier. Why were scars so hot on a man?

He climbed in next to her in the dark blue sweats he'd been wearing when she'd arrived. He slid an arm around her shoulder and pulled her in close, sitting back against the pillows piled against the wall behind them. It felt good to be close to him, to feel the reassuring strength of his big body next to hers. But it still felt a little strange, more intimate than the things they'd done at the club together. More *real*.

"Travel TV, still?" he asked.

"I can't believe you remember."

"I remember a lot, Allie."

She let herself relax a little into him. He flicked on the flat screen television with the remote and found her channel. They watched in silence a piece on California's Mendocino Coast, and as the narrator's voice spoke about the rugged beauty of the cliffs, the sea lions swimming off the shore, her shoulders loosened and she leaned into Mick's arm around her.

After a while Mick muted the volume and said quietly, "Tell me about your dad, Allie."

Her body instinctively stiffened for a moment. It made sense that he'd ask after what she'd said, but she still hesitated. "My dad?"

Mick tugged her closer. "I've known you all these years and that's the one thing you never really talked to me about. I know he died when you were a kid, I know he was a musician. I know your mom adored him, and still does. But you've never told me much more than that. Since it came up tonight, I thought this might be a good time to tell me."

"Maybe." She had to digest the idea for a few moments. "My dad was . . . I sort of idolized him, I guess," she said, the words trying to stick in her throat. "He spent a lot of time with me growing up, but I think you already knew that. And I guess what you want to know is how his . . . death affected me."

"Only because it obviously still does. And this is not just me being the Dom getting to know the psychology of his partner. This is *me*, Allie. And if we're going to get closer . . . well, it seems we are." He paused, and she looked up to see him blink a few times. "Yeah. We are. So we have to build trust."

"I know." She paused, swallowed the ache in her chest that was partly from thinking about her dad and partly from Mick caring about her and being willing to show it. Being willing to admit that the two of them being together was possibly going somewhere. But that was too much to think about and have this discussion at the same time.

"I don't talk about this," she said, her fingers picking at the edge of the cotton sheet, her gaze focused there. "Not with anyone. But you're right. I have to. And it's you. Even though we're in kind of a scary place right now, I still understand we've known each other forever.

"So . . . you know that it was mostly Dad who got me ready in the mornings while Mama was at the bakery. He would play the piano for me sometimes while I was eating breakfast, or brushing my teeth—sometimes it would be a classical piece, sometimes jazz. Sometimes just silly stuff, cartoon music. That last morning . . . he was playing Mozart's Piano Concerto number twenty-one. I'm sure you've heard it. It's a light piece. Supposed to be cheerful. Well."

She stopped to draw in a long breath. She wasn't sure how to say the words out loud. "That morning . . . the music stopped suddenly, and I came downstairs demanding that he play some ragtime for me, which I did a lot. I just skipped into the room and . . ." She stopped again, swallowed hard. "He was sort of slumped over the piano." She had to close her eyes. She could see him there, his blue striped shirt, his dark hair shining in the morning sun streaming through her mother's lace curtains, the pattern of light and shadow it made on the floor. She drew in another breath and went on. "Even in my ten-year-old brain I knew right away he was gone. That he wasn't coming back. I started screaming. Apparently a neighbor heard me, because suddenly there were a lot of people in the house. I don't remember much more after that." She stopped and gulped past the hard lump in her throat, tightening her chest. "All I knew—all I *believed*—for a long time after was that he'd left me."

Mick tightened his arms around her. "Jesus, baby. Poor girl."

She shook her head—or tried to, which was difficult being held so hard against his muscled shoulder. "Don't, Mick."

"Don't what? Feel bad that you had to go through that?"

"Don't feel sorry for me. I don't feel sorry for myself. Life happens, right? Everyone's gone through something difficult."

"Yeah, I guess so. But not that." His voice was rough. "No one should have to go through that. I get that you'd probably carry those feelings with you through your life. And I guess I get how you might have felt the same way when I didn't call you, that it would have been a trigger. If I'd known more . . . maybe . . ."

They both let the sentence fade and quiet descend as they held each other.

It had felt good to tell him, somehow. And bad, like opening an old wound that would now have to grow a new scab. But if things were going to continue between them, she was going to have to get used to being vulnerable with him. It was different with Mick than it was with the other Doms she'd played with, the men she'd had relationships with. Mick *knew* her in ways no one else did, and that made the rawness all the more wide open. She didn't like that part.

She sniffed, rubbed at the makeup that had undoubtedly run under her eyes.

"Mick?"

"Yeah?"

"Will you tell me something now?" she asked.

"What?"

"I sort of feel like I've just laid my soul out to you on a platter, and I'd feel a lot better if you did a little of the same with me."

He shifted her in his arms so he could see her face.

"Really? That's the only thing that'll make you feel better?" he lowered his voice an octave. "What about this?"

He leaned in and kissed her softly, his lips pressing to hers, then pressing again, gently, sweetly.

"That's nice, too," she admitted.

"Tell me if this is any better."

He kissed her again, this time teasing her lips open with his tongue. He slid the tip of his tongue between her lips, giving her just a taste before pulling away. Cupping her face in his hands he did it once more, this time sliding in farther, pulling back, doing it again, a lovely tease that built desire in her body like a slowly heating flame. She couldn't help but moan. Couldn't help the way her body—her need—betrayed her.

There would be time to talk later. For now, there was Mick. She'd never been able to resist.

CHAPTER
Nine

HIS HANDS SLID down to her shoulders, and he kissed her lips, her cheek, her neck, as he slipped her tank top over her head. One strong arm wrapped around her back and he unhooked her bra, and that came off, too. His mouth was on hers once more as he pulled her in close, sliding down into the sheets with her. He held her in his arms, their bodies pressed close, until she could feel his erection against her belly. The gears had shifted, her mind emptying out, her body filling with desire, her sex aching and wet.

"Here, baby girl," he said, kicking his way out of his sweats, then helping her slide her underwear off before rolling her onto her back and climbing on top of her.

God, his body felt so damn good, the weight of him pressing her down. He folded her fingers into his, raised her arms over her head and held her there while he kissed her, teasing her with lips and tongue and teeth while his hard cock pressed into her abdomen, his hard thigh pressing against her swollen mound.

"Come on, Mick," she begged.

"Shh, baby. Just lie here and take it for now."

No, she'd never been able to resist him. Certainly not his command. Her body responded even before her brain did, her muscles going lax.

"Perfect," he murmured before bending to kiss her neck, to bite there. Then lower until his teeth were grazing her nipple, making it go hard, making her muscles go limp with need.

His teeth grazed her skin as his mouth traveled all over her breasts—light nibbling at first that gradually built to harder nips. The bites were quick, leaving tiny shots of pain behind, creating a lancing pattern of sensation all over her breasts. Her nipples were so damn hard they hurt, aching to be touched. Begging for the pain.

He moved down her side, over her rib cage, down to the tender skin at her waist. He bit her there hard, his teeth sinking in, making her yelp.

"Oh!"

"Does this hurt you, baby?" he asked, his voice muted, his mouth a breath away from her body.

"Yes," she moaned.

"But you like it?"

"Oh, yes."

"Do you want more? Tell me."

"Yes, please, Mick."

He kissed the sore spot where he'd last bitten her, making her sigh with pleasure. "Your skin tastes like fucking heaven, baby girl. I'm going to bite you hard now. I'm going to eat you up. And you must hold very still for me. Don't make me tie you up. If you do, there will be consequences."

Consequences.

Oh . . .

Her sex clenched, went soaking wet at the thought.

He bent and sank his teeth hard into her flesh, right at the curve of her waist, and she had to breathe through the pain. It was exquisite, searing, and followed quickly by a lovely rush of endorphins. He bit again, a little higher—the fragile skin over her ribs—and this time the pain was more severe. She gasped, tried to breathe through it.

"You can take it. Come on, baby. For me."

She nodded, forced her body to calm, waited for the next bite.

This time it was the underside of her breast, and he bit down hard.

"Ah, God!"

Her fingers dug into the bedclothes until her knuckles ached, but somehow she managed not to move as she struggled between her body's natural instinct for flight and the desire to please, between the pain and the shimmering, tenuous pleasure of the chemicals beginning to seep into her brain.

He held on, her flesh gripped between his sharp teeth, and the pain threatened to overwhelm her.

"Mick . . ."

He bit harder, and a tear slid down her cheek. She was panting, trying to convert the pain to pleasure. After a few difficult moments it worked, and she was rewarded by a flood of endorphins. She went limp with it, let her body process the intense pain and the even more powerful pleasure. The powerful sensation of Mick doing these things to her. The lovely, sweet sensation as he lapped at the bite with his soft tongue.

He finally pulled away and knelt over her, looking down at her. He didn't say anything, but she knew from his expression he was pleased with her. He urged her thighs wide apart with his. She was weak with her need for him. Aching with wanting.

He reached between her thighs, and she arched her hips as his fingers slid into her.

"Love this, baby girl," he murmured. "Love how damn wet you get. I want to be inside you. To fuck you. And I will."

He pressed down on one of her thighs with his hand, hard and hurting, and spread her even more, left his hand there, the pressure letting her know he was completely in control. With his other hand he began working her clit, rubbing, tugging, pinching, then moving to push his fingers inside her and pumping a few times before going back to her swollen clitoris.

"Hold still, baby," he demanded.

She did her best. But pleasure was building inside her, making her dizzy. Finally, she couldn't take it and she arched her hips hard against his hand. He immediately pulled back.

"Ah, now you know that won't do, princess."

He pushed himself off her and leaned over her, reached under the center of the mattress at the top of the bed and pulled up a length of black rope. He pulled her arms up over her head and tied her wrists together so fast she didn't have time to consider what he was doing. But she instantly sank into the sensation of safety in the arms of his ropes. Her head really began to empty out, and she was vaguely aware of how much easier it would be to take the pain and the orgasm control if she were bound.

He moved around the bed—she couldn't really see what he was doing, but figured he had ropes attached to the bed frame— and soon he had her ankles tied, legs spread to the corners of the mattress, as well as a doubled length of rope pulled tight across her stomach and over the middle of the bed.

"Better," he said as he moved back to kneel between her thighs.

"I love the way you look like this. Stilled by my ropes. The contrast of the dark rope against your skin, the surrender in your eyes. That just about kills me—I don't mind telling you that." He paused, ran a hand down her body—in between her breasts, over her stomach, until his fingers were surging into her once more.

"Oh . . ."

"You know I like to hear that—your sounds of pleasure. Come on, baby, give it to me. Let me take you right to the edge."

He pumped his fingers—two, maybe three—curving them to hit her G-spot, and she groaned.

"Yeah, that's it."

With his other hand he pinched her pussy lips, the pain sending pleasure rocketing through her system.

"Ah, Mick . . . yes . . ."

He thrust hard into her, and her pussy clenched hard around his fingers. He withdrew them.

"Not yet. Breathe for me."

She did as she was told, pleasure so keen in her body she could barely hold it back, even though he was no longer touching her.

"That's it. Get it under control. You can do it."

He pressed into her once more, adding more fingers and spreading them so that it hurt her a little. But pain *was* pleasure to her, and she had to work to hold back her climax. He held his hand still inside her, his fingers still spread wide. With the other he started to caress her body: her stomach, her breasts, her hips, her thighs, tracing over the bite marks and the tender welts from their previous play. His touch was lovely, his gentle fingertips a sensual contrast to the way he filled her sex with his hand. Desire was sharp, surging hard through her system, and only Mick's command and his ropes held her orgasm at bay.

He held her there, suspended for endless moments while she took in a breath, let it out, rode that exquisite edge.

"You need to come," he said. It wasn't a question.

"Please."

"Beg me for it, Allie. Beg for your release. Make me know how much you need it."

"Oh, God. Please Mick. Let me . . . please make me come. *Make* me, Goddamn it."

He laughed as his fingers surged into her, as he bent to suck her hard clit into his mouth.

"Ah!"

She screamed as she came. Screamed his name over and over as pleasure made her shatter, made her shiver. Then made her mutter senselessly as her mind clouded, her body lost in sensation.

"Yes . . . oh, Mick, please . . . yes, that's it, so good . . . Mmm . . ."

Finally her body calmed, and she was left with tiny sparks of pleasure shimmering through her. Mick pulled away.

"And now, my girl, you are ready for me to fuck you."

She could only sigh.

Yes . . .

She watched through climax-clouded eyes as he sheathed his thick cock, licking her lips in anticipation. He lowered his body over hers, one arm holding him up as he gripped his cock and guided it to her entrance.

"Do you want it, Allie? Tell me you want me to fuck you."

"I need you, Mick. Need you to fuck me. Ah . . . yes . . ."

He angled his hips and plunged into her, all at once and hard, filling her with his flesh.

He immediately started with a fast, punishing pace, his hips ramming against hers, his pubic bone slamming into her mound over and over. Above her his face was a concentration of lust, his eyes gleaming, his wicked mouth loose with pleasure. And pleasure filled her every bit as much as his lovely, big cock while she lay helplessly, unable to do anything but accept the pleasure he gave her. Safe in the ropes.

At this moment what happened between them was *his* responsibility. Under his control. She reveled in that thought. In his hard fucking. In his utter and absolute command over her body.

His hips arched hard, faster and faster, his breath coming in sharp gasps. Pain and pleasure blended, surged together, and once more her body rose toward climax. Pleasure and pleasure, pain and . . . she came in hard, shuddering spasms, stars exploding behind her eyes.

"Mick! God . . ."

"Ah, baby . . . coming, my baby girl . . ."

She felt him shiver, then his hips jerked hard, and he bent to latch on to her neck, his teeth sinking in.

They were both out of control, beings of pure sensation, needing nothing but this moment.

He fell onto her, his weight pressing her down until she could barely breathe. But she wanted it. *Needed* it.

Needed him.

MICK GASPED FOR air—the power of his orgasm had stolen every bit of breath from his body. He knew he was crushing Allie beneath him, but it was several minutes before he was able to move. Finally he rolled off her, propped himself up on one elbow beside her. She was watching him, her eyes glazed, a sheen of pure gold over the deep brown. Beautiful. Her cheeks were flushed, her full lips that gorgeous dark pink. He leaned down and kissed her mouth, just brushed her lips with his. She was so damn sweet he had to do it again, and then again.

Something in his chest tightened and he pulled back. She blinked, but remained quiet, only the hitching rhythm of her breathing telling him that she felt something, too. Something that went beyond the sex.

No.

But it was the truth, and right now it was too damn hard to hide from, naked as they were, both of them raw and open.

He'd always managed to keep certain parts of himself locked away from the women he played with, slept with. But this was *Allie.*

"Mick?"

"It's okay, baby. Let me get you out now."

He knelt up and untied the doubled rope that held her body down on the bed, swept his palm across her stomach, heard her breath catch as he brushed over the already-bruising bite marks at the curve of her waist. The ropes had left a pattern of shallow indents in her skin, and he smoothed his fingertips over the grooves for a moment before turning to untie her ankles. He did the same there, stroking the rope marks, massaging her feet for a minute or two to ensure the circulation returned, then he massaged her slender ankles, loving the delicacy of the bones there. Finally he moved up, kneeling over her to untie her wrists.

Her arms immediately reached for him, wrapping around his neck as she whispered, "Mick, I need you to hold me. Please."

He pulled her into his lap and she curled against him, her head on his shoulder. She was all soft, fragrant skin, lean curves and pure yielding girl. He'd never felt any woman's submission in the way he did with her—giving herself over was so acute because it was something she struggled with. And there was something about her submitting to *him*. He didn't think he could fight against it.

He didn't even know what that meant.

Christ.

His stomach knotted. He wanted to get away. He wanted to never let her go.

He couldn't let her go yet. He owed her aftercare.

Fuck. He was being an asshole.

What else is new?

Fuck.

She leaned her head back to look up at him. Her eyes had cleared a bit. He shifted her, settling her against the pillows, and sat next to her.

Do what you're supposed to, damn it.

He reached out and tucked a silky strand of her hair behind her ear. "You doing okay?"

"I'm fine. That was . . . amazing."

"Yeah, it was," he said truthfully.

Too amazing. Too good.

Panic was a hard flutter in his veins. He tried to swallow it down.

"But now you need to talk to me," she said, softly but insistently.

"We can talk any time, baby. Are you hungry? Do you need something to drink? I'm getting some Gatorade."

He got up before she could answer him, and went to the kitchen, where he paced the length of the dark slate floors, his heart slamming into his ribs.

He couldn't fucking talk to her—not the way she wanted him to.

It was Allie, for God's sake. He owed her.

No.

Not that. Not anything he wasn't able to give. And to really be himself? To let go of the reins he'd used for years to hold himself in check, to contain the beast? He just wasn't capable. He'd always known it. That was why they hadn't been together all these years. She deserved more.

He needed to calm the fuck down.

He yanked open the brushed-steel refrigerator and pulled out a bottle of Gatorade, cracked it open and took a few swigs.

He couldn't leave her alone in there for too long—she was going to wonder.

He pulled in a breath, closed his eyes as he blew it out. What he really needed right now was to go for a long run, to lose himself in the New Orleans heat, in the pumping of his legs and his lungs. Even in the pain from his damn leg—the pain that was always there when he went running. But she was waiting for him, and he had to handle this somehow.

"Okay," he muttered, scrubbing at his goatee. "Okay."

He grabbed another Gatorade and went back to the bedroom. Allie was right where he'd left her, her hair a tumble of dark silk around her shoulders, her breasts bare above the sheet she'd pulled up around her waist.

He handed her the Gatorade, pulled his sweatpants back on and sat next to her on the bed.

"Drink some," he told her. "I want to be sure you're not dehydrated."

She opened the bottle and took a few sips.

"Is everything okay, Mick?" she asked.

"What? Sure. Everything's great. You were perfect."

He took her hand and pressed a kiss to the back of it before letting it go.

"You seem kind of . . . disconnected."

"I'm right here, baby."

"Are you?"

He smiled. "Yeah, of course. Hey, I'm going to have to get

up at the crack of dawn tomorrow to catch my plane. I don't know if you want to stay. You'll have to be up early with me."

She looked at him warily. "I'm . . . not sure if you're asking me to stay or to go."

"You're welcome to stay if you want."

"That wasn't exactly an answer."

"Sure it was."

He was such a liar. And a bad one, at that.

Asshole.

"Jesus, Mick. What's going on here?" she demanded.

"What do you mean? I'm just saying I still have to finish packing, and I have to be up early. And I thought you were coming over to talk for a while. But now that you're here and naked in my bed, you can stay if you want to."

He had to be up early? Fuck, he was a Grade A piece of shit. But the panic inside him had to be quelled.

"Do *you* want me to?"

"Sure."

"Wow, that is *really* not an answer." She pulled the sheet up to cover her chest. "Tell me what's going on with you, Mick. Tell me why you're shutting down on me."

He shrugged. "Everything's fine, babe. But I have to get ready for this trip. It's business. And as much fun as I have with you, I still have stuff to take care of."

Fun? He felt like such a bastard as the words came out of his mouth. Part of him couldn't believe he was doing this to her. But the other part—the part that felt the urgent need to escape— couldn't help it. He didn't even want to think about the control he'd schooled himself in for years, or the fact that he'd obviously lost it completely.

She threw back the sheet and stood up, rummaging on the floor for her clothes. "I can't believe you're doing this."

"Doing what?" he defended himself, knowing full well it was bullshit.

"I opened my *pain* up to you, and now you refuse to give me anything back. Is that what we're doing here, Mick? Is it all about 'fun'? Because I thought it was something more than that. I thought it was us getting to know each other again." She paused while she slipped back into her underwear. "How the hell am I supposed to do that when all you do is hide your real self from me? Your truth?"

"I didn't ask you to open to me like that."

She straightened up and pulled her tank top over her head. "Didn't you?"

She was glaring at him. He didn't blame her.

"Maybe this *is* my truth, Allie. Maybe this is all I can do. Maybe that's what I've been trying to tell you for years."

She shook her head. "That is such a cop-out. Poor Mick, so fucked up he hasn't learned a damn thing about himself in eleven years."

"I've learned to accept who I am," he said, hating that he sounded so churlish.

She crossed her arms over her chest. "Really? Then why don't you share it with the class? Who do you think you are?"

"I think I'm fine."

"Fine?" she challenged. "It must have taken a lot of soul searching to come up with 'fine.'"

"Christ, Allie. Why does this have to be some psychological examination of me? Why do you have to fucking force it?"

She stood looking at him, a flush coming over her face, her eyes glittering. It was several moments before he realized it wasn't anger but tears that gleamed there. "That was a horrible thing to say, Mick. Take it back."

"Fuck. I shouldn't have said that. I know it's not true." He got up off the bed, unable to bear the hurt in her eyes, knowing he was the cause. He reached for her hand and leaned in to brush a kiss across her cheek. "Come on. Let's not argue anymore. Not tonight. Stay with me. Please."

She shrugged her shoulders. "Only if you want me here. If you *want* me to stay. I can't do this half-assed thing where I'm the only one who wants me here with you."

"I do want you here. I really *am* going to have to pack. But I want you here where I can see you. Talk to you. Touch you."

She blew out a breath. "I don't mind the packing."

He pulled her in and pressed his lips to hers. He wanted to ignore how soft she was, how sweet, but he had to kiss her once more before pulling back.

"I'm going to be gone for a few days. Can we not get into anything heavy right now? We'll talk more when I get back from my trip. I still . . . obviously have some stuff to wrap my head around."

"Okay. It can wait," she agreed.

He wrapped her in his arms and she leaned into him. He didn't want to think about how good she felt. He didn't want to think about anything.

"Why don't you curl up in bed while I pack? You can help me figure out what to take."

She climbed back into bed in her tank and her panties. She was fucking adorable.

"How have you managed on your own all these years, Mick?"

"Probably by running out of socks on every trip."

"Men."

"Why do I have a feeling you're quoting Marie Dawn?"

"Because from her comes the wisdom of the universe," she said soberly.

"That's what she keeps telling Neal, anyway."

Allie laughed, and he felt the knot in his gut loosen a little as he went into his office to grab his suitcase from the closet. It seemed he'd gotten around the tension. For now. But he'd think about that later, after his trip. Right now things were okay with Allie—or at least in a holding pattern—and a little less intense. He had a few days just to chill, which was what he needed.

You need her.

Yeah, that too. Which was why the timing of this trip couldn't have been better. He couldn't think straight with Allie this close, this accessible. A few days away would give him perspective.

MAY IN ATLANTA was almost as hot and muggy as New Orleans, but Mick had always liked this town. He was booked into his usual hotel, the Omni—it had a killer view of the Atlanta skyline and was central to his business contacts. And to the local dungeon, 2112, where he was meeting his friend Finn tonight.

He and Finn had met each other on the kink circuit five years earlier, and they hung out together whenever they were in each other's cities, or at the fetish conventions, where Finn often lectured on BDSM safety and his favorite topic, mind-fuck. He was a true sadist, one of the best Doms Mick had ever seen, and a good friend.

Mick stared out at the incredible view, the city lights a sea of color against the dark sky. The sky was clearer here than in New Orleans. His head was clearer here than in New Orleans.

He'd spoken with Allie several times in the last few days, checking in on her. They'd kept the conversation light. He hadn't mentioned to her that he was extending his trip by a day or two so he could play at 2112. No, he'd texted a short message to her a few hours earlier saying business was keeping him longer than expected.

He hated that he'd lied to her. But he'd excused it by telling himself that letting her know he was going to play with someone else would only hurt her.

It wasn't as if he'd promised to play exclusively with her.

He turned from the window and grabbed the keys to his rental car. There was no point in beating himself up about it. He was doing what he needed to in order to get his head on straight. It was that simple. He fucking needed simple.

The drive to 2112 in Atlanta's historic Adair Park area only took fifteen minutes. He found parking across the street from the club—although from the outside no one would have known what went on behind closed doors.

The place was a beautifully restored Craftsman bungalow set on a large hill lot at the end of the street, three stories of gorgeous old architecture, outfitted from top to bottom for kink. He'd been a number of times before and knew many of the regulars. Still, he'd called Finn and asked him to set up a play partner or two for the night.

He grabbed the small play bag he often took when he traveled from the trunk of the rental car and walked up the long driveway to the house. It was only when he stepped onto the porch and knocked on the door that he could hear the music playing inside.

The ornately carved door was opened by a hulking man in a black leather vest.

"Evening, Mick," the man greeted him.

"Evening, Richard," Mick said as he moved past him into the club.

He nodded at the pair of collared subbie girls corseted in white leather at the desk, a matching pair of blondes. 2112 always did it up right.

"Good evening, Mick, Sir," they chorused.

"We have your online check-in, Sir," one of them said. "You're welcome to go on through."

"Thank you."

He moved through the door to the right and into what was originally a parlor but was now a sort of lounge for members of the club. It was decorated in early Craftsman style, with a few additions. There were large eyebolts in the floor next to chairs and sofas to which a leash or rope or chains could be attached, and an old gun case against one wall held a nice array of paddles, floggers and crops. Another young woman in the club's official white leather corset and collar approached with a carefully balanced silver tray holding a decanter of whisky and several crystal glasses.

"A beverage for you, Sir?"

He rarely drank on a play night, but a little extra relaxation sounded good.

He nodded, and watched as the pretty girl balanced the tray with one hand and managed to pour with the other. She smiled as she handed him the glass.

"For your pleasure, Sir."

"I'm sure it will be."

He smiled back, paused a few moments to look over her soft curves, the mane of red hair cascading over her shoulders, before nodding his dismissal. She was a pretty little thing, but even if she hadn't been contracted to train at the house, he wasn't interested in the slave mentality. Still, he wasn't dead. He watched her hips sway as she walked away to offer a drink to another member.

He moved through the lounge and back into the second parlor, known as the Spanking Room. This room was more dimly lit and more comfortably furnished, though still in Craftsman style. Here the submissives were mostly naked. Several were draped over a lap and being soundly spanked. Small sighs and cries of pain or pleasure filled the air, and he felt that familiar tingle of anticipation deep in his bones.

He walked through, keeping an eye out for Finn—and finally found him standing in the opposite doorway, heavily tattooed arms crossed over his massive chest, watching the action. Finn was an enormous man, with tribal Maori ink covering most of his body and a short crop of spiky platinum blond hair. His appearance could be intimidating to those who didn't know him, but despite his wicked Dom side he was a real gentle giant, someone who laughed a lot. His thick Australian accent added to that sense of ease, and he was damn good company.

Finn clapped Mick on the back, his huge hands giving him a good pounding.

"How are you, my friend?" the big man asked.

"Doing okay."

"I'm not so sure that's true, but we can talk more later. I've set up a few potential play partners for you. Would you like to meet them? Or do you want to relax first?"

"I'd like to finish this drink and hang out for a while."

"Sounds good. Think I'll join you. I'll meet you in the main room in a minute."

"Sure."

Mick turned to let himself through the glass-paned double doors that led to the largest play area on the main floor of the house. The lights were even dimmer in there, red, purple and amber lamps casting color and shadow in the room, which was a real dungeon room with padded spanking benches, the big St. Andrew's crosses that looked like giant Xs made of wood, some of them freestanding in the center of the room and double-sided. There were enormous bondage frames made of heavy wood in the Craftsman style, even with the faux exposed rafters mimicking those under the eaves of a Craftsman building's roofline. There were other pieces of equipment: chains hanging from the ceiling with thick iron spreader bars or heavy leather cuffs attached, special thronelike chairs made for interrogation scenes, cages lined with fur rugs. In between the equipment were comfortable seating areas for those who wanted to watch and for aftercare use. A number of people were already playing, and the room was filled with naked bodies and an air of wanting that reminded him too sharply of what he'd needed to get away from.

But she's not here.

No, it was just him, a club that was familiar enough for him to feel at home, a good friend, and the girls he would play tonight to work some of this tension out of his body, and hopefully his damn head.

Finn found him, drink in hand, and they chose a long sofa to sit on.

Finn raised his glass. "Cheers, mate."

"Cheers." Mick raised his glass in salute, then tipped it back and swallowed. "Damn good Scotch," he remarked.

"As always. Do you need another?"

"Not yet."

His friend studied him for a moment. Even in the dusky colored light he could see Finn's piercing blue gaze searching his face.

"So," Finn started.

"So," Mick finished—or so he thought.

"So, you going to tell me about it?"

"Tell you about what?"

"Don't try to bullshit me, mate. I'm the mind-fuck expert, remember? My psychology degree has trained me to run circles around people's minds."

"Don't even fucking consider crawling inside my head, old friend. You might not like what you see in there."

"Do you really think anything could shock me? And that's starting to sound like whining, if you don't mind me saying so." Finn raised a hand when Mick started to protest. "Yes, I'm sure you do mind. Whatever. I say what I think. As you well know."

"Don't think I didn't come here knowing that."

"In which case you must have wanted to hear what I have to say."

"Since it's fucking inevitable," Mick said, not even trying to keep the wry sarcasm out of his voice.

"Damn right." Finn leaned back and slung an arm across the back of the couch. "Shall we dance around this a little more, or are you ready to spill?"

Mick blew out a breath, leaned forward and rested his elbows on his knees, avoiding Finn's knowing gaze. "I hate this transparent communication shit sometimes, you know?" he muttered.

"Then you shouldn't have become a Dominant. Not in this circle, anyway."

"Yeah, yeah."

"Out with it. There's no other way, mate."

"Fuck." He ran a hand back through his hair. "There's this woman," he began.

Finn's grin was blissful. "Isn't there always?"

"Yeah. But not like Allie. She's the one who's been haunting me since high school. The one I can't forget. She's back in town after being gone . . . well, a long time. Years. And she's into it, the kink. Hard core. We're playing. And it's totally fucking with my head."

"Because you want her or because you don't? And you don't have to answer me. You're the one who has to know."

Mick shook his head. "I don't have that answer. I mean, of course I want her. Christ, I've never wanted a woman as much. But ask me if I can give her what she wants? What she needs?

That I can't figure out. To be honest—hell, with myself, even—I just don't know that I'm up to it. What do I know about relationships? The last real one I had was with her in high school."

"Yeah, fucking pathetic. But from what you've told me, that was the real thing. Love, right?"

"Yeah, it was," he said, an edge of fierceness in his voice.

Love. Christ, he had loved her so damn much. It made his chest ache even now. He'd carried it with him all these years. Carried *her* with him, unable to ever let her go.

He sipped his drink, his fingers flexing hard on the glass. "I thought some time and distance would clarify things, but it hasn't done a damn thing. I'll have to deal with it—with her—when I get home. I came here tonight to forget for a while."

After several silent moments Mick turned around to look at Finn. His expression was thoughtful.

"It's your thing, you know, Mick. Your decision to make. I'm thinking maybe you're too much in your own head."

"Yeah. Probably."

Finn grinned. "I know a good way to get out of it."

"That was my thought, too."

"Ready to meet Princess, then?"

"Princess?"

His nickname for Allie since high school. Fuck.

He knew the subbie girls often chose cute nicknames, but why did this one have to be Princess?

"She's a real beauty. Goes down nice and easy. Loves the ropes."

Shake it off. It's not her.

"Where is she?"

Finn made a gesture, and Mick followed the direction of his hand to see a petite woman with luscious curves and long hair dyed hot pink. She was dressed in nothing but a pale pink thong and pink knee-high boots. As she drew closer he could see that her nipples were pierced. She smiled shyly as she approached.

"Princess, this is Mick, our visitor from New Orleans. Be nice to him."

"Of course, Finn," she said, her voice soft, feminine.

His cock should have been hardening at the sight of her. She had a gorgeous, hot little body, her breasts large and firm, and a beautiful face to match. A prime girl—he was certain her time was vied for at the club.

"Hi, Princess."

He couldn't stand to call her that. Could not. Fucking. Stand it.

"Hello, Sir. Or . . . should I call you something else?"

Allie called him Mick.

" 'Sir' is fine."

"I would be very happy to play with you, Sir," she said, looking up at him through long lashes. Her eyes were blue. Not that rich golden brown, like Allie's.

Stop thinking about her.

That was the whole point in being here. So why was he finding it so damn difficult to do the things he always did with the greatest pleasure?

Finn rose to his feet. "You two seem to be doing just fine. Unless you'd prefer I stay for negotiations, Princess?"

"No, Finn, Sir. I'm fine, thank you." She smiled, dropped a small curtsy. She was absolutely charming.

Except he was still left entirely untouched by her.

Mick stood, grabbed Finn's arm, said quietly, "I don't know about this, Finn."

"Is she not to your liking? I have Tina waiting for me, but I'd be happy to trade out. She's an amazing player. Sassy. You'd like her. Of course, Princess is top-notch, too. But if there's no connection . . ."

Mick shook his head. "It's not that. She's as gorgeous as you said and I can tell she's well trained. But I'm not . . . fuck all, I don't know what my problem is."

Finn looked thoughtful, then he gestured to Princess. "Sweetheart, go and wait for me with Tina, that's a good girl."

Princess blushed, curtsied to Mick and left. But not before he saw the disappointed pout on her pretty face.

"Oh, that girl back in New Orleans has your head twisted the fuck up, mate, doesn't she?"

"Yeah. She does. Sorry, Finn. I thought this would be the best thing for me, coming here to play. To work some of this . . . whatever it is out of my system."

"You know, I've seen a few guys in your position, and it seems the only thing that'll really work is to work *her*."

"Maybe. I don't know," Mick said, his hands fisting at his sides. His head was spinning. "I can't believe I can't do this."

"Don't worry about it," Finn said. "Just do what you need to. Go home and fuck her right through the walls. Play her until she screams. Go to the gym and pummel someone's head in. Go to one of your fights. Work it out, mate. You can handle it."

Mick clapped Finn on the back. "Thanks for understanding."

"No worries. I won't let her go to waste," Finn said with a wide grin.

"I'm sure you won't."

"Good to see you. Try a longer visit next time. Or I'll come and see you soon, anyway, to talk about working with you. And Mick, let me know how it goes, will you?"

"Yeah, I will."

He passed back through the club, his brain in a tangle—images of Allie, of the woman called Princess, and a slow, simmering anger. It was himself he was pissed at, though.

Maybe Finn had the right idea, he thought as he got back

Dangerously Bound 197

into the rental car and started the engine. Maybe he needed to go home and go to the fight club.

Punching someone in the face—in a consensual environment, of course—would feel fucking great, he had to admit. Didn't matter if they hit him back. Hell, that was part of it all, anyway—the chance of being hit. Even the pain, Dom or not.

He needed to find the next flight out of Atlanta. Had to get back to his city.

And fuck it, he had to see Allie.

CHAPTER

Ten

Allie brought up her PowerPoint presentation on her laptop, and the first image popped up on the projection screen she'd set up on one of the tables at Dolcetti.

She breathed in the familiar dry warmth of her family's bakery and glanced around. The tall jars of biscotti still lined the top of the counters, as they always had. The glass case was filled with fresh walnut shortbread cookies and macaroons, the luscious panettone with the almond and hazelnut icing that was her great-grandmother's recipe, the colorful torta di frutta. She inhaled the scent of fruit and sugar. The scent of memories.

How many times had Mick strolled in to visit her when she worked in the bakery after school, all swagger even in their high school days? He'd stolen kisses when her mother and her aunts weren't looking . . .

Her aunts Felisa and Renata, her mother's younger sisters—

identical twins Allie had had a hard time telling apart as a child—were already seated with their cups of coffee. She was just waiting for her mother to finish some work she was doing in the back.

It was Friday evening and the bakery was closed. She knew they were all tired after working all day, but the only day the bakery shut their doors was Sunday, when her mother and aunts spent much of the day in church. And she was ready—she didn't want to wait any longer.

Where was her mother?

"Are you going to show us a movie?" one of her aunts asked.

"No, *Zia* Felisa. It's more like a slide show."

Her aunt folded her arms. "Hmm."

When Mick had texted that he was back in town and wanted to see her, she'd put him off, telling him she was presenting her business expansion plan tonight. He'd wished her luck and told her not to be nervous. Which was, of course, totally impossible. This had been her dream for years. It was why she'd learned to be a pastry chef. And it was the one bridge she'd been unable to cross in her life. Well, other than Mick. But they were working on it.

At least, she thought they were. But he was so damn confusing. In one minute and out the next. She never knew where his head would be on any given day. His behavior the night before he'd left town had only muddied the waters that was their relationship even more. If one could even call it a relationship.

Frankly, she didn't know what the hell they were doing, and she was about out of patience with it. She'd agreed to table any heavy conversation until Mick got back from his trip. Well, he was certainly going to get an earful tonight. Right after she gave her family the earful they'd had coming since she'd first gone to culinary school.

"Mama," she called, out of patience. "Please come and sit down."

"I was just cleaning up," her mother said, drying her hands on her apron as she came out from behind the counter and threw her arms around her. She sank into her mother's warm embrace—her mother who smelled of sugar after all her years running the bakery. Allie inhaled, smiled.

Her mother pulled back, still holding her shoulders. "You're too thin, Allesandra," she said.

Her mother was still a beautiful woman, her hair still the same dark brown as Allie's, with only a few strands of silver.

"I know, Mama. You told me the same thing when you saw me last week. And I'm sure you'll feed me up tonight, like you always do. Three months back in New Orleans and I'll be plump as a Halloween pumpkin."

"A few curves on a woman are not a bad thing," her mother said, squeezing her hand.

"Don't be silly," *Zia* Renata put in. "We're fourth-generation bakers—sugar runs in our blood."

"That's right," her mother agreed. "I can still fit into my wedding dress. Don't I look just as I did the day I married my Bertrand?"

Allie stiffened. She hated that she did it automatically every time her father was mentioned. But it hurt to see how much her mother still loved him. All these years and it still hurt that he was gone. She'd been a daddy's girl, and wasn't ashamed to admit it. She hadn't been anyone's girl since he'd died.

Except for Mick, for that lovely time when they were teenagers, when everything had felt so perfect. She'd been utterly convinced they were indestructible. The naiveté of youth, maybe.

Her mother pulled one of the iced panettone from the jar on the counter and handed it to Allie with a smile.

"You always know how to get to me, Mama." She took a bite, let the familiar flavors melt on her tongue. Forced her thoughts away from Mick.

"I hope so. Now, tell us what this is all about, Allesandra."

"Have a seat and I will."

She waited for her mother to get settled, taking a few deep breaths to calm herself, then hit the space bar on her keyboard to start the presentation. She saw the screen light up with the graphics she'd made featuring the front of Dolcetti.

"As you can see, this image of Dolcetti includes the storefront next door, because what I'm addressing here today is the expansion of the bakery. And I know, Mama, I've talked to you about it before, but please just hear me out. I've done a lot of market research, and I have new information for you on the viability of this plan. These are copies of my business plan, one for each of you," she said, handing them the packets she'd prepared.

Her mother's features were shutting down, but she remained quiet.

"I've already looked into it and the boutique next door ends their lease on August first. They haven't been doing well, and the manager has admitted to me that she doesn't think they'll be able to continue. Not that I'm celebrating the demise of a small business, but the timing would be perfect for expansion. The business is booming, we're in a great location, so things can only get better. Frankly, right now the only thing holding Dolcetti back from making more money is the limited size—and the limit in menu and services because we simply don't have enough space."

She took a breath and continued without looking too carefully at any of them—she didn't want to see the closed expressions she assumed she'd find there. "This next slide shows a possible floor plan. As you can see from this color-coded chart, taking over the space next door means an increase in usable space by forty-five percent, which would mean more ovens and prep space, a new walk-in refrigerator, more seating in front and another office especially for meeting with catering clients."

"Honey, we don't have the time or the staff to do more catering," *Zia* Felisa protested.

Allie smiled. "Which is exactly why you need me. I've been doing just that—running pastry catering for some of the best restaurants in San Francisco for years. I *know* how to do this. I know how to make this aspect of a business successful. And because of my background in European pastry, I can re-create our entire menu to appeal to a more modern clientele."

"We like our old clientele. We have loyal customers who have come to us for years," her mother said. "Allesandra, I know you mean well, but this just sounds like a big headache to me. And there's no way this could be done without shutting down for a while. What happens to our customers then?"

"I've been thinking about that and I've talked with Allister— Jamie's brother—about doing the build-out. He's assured me there are ways to do it so we're not closed for more than two to three weeks at the most."

"Three weeks?" *Zia* Renata crossed her arms over her chest. "We can't be closed for three weeks. We were open two days after Katrina."

"I agree," her mother said. "And you know how contractors are—they always go over budget and over on time. My darling, I know you mean well, but why can't you just come to work with us here, as things are? We could do a little more catering with you here."

Her heart sank. They weren't going to listen to her. "More king cakes and a few weddings and birthdays? Mama . . ."

"I know, you think it's boring, but this is what we've always done, Allesandra. We're all perfectly happy with it. We don't feel any need to make changes. Other than you baking with us. We would welcome you any time."

"It's true," *Zia* Renata agreed.

Felisa nodded her agreement.

"But we're not changing the business," her mother stated with an air of finality. "Let's not discuss it anymore. Why don't you come home with us for dinner? I'm making my famous ziti."

"I . . . I can't, Mama. I have to be somewhere."

And even if she didn't have plans, she'd need some time to swallow her disappointment. Why had she been so convinced her professional presentation would make any difference? Her family still saw her as a child.

Just like Mick.

Her mother stood up and drew her in, kissed her cheek. "We love you, darling girl. Don't be upset with us. This simply isn't for us."

"Okay, Mama."

Her aunts kissed her cheeks as she closed her laptop and took down the screen. Her mother waited for her to gather everything, and they walked out together. Her mother locked the door behind them.

"We'll see you soon, yes?" her mother asked.

"Yes. Of course."

She kissed her one more time before making her way around the corner to where her car was parked. Allie watched her mother walk away, feeling utterly rejected, utterly invalidated.

Not exactly how she wanted to feel seeing Mick tonight, and needing to confront him. She'd go home, drop her things off at the house and go for a long walk to clear her head, then a quick bath before going to his place. Mick Reid, for once, was just going to have to wait.

IT WAS ALMOST nine before she made it to Mick's place. She'd taken a long walk around her neighborhood, which had done her good, then she'd dallied getting herself put together.

She'd missed him so much it made her chest ache with every breath. Missed him so much she'd spent long spans of time simply looking at the darkening bite marks he'd left all over her skin in the mirror, tracing the shape of his teeth. Missed him so much that she hung on to even this memory of their bodies together, the intimacy they'd shared. And yet, she'd lingered rather than running right over to his place. At this point she didn't know that she wanted to have this necessary conversation about him pulling away any more than he did. She simply wanted to see him. To make the empty ache go away. She didn't want to talk.

It had to be done, or they weren't ever going anywhere. Not together, anyway.

Still, when she rang the bell and heard his footsteps on the stairs, her pulse fluttered with anticipation. When he opened the door, dressed in worn jeans, like her, and a tight white wife-beater, his bare feet making him look sensually naked somehow, her body started to melt into a pool of heat and need right away. The turmoil in her head began to fade.

She kind of hated that his sheer, masculine beauty could make her forget everything else so easily, but it had always been like that with Mick.

"Hey, baby," he said, leaning over to press a kiss to her forehead, then her mouth. "Come on in."

He waited for her to start up the stairs before him, and when she got to the top she set her purse down on the living room floor before settling onto the big leather couch. Mick came to sit beside her.

"You okay?" he asked.

She shrugged. "Rough day."

"You said in your text you needed some time before you came over tonight. Is everything all right?"

"Yes, I guess so. I mean, my life hasn't actually been changed for it. Which I sort of expected." She turned to face him. "Does your family still treat you like you're a kid, Mick?"

"No. They treat me like I'm the bad news teenager. I was, so I guess I can't blame them. Maybe I still am. They hate my fighting."

"Well, that totally makes sense," she muttered. "I'm on the same page with them."

"Thanks for that."

She shook her head. "I'm sorry. Maybe I shouldn't have come tonight. I'm in a lousy mood."

"It's okay, baby. Talk to me. Tell me what happened."

She pulled a throw pillow into her lap, running her fingertips over the fabric. "Oh, I was dumb enough to think if I presented my business plan to Mama and the aunts in a professional manner they'd take me seriously. But of course they just shot me down. The same way they did when I tried to talk to them fresh out of culinary school. But Jesus, I have years of practical experience now—you'd think that would make a difference."

"It should. You've had some of the best training in the world—all over Europe. From what Marie Dawn and Neal and Jamie have told me over the years, you've worked at some of the top restaurants in San Francisco, that you're a highly sought-after pastry chef there. Did you tell your family all of it?"

"I don't know. I've always kept them up to date about where I'm working."

"Maybe they don't understand the prestige of the places you've baked for. You know how New Orleans is—we're convinced nothing else really exists outside the walls of this city. It's an incestuous culture here, especially for the city's old-guard citizens, and your family has been here for how many generations? I get it because my family has been, too. They don't always see the rest of the world. Isn't your mother's argument that Dolcetti's recipes were brought to this city by her great-grandmother from Italy?"

She tossed the pillow aside with a sigh. "And it's like the art of pastry making just stopped there. Recipes that are a hundred years old. Not that they aren't fantastic—they are, or the business wouldn't have survived. But what happens when the old loyal customers are gone? So many new people are moving to the city now that it's being rebuilt. The old magic always attracts new people. We have to keep up with the times or . . ." She paused, ran her fingers through her hair. "I'm sorry. You seem to know all this already. Guess I'm preaching to the choir."

"Yes and no. Look, Allie, do you want to go over your presentation and business plan with me? Because it sounds like you have the right idea. I might have some suggestions for you. And the bottom line is, if you believe in this, then you can't let their stubbornness make you back down. If this is your dream, you have to go for it."

She had more than one dream.

"Maybe. I don't know. Right now I'm too tired to think any more about it."

"Do you need some Travel TV?"

What she needed was for him to take her in his arms and tell her everything would be okay. Her dreams for the family business. Things with him. But even though he seemed to be supportive, thoroughly immersed in the conversation, he was still . . . not quite there with her. That brief kiss when she'd arrived hadn't been followed up by any further show of affection, and it was making her feel worse. She didn't know if she should just leave . . . or stay and see if they could manage to find their way to each other tonight.

"I'm . . . not sure what I need," she lied.

"I have some fresh raspberry sorbet in the freezer. It's been calling to me for the last few hours."

"Sure, that sounds good."

Mick headed into the kitchen, and Allie got up and went to the bookcase against one wall—an old, heavy Spanish-looking piece. On it were a few photographs of his family among the books. She ran her fingers over the spines, peering at the titles. Books on martial arts, which didn't surprise her, more on shibari rope bondage, which was even less of a surprise. Mixed in were a few fiction titles—thrillers, mostly—a small book of the Tao, which did surprise her, as well as some books on Buddhism by Thich Nhat Hanh. Strange reading for an Irish Catholic, fallen though he may be. But it opened a small window into the man he was today—the man she yearned to know better, and who seemed to be refusing to let her.

Mick returned with the promised sorbet in its carton and two spoons, and she joined him back on the sofa. He handed her one of the spoons.

"I've been looking forward to this all day," he said.

Not looking forward to seeing her.

Was she simply feeling sorry for herself? Or was that a realistic expectation? She hated that she had to doubt herself so much.

They sat eating the sorbet for a few minutes in silence.

"I really do think you need to talk to them again," Mick said.

"I will. You're probably right."

"And I do like to be right." He grinned at her, but she swore some of his usual natural charm was missing.

"Yes, you do." She smiled, trying to lighten the moment.

She felt desperate suddenly to find a way back to those intimate moments. To find their connection, despite the unspoken issues hanging in the air—or maybe more so because of them.

She stuck her spoon into the middle of the sorbet left in the carton, pulled Mick's spoon from between his lips and did the same with it. He watched her, an eyebrow raised in question. She set the carton on the big coffee table, then climbed onto him, straddling his lap.

"Hey, what's going on here?" he asked softly as she settled her arms around his neck.

He wasn't touching her, no hands on her waist.

She had to remind herself about Marie Dawn's stupidity ruling.

"Mick, you're going to kiss me. And touch me. And we're going to have sex."

"Okay . . ."

"And we're going to find a way to reconnect. Because I can't figure out any other way at the moment, and I can't stand how distant things are between us right now."

He had the grace to look a bit sheepish, but only for a moment.

"You know I prefer to be the one calling the shots. Usually I demand it."

"Believe me, I know. But tonight I don't want any bondage or pain play. I think it just needs to be . . . us. Just us here, without all the fancy window dressing, you know?"

He was quiet a few moments, simply looking up at her. She didn't have a clue what was going through his mind, and it was making her uncomfortable as hell. She was sitting on his lap, and he still hadn't put his hands on her.

"Mick," she whispered as she leaned forward, bringing her mouth within inches of his. "I need you to kiss me. I need you to touch me. Don't argue it. Just do it."

"Bossy girl."

"Yes. Just . . . for now. Just for now, stop talking and kiss me. Kiss me hard. Make me remember it."

He blinked up at her, then his shadowed eyes lost their darkness and began to gleam, a pure, crystalline gray.

"I need to remember, too," he said quietly.

The energy between them shifted and so did he, grasping her hips and bringing her pelvis in until it was seated hard up against his. Then he grabbed her face and kissed her. He pressed his lips to hers, hard, harder. Just the urgent press of his lips until she could barely breathe, his hands loosening their tight hold on her cheeks, going gentle. Then his mouth gentled, too, and it was a pure, sensual fire between them, his tongue sliding into her mouth, so sweet and soft she wanted to cry for everything she felt in his kiss.

It was too much—too much to feel. She took his face in her hands and deepened the kiss, pressed her pelvis into his. Everything changed in an instant. He kissed her harder, *taking* her mouth. His kiss was primal, wild, taking command. He always would, one way or another, and she was fine with that. More than fine—she loved it. Her body was coming alive, every nerve ending on fire. She ground her hips against him, felt the solid ridge of his erection through his jeans and hers. Wanted—needed—more.

She broke from the kiss long enough to strip her tank top over her head. As she started on his he helped her, then he bent to kiss her breasts roughly. She let her head fall back as he gathered her breasts in his hands and pushed them together, used his thumbs to work his way over the still-dark bite marks, past the lacy edge of her bra to find her nipples. They were already hard. His circling thumbs only made them harder.

Pleasure suffused her, washing the worry away. This was exactly what she needed—to lose herself in body to body, lips to lips, pleasure to pleasure.

Mick unsnapped her bra and tore it off, then he started to unbutton her jeans. She went for his at the same time—and was rewarded by the hard, golden head of his bare cock as she pulled his jeans open. She stroked him, her fingers curling around the tip, and he groaned.

"Ah, Allie."

"Come on, Mick."

"You don't have to ask me twice, baby."

He stood and set her on her feet, stripped her out of her jeans and panties in mere seconds, then tore his jeans off.

"Damn it. Condom. Hang on."

She watched his finely molded ass as he strode toward his bedroom, noticed that he was limping a little. The trip must have been hard on him. Seconds later he was coming at her, a string of condom packets in his hand, his beautifully erect cock leading the way.

God, the man was really something.

He sat back down on the sofa, wrapped his hands around her waist and pulled her on top of him, seating her against him the way he had earlier, with her straddling his lap—only this time, naked. His cock was pressed against her mound, the ridge of it hitting her swollen clit. Immediately she grabbed the back of the sofa to steady herself and began a slow, sinuous grind against him.

"Christ," he groaned. "You're gonna kill me with that thing, Allie girl."

"Oh, I intend to," she said, sliding her wet pussy up and down the length of him, every stroke sending desire shivering into her system.

She moved faster, the slip and slide of their bodies hitting her in all the right places, and pleasure rose higher, built like a tight knot deep in her sex.

"Ahhhh," Mick groaned, driving her on.

She arched her hips, really grinding into him, wanting release, needing it *now*.

"Allie, slow down, baby."

"No," she growled.

She let go of the sofa cushions and grabbed his shoulders, dug her nails into the heavy muscle there. He moaned, arched up against her.

"Oh, yes . . ."

He buried his face between her breasts, kissing and licking at the skin there. "Need to fuck you," he murmured. "Need to fuck you so hard."

"Not yet."

"You are . . . fucking sexy when . . . you're toppy," Mick told her between gasping breaths.

She sighed as she slid along the length of his shaft, up, then down, making the pressure just right. He grabbed her ass and helped her move her arching hips, holding her tight against him, making his cock press harder against her. Pleasure spiraled, crested, and finally erupted like a burst of thunder deep in her body.

"Oh! Oh . . ."

She was coming so hard she was shaking. Mick held on to her, held her tight, kissing her bruised breasts as she came. She kept thrusting her hips, sliding her clenching pussy up and down his hard shaft, her climax still skittering over her skin.

Before she was certain she was done, Mick flipped her on her back on the coffee table so fast she never saw it coming—the wood was hard and cool against her back—and in moments he'd rolled a condom over his cock. He held himself over her, and as she wrapped her legs around his waist he thrust into her.

"Mick!"

His cock was big, but she was wet enough to take him all at once. He surged into her, slid out, every motion driving pleasure deep and hard. He was kissing her breasts again, using lips and tongue, punctuated with small, nipping bites that only drove her pleasure higher.

He paused, gasping. "Allie . . . I'm going to come."

"Yes. Do it. But kiss me, Mick. Just fucking kiss me."

He lowered his head and crushed his lips to hers as he rammed into her. She held his face in her hands, needing to feel him, to feel connected in some way, even if it was just their two bodies, their hot, wet mouths, joined together.

He pulled back with a sharp groan, and she looked into his eyes as he started to come, hips jerking, gaze locked on hers. Something in his eyes looked lost in wonderment, making her heart twist in her chest. At that moment, she knew he was right there with her.

Right there.

He shivered all over, shook in her arms, that intense, wide gaze never leaving hers. Then he buried his face between her breasts once more as he caught his panting breath, his hands tangling in her hair.

They stayed there for several minutes before he pulled away, helped her sit up on the edge of the table.

"Bed?" he asked, still not quite all there after his orgasm.

She nodded. He drew her to her feet, and she followed him into the bedroom, where he helped tuck her in beneath the covers. He climbed in beside her, lying on his back. When she nudged his arm he opened it and invited her in. She laid her head on his chest and listened to him breathe. Waited for him to really wrap her in his arms. To kiss her again. But all he did was lie perfectly still in the darkened room. There was just enough light coming from the living room for her to see the silhouette of his eyelashes. His eyes were open—he wasn't sleeping. But he was silent. Unmoving. As if she weren't even there.

She'd needed to be with him, for him to be with her. Present. Engaged. Connected. But it hadn't worked in the end, had it? Other than those brief moments when he was coming, when he looked into her eyes and *saw* her. *Felt* her. And now she felt even worse than she had when she'd arrived.

A slow tear made its way down her cheek, but she didn't dare brush it away. She didn't want him to know. She bit her lip to stifle any sound, forced herself to stop the crying.

How many tears had she cried over Mick Reid? How many times had he turned away from her? And yet she still kept after him.

It was beginning to be humiliating.

She couldn't be the only one with all her cards in the game. And damn it, it wasn't a game to her. It was her heart, a heart that had carried these wounds for far too long. She'd never been able to fall for another man—*really* fall, although she'd tried a few times—because Mick had always owned her heart.

He still fucking did. But maybe she was only helpless against it if she chose to be.

Hours passed while the same ideas whirled through her mind with the force of a tornado. When she checked the clock at five thirty in the morning, she still didn't have the answers. But one thing she knew: continuing to do this—accepting Mick's crappy behavior toward her—wasn't getting her anywhere.

She needed distance to figure things out. To decide if she was willing to accept this from him or if she was stronger than that. And maybe only once she'd gone—gone of her own accord and not because Mick needed space—maybe then he'd realize what was at stake.

She listened for his breathing, wanting to make sure he was asleep. She couldn't handle another conversation. He always managed to talk his way around her, or seduce her into forgetting what it was she wanted to talk about. The man was too clever for his own good—certainly for hers. She slipped quietly from the bed, found her clothes, her purse, and left the warmth of Mick's body, his bed, behind. But she knew that warmth would never be anything but temporary if she didn't go.

Have to go.

She wiped the tears away as she started her car, the engine a loud rumble in the still, early morning air.

The sun was rising as she headed home, the sky a wash of pink and gold. It was lovely. Heartbreakingly beautiful.

Like him.

She was tired of Mick breaking her heart. Maybe it was his turn.

She wanted to feel some satisfaction at the thought. But it was Mick, and she loved him. Knowing he might hurt when he woke up alone only made her own pain more wrenching.

It was still the right thing to do.

Sometimes, being right sucked.

MICK WOKE WITH a start. He reached for Allie but found only cool sheets next to him.

"What the hell?"

He ran a hand over his head, rubbed his eyes. Maybe she was in the bathroom? The kitchen?

He glanced at the clock as he got up. Seven in the morning. Dusky light shone from behind the curtains—another hazy spring day in New Orleans. It was probably already warm out there. Why did he feel chilled?

He found the bathroom door wide open, moved into the kitchen. It was empty.

"Allie?" he called, knowing there would be no answer.

He grabbed his sweats from the living room floor, pulled them on, then moved around the apartment looking for a note, then his cell phone. No voice mail, no texts. He went into his office and booted up his computer, tapping his fingers on the desk while he waited.

Maybe she was sick? But she would have left him some kind of message or even woken him up to tell him. Wouldn't she?

He remembered in a small flash the look on her face when she'd shown up at his place last night. She'd looked . . . haunted. He damn well knew why. He just didn't know what the hell to do about it. But now she was gone. She should at least have had the grace to tell him she was going. Not that he'd treated her any better all those years ago, in college, when he'd split in the middle of the night.

Tears sliding down her cheeks—he'd been too damn caught up to notice. Hell, he was still hard. After the hottest sex he'd ever had in his life. Hot because it was her. *But he'd made her fucking cry! What kind of sick fuck was he?*

Something in his chest tore, even as her warm body pressed against his, her arms winding tight around his neck. He swore he could see through the gaping hole that had opened in his chest to the darkness that lay underneath, a darkness he'd unleashed on Allie. Allie, of all people!

He held her tight, whispering to her—all the things he thought she might need to hear, feeling like he was flailing around, trying to find some way to make it right.

"Shh, Allie girl. It's okay."

Christ, what a liar he was.

"Mick . . . I just . . . I didn't know. I had no idea this was . . ."

She cried harder, her hot tears falling onto his chest.

Nothing would make it right. Because he was all damn wrong.

Fuck.

He tried to shake it off.

Was this payback?

He deserved it—there was no arguing with that. But he'd have thought better of Allie.

He paced the apartment, the wood floors cold beneath his bare feet.

Fuck it. This was inevitable, anyway. They'd never been meant to be together.

Except that the dull, thudding ache in his chest told him otherwise.

She belonged to him.

No.

"Fuck," he muttered, stalking into the bedroom and grabbing a shirt and his running shoes, shoving his feet into them.

He needed to run. Just fucking run this off—the thoughts and emotions he had no control over.

He grabbed his keys and a small water bottle and headed downstairs, his shoes making a slapping sound on the old wood treads. He shot out the front door and went into a full run as he hit the streets, the lack of warm-up making his muscles go tight, but he needed it. If he slowed down, his brain would catch up with him.

Can't handle it right now. Not now.

His bad leg began to ache right away, but he didn't care. He kept running, his feet hitting the damp pavement—it must have rained at some point in the night. He could smell it all around him. Damp cement, the scent of the old bricks and plaster on the buildings he passed. The green scent of the flowers and plants and weeds that grew in pots on porches and balconies, in every possible crevice. He drew in a deep breath, wanting the damp and the green to cool his burning lungs. He should have started out slower, he knew. But right now all that mattered was running as fast and hard as he could.

Ha. That was fucking obvious.

Don't think about it. Nothing is going to make sense now.

Not his anger at Allie for taking off. Not his anger at himself for being an asshole to the woman he loved.

Fucking loved!

Still. Always.

Allie.

That was never going to change. What had changed was that she finally understood what he was and wasn't capable of. And she was telling him loud and clear she wasn't having it. He didn't blame her.

Except that he did.

He was fucking mad. Hell, he was in a rage.

He needed to fight. Needed to purge the animal from his body, from his Goddamn soul. And he knew exactly where to go.

He was about to change direction when he realized his feet had already taken him down Dauphine to Canal Street. He crossed Canal, still quiet this early in the day, and Dauphine turned into Baronne. He ran on, his lungs on fire, toward the Pontchartrain Expressway and the row of warehouses that housed the private fight club hidden in the underbelly of the city.

He headed south, following the line of the freeway, his mind empty of everything now but his absolute need to hit something, anything. To be hit back. He *needed* it—to feel his fist connecting. To have some of the piss knocked out of him. Needed not to think, to feel. And nothing made him go numb better than fighting.

He flexed his fingers, almost dropping his water bottle when he got to the club. There was no address on the old corrugated metal structure. The big door was closed, but he knew there was someone to be found inside at almost any time of day or night.

He paused outside, sweat dripping into his eyes, and he tasted salt. He shook his head, shook the sweat out of his hair, took a swig from his water bottle and pushed the door aside. And walked into the darkness.

CHAPTER

Eleven

S HE WOKE TO a dull throb in her head.

Bang, bang, bang.

Blearily, she glanced at the clock on her nightstand and found she'd only slept an hour.

Bang, bang, bang.

She should get up and take some ibuprofen for her aching head. Too bad they didn't make a medicine for an aching heart.

She rolled over and realized she was still lying on top of the covers, fully dressed. She'd come home and fallen onto her bed, turned on Travel TV and mostly just stared at it, unfocused, pretending not to think, crying a little. But not too much. She just wouldn't stand for much of the damn crying.

"Allie?"

The voice was muffled, and it was then she realized the banging was the front door.

Not Mick. Thank God.

And fuck, why not Mick?

She ran a hand through her hair as she padded on bare feet to the door.

"Allie, it's Jamie. You in there?"

"Hang on."

She checked her reflection in the hall mirror. She looked like hell. She shrugged helplessly before turning to open the door. The morning sunlight made her squint.

"Hi, Jamie."

"Jesus. You sick or something?"

She shook her head and stepped aside to let him in. "I don't know. Maybe the 'or something,' " she mumbled as he moved past her into the house.

"I brought you some coffee and beignets from Café Du Monde. Maybe that'll help?"

She followed him into the kitchen, where he set the cardboard tray of paper coffee cups on the table, as well as a white paper bag.

"They smell good."

He pulled her in for a hug, and she burrowed into his arms and immediately felt like crying. But she would not do it. She would *not*.

"Hey, you okay, sweetheart?"

She nodded into his chest.

He squeezed her shoulders. "Allie?"

"I will be."

"That sounds cryptic. You want to talk to me about it?"

She nodded against his chest again. "Okay," she said, her voice muffled.

"Okay. Let's sit down and we'll both get some coffee in us."

He helped her into a chair, then pulled out another and folded himself into it, trying unsuccessfully to tuck his long legs under the table, finally settling on sprawling them out to the side and leaning his back against the table.

Allie sipped at her chicory-laced coffee, grimaced.

"Is it a sugar day?" Jamie asked, already getting up to poke through the cupboards.

It touched her that he remembered she only took sugar in her coffee when she was stressed.

"Top cupboard on the right, bottom shelf," she directed him.

He came back with the Tupperware she kept the sugar in— it was too humid in the old house to keep it in a bowl—and a spoon and offered it to her. She added a good rounded spoonful to her cup and stirred.

"Better?"

"Yes. Thanks."

"So?"

She shrugged. "This thing with Mick . . . it's not going so well."

"We both knew it wasn't going to be easy."

"Yes, but I don't think I realized it might actually be impossible."

"Is that how you're feeling right now?" Jamie asked.

"Maybe. I don't know. We started getting closer—too close, maybe—and he totally shut down on me. One minute we were perfectly fine, then suddenly there was this glaring disconnect. And he can't seem to come back from it. I was with him last night and it was . . ." She paused, her throat closing up. She ran her hands through her hair, pulling it tight, needing the sensation—the little bit of pain—to help her loosen up enough to say the words. After several moments she let it go. "It was bad, Jamie. I was up all night thinking about it. And this morning I just . . . left."

"What do you mean?"

"I got up and sort of . . . snuck out while he was still sleeping."

Jamie chuckled quietly. "Oh, he's going to love that—Mr. Control Freak."

"He hasn't tried to call."

"Either his ego is too sore or he's too pissed off."

"That's his problem," she said, anger suffusing her. "I'm tired of being the one to babysit things along. We're supposed to be reconnecting but I can't be the one who does all the work."

Jamie put a hand on her arm. "Calm down, sweetheart. I'm with you on this one."

"I know. So tell me—what do I do?"

"Honestly, leaving may have been the best bet. We guys are cavemen—we need to retreat when we're overwhelmed, and it sounds like that's what he's doing."

"Well, he's retreating his way out of any chance at a relationship with me. I don't know how much more I'm willing to deal with. I'm not about to just lie down and take it—not even for him. Anyway, I've done enough of that with Mick already. I did it for years, whether we were together or not. I let the distance he imposed between us keep me from New Orleans, even from seeing my family, because I couldn't stand it. But I'm not that girl anymore."

Jamie smiled at her, drew his hand back and took a sip from his coffee. "No, you're not. And I'm glad to see you remember that. Mick will be, too, once he gets his head out of his ass."

"When do you think that'll happen?"

"Not sure. If it wasn't about you, I'd probably say when pigs fly. But it *is* you. And maybe I can help him along. Want me to try to talk to him?"

"I don't want to put you in the middle."

Jamie grinned at her crookedly. "Sweetheart, you put me in the middle from day one."

That made her smile. "So I did."

"Anyway, I don't mind having a reason to tell Mick he's an idiot."

She shook her head. "You boys."

"Don't let him catch you calling him that."

"As if. So, tell me what's been going on with you. I don't mean to make this all about me. I'm sorry."

"Don't be. Nothing much has been happening, anyway. Except . . ."

"Except what?"

"You know . . . Summer Grace stopped by the shop yesterday."

"Did she?"

He nodded. "I was out, so I didn't see her. She didn't tell any of the guys what she wanted."

"Maybe her car needs work? Or maybe you should give her a chance, Jamie."

"And maybe you should have your head examined. You know damn well why that's not going to happen."

"Another case of stupid man, maybe," she muttered into her coffee. "Must be an epidemic."

He picked up his cup before responding to her barb. "You seem to be feeling better."

"You're just doing a good job of distracting me." But she reached for the bag and extracted a beignet, bit into it and chewed as she leaned back in her chair. "These are still pretty damn good even after they're cold."

"Have as many as you want. I ate mine on the way over."

"I didn't think that white powder meant you'd developed a cocaine problem."

Jamie wiped at his chin and she laughed.

"You *are* feeling better."

"I'll really feel better when Mick calls me and apologizes for being an ass. And follows it up by being appropriately attentive and actually working toward something with me."

And by "appropriately attentive" she meant more than just great sex.

"He will. He's never forgotten about you. I don't think he can, no matter how checked out he's been lately. It's part of him transitioning into this. It's a lot to accept all at once after the years he's put into being stubborn when it comes to you."

"So, you think talking to him will do some good?"

"It'll be a little push. Or a big one if he's in bastard mode. But mostly it'll be the fact that he still loves you, Allie."

Her eyes misted—she couldn't help it. "I wish I didn't need him to so damn much."

"That's the bitch about love—people don't have much control over it. That's what's eating him up, sweetheart. It's not you."

That was the part that hurt the worst—knowing he couldn't drop the control issues long enough to just love her, to let that old amazing love they'd shared rekindle into something current and real. They could have so much together if only . . .

But "if onlys" didn't make a relationship—not the one she wanted to find with him.

She wanted to be able to say she could walk away forever if Mick couldn't let his walls down with her. She wanted to. She wasn't entirely certain she could.

Meanwhile, she had better learn how to pray.

IT WAS NEARLY ten that night when there was another knock at her door. She'd been halfway anticipating it, but her heart thundered in her chest as she smoothed her hair and went to answer it, knowing it would be him.

When she opened the door, he was a shadow silhouetted against the amber porch light, but she'd have known that big frame anywhere, his cocky stance, the familiar scent of him that immediately drifted to her, even against the backdrop of the magnolia blossoms and the crepe myrtle starting to bloom in her yard.

"Can I come in, Allie?"

Somehow he managed to sound demanding and humble all at the same time, but she moved back to let him pass. He went into the living room and stood facing the mantel, which was cluttered with items she hadn't managed to put away yet: a collection of glass candlesticks, her sewing box, a folder full of the postcards she'd collected from all over the world during her travels. She followed him in and switched on a lamp.

"You still unpacking?" he asked.

"The cardboard boxes make it that obvious?" When he didn't answer she prompted, "I suppose you didn't come here to talk about my boxes."

"No."

He turned around and she gasped. "Jesus, Mick. What did you do to yourself?"

"It's just a split lip."

She marched across the room and held his chin in her hand. "Let me look at that."

"I'm fine."

"Have you had any medical attention?"

"I don't need it, babe. It's nothing."

She dropped her hand and crossed her arms over her chest. "Don't you 'babe' me. You've been fighting."

He nodded.

"An illegal fight." When he didn't say anything she went on. "Mick, I know damn well it was one of those stupid club fights. If you'd been sparring, you would have just told me."

"I didn't come here to upset you, Allie. I've done enough of that already."

Her blood went cold, a slow knot forming in her stomach. Was this where he told her—again—that she was better off without him before he walked out of her life once more?

She couldn't speak, so she just nodded.

He was quiet for several long moments while her breath stalled in her lungs. He was so damn handsome, his lush mouth drawn tight around the swelling, his gray eyes full of shadows.

She waited.

He ran a hand over his jaw, winced when he came too close to the swollen lip. Finally he said, "I guess you know Jamie came to talk to me today?"

"Yes."

"He made a lot of sense after he finished verbally beating the shit out of me. Which I deserved—I know it. He told me about his conversation with you. And it wasn't like I wasn't thinking about this stuff already. But fuck, Allie, when I woke up this morning and found you gone . . ."

"What?" she demanded. "You found me gone and *what*, Mick?"

The anger was rising again, making her throat go tight, but it was better than the pain, the panic at the idea of not having him in her life.

"And I couldn't stand that I'd done it. That I'd been so dense. Needing to escape the issues so badly I acted like a twelve-year-old."

She smirked a little. "Maybe fifteen."

"Yeah."

"Is that a half-assed apology, Mick?"

"No. This is. I'm sorry, Allie. I'm sorry it's been so hard for me to let you in. I'm sorry I'm not coming through for you no matter how much we negotiate and talk and agree to try." His gaze locked hard on hers, and he looked right into her in the way he always had, making her feel naked right down to her bones. "I want to try."

Her heart twisted. Tears burned but she swallowed them down.

"Do you, Mick? Really try? Because this half-assed stuff is not going to work for me."

"I know. That's why you left. I get it. I would have left, too, if I were you."

She bit her lip. "Mick, I think . . . there has to be more than simply trying, do you know what I'm saying? I feel like you have to sort of transcend what's happened in the past. You accused me—rightfully so—of living in the past where we were concerned. But I think you do it, too. About a lot of things. Us. The accident. Your self-image when you were younger. I don't think you've really let it go yet."

He dropped his head and stuck his hands in his pockets, looking absolutely humble—so out of the ordinary for him that she waited with bated breath for what he might say. Either that, or for him to bolt.

Finally he lifted his head. "Okay. You've got me there. I was the troublemaker in my family. Neal pulled some pranks, but it was normal teenage stuff. I've always been a little darker. Not just the kink, although that probably had a lot to do with how I viewed myself back then. But the staying out late, cutting school, stealing my dad's good Scotch."

She couldn't help but smile. "I always did like a bad boy. But Mick, none of that was really that terrible. You weren't stealing cars or dealing drugs. You were just a kid with a bit of a wild streak. So what?"

"So you were the A student with aspirations and virginity intact."

"And you were a high school man-whore. Again, so what?" she countered.

"Only until I met you," he said, his gaze softening. "Once I met you . . ."

God, he had loved her so much once. She remembered the way he looked at her. The way he held her. As if nothing in the world mattered but the two of them being together.

"Mick, there was an innocence to you back then, too."

"Me?"

"You were just a kid! Think about a sixteen-year-old now, from an adult perspective. If your nephew cut classes or slept with a few girls, would you think he was a terrible person?"

"What? No, of course not."

"Then maybe it's time you cut your teenage self some slack, too."

"Fuck, Allie . . ."

He looked away, but she could tell she'd gotten through. She waited for him to absorb what she'd said.

He turned back to her and there was the edge of a grin on his handsome face. "But if he tied a girl up, we'd have to have a talk."

"Yes, you would. And when he was eighteen you'd show him how to do it the right way. The safe way."

"Yeah."

"So, maybe not so terrible, are you, Mick? And if it's the kink issue—"

"No, I'm starting to get that."

"Okay. That's good, especially because I feel like that's what's brought us back together."

"I think so, too."

"And you're here. You came for me, and that's important to me. But Mick, there's still the damn fighting."

"Sometimes I need it, Allie."

She shook her head. "You are so stubborn, Mick Reid! You

just make me want to . . ." She shook her head again. "And would you just . . . God, you really are dense!"

He moved in and grabbed her, pulling her in tight. The still-mad part of her wanted to scramble away from him, make him work for it, but she melted right into him, as she always did. Nothing in the world felt better than Mick's arms around her, his scent, the *feel* of him. The mad faded away.

He held her head close to his chest, his fingers buried in her hair. She laced her arms around his waist, her palms smoothing his muscled back.

"Hey," he said softly.

"What?"

He grasped her hair just hard enough to tip her head back until he caught her gaze with his.

"This," he said before kissing her gently.

"I don't want to hurt your lip," she whispered.

"I don't care."

He kissed her again, harder this time. She felt the swelling on his mouth, and it made her want to cry. But Mick was there and he wanted to be with her, he was willing to talk stuff out, and the crying was over.

He slid his tongue along her lower lip and she opened to him, her tongue darting out to soothe his injury.

He groaned deep in his throat.

She pulled back. "Did I hurt you?"

He smiled at her, a crooked grin. "Yeah. That doesn't mean I didn't like it."

"You're so kinky."

"Luckily—thank the fucking heavens—you seem to like that about me."

"I do." She smiled back at him, stepped away from him and took his hand. "Come over here and let me show you, Mick."

He gripped her hand and yanked her back into him roughly, making her gasp. "Oh, no. I've had enough of you trying to be boss, princess."

She yelped when he picked her up and threw her over his shoulder. "Hey!"

He gave her ass a sound spank. "Don't argue with me."

He carried her into the bedroom and flopped her down on the bed and immediately started to undress her. Her yoga pants came off, followed by her tank top, then her underwear. With only a few fingertips, he pressed between her breasts, using one finger to make a hard pressure point that told her in no uncertain terms to do what he wanted. She lay back and watched as he tore his T-shirt over his head.

She never got tired of looking at his muscled chest, the ridges of his abs. The narrow line of dark hair leading into the waistband of his jeans. She bit her lip as he unzipped them, knowing he always went commando. In seconds he was kicking the denim away and, naked, he lowered himself over her.

She reached for him, her hands hungry for the weight of his already hard cock, but he took both wrists with a low growl and spread her arms out to the sides. He lowered his mouth, and she felt the heat of his breath on the side of her breast before he bit in savagely.

"Ah! Mick . . ."

But the pain was immediately washed away in a flood of endorphins and that sense of being *his* she craved down to her bones.

She moaned quietly, and he licked at the sore spot, sucked the tender skin. She was going wet, loving his mouth on her, his teeth.

"God, when you bite me . . ." she said, groaning.

"When I bite you, what?" he murmured against her skin.

"It makes me feel . . . owned."

"Do you want that? Do you like it when I leave marks on you? Tell me, Allie girl."

"Yes. I love to be marked. I love to look at them and remember it was you."

"Did you look at your marks while I was gone, baby? Did you want to remember me?"

She licked her lips. "Always. Always, Mick."

"Allie . . ."

He moved down to her stomach, kissed her there softly, his mouth hot and lingering before he nipped at her flesh.

"Oh . . ."

He paused for a moment, blew onto her skin, tickling her, then he bit. Hard.

"Oh!"

She reached for him, buried her fingers in his hair, but he pushed her hands away and she knew she was to try to hold still. She lowered her arms, spread out on each side, a lovely, liquid sense of obedience flooding her.

He moved to another spot and bit again, and once more she cried out but she didn't move.

It hurt like crazy. Her body was lighting up with need.

He bit her again and again, moving lower until he was at that tender juncture between hip and thigh. He bit down hard, pulled back just long enough for her to take in a gasping breath, to fist her hands in the duvet. Then he did it again.

"Fuck, that hurts!"

He chuckled. Held her down with both hands on her thighs and did it once more, biting her so hard she didn't know how much more she could take.

"Ah!"

"Is it too much? Tell me."

"It's . . ." She was panting hard from the pain, from the plea-sure. "It's almost too much. And not enough. Please, Mick. I need more."

His voice was a guttural growl, rasping steel on gravel. "Do you have any idea what it does to me to hear you say these things?" He grabbed her by the waist and picked her up, shoved her farther up the bed. "Do you know how fucking rock-hard I am for you right now?" He got on his knees, sitting back on his heels, shoved her legs apart and yanked her body in, his arms wrapping around her back as he lifted her until she was strad-dling his lap, his fingers digging into her flesh. She grabbed onto his arms to steady herself.

"This is why," he gasped as he pressed her hips into his, her open, soaking wet sex coming up against his solid shaft. "This is why I was always so damn careful with you. Because with you . . . Fuck . . . You unleash the beast inside of me, Allie girl. And now it's been pushed too far to contain."

"Please," she whispered, her arms winding around his neck.

He paused, his breath coming in ragged pants. "I'm going to hurt you."

Her body was on fire. His pulsing cock pressed against her pussy lips, his hard chest crushed her breasts, and every inch of her skin needed him to touch, bite, strike, scratch.

"Yes. Do it, Mick."

He picked her up, and there was one brief moment when she was held, suspended, his gaze boring into hers, his mouth beau-tifully loose with unbridled lust. Then he impaled her—there was no other word for it—stabbing into her so hard and fast she couldn't breathe.

Right away he began a hard, punishing stroke, his thick cock plunging into her over and over. Pleasure spiraled, pain soared: his big ramming cock, his fingernails digging into her ass as he moved her up and down on his heavy shaft as if she were nothing more than a doll. And all the while he growled like an animal sprung from its cage. He fucked her like an animal. Mindless. Primal. Heat and pleasure and pain.

Her nails dug into the back of his neck, and all she could do was hang on to him while sensation took her over completely. She was helpless against what he was doing to her. Helpless against the waves that threatened to drown her as she started to come.

"Yeah, baby . . . Ah, Christ, baby girl . . ."

The words turned into a low muttering, then a thunderous growl until he threw his head back and yelled, bucking into her so hard it shook her all over, her climax shattering her to the core, her mind reeling.

"Mick!"

Pleasure and pleasure and pleasure, drowning out the pain. She clung to him, helpless in his arms. Rendered helpless by this pure need for him. For whatever he wanted of her. She wanted him to ravage her just like this. Wanted to be flesh to his flesh, and nothing more. It felt pure to her in some way she would never be able to explain.

The beast had been unleashed. And met the wildness inside her. And it was perfect.

"Hey."

They were still panting, her arms and legs wrapped around him so tightly he could feel her heart beating against his chest. He could feel the warmth of every luscious curve of this girl's body. *His* girl.

They were covered in sweat. He could smell it, their pheromones seeming to blend together perfectly, the perfume of sex. And beneath it something metallic . . .

"Baby, you're bleeding," he said, bringing his hand up to see the red spots on his fingertips.

"Hmm, what?" she asked sleepily.

"My nails must have scratched you when I grabbed your ass."

"No big deal. I liked it."

"I know you did. But let's get you cleaned up, baby girl."

He picked her up and carried her, still wrapped around his waist, her head resting on his shoulder in a show of utter trust that made his chest ache.

"I'm going to need to put you down for a sec."

He unwound her legs from his waist, then her arms from around his neck, and sat her on the edge of the old claw-footed bathtub while he ran hot water in the stall shower.

"Come on. I've got you," he told her as he helped her to her feet, held her close against his side and took her into the shower, the water cascading over their bodies.

"Mick?"

"What is it, baby?"

"That's the nicest thing anyone has ever said to me."

"Get ready to hear it a lot. 'Cause it's true. I've got you, Allie girl. *My* girl."

She laid a soft kiss on his chest, her hands slipping over his back under the hot water. She looked up at him, her gorgeous golden-brown eyes glowing, the pupils wide. Water tipped her black lashes.

"Am I, Mick? Am I your girl?"

"You know how this works. Safe, Sane and Consensual. Do you want to be mine? Do you want to belong to me?"

His heart was like a hammer in his chest. Why did this feel so important? But hell, nothing had ever been as important as Allie. That was what he'd been running from since he was eighteen years old.

"Only if you want me. Really want me, Mick. Do you?"

He bent and kissed her sweet mouth, her cheek, her forehead, pulled her hand to his lips and brushed kisses over her fingertips.

"Allie. My baby girl. You're everything I've ever wanted. And everything I ever will. God help me if I'm ever too stupid to see that again."

She blinked up at him. "I'm a little spaced. Or maybe a lot. Can you tell me that again when I have my head on straight?"

"Until you get sick of hearing it."

"I never will."

He put his hands into her hair and kissed her long and hard, ignoring his split lip. Their tongues were wet, tangling, joining them together. Their arms were so tight around each other he could feel every bone in her lovely body.

His.

"Let me take care of you now," he said, grabbing a big sea sponge, lathering it with soap, then turning her around so he could clean the small wounds left in her buttocks and hips. He ran the sponge over her skin and she sighed, pliant in his arms.

He'd never thought to see her like this, so completely submissive. So spent and loose and relaxed. He loved the fire in her. Loved her in this state even more *because* of that. He understood it meant more.

"Can you stand on your own, baby?"

"Yes."

He took the sprayer wand and used it to wet her hair, then squeezed some shampoo into his palm and began to work it in.

"Oh, that's nice," she said, her voice a quiet sigh.

He massaged her scalp, working up a good lather before rinsing it out, then doing the same with the conditioner, working it through the ends of her long hair, then rinsing again.

She was waking up a bit more by then. She turned to him, wrapped her arms around his neck, and he winced.

Her brows drew together. "Let me look."

He turned around and she laughed. "Boy, did I scratch the hell out of your neck and shoulders."

"Good girl," he murmured, smiling to himself.

"The skin opened in a spot or two."

"Just wash it off for me."

She did as he asked with gentle hands, pausing to stand on her toes and kiss the sore skin.

No one had ever treated him this way. Hell, he wouldn't have allowed it. But this was *Allie*. And he couldn't help but show her every side of him. Driven animal. Sensual being. Man who loved her.

Fuck.

He did. He loved her. Always had. Still did. Always would.

But . . . it was too soon to tell her. They needed to spend some time simply being together. See where it took them. Get to know each other all over again, like they'd talked about.

They had all the time in the world now, didn't they?

The water was growing cooler. He shut the shower off and reached out to grab a thick, white towel from the rack, pulled it into the shower with them and wrapped Allie up in it before he stepped out and found another rolled up in a basket on the floor for himself. He slung it around his waist, helped her step out onto the white bath mat and dried her carefully: her slender arms, her long legs, the sleek curve of her shoulders, the rounder curves of her beautiful breasts. She stood quietly, letting him do it while the steam wrapped around them, keeping them as warm as the soft New Orleans air.

He slipped the towel between her legs to dry her there and she pulled in a small, gasping breath. Their eyes met. She smiled, stood up on her toes to kiss him and reached down to grasp his cock in her hand. Two long strokes was all it took. He grew rock-hard in an instant, tearing the towel from his waist with one hand while with the other he drew her in tight. He grabbed her and sat her on the edge of the tiled counter and spread her thighs. Her legs wound around him.

"Yes, Mick. Come on." She reached between them, taking his cock in her soft hand again, her fingers feathering over the head.

He groaned, arching his hip into her fisted palm a few times, pleasure simmering low in his belly, making his cock pulse already. He grabbed her hand and pulled it away.

"Hey."

"Shh."

He quieted her by covering her lips with his, kissing her hard, his tongue forging into her mouth even as the split in his lip stung. She kissed him back hungrily, eating up his mouth. He was so fucking hard he couldn't wait.

He grabbed her ass, raising her hips, and plunged into her.

Christ, she was all hot, sleek silk inside, wet and ready for him, taking him all.

She moaned, her head against his mouth. "Fuck me, Mick," she whispered. "I need you to. I . . . need you."

They were bucking into each other, and he reached between them to work her clit with his hand. In moments she was coming, her hot sex clenching around him as she called his name. Then he was coming and his voice was a howl. The world went black, his orgasm ripping through him, ripping his heart out and serving it to her on a platter.

Allie.

His.

Together.

He latched on to her neck, bit into her, licked at her skin, then kissed her as his body calmed.

He saw he'd left more teeth marks on her. But she didn't mind. And he didn't mind that he'd marked her, made her his in some tangible way.

Some distant part of him realized he was lost. Lost to her.

Didn't matter.

All that mattered was that Allie—his Allie girl—belonged to him. Finally.

SHE WAS AWAKE but didn't want to open her eyes in case she'd imagined that Mick was there with her, that everything would be okay. But in moments she realized the weight on her stomach was his strong arm flung across her body. Still without opening her eyes, she reached down and linked her fingers with his, smiling.

"You happy, baby?"

She opened her eyes to find Mick looking at her, his gray eyes clear as crystals in the soft morning light. "You're up."

"Well, I'm awake. Not up yet, but I'm sure we can take care of that in about . . . three seconds."

He kissed her shoulder, then slid his hand over her stomach and between her thighs. "Ah, already wet for me, baby girl. And now I'm up."

She giggled. She couldn't help it. Heat shimmered through her when he teased her hardening clitoris. "And what are you going to do about that?"

"Anything I want. Isn't that right?" He stroked her damp slit, pressed a fingertip inside her, making her groan.

"Yes, Sir."

He pulled his hand away.

"So . . . the first thing I want . . . need to do is to ask if you're on some kind of birth control, since I was too carried away to remember to use a condom. And just so you know, that has never happened to me before."

"I always practice safe sex unless I'm with a long-term partner. But yes, I'm on the pill. And we've seen each other's paperwork. God, you really know how to kill the mood, Mick."

"On the contrary." He threw back the covers and she saw his glorious erection. "I'm as hard for you as I was five minutes ago."

"See? So kinky."

"Are you going to try to tell me you're not?" he challenged her.

"Not what? Kinky? Or still hot for you?"

He spread her thighs wide with his hand, pressed his fingers against her opening. They slid right in and she moaned, desire making a tight knot in her belly.

"Question number two answered. Let's see about question number one."

He scooted up until his back was against the pillows, and she watched him, wondering what he had in mind. But before she could figure it out, he grabbed her and flipped her facedown and naked on his lap.

"Mick, wait."

"Nope. This is a test of your kinkability, baby. Now be quiet while I do horrible things to your delicious ass."

He smacked one cheek hard enough to make her yelp.

"Quiet, now," he ordered.

"I can't!"

He smacked the other cheek just as hard.

"Oh!"

"If you can't stay quiet, then I'm going to have to make you count."

"Jesus, Mick." She laid her head down on the cool sheets and waited.

He gave her a good hard slap. Her ass stung like mad. "That's an extra one for you sassing me. Now count."

He smacked her cheek and she had to work to convert the pain to pleasure. Before she had a chance to do that, he smacked the other cheek.

"You're not counting."

"Two."

"Nope. That was one. The second one was to remind you." She bit her lip.

"Good girl."

Another hard slap.

"Two."

And another.

"Three," she said breathlessly. It was really beginning to hurt as he layered sensation over her tender skin.

She heard him pull in a breath, and his hand came down again, catching both ass cheeks, right in the center.

"Oh! Four."

The next few came in such rapid succession she squirmed in his lap.

"Oh no you don't, princess. You're not going anywhere." He held her down with one hand on the small of her back. "How many is that?"

"Five, six and seven, damn it."

"Excellent."

"Fucking sadist," she muttered.

He smacked her hard, the pain reverberating through her entire body.

"Ouch! Fuck, Mick! I suppose that one didn't count?"

"It sure as hell didn't. How many more do you think I've got for you?"

"Hundreds, I'm sure."

He chuckled, slipped a hand between her thighs, found her sex wet with wanting. "You don't seem to mind. Which I love about you, baby girl. And I know you can take a few more."

He slapped her ass over and over—she had a hard time keeping up with the count.

"Eight, nine . . . eleven," she gasped. "I think. Ah! Twelve?" She was panting, squirming hard in his lap, her hip coming up against his hard cock.

"Ten. You're bad at math, baby," he teased.

"I am not. It was twelve." She kicked her feet, squirmed again. She was loving every minute of this delicious torture.

"Still," he ordered. She complied, her body going loose at the mere tone of his voice.

He spread her thighs apart, pressed his fingers into her aching sex and began to pump.

"Mmm . . ."

He slipped them out and smacked her ass again, really hard this time. But the pleasure he'd given her allowed her to ride the pain out.

"What's the count, baby?"

"Thirteen."

"Ah, unlucky number thirteen. But you know, it's lucky for some of us. It's lucky for you today. And lucky for me."

He lifted her and positioned her so she was on her hands and knees on the bed, and he came up behind her and grasped her hips.

"I am going to fuck you so damn hard, Allie girl. And you're going to come and come until you scream."

She hung her head, loving the sensation of yielding he'd created in her flesh, her mind.

She felt the heat of his body as he rocked his hips forward, even the fine hairs on his thighs abrading the hot, tender skin from the spanking. But she loved it. Loved it even more when he surged into her an inch at a time, holding her still with firm hands, not letting her ease back onto his cock.

Finally, slowly, he buried himself deep in her pussy.

She let out a soft sigh of pure pleasure at being filled by him.

"Shh, hold still for me, baby."

He reached around her and filled his hands with her breasts, kneading the full flesh. She wanted to arch into his touch, but she knew to follow instructions. She bit her lip. Waited while pleasure suffused her, making her go warm and weak all over.

Finally he took her stiff nipples between his fingers and pinched, tugged, sensation a keen edge in her body, making her moan aloud. Making her arch her neck, her head coming up. He pinched harder, bringing pain sharply into the mix.

"Ah!"

Still holding her nipples firmly between his fingers, he used his strong forearms to bring her body up until she was almost sitting up on her knees, his cock still deep inside her. And slowly he began to fuck her.

"Ah, God, Mick . . ."

His thick cock slid in and out, in this position easily hitting her G-spot, and pleasure built quickly, a deep, thrumming rhythm. His cock and his hard, pinching fingers on her nipples causing sensation everywhere—thrilling, dazzling. Even better when he bit into her shoulder, his teeth sinking deep while his tongue swirled over her skin.

Her mind was spinning, out of control, pleasure and pain all one thing. He fucked her harder, his cock jackhammering into her, making her gasp with each punishing stroke. His hands wrapped around her breasts, pressing hard, hurting her. Making her dizzy with the desire for *more*.

He bit her harder. She felt his body tense and knew he was ready to come. And at that moment he reached down to pinch her clit, using his nails to bite hard into the sensitive flesh.

"Ah, God!"

It fucking hurt. But she was coming and coming, her hips arching into his hurting touch, back to take his big cock in deep. He was growling, panting, his teeth sinking deeper. And she was coming so damn hard the coming itself was painful, the pleasure almost too much to take. He fucked her harder, slamming into her, and she was drowning in the heat of his body, his scent filling her head as her climax crashed over her again and again.

"Ahhhhhh! Mick!"

"Baby, baby . . ."

They collapsed on the bed together. He was still inside her, still hard even though she knew he'd come. They lay on their sides, his taut stomach pressed against her back, his arms still around her. They were both slick with sweat. Lovely, that slippery friction of damp skin against damp skin. He slung one leg over her hip and pushed in and out of her almost lazily, his slowly softening cock causing small frissons of orgasm to shiver through her.

"Oh, that's good," she murmured, locking her fingers with his. He held on tight, brought their clasped hands up to her chest and nestled them between her breasts.

"I can feel your heart pounding," he whispered into her hair. "So is mine."

"I can feel it against my back," she told him, "I can feel your heartbeat echoing all the way up my spine."

They were quiet for a long time, simply relaxing, trying to catch their breath.

Finally he said, "This is it, you know. This is what I want."

Her heart surged at hearing him say it. She'd thought that was what he'd meant when they'd talked the night before. But the confirmation was lovely to hear. She'd needed to hear it. "Me, too."

He slipped out of her and rolled her over then, pulling her in close to his big body. He propped himself up on one elbow, looking down at her. He was watching her again, searching her face.

"What is it, Mick?"

He shook his head, leaned in and kissed her cheek, her jaw, her neck, her shoulder. He was being so tender with her, so sweet it made her heart thump, her stomach flutter. Her nerves sang with the one truth she had known almost her whole life.

She loved him.

She nearly said the words. But she didn't want anything to ruin this moment. She didn't want to risk chasing him off with too much, too soon.

Instead she reached to trace the scar on his ribs. He flinched for a moment, but she looked up into his eyes and said quietly, "Let me, Mick. Share this with me. It's a part of you."

"It's an ugly part."

She shook her head. "It's still you. It's one of your life's stories. It's one you've never shared with me."

"It's one I'd rather not talk to anyone about."

"This is *me*, Mick. Tell me. Please. It's part of that transparency, right? How can we be together in the BDSM realm if I don't know you as well as you know me? How can we have that ultimate connection—the power exchange—that's so much a part of BDSM relationships if it's not an *exchange*? I want that with you."

He shook his head again and she thought he would argue. But after a few moments he said, "You're right. But only because it *is* you, Allie." He paused, ran a hand over his jaw, his eyes going dark and a little stormy. "Okay. I'll tell you."

CHAPTER

Twelve

M ICK SMOOTHED A hand over her stomach, taking the heat
of her body into his palm, his fingertips. He concentrated
on that sensation for several long moments while he tried to get
his head together, his thoughts organized.

"Okay." He took in a deep breath. "So . . . when I went away
to Louisiana State in Baton Rouge, I sold all my older, crappy
bikes I'd worked on and rebuilt through high school and got the
new Yamaha. I loved that bike. It was fast. Beautiful. All shining chrome, and I swear that thing purred at me when I really
opened her up."

"Jamie mentioned it a time or two when I saw him after you
left."

"Did he also mention I liked to drive too fast?"

She shrugged. "I already knew that. Anyway, Jamie and his
muscle cars . . . he was nineteen, too. I doubt he even noticed."

"Yeah, probably true."

She laid a hand on his chest. "So, what happened, Mick?" she asked softly.

He focused again on the heat of her touch, using it to calm him. He did not want to talk about this. But it was Allie, and he would do it for her. "Motorcycles are tricky things. Especially when someone too young and arrogant thinks he's in control of that kind of machine. All it takes is one pebble on the road. One moment where you don't let out the clutch just right taking a turn, or you're not focused enough on what's right in front of you. That's what happened, I guess. I wasn't focused, wasn't paying enough attention. Wasn't giving the bike and the speed the respect those things deserve.

"I don't even know exactly what happened, as stupid as that sounds. It *was* stupid. Totally irresponsible. I woke up in the hospital and they told me I'd wrapped my bike around an old oak tree in someone's front yard. In the middle of the Goddamn day. Could have been someone's kid out there, you know?" His chest pulled tight. It wasn't any easier to say it now, even after all the years that had passed. It felt like the damn words were choking him. He could barely stand to look at her while he said these things. "Thank God it was just my reckless, idiotic ass out there. But I couldn't stop thinking about it—that I could have hit someone. I could have fucking killed someone. It's still there in the back of my mind. It's always there."

"You can't do that to yourself, Mick."

"No? How can I not hold myself accountable? For what happened. For what could have happened. Especially after Brandon. We all saw firsthand what that did to his parents, to Summer. To all of us—his friends—especially Jamie. I knew better. Or, I should have. And Allie, I come from a family of men who care for the people of our community. Not only did I take a stupid-ass risk with other people's lives, I took away my own . . . shit. It sounds selfish as hell to even mention it."

"What?" she asked, her tone gentle. "Tell me."

He looked away, shook his head, but he went on, his blood pounding in his temples. "I took away my chance to . . . my *ability* to serve this city the same way my family has for generations. That accident ate a part of my soul. A part I'll never get back."

"Oh, Mick."

He flinched. "Ah, stop it, Allie. I can't take anyone's pity and you know it."

He felt her fingertips soft on his cheek, and he allowed her to turn his face back to hers. Her brown eyes were sheened with tears, gleaming golden in the misty morning light.

"This is *me*, Mick. You know it's not pity, that hearing you say it makes my heart break for you. To know you've carried that kind of guilt all this time. But I've never pitied you. I thought you were just mad."

"Oh, I'm mad. I'm pissed as hell at myself."

"I don't blame you. I'd probably feel the same way. I *know* I would. But Mick, at some point you've got to let it go."

"Do I? Or more to the point, should I?"

She tilted her chin, her brows drawing together. "I don't understand."

"The guilt is nothing less than I deserve, Allie. It's my burden to carry with me."

"But you didn't hurt anyone else," she protested.

"That's not true. Every single day I'm not a firefighter like I should have been, like my family and my city had a right to expect of me, I hurt someone. Every day there's one less man on the force to protect people."

She shook her head. "That's not realistic, Mick. You can't blame yourself for things you *might* have been able to prevent. And you have found a way to protect people. Your security business—"

"I work boxing matches and rock concerts. I protect drunken fools from other drunken fools. It's not the same thing."

"It's something, Mick," she said quietly, maybe understanding that he simply wasn't able to hear it, no matter how she put it.

"Yeah. Something." He shrugged.

"Thank you for telling me. Even when you didn't want to. Especially because you didn't want to."

But he *had* wanted to. That was the strange thing. Or maybe the strange thing was that they were there together, in her bed, naked. Strange that it had finally happened, the two of them together again.

A part of him felt like it was fate. Another part still believed she was too damn good for him.

He had to shake that shit off.

He lifted her hand, kissed it, shifted the gears in his head.

"Enough of this. I'm taking you out to breakfast." He silently thanked God for the male ability to compartmentalize. "Get your gorgeous ass in the shower and get clean while I make some coffee for the road."

"Yes, Sir."

She was smiling at him, going along with the game. Good girl.

She was a good girl. The best. More than he deserved. But he was done trying to convince her of that. She'd chosen him. And he wasn't that stupid anymore. He wasn't letting her go again.

LESS THAN AN hour later they had made their way uptown along St. Charles Avenue to The Camellia Grill, one of the best breakfast spots in the city. It was the usual packed Sunday morning. They stood together on the sidewalk in front of the old colonial structure, with its white columns and dark green shutters, another of the city's local landmarks to resurrect after Katrina.

It felt strange to be out with Allie, doing this kind of normal thing like going to breakfast. They'd been to this place a dozen times as teenagers, and it took him back. Him in his ever-present leather jacket. Allie's long hair shining in the sun, her laughing with him. Everything had seemed a lot simpler then. So much less at stake. But wasn't that always the difference between being a teenager—just a kid, really—and being an adult? Yeah, a hell of a lot more at stake now.

Don't trip on it. Just enjoy the day.

What had happened to the compartmentalizing he'd been so good at only a little while ago? Hell, he'd had years of practice at shutting things down. He knew it was Allie that was making things harder to keep under control. And control had been the key to managing his life since those days . . . the days before his life had come crashing down around him piece by piece. Brandon's death. Seeing Jamie's reaction—his grief going way beyond what the rest of them had experienced. Coming to terms with the fact that he had to leave Allie behind when he went away to college. That one night when he'd seen her again. When he'd done those things to her. The way he'd felt the next morning, as if he'd fucking murdered someone . . . and the damn accident that he swore was not a death wish.

"Mick? You look like a cloud just passed over your grave. What are you thinking about?"

"What? Sorry, princess. Just woolgathering."

"You are so not the kind of man to mingle with sheep," she teased.

He had to smile. "Nope. Subbie girl though you may be, you're definitely not the sheep type."

She laughed, and some of the ice that had been running through his veins melted. "You've got that right. God, I can't remember the last time I ate here."

"The last weekend in May, my senior year. Jamie and I were cutting school, which was our right as seniors, and you were playing delinquent with us."

"I can't believe you remember all that."

He reached out and tucked a long strand of her dark, silky hair behind her ear. "You were wearing a cotton sundress with tiny pink roses all over it. They were the same shade as your lips."

Her smile widened, her eyes shining. "You're a romantic at heart, you know that, Mick Reid?"

"Never."

She slunk up against him. "Always."

He grabbed her by the waist and bent to brush a kiss across her lush mouth. "If I agree with you, will it get me some later?"

"Do you really have to ask?" Her voice was a quiet purr. "You buy me breakfast and you are so getting laid."

"Am I, now?"

"Yep. Sir. Yep, Sir."

He laughed and picked her up until her feet left the ground. "Hey!"

He set her back down, took her hand and kissed it, held it tightly in his.

If he could just keep the bullshit from invading his brain, this might turn out to be a perfect day. A perfect life.

Gotta take it one day at a time.

That was the smart thing to do, wasn't it?

Wasn't it?

*   *   *

THEY WERE FINALLY seated at the long counter facing the gleaming steel kitchen, the only seating there was at the crowded, noisy Camellia Grill. Mick seemed almost too big to fit on the stools lined up at the marble counter—he had to sit half-turned toward her, one long leg crossed over hers, but Allie didn't mind. She was enjoying the closeness she felt with him today.

Maybe part of it was that he'd opened up to her and told her a bit of his story about the accident. But it was also that he'd remained open to her—a good chink in the armor, anyway—and she loved the vulnerability he was allowing himself with her.

She knew it was that he *allowed* himself—there was no doubt about it. Mick was still almost perfectly controlled. The Dom thing. The Mick thing. It was that lovely, melding combination of control and vulnerability that just killed her. He could ask anything he wanted of her right now and she'd have to say yes.

"What are you having, baby?" he asked.

"A veggie omelet."

"Really? That's no fun. I'm having the waffles."

"Oh, that sounds good."

"You should have them, too."

"I'm a pastry chef, Mick. I have sugar in my mouth on a daily basis. Or, I will when I start working again."

He leaned in and murmured against her ear, his breath warm on her skin, "I'll put some sugar in your mouth, girl."

She shivered, lust infusing her system so fast it made her go hot all over.

"Yes, please," she answered.

He grinned. "Good girl."

"Oh, God, don't do that to me here, Mick."

"I'll do plenty to you later. Just leaving you with something to think about."

"You're a wicked man."

"You like me that way."

"Yes, I do. But shall we change the subject?"

His gray eyes were sparkling. "Why, when I'm having so much fun torturing you?"

"Change of subject, please."

He looked like he was about to protest when a waiter approached their section of the counter and poured two cups of coffee for them without being asked.

"What'll you have?"

Mick ordered for them, and the waiter, in classic Camellia Grill style, shouted the order at the cooks.

Mick turned his attention back to her.

"Okay. Change of subject, but only because you asked so nicely. Tell me how your family's doing."

"They're fine. I've talked to Mama and *Zia* Renata on the phone. No one brought up my business plan, which is just as I'd expected. Brush things under the rug and they disappear—that's our family motto."

"That's everyone's family motto."

"Maybe. How is your family? I only get regular updates on Neal through Marie Dawn."

"Doing well. Gareth's kid just had his fourteenth birthday. Makes me feel old. I remember when he was in diapers. Nolan's wedding is coming up in the fall . . . hey, you should see if they need someone to do the cake."

"Oh, I'm sure they've got that arranged by now."

"Maybe not. I'll give you his fiancée's number. Katie's great. You should call her."

"I actually love to do wedding cakes."

"Where did you learn how?" he asked as their food arrived.

"Veggie omelet hold the onions and the house waffles for the beautiful couple!" the waiter shouted for effect as he set the plates in front of them.

"Thanks." She smiled at the waiter before turning back to Mick. "A bit at culinary school—just doing cakes, I mean—but I apprenticed at this incredible place in Vienna for about six months and they really put me through the drills. Made me stay up literally all night rolling and rerolling my fondant until I learned to do it right."

"Fondant?" He took a big bite of syrup-covered waffle. "Ah, this is damn good," he said, the words muffled.

"It's like icing, except it's heavier and more moldable. You can make flowers out of it—almost anything."

"Ah. And now I know as much as I did before."

"I can give you baking lessons if you're interested."

"No thanks. I'll leave the art up to the artist. Tell me more about Vienna."

She chewed a bite of her omelet, washed it down with a sip of coffee. "What do you want to know?"

He shrugged, shoving another forkful of waffle between his lips. "I don't know. Whatever you want to tell me. What did you love about the city?"

"The history, I guess. It's everywhere. Ever present, if that makes sense. It's in the architecture, which is gorgeous—the museums and the opera houses and the cathedrals. In the old cobblestone streets. In the way people go about their lives there, for the most part. I mean, there are really sleek, modern structures that rival contemporary architecture anywhere in the world, like the Haas Haus. Have you ever seen it?"

"You mean that big mirrored building? I've seen pictures. Looks incredible."

"It is," she agreed. "It's stunning. But despite places like that there's still a sense of antiquity about the city. Sort of like there is here. I guess that's why I felt so at home in Europe."

"What else?"

"About Vienna in general? Or about the architecture?"

"I just want to know about your experiences in Europe. It must have been amazing to see so many countries. To live in so many places. I couldn't have done it. I can't bear to be away from New Orleans for too long. You're braver than I am, Allie girl." He put his fork down and turned to her. "In a lot of ways."

His gaze was steady, *deep* somehow. It made her breath catch in her throat.

"I'm not," she protested weakly.

"But you are. It takes a lot to be a sub. Don't think I don't know that. It takes strength. Courage."

All she could do was blink for a moment. "Thank you for saying that. It does. In my experience not everyone sees it that way. But . . . you and I see a lot of things the same way. We always have."

He nodded slowly. And in that moment she felt something blaze between them, their mental as well as physical chemistry like the sharply burning edge of ozone in the air.

He took her hand and lifted it to his lips, brushed a hot kiss across her knuckles. Her body shivered in answer.

"You are one beautiful girl," he said, a sense of wonder in his voice.

She smiled. He smiled back, his strong white teeth framed by his wicked goatee.

She'd always loved a goatee on a man. Loved that evil edge it gave a man's face. And on Mick's face . . .

"More coffee for you two? Yes, and drink it while it's hot," the waiter asked and answered in the same breath, already pouring, bringing them both back to the world around them, full of sound and the warm scents of breakfast cooking.

Mick shook his head as he lifted his cup, one corner of his mouth quirking. "If these waiters only knew who they were bossing around," he said quietly, humor in his low tone. He took a sip, set the cup down and picked up his fork once more, spearing a piece of waffle and offering it to her lips. "Here, have a bite before they get cold. And before we cause a scandal in the middle of this restaurant."

She grabbed the fork. "In the interest of not causing a scandal," she said, slipping the bite of waffle into her mouth. "Mmm, good." She finished chewing. "Can we get out of here now?"

"You insatiable girl."

"Luckily you like me this way."

"Lord, do I ever."

They finished up and paid the bill, and soon they were in his truck, moving back through the city toward the French Quarter.

Mick took her to his place, and they parked in the garage he rented for his truck a few blocks from his house. They walked hand in hand down the street, and it was sweet strolling with him through the sleepy Sunday city that smelled of ancient wood and brick, flowers and spices, along with the familiar edge of decay from the tropical air. Sweet, and yet her heart was racing, her body burning for him just from the feel of his big hand around hers. From knowing it was *Mick* she was walking with. From knowing what would happen when they got to his place. They reached the second block, having walked in silence when she turned to him.

"Why so quiet?"

"I'm concentrating."

"On what?"

"On not tearing your clothes off in the middle of the street."

"Oh . . ."

Heat shimmered through her, reached deep into her belly, in between her thighs to that warm spot that was nearly always just a little wet for him. It was tingling now. Needy instantly.

She gripped his hand tighter, and they both moved faster until they reached his door, where he let her hand go long enough to fit the key in the lock before taking her hand again and pulling her inside. He kicked the door shut behind them and grabbed her, yanking her body in tight and kissing her hard.

She moaned into his mouth as he opened her lips with his wet, seeking tongue, and her hands slid into his hair, holding him closer. In moments they were both panting, their bodies pressed close together, hips moving in rhythm.

Mick pulled away. "Fuck it," he growled as he yanked her tank top over her head, and she was grateful she'd gone without a bra today. His gaze lingered on her bare breasts, making her feel all the more naked for him.

She helped him slide his T-shirt up. It caught on one arm, and they both yanked together, the fabric ripping before they were able to work it free. She groaned as she slid her hands over his chest, over his flat, hardening nipples, leaned in to taste his skin.

"Christ," he muttered. "Come here, baby."

He wrapped a hand around her hair and pulled her head back, biting into her throat, then sucking at the skin, while with the other hand he unbuttoned her jeans and shoved them down her legs. He slid a few fingers under the edge of her underwear, and she heard the tearing of lace as they came off.

"God . . . yes, Mick."

She went for his jeans, and his hands were there, too. He

shoved them down around his ankles. They got stuck and he kicked off his boots, the worn denim of his jeans slipping off easily, and she found his big cock hard as granite, her fingers wrapping around it.

He filled his hands with her breasts, squeezing, caressing. Her body was on fire, desire a fierce blaze, building so quickly she couldn't think straight. She didn't want to. All she knew was this panting desperation, this tearing of clothes, the need to touch and taste and feel.

He bent to take one nipple into his mouth and she surged into him. He licked until it was hard, began to suck while she moaned and held his head, her fingers digging into his scalp. When he bit her she only sighed. And began to stroke his cock.

"No."

He grabbed her hand and pulled it away, and before she could protest he turned her around, had her on her hands and knees at the bottom of the stairwell.

"Can't wait to be inside you," he said from between gritted teeth, picking her up and moving up a few steps.

"Don't wait, Mick. Come on."

She reached back for him, digging her fingernails into his thigh as he gripped her hips with firm, hurting hands. She welcomed the pain, welcomed his command. She spread her thighs wider.

"Hang on, baby," he ground out as he plowed into her.

"Oh!"

But it was all good—the pain and the pleasure as he thrust into her in one long, hard stroke. The hard surface of the old wooden stairs pressing into her knees. He pulled back, stabbed into her. She swore she could feel the tip of his cock ramming against her G-spot over and over. Pleasure speared through her, desire rising to a dizzying height instantly.

"Come on, baby. I'm going to fuck you so hard. You can take it. Tell me," he demanded.

"I need you, Mick. Fuck me hard. As hard as you can. Please," she gasped.

He bucked into her so hard she would have collapsed on the stairs if he hadn't been holding on to her. And along with the exquisite pleasure was the warm sense of yielding to his command, like lightning filtering through her veins in small electric jolts.

"Oh, fuck, baby girl. You feel so. Damn. Good."

He rammed into her, again and again, bringing her to the edge.

"Not yet," he ordered her. "Don't come yet."

"God . . ."

But she bit it back, forcing her climax to hover at the precipice. He reached around her and pinched her clit.

"Oh!" She shook her head, her hair flying around her face.

"Not yet," he ground out, his body shivering so hard she knew he was fighting it, too.

She inhaled, struggling against sensation that threatened to overload, her sex squeezing his big cock with every punishing stroke.

"Gonna come."

"Please," she begged.

"Wait."

To her surprise he turned her over until she was sitting on the stairs. He wrapped her legs around his waist, pausing with the tip of his cock at the opening of her hungry, aching sex.

"Mick," she breathed.

"Look at me, Allie."

She locked her gaze to his as he reached under her, lifted her, and impaled her.

"Mick . . . oh . . ."

Her arms went to his shoulders and she hung on while he surged into her.

"Ah, baby girl."

Something shifted. He tilted his hips, in, then out. Slowly. Excruciating. Wonderful, as pleasure coiled inside her, waiting. And his glittering, gray gaze never left her face.

One big hand cupped her ass, and with the other he reached between them to press on her swollen clitoris.

"Now, baby. Come for me now."

His voice, his command, triggered her climax. She came, and came apart, her orgasm rippling over her skin, deep into her belly, her sex. Sharp and soft all at the same time. Hard yet liquid. She was shaken by the intensity of his gaze on hers.

"Say you're mine. Allie," he demanded, his voice rough. "Say it."

"Yes. God . . . yours. Always."

"*Mine.*"

His body went stiff all over and he plunged into her, shaking as he came.

"Mine, my girl," he muttered, his mouth going beautifully soft with pleasure.

The reverberations seemed to go on forever as they trembled together, coming and coming. And she saw it in his eyes, in his pleasure-torn expression.

Love.

There was no mistaking it—naked on his face, all of it written there as if in indelible ink, as stark and raw as she felt at that moment herself.

Love him. Always.

She loved him. With all her heart, with every cell in her being. And it was a love strong enough to hold up to the years, the times he'd broken her heart. But even broken, the love had remained. Had only grown stronger in knowing the man he'd become.

Tears stung her eyes. She blinked them away even as her heart dared to soar.

Love him so damn much.

He loved her back.

She'd known it in some cerebral way. But now she *felt* it. And that was something entirely different.

She blinked. Blinked again in wonder. "Mick."

He tilted his head, his brows drawn together as if he were thinking very hard. Then he leaned in slowly and kissed her mouth. He pulled back a few inches, then kissed her lips once more. Then her cheek, over and over as she melted into his touch. Then her temple, her ear, her hair, before pulling back to look at her again.

His hand went around the back of her neck, cradling her head in his palm.

"Allie . . ." He paused. Started again. "I love you, Allie girl. *My* girl."

Her heart twisted in her chest, wanting to sing, to leap. "I am your girl."

"You love me," he said. It was a statement, not a question.

The tears welled in her eyes, making his face swim before her. She blinked them away. She needed to see him. "I do. I love you."

"I never stopped," he told her. "Never. I was just . . . stubborn. Stupid. I never gave you enough credit."

She pressed a fingertip to his lips. "Shh. Don't. You never gave yourself enough credit, either. But we're here now. That's what's important."

He nodded, kissed her fingertips, took her hand in his and held it to his cheek. "How can I ask you to forgive me for what

I did to you? You loved me, and I didn't believe in either of us enough. I fucking *hurt* you."

"Yes. You did. But it's time to put all of that behind us. We have to if we're going to be able to hang on to each other. If we're going to be able to love each other." She slid her hands down over his shoulders, gripped the bulging muscles of his biceps. "Mick, tell me you can do that. Tell me you'll try."

Suddenly her heart was thundering in her chest. What if he didn't know *how* to let himself love her? What if he couldn't let the past go and move forward with her? Simply saying he loved her was only the first step.

"I don't have any other choice. Not now. I love you, my baby girl. I love you. I don't know how I've lived without you all these years." He stroked her hair from her face, his fingers lingering there. "You're mine now. The way you always should have been."

"Mick . . . can we really do this? Can we really start over? I'm not foolish enough to think we'll be starting with a clean slate. No one does that. We can't pretend the past never happened—"

"I don't want to. You're as much a part of my past as you are my present. As I hope you'll be of my future."

She smiled, stroked his cheek. He turned his face into her palm and kissed her there. Softly. Lingeringly.

"But things may come up that we'll have to deal with," she said. "We have to communicate with each other."

"You know I kind of suck at that sometimes. If it's kink related, I'm all about the transparency, but the emotional stuff . . . that's a lot harder."

"I know. I promise I'll cut you a little slack. For being male, if nothing else."

"Oh, will you now?"

She grinned up at him. "I will. I'm generous like that."

"I'll show you generous, my girl. I'll be generous all over your fine ass."

"Promises, promises," she teased.

She yelped as he picked her up, threw her over his shoulder and started up the stairs.

"You're a caveman, Mick Reid!"

"Tell me you don't love it."

"I . . . plead the Fifth."

"Ha!"

"Where are you taking me?"

"To bed, where I can do terrible things to your gorgeous body. Do I hear more arguments?"

"Um . . . no."

"No, what?" he demanded.

"No . . . please?"

He laughed. "That'll do."

They reached his bedroom, where the afternoon light was seeping through the curtains, illuminating it with the kind of soft golden sunlight that made dust motes dance in the air. His muscles flexed under her palms as he bent and laid her on the bed. He was so beautifully built. She'd always loved the breadth of his shoulders, his narrow hips, the pale gold hue of his skin. She loved the wicked gleam in his eyes, the cocky half smile on his face. The mix of bad boy and occasional tender lover and the sadistic streak that ran through it all.

"What are you going to do with me?" she asked.

He rubbed his chin. "I'm working on it. I just had a mind-blowing orgasm and told you I love you. I might need a minute to recover."

"Mind-blowing?"

"Every damn time."

"Really?"

"Don't think that gives you any bargaining power."

"Doesn't it?" She batted her lashes.

He chuckled. "All right, I give up. You know damn well it does."

"I rather like that idea."

"Don't get too comfortable with it. I'm still the Dom."

"I'm pretty sure you won't ever let me forget it."

"Damn right," he said as he lunged for her.

"Mick!"

"Shh."

He flipped her over onto her stomach and straddled her, pinning her down with his legs while he found the ankle cuffs he kept attached to his bed, and shackled her with lightning speed. Immediately he began to spank her, a quick, sharp volley of slaps. They came too quickly for her to have time to convert the pain. She was overloading, squirming, panting. He smacked her harder—her ass, the backs of her thighs. The pain built and built. She couldn't give herself over to it—it was too much, too fast.

"Mick!"

"My name is not a safe word, princess."

She almost laughed, but his hand came down again and again, fast and stinging like crazy. Her flesh was burning hot.

"Do you need to safe-word?" he asked, still spanking her.

"Mick," she said, her breath rasping in her lungs as she struggled uselessly to get away from him, from the padded cuffs holding her ankles so securely.

"Yes?"

He smacked her again, impossibly harder.

She did laugh, then, as the lovely brain chemicals broke free and swarmed her head, her body. She went limp all over.

He stopped, unbuckled the cuffs, turned her over and held her in his arms.

"Lord, I love to see you like this," he said quietly, almost reverentially. "Your pupils wide, your cheeks flushed. Your lips . . . so damn beautiful. I always love you, but when you're like this, yielding to me so completely, well . . . that's when I really fall for you all over again. Every damn time. Because I know you've given yourself into my hands. You make yourself so vulnerable it makes my chest ache. And I have never said anything like that to anyone in my life." He paused to stroke her cheek, her jaw, her throat. "Love you, baby girl."

"Love you, too, you beast."

He smiled, leaned down to kiss her. When she tried to curl her hands behind his neck, he gently pried them away, held her wrists as he lowered her arms to the bed and laid her down once more. He lowered his body over hers, and it was only when he brushed up against her stomach that she realized he was hard again.

"You're such a nymphomaniac," she murmured, her body heavy and languid with endorphins and an aching renewed desire.

"Men can't be nymphomaniacs," he argued as he took his rigid shaft in his hand to guide it to her. "And it's only with you, Allie. Only you." He paused, the tip of his cock resting just inside her. "Tell me again."

"I'll tell you everything. Anything. I love you, Mick. I'm yours. Always."

"Always," he said, slipping inside her.

She was so wet she took him all in one smooth thrust, gasping as sensation trembled through her.

"Mmm . . ."

He kissed her lips, took her bottom lip between his teeth and nibbled, pulled back and bent to kiss her breasts.

She reached for him, holding on to his strong forearms, loving the corded muscle there. And as he arched into her, taking his time, kissing her neck, her shoulders, she explored his hard frame with her hands. She slid her palms over his sides, pausing to touch the scar on his ribs before slipping her hand between their bodies to stroke the rock-hard surface of his abdomen. She smoothed her fingers over every ridge, loving the contraction of muscle as he arched his hips, pressing his cock deep inside her.

Pleasure was a slowly building blaze. Scorching her, lighting her up inside. He moved faster and she held on to him, her arms around his waist, her hands spread wide over his back.

Desire rose, spiraled, her sex impossibly wet, clasping his rigid flesh inside her.

"You feel so good, baby. So good," he murmured. "Love you, my baby."

"Love you, Mick. Oh . . ."

"Yeah, that's it. I can feel you . . . come with me, my girl."

"Oh!"

Their bodies rose at the same moment, arms winding tightly around each other. They shook together, burned together, cried out. Her mind spun, light flashing behind her eyes as if all the stars in heaven were reeling past.

"Mick!"

"Love you, my baby," he whispered into her hair. "Love you . . ."

The night was quiet around them. She couldn't even hear the cicadas that sang all over the city of New Orleans. All she heard was his steady breathing. The sound of her heart beating in time with his.

Together.

This was everything she'd ever wanted.

She loved him.

He loved her.

She was scared to death.

She buried her face in his muscled shoulder and let the tears come.

CHAPTER
Thirteen

"Hey." He rolled onto his side, taking her with him. "What's this?"

She sniffed. "It's nothing."

"Transparency, baby."

"Sorry. You're right. It's just that . . . I'm scared, Mick. Aren't you?"

"Hell, yes. But I'm trying not to run anymore."

She pressed her cheek against his chest, taking comfort in the solidity of his big body. "That makes me feel a little better."

He laughed. "That I'm not running or that I'm still scared?"

"Not that you're scared. I mean, yes, that you're scared, but not because I want you to be." She wiped the final traces of tears away. It just makes me feel a little more . . . normal."

"Baby girl, there is nothing normal about us."

"No, I guess not," she agreed, smiling. "A pastry chef with no bakery who likes to be beaten, and a security expert who gets into illegal fights and likes to hurt pretty girls. Pretty fucked up, huh?"

"I only want to hurt *you*, from now on. In the good way. And yeah, pretty fucked up. Anyway, about the bakery . . ."

She pulled away and looked up at him. "I'm going to start my own business doing bakery catering. I'll rent kitchen space somewhere. I don't want to work for anyone else anymore."

"You should keep at it with your family—you can get through to them eventually, get them to see your ideas are the best possible plan for Dolcetti. That's where you're meant to be. Where you've always belonged. Like you do with me. Like you do in New Orleans."

"They're never going to listen, and I'm done banging my head against that particular wall. I need to redraw my business plan with this other course of action in mind. I can't wait on them forever. And Mick? Can we argue about this another time?"

"We're not arguing. I just want the best for you. You know that, right?"

"I do. But right now I need to just be here with you. I don't want to have any serious discussions for a while. Is that okay?"

"Anything you want."

He pulled her in close, and she sighed as she breathed in his familiar scent. Smiled when her sex went wet all over again. But she didn't need sex right now. His arms around her, their bodies pressed close, knowing he loved her, was enough.

"Don't fuck it up, Mick," she murmured, smiling to herself.

"You are one sassy little wench, girl."

"You love that about me."

"Yeah, I do. Doesn't mean I don't owe you one hell of a spanking later, though. With a small club."

She closed her eyes, burrowed in closer. "You would never spank me with a club."

"I'm beginning to consider it."

He bent and kissed the top of her head, pushed her hair back and kissed her cheek, her lips. He pulled back and she looked up to see him shaking his head.

"What?" she asked.

"Who would have believed this? After all this time."

"Marie Dawn did. Jamie sort of did or he wouldn't have helped me."

"Remind me to take that club to his ass, too."

She giggled. "Like that'll ever happen."

His face grew sober. "*This* happened. I feel like it's a miracle, Allie."

So did she. No matter how much she'd wanted to believe they could be together again, she'd always harbored doubts. A screaming fear she couldn't quite put voice to—it was too painful to really consider. But here they were. Together. Happy.

"You're right. It is a small miracle. It's what I wanted for so long. Thank God I was stubborn enough to get it."

"Thank *you*," he whispered as his arms tightened around her.

THEY SPENT THE next several weeks, in between Mick's work gigs, visiting all their favorite old haunts, like the Court of Two Sisters, where they feasted on peppery shrimp wrapped in bacon and cold beer over long conversations about politics, their families, their high school days. Art and movies and kink. Friends and books and travel. They stopped at Café Du Monde sometimes twice in a day to drink the chicory-laced coffee and eat the sweet, scalding-hot beignets, or sometimes just to see how much powdered sugar was on the sidewalk surrounding the canopied patio before wandering across the street to hang out in Jackson Square, making out on the benches like they had when they were teenagers.

They discovered new common interests, things they'd never done together before. They both loved the old architecture of the city, and they visited the famous homes that were part of the official Historic New Orleans Collection. They both particularly loved the Perrilliat House, with its spiral wooden staircase.

They had dinner with Neal and Marie Dawn, and Allie realized how much she'd missed seeing Mick with his family, the two men joking with each other in the rough way brothers often did. And it felt right somehow, everyone being together as couples. Of course, she'd told her best friend that she and Mick were together, but neither Marie Dawn or Neal questioned them too closely. Everyone had simply accepted their being together, almost as if it were expected. Perhaps it was.

They had a late brunch with her mother and her aunts and uncles after they'd all returned from church one Sunday. Mick was immediately taken into the family as if it hadn't been thirteen years since he'd last been in her mother's house, eaten her coq au vin, the wonderful French peasant stew recipe that had been passed down from Allie's long-gone *grand-mère*, her father's mother. They sat around the table and drank wine and talked and argued for hours, a ritual that had always been part of her family, from both her mother's Italian side and her father's French side—something Allie realized she missed, too, and she vowed to spend more time with them.

In June Mick invited her to his parents' house for their annual Father's Day barbeque. They'd been back together for almost six weeks, and she still hadn't seen any of Mick's family aside from Neal. She was trying to decide what to wear when her cell phone rang.

"Marie Dawn—just the person I needed to talk to."

"What's up, *chérie*? Everything okay with you and Mick?"

"Everything's great."

"Is he there? Or are you at his place?"

"No, I'm at my house, alone. Why?"

"Just making sure that wasn't girlcode because he was standing right next to you."

"Things really are great. Better than great. It's been amazing with us."

"Then what did you need to talk to me about?" Marie Dawn asked.

"I need my best friend for more than relationship advice, you know."

"Like what?"

"Like fashion advice."

"You're the one who traveled the world and came home with that sense of simple European sophistication, *mon amie*."

"I did not," Allie protested, digging through her dresser drawer while holding her cell phone between her ear and shoulder. "I came back with oven burns and an overwhelming urge to kiss everyone's cheeks."

Marie Dawn sighed. "All you do is add one of those tissue-thin scarves to a wifebeater and jeans, and you look like a million dollars. It's so damn . . . French."

Allie laughed. "Okay, the scarf trick *is* French. But what I really need to know is what to wear to this barbeque."

"It's a barbeque. Wear your jeans and that scarf."

"But it's Father's Day and I haven't seen his family for years, other than you guys. Shouldn't I wear a dress or something?"

"Sure, a sundress, if you want. This is New Orleans, in case you've forgotten. It's going to be almost ninety and humid out there. My only advice would be to put your hair up."

Allie bit her lip, holding up a dusky pink cotton tank trimmed in lace. "Hmm . . . okay, I'll do that."

"So . . ." Marie Dawn started. "How are things with you two . . . you know . . . at the club?"

"We haven't been going. We've just kind of wanted to spend time reconnecting. We both feel the same way about it—like the club would almost be a distraction right now. We just want it to be about the two of us."

"That sounds really good. I'm happy for you, *chérie*."

Allie straightened up, smiling. "So am I."

"So you've put the kinky stuff on hold, then?"

She laughed. "You are so nosy! But no, we haven't put the kink on hold. We're just doing our thing at home. Technically. There was that one time in his truck . . . and maybe one time on a bench at Washington Square Park."

"Allie! You had sex at a *park*? Where there are kids?"

"It was right after sunset, and the park had emptied out because it started to rain. And we didn't have sex. He was just sort of . . . holding my hands behind my back and kissing me really hard and pulling my hair and . . . you really don't want to know any more than that."

"Oh, but I do. Brother-in-law or not." She paused for a moment. "You know, I've been thinking lately that Neal and I could spice things up a bit. I may need to come to you with some questions."

"Anytime. Except for at this Father's Day thing."

"Oh my God—can you imagine their mother overhearing a conversation like that?"

"Please. She'd die of shock."

Marie Dawn giggled.

"Promise me you'll behave," Allie demanded. "You've been part of the Reid family longer than I have."

"Longer than . . . ? Allie, are you guys planning on getting engaged or something?" Allie heard her take in a breath. "Did you get engaged and not tell me? Are you two going to announce it today?"

"What? No. Of course not."

"Why 'of course not'? You just said—"

"It was a slip of the tongue. We're not there yet, Marie Dawn. We haven't even been back together for two months yet. We haven't talked about anything that far in the future. If we had, you know you'd be the first person I called."

But they sort of had—they'd both used the word *forever*. Still, now that Marie Dawn had asked, Allie couldn't help but wonder if either of them truly had a grasp on what *forever* meant.

Part of her wanted it. That commitment. That promise of enduring love.

No. This is enough.

She and Marie Dawn hung up, agreeing to talk more later, and it came to Allie all at once that she'd been trying to allow it to be enough. But some part of her was left unsatisfied.

She hated to be such a girl. But when had she ever imagined walking down the aisle with anyone but Mick Reid?

She shook her head, slammed the dresser drawer shut. She was being ridiculous. She was happy with things as they were. *They* were happy. And did she really have any better grasp on *forever* than Mick did? Wasn't the idea of that what scared her?

Or maybe it was the idea of something as wonderful as the love they had for each other being taken away. It felt . . . inevitable.

Don't think about it.

She'd been pushing that thought to the back of her mind ever since they'd talked about love. But she couldn't help that it came creeping back in sometimes. Like after they'd made love staring into each other's eyes and it felt like a gift, and she'd have to swallow down her tears.

She'd gotten good at pretending, hadn't she? Pretending the fear wasn't always there, hovering. Waiting.

No.

She had to shake it off or the fear was going to ruin everything. It was the one thing she couldn't talk to Mick about. The one thing she had to keep locked away in a dark corner.

She opened the dresser drawer again and stuffed the tank top back in, going to the closet to distract herself more than anything, maybe. She finally decided on a long cotton-knit sundress in a modern print in shades of orange and brown. She grabbed her favorite flat brown leather sandals she'd bought in Barcelona years earlier, and added a pair of silver hoop earrings after putting her hair up, as Marie Dawn had suggested.

Looking at her reflection in the mirror she told herself not to be silly—his family had always liked her and there wouldn't be a problem. But the real problem was the nagging voice in the back of her mind that worried about this being one more step in a serious direction.

"What are you even thinking?" she asked her reflection aloud. "You're with the man you love, who loves you back."

She was too afraid to assure herself it wouldn't all disappear at some point, just dissolve like soap bubbles on the wind. *Because* she loved him. She didn't dare believe in it too much. It made her so sad—it hurt to the core—if she let herself dwell on that thought.

She squared her shoulders. "So I just won't."

But the mirror didn't lie. She could see for herself the haunted look in her eyes. She'd have to do better before she saw Mick.

*   *   *

MICK HELPED HER out of the truck in front of his parents' home, a perfectly kept two-story wood-sided colonial built in the 1930s.

"Ready to see everyone?" he asked, holding on to her elbow as they made their way up the front steps.

She turned to smile at him. "I can't wait."

It was true, even if her stomach had a few gently fluttering butterflies.

He opened the door, and Mick's father was on the other side, waiting for them.

Emmet Reid was nearly a carbon copy of Mick. He was almost as tall, with the same dark hair and gray eyes, the same hard, handsome features, if a bit more weathered. And the same air of command that had helped make him fire chief. Even after being retired for several years, he still carried himself with a natural air of authority. But his broad, warm smile was full of welcome as he pulled Allie in for a hug, and she found herself relaxing into his embrace.

"Allie, it's been too long since we've seen you, girl." He patted her back and pulled away to look at her. "I'd heard you'd grown into a fine-looking woman, but my oh my. No wonder Mick's so taken with you."

She glanced at Mick, who rolled his eyes, but he was grinning proudly.

"It's so good to see you," Allie said. It was. It was good to be back in their comfortably familiar house, with its broad wood floors and the familiar lemony scent of furniture polish.

"Hands off her, Dad. She's mine."

Emmet released her, gave Mick a hard clap on the shoulder and waved them through the living room. "Your mother's in the kitchen. Go say hello to her. Everyone else is out back. Which is where I should be, tending my grill. I have some gator sausage going that'll set your tongue on fire—so hot it'll take all my boys and me to put the flames out."

She caught Mick's silent wince. She knew he hated when his father in particular made reference to his other sons being firefighters. Not that Mick begrudged any of them. But she knew he still felt it like a stab to the chest that he hadn't been able to be a part of that noble family tradition.

They moved into the kitchen, where Mick's mother—still a beauty with a head of gorgeous dark curls even in her sixties—was spooning coleslaw from an enormous Tupperware container into a festive plastic bowl. She set it down and wiped her hands on her apron, coming around the counter to take Allie in her arms.

"Oh, honey, I'm so glad you're here. Thank you for joining us."

"Thank you so much for inviting me, Maureen."

"Of course." Mick's mother let her go and looked her over. "All grown up. I can remember you at sixteen like it was yesterday. How's your mother doing?"

"She's just fine. Still up at four a.m. every morning to bake, same as always."

"Good. That's good. Mick, you come give your mother a kiss."

He leaned down to place a kiss on her cheek.

"Has he been nice to you, Allie?"

"He has. You've trained him well."

"That's my boy," Maureen said, beaming. "Now, what can I get you to drink? Sweet tea? Lemonade?"

"A cold beer for us both, I think, Mom. Allie? Yes? I'll get it."

"I'd heard Allister did your kitchen remodel," Allie said as

Mick grabbed two bottles from the refrigerator. "It's gorgeous. He's started work on my place. I can't wait for the dust to settle, especially if it turns out anything like yours."

"Thank you, honey. I'm thrilled with it. And Mick told me about the work being done on your house. I'm awfully sorry about your aunt Joséphine, by the way. You weren't close with her, were you?"

"I don't think anyone was. I'm not even sure why she left the house to me. Maybe because I was the only relative left in the States, although she did have some family in France."

Maureen took her hand and looked her in the eye. "Some things are just meant to be."

She resisted the urge to pull away and smiled instead. "Yes, I guess they are."

"You two go on out back and see the rest of the family. Allie, you haven't even met my grandson, have you?"

"I haven't."

Mick reached into the bowl and pulled out a piece of cabbage, stuffed it into his mouth. Maureen gave his hand a slap. "Go on, now. I've got work to do in here."

"Can I help with anything?" Allie asked.

"Don't be silly—you know I have control issues when it comes to my kitchen. You go visit. Enjoy yourself. I'll be out in a bit."

"Come on."

Mick took her hand and led her through the pantry and out the back door that led to the screened-in deck. She smelled the sausage and shrimp cooking on the grill right away, mixed with the summer scent of the sun hitting the green leaves of the big lacebark elm that grew in the Reids' yard. Marie Dawn was next to her in a moment, pulling her away from Mick to greet his brothers. Gareth and Nolan both looked a bit more like their mother's side of the family, with rounder features and her blue eyes. They introduced her to Nolan's fiancée, Katie, and Gareth's wife, Leanne. Their teenage son, Colby, was throwing a Frisbee on the grass for Emmet and Maureen's old yellow lab, Scratch, who had been a puppy the last time she'd seen him.

She felt that sense of family right down to her bones—the bond they all shared. It was one of the things she and Mick had in common. Except that he always held a part of himself at a distance from the people she knew wanted to love him, to take him in and accept him completely. She could almost sense his walls coming up the moment they'd walked in the door.

Did he live with that pressure constantly? Carry it nearly every day of his life?

"Come and talk wedding stuff with Katie," Marie Dawn said, pulling Allie out of her musing to sit with the Reid family's newest member-to-be. Katie was a lovely young woman, sweet and friendly, and it was easy for Allie to lose herself in discussions about wedding cakes and flowers.

By the time the food was ready, she was much more relaxed, remembering what it felt like to be at home in this house as if by muscle memory. Everyone ate at long wooden trestle tables set up in the yard under a tent of mosquito netting. There was a veritable feast: the promised barbequed shrimp and spicy alligator sausage, Maureen's coleslaw and cornbread and icy lemonade, red beans and rice, and pecan pie for dessert. Allie ate until she couldn't move, and everyone but Colby stayed at the table for hours, telling all the old stories about New Orleans's great fires and the Reid men being there to battle the flames. Gareth was cajoled into showing off his scar from a bad warehouse fire that had almost gotten him killed saving a fellow firefighter from a back draft, and all of Emmet's sons talked with pride about their father having served the city for almost forty years.

Everyone except Mick.

He sat beside Allie like stone. He tried to smile, to nod his head, but the fact that he couldn't be an integral part of the conversation was killing him, she knew. The family didn't do it on purpose, of course, and she understood there was no way they could have ignored Emmet, Gareth, Nolan and Neal's accomplished careers in the department. But for the first time she came to understand how it must grate on Mick's nerves, like drilling on a bad tooth, every time the family got together. She hurt for him.

"Mick," Maureen started, turning to him, "tell us about the time you saved that young girl from being trampled to death at that concert." She glanced at Allie, pride and something else in her blue eyes. "He was bruised all over by the time he got her out, but there wasn't a scratch on the girl. Her parents sent him so many thank-you cards you'd think they bought stock in the company."

"No, Mom. It's Dad's day."

"Ah, come on, Mick," Neal urged, jostling his shoulder. "It was pretty damn heroic."

Mick just shook his head and raised the bottle of beer he'd been nursing all day. "To Dad. Happy Father's Day, chief."

"To Dad," the entire family echoed.

There was much clinking of bottles and plastic cups, then everyone fell into different conversations, including Mick and Neal. But Allie was acutely aware of what that bad moment had cost him.

Eventually the party broke up and they said their good-byes, Maureen making Allie promise she'd come by the house again, and Katie having gotten Allie's number to talk more about making her wedding cake.

Mick was quiet on the drive back to his place. Or, she'd

thought they were heading to his place, but he took a turn that led into her neighborhood.

"Where are we going?" she asked.

"I'm taking you home."

"But . . ." She paused, chewing on her lip for a moment. "Mick? Do we ever see each other and not spend the night if you're not going out of town?"

He kept his eyes on the road. "I guess not."

"So, this is different because . . . ?"

When he didn't answer she looked out the window, waiting. He was quiet as they passed a row of houses laced with scaffolding, another row of homes that had been newly rebuilt. There were shops on the next block, one a produce market with stands on the sidewalk, stacked high with melons and cabbage and beans, oranges and peppers in every imaginable color. She was glad to see the city had gained so much of its old vibrancy.

She wondered if Mick ever would.

When they got to her place, he parked and sat staring out the front windshield.

"Are you coming in, at least?" she asked.

"I'd rather you not see this."

"See what, Mick?"

She laid a hand on his arm but felt him stiffen under her touch.

He shook his head.

She waited.

After a few moments she said quietly, "You know, I'm not getting out of this truck until you give me some sort of answer."

"I kind of figured you wouldn't, you being you."

"What does that mean?"

"You're stubborn as hell, Allie."

"I thought you liked that about me."

"Maybe a little less right now."

That stung.

"Fuck you, Mick," she said quietly.

He whipped his head around. "What did you say?" His eyes were blazing.

"You heard me." Anger was hot in her veins suddenly, burning her up inside. "You and your surly attitude. I used to think it was sexy. Damn it, maybe I still do. But I don't like it one bit when it's turned on me. When it's turned on *us*. I get it. I have some family issues, too, you know, but maybe you're too caught up in your own shit to notice. So go on. You do whatever you need to do about your issues—indulge in your juvenile desire to get your face bashed in or whatever the hell helps you get it out of your system—but don't take it out on me." Her hands fisted at her sides. "Don't you do it, Mick."

He looked stunned. Then his tight features relaxed, his mouth going wide until there was nothing short of a grin there.

"Are you laughing at me?" she asked in shock.

"Maybe I'm laughing at me. But Lord, were you mad."

"Maybe I still am," she said, not entirely certain herself.

He watched her for several long moments, then he launched himself at her.

It wouldn't have been possible had his truck been any smaller, but in seconds he was on top of her, having pushed her down on the seat, and he was kissing her hard, one hand fisted in her hair, holding on tight.

She tried to push him off her, but she may as well have been shoving at a brick wall. He kissed her harder, his tongue pushing its way into her mouth, and he tasted of beer and spices and only a little of quickly recovering ego.

*   *   *

MICK PULLED BACK, watching her. He'd felt her surrender, had forced past her stubbornness and her anger to get there. But she was still pissed, he could tell from the way her fingers dug into his shoulders, still pretending to push him away.

"You angry with me, baby?"

"Yes."

"You're damn pretty when you're mad."

"Didn't we talk about condescension being a hard limit?" she asked, only partly fake fuming.

"We did not."

"We should have," she muttered.

He grabbed her and pulled her closer, heard her small gasp as he lifted her hand and bit into her palm.

"We can have that talk in bed. While I'm fucking you into a better mood."

"My mood was just fine! Yours is the one that sucked."

"I never specified whose mood we'd be improving."

"But . . ." she sputtered. "Whatever."

"Whatever what?" he demanded.

"Whatever . . . Sir?" She rolled her eyes, but there was a small grin on her face.

"Ah, that's my girl. Come on."

He got out and pulled her, sliding her across the seat and out his side of the truck. He took her hand and hurried up the walk, took her keys from her and opened the door, slamming it shut behind them. He led her into the kitchen.

"You. Here," he ordered, yanking her in hard, until he could feel every soft female curve pressed up against him. His cock went rock-hard.

She was a little breathless already. She licked her lips. He leaned in and bit them—he couldn't resist.

"Mmm."

She smelled so damn good—he could smell the sun on her skin, in her hair. He reached behind her and pulled out the clip, and she shook her long tresses free. He buried his face in her hair, inhaled. Dug his fingers in and pulled tight.

He whispered in her ear, "I'm going to fuck you over the kitchen table, princess. Take your panties off."

He let her go and she took one step back, lifted her dress to reach under it, bent and came back up with a small handful of pink lace. He took them from her and tossed them on the floor before turning her roughly and bending her over the edge of the small, round table, using a hand to press her down onto the wood surface until her cheek laid there.

"Mick . . ."

"Shh."

He flipped the hem of her dress up, baring her perfectly rounded ass, pulled open the buttoned fly of his cargo pants and pulled his cock out. Christ, he was so hard it hurt. Had to be inside her.

"Spread," he told her, and she complied.

He reached under her, found her pussy already wet.

"Have to just fuck you, baby." He guided his cock to her opening, rammed inside her all at once. "Fuck, yeah . . ."

"Oh!"

He pulled back, thrust hard again, needing it to be hard and fast and merciless for reasons he didn't understand. He took one of her arms and twisted it behind her back, held it there as he plunged into her over and over.

Pleasure was like a hammer, pounding into him. She was moaning, crying out, and he felt her sex tighten around him.

He reached around her and found the tight nub of her clit. He tugged on it, pinched, twisted the tender flesh between his fingers as he rammed into her.

"God, Mick!"

She came, her sweet pussy clenching around him, then drenching him with her pleasure. It was too much for him. He came in a torrent of fiery sensation, fucking her harder and harder, pleasure and heat blinding him as he shivered inside her.

"Baby, baby, baby . . ."

He could barely breathe. He'd barely stopped coming and he needed her again already.

He slipped out of her, turning her and pulling her into his arms. Hers went around his neck.

"You okay?" she asked.

"What? I'm so good, baby girl."

And it was true. Partly. The other part he'd either ignore until it went away, or he'd just keep fucking Allie until it disappeared. It was either that or go fight. He had to admit the fucking was better.

She stood on her toes and kissed his neck.

"Come on," he said. "I'm going to need you again in about five minutes."

She stepped back, kicked her way out of her sandals and pulled her dress over her head. Her eyes were a smoldering gold. "Ready when you are."

She offered her hand to him and he took it, let her take him to her bedroom, where he got out of his clothes and pushed her down on the bed.

"Hands and knees," he told her.

He wasn't even certain himself why he was being so curt with her. But she wasn't fighting it, didn't seem to mind. But when he came up behind her and started to wrap his T-shirt around her eyes, she pushed it away. "Hard limit, Mick," she reminded him. "I just can't."

"No problem, baby."

He dropped the shirt and reached under her, sliding his hands over her breasts and playing with her nipples. They went hard immediately.

"Does that feel good, Allie girl?"

"I like it."

"But . . . ?"

"But I need you to pinch them."

"Like this?" He twisted the stiffening flesh between thumb and forefinger. She groaned. "I take that as a yes?"

"Mmm, yes . . ."

Hearing her moans, feeling her heat up beneath him, was making him hard again. He felt the desire like a pressure inside his body, his balls, his cock.

"Gotta fuck you again," he said, as much to himself as to her.

He arched his hips until his cock pressed against her sex. She was wet, the lips slick and swollen.

He let the tip slide there, back and forth in the liquid heat of her body, before he pushed inside.

Yes, this was what he needed. To lose himself in her. In pure, mindless pleasure. In the primal nature of fucking.

He plunged into her over and over, his grip on her lush body tightening, his fingers digging into her hips. But it wasn't about giving her pain. It wasn't about kink at all. Maybe it wasn't even about sex. It was more about forgetting.

He came, his body shaking, and collapsed on top of her. It was a long while before he caught his breath and realized he was probably crushing her.

"Fuck. Sorry, babe."

He rolled off her and she turned onto her side, looking at him. She laid her hand on his chest.

"You okay?" she asked again.

"Fine. You keep asking me that."

"I'm just . . ." She paused, bit her lip. "Checking."

He wasn't quite fine. Not yet. But he would be. There was just something about seeing his family—seeing them with Allie at his side—that made things more painfully clear. But he couldn't think about it now. He didn't want to.

Some things were just too dark and ugly to look at in the light of a Sunday afternoon.

H E WOKE AT six a.m., the morning gray and overcast. Allie was asleep beside him, unmoving except for the gentle rise and fall of her breasts. He'd kept her up late, had gone out to his truck to get his rope bag at one point and tied her up, practicing some complicated knots on her. This morning he had to admit it had been mostly so they didn't have to talk more than it was the pure pleasure of the rope work—either hers or his own.

He hated himself a little for that.

Flash of that cold morning when he'd gotten up and left her sleeping all those years ago. His heart in his throat as he looked at her one last time, so fucking beautiful, her head pillowed on one arm, eyes closed, long lashes against her cheeks. That tearing sensation as he left her behind. The churning in his gut for days after. The bottle of Scotch he'd finished that night while he'd justified his actions to himself over and over.

He wasn't good enough for her.

Never had been. Allie was a good girl. What the hell had he done?

He'd hated himself then, too.

"Fuck," he muttered, sitting up in the bed and running his hands over his head, rubbing the grit out of his eyes. "This is different."

But was it, ultimately?

He felt twitchy, and he hated feeling twitchy. It only meant one thing.

He got up and found his clothes and came back to the bedroom, intending to tell her he was leaving. But she looked too peaceful to wake—that was what he was telling himself, anyway—one arm thrown over her eyes, her hair spread out on the pillows. He watched her sleeping for several minutes before he turned to leave.

New Orleans was quiet this early on a Monday morning. The quiet was giving him far too much time to think. About everything he could have—should have—been. And he didn't want to go there. But it was too late, wasn't it?

His head was pounding, his heart racing, as he turned on some music, loud, head-banging metal, and let it drown out his thoughts as he drove the all-too-familiar route to the club on the Pontchartrain Expressway. He parked and jumped out. The warehouse doors were closed. He pulled and found them locked.

"What the fuck?"

There was always someone at the club. Unless it had been raided over the weekend and he hadn't heard about it.

He kicked the door with his boot. It hurt, the pain reverberating up his leg, but he did it again, anyway.

"God fucking damn it."

He needed the club right now. Needed to fight.

He jumped in his truck and gunned the engine, heading for his gym instead.

It didn't take him long to get there, only minutes to change. The place was mostly empty this early in the morning. The before-work crowd would arrive any time, though. He found Antoine on his back, bench pressing as he came out of the locker room.

"Spar?" he asked him without preamble.

Antoine set the bar back on the stand with a puff of breath. "Sure. You want to warm up first?"

"Not really, but I will," he muttered, ignoring Antoine's curious stare.

He did a quick tape job on his hands and worked the speed bag first, really laying into it, working up a quick sweat. It felt good, that burn in his muscles, the impact of the bag against his knuckles. But he needed a challenge. He went to find Antoine, who was still working out with the weights.

"I'm ready," he said.

Antoine looked up, set the heavy dumbbells down. "Okay. Let's go."

They ducked under the ropes and stepped into the ring. Antoine started to move right away—he was always good with the footwork. But Mick felt his brain settle into laser-focus. He threw the first punch, but Antoine ducked. And it pissed him off.

He went after him, managed to land a fist on his chest, a kick to the thigh, then another punch to the body.

"Hey! What the hell is up with you, man?" Antoine yelled.

But he didn't stop. He couldn't. His bad leg ached. It only made frustration boil through him. Made him think the words that had haunted him most of his life.

Failure.

He remembered in a flash the doctor coming in after his leg surgery, telling him he'd never be able to pass the physical required to be a firefighter. He remembered the look on his

father's face, the shock and dismay he'd tried to hide. But Mick
had seen it. Had felt it every damn day since.

Fuckup.

He remembered all the times he'd come home after curfew.
Cut school. Hurt Allie. Hurt his family. Hurt his own chance
at the life he *should* have fucking had.

Antoine fought back, finally taking Mick down to the mat
with a roundhouse. He held him down.

"What the *fuck*, Mick? You gone crazy?"

He was breathing hard, his airway partially constricted by
Antoine's elbow across his throat. "Let me up."

"Not until you explain yourself."

"I can't."

Antoine was silent for several moments before shoving
himself off him. He stood up. "You need to figure your shit out,
man. Go take a sauna or something."

Mick glared at him.

Antoine crossed his arms. "You wanna tell me what you're
trying to prove? Fucking coming after me in a spar, man. If I
didn't know you, I'd think you had some kind of death wish."

Hadn't he thought the same thing not that long ago? Mick
sat up, then got to his feet. "Nothing. It's nothing." He wiped
the sweat from his face with the back of one arm. "Sorry I'm
being an asshole. Rough morning."

"Yeah, well go spread that sunshine somewhere else. I don't
need it." Antoine shook his head and walked away, leaving Mick
in the middle of the ring, anger still bubbling like some black
cauldron in his belly.

He needed to fight. But the fight he needed wasn't with Antoine.

He left the ring, left the gym, driving home too fast in the
morning traffic.

What he needed was dirty and rough and illegal. He'd make some calls until he found it.

ALLIE WOKE ALONE. She knew even before getting out of bed that her house was empty, Mick gone, and it weighed on her heart. It wasn't like him to leave without saying good-bye.

She got up and checked her phone. Nothing.

He'd been so weird the night before. Even the sex had been weird. Strained. Desperate. But she'd had some sense of giving him something he needed. She'd thought it would be enough.

Her body was sore from the workout he'd given her. It would have felt good if she didn't feel this sense of dread. She got in the shower, blasting the hot water to ease some of the aches, trying to figure out what to do as she washed her hair.

Should she try to call him? Or give him the space that men sometimes needed to clear their heads?

It was obvious he didn't want to discuss how the conversation at his parents' house had left him feeling. She understood it—as much as she could, anyway. She tried. But his family obviously adored him—they certainly didn't find him lacking, didn't treat him any differently. He did it all to himself. Didn't he have to find some way to deal with it eventually? That's what she didn't quite get. Didn't he want to?

If only he would let her help him.

She shut off the water, stepped out to dry herself and saw her bruises in the mirror—the marks on her thighs and arms and breasts from the ropes. They hadn't even done any heavy impact play, but he'd used a lot of knots—that was what had marked her. That and his teeth in a few places. Normally she would have gloried in her marks, but this morning she knew they'd come from a place of desperation and pain, and it only made her chest go tight with concern for him. And a little impatience.

Where the hell was he?

She wrapped her hair in a towel and herself in her robe and went into the living room to boot up her laptop and check her email. Sure enough, there was one from Mick.

Allie,

Sorry about my early departure—I woke up and found a message on my phone from one of my clients. I didn't want to wake you. I'll be tied up with this job all day. Talk to you later, babe.

Mick

Babe. That's what he called her when he needed to distance himself. Not *baby*, like he usually did. Not *princess*. Not that she needed to see that to know. He'd called her *babe* last night. Had had sex with her only from behind. Had hardly looked into her eyes since they'd left his parents' place.

She'd felt his emotions, even though he'd tried to hide them from her. She *knew* him, and she'd felt it bone deep. And she understood with just as much clarity now that the email was a lie. There was no client. No message. No job. Only his anger and the guilt that had been eating him up for most of his adult life.

And there was nothing she could do.

She'd be thoroughly pissed if she didn't get how much he was hurting. It made *her* hurt.

Tears welled in her eyes. She wiped them away, frustrated. Mick was just going to have to work through this himself. There wasn't a damn thing she could do for him. Because he wouldn't let her. She'd have to wait and see if what they had together was reason enough for him to do what he hadn't done in years. Move on.

IT WAS ALMOST ten that night when her cell phone rang. She looked at the caller ID before answering.

"Hi, Jamie."

She wasn't in the mood to chat—it had been one of those endless, dragging days while she pretended her feelings weren't hurt, pretended she hadn't been practically sitting on top of her phone—but maybe he'd talked to Mick.

"Allie, Mick's hurt."

"Well just launch right into your agenda without even saying hello, why don't you? And he's the one who left this morning without saying a word to me."

"No. *Hurt*, Allie. He's in the emergency room."

"What?" Shock coursed through her, then panic. "Tell me."

"He took a pretty hard hit to the head. Lost consciousness for at least a few minutes, apparently. Someone dropped him off here—I don't even know who. The hospital called me—I'm in his cell phone as his emergency contact."

"Oh my God. How bad is it?"

"He's having a CT scan now. But he was awake. Alert enough that he made me promise not to call you."

"He asked you *not* to call me? Did he think I wouldn't find out? Jesus." She pushed her hair out of her face, blew out a breath. "Okay. Okay. I appreciate you calling. Thank you, Jamie."

"Of course. I thought you should know."

"I'll be there as soon as I can."

"I don't think you need to come down here. Mick said—"

"Are you kidding? I'm coming!"

She hung up before he could argue any further. She didn't care what Mick had told him. They didn't even know how bad it was, and wouldn't until they got the scan results. She wasn't going to just sit at home waiting for the bad news.

She slid into a pair of sandals, remembered to grab a sweater along with her purse and headed out the door.

WHY WERE HOSPITALS always so white?

She hadn't had the need to walk into a hospital too many times in her life—once as a kid when she'd sprained her ankle falling off her bike, again in Paris when she'd burned her hand on an oven, the last time to visit a friend who'd been in a mountain bike accident. And of course in high school they had all rushed to the hospital the night Brandon died, everyone huddled together in these same sterile, garishly lit hallways. She got the chills just thinking about that awful night.

But this was where Mick was, and she *had* to see him. See if he was okay. She didn't think she could stand it if he wasn't.

Her jaw clenched as she walked into the emergency room and up to the desk.

"I'm here to see Mick Reid. He was brought in tonight."

"Are you his wife?" the woman at the desk asked.

"I'm his . . ." But what was she? "Are you going to let me in if I'm not?"

"I'll have to check."

She blew out a breath. If he hadn't wanted Jamie to call, he certainly wasn't going to invite her back there to see him.

She leaned over the desk and said quietly, "Look. Mick is my boyfriend, for lack of a more grown-up term. He's been injured. I need to see him. Please. Or find our friend—he called me to come down here." A small lie, but she didn't care.

The woman was quiet for a moment. Then she said, "Okay. You can go back. He's in . . ." She tapped a few keys on her computer. "He's in number four."

"Thank you."

She gripped her sweater in her hands as she moved through the heavy automatic doors.

She passed an open curtain, caught a glimpse of an empty gurney. Her stomach knotted.

Papa being taken away on the big metal bed, his face covered. Why did they have to cover his face? He couldn't breathe right if they covered his face.

Except he hadn't needed to breathe.

Her heart hammered, a fast, staccato beat. She walked faster, found curtain number four. She took a breath, pulled it aside and stepped through.

Mick lay on the hospital bed, his eyes closed, his face white as a sheet except for the dark bruise forming on his temple.

God, please no . . .

Papa being loaded onto the white bed on wheels, his head bruised where it must have hit the piano when he'd . . .

Mick opened his eyes.

"Allie? What are you doing here?"

She shook her head, unable to speak as fear and love and anger suffused her, forming a cold, nearly incomprehensible ball of emotion.

"What am I doing here? What are *you* doing here?"

"I guess . . . you can probably guess."

"How badly are you hurt?" she asked.

"It's just an MTBI."

"A what?"

"A concussion. The scan looked fine. No blood clots or anything. I'll be fine. It's fine."

"Jesus, Mick. This is not fine! What happened?"

"Someone got the better of me. I was . . . distracted. It's bound to happen once in a while."

"This happened because you were fighting. On purpose."

He didn't even have the decency to look ashamed. The anger boiled over.

"It's only bound to happen when you put yourself in stupid situations. *Illegal* fights. Come on, Mick—this isn't *Fight Club*."

He blinked, seemed to be thinking for several moments. "Except that it is. That's why I do it. It's what I need."

"*That's* what you need?" she demanded. "What about me, Mick? What about what I need, huh? How about I need a man who doesn't think punching something or getting the shit kicked out of him is the way to solve a problem? A man who doesn't *lie to me* and push me away after showing me how amazing we could be together? A man who isn't going to *die* on me."

Tears made her throat tight. She used the rage simmering in her system to swallow them down.

"Seriously, Allie? I'm not going to—"

"You might! You're the one determined to keep punishing yourself for every kitten you didn't rescue from a tree instead of seeing what you have right in front of you. You're the one fighting without gloves, without rules, without letting anyone know where you are in case something happens to you, for God's sake. How fucking stupid do you have to be?"

His face went even paler, his lips tightening into a thin line, and she knew instantly she'd said the absolutely wrong thing. But she couldn't stop now.

"Mick . . ." The damn tears again. She blinked hard, but they welled in her eyes. "I can't watch you do this to yourself. I can't watch you do this to me. If something happened to you . . . and it will if you won't stop doing this."

"You don't understand."

"You're right. I don't. I'm never going to. You could have *died*, Mick. Just like my dad."

"Allie. Baby. He died of an aneurism."

"So could you if you keep taking hits to the head. There were no blood clots this time, but what about the next time? Or the time after that?"

"Come on, Allie. That's not going to happen. We can talk about this when I get out of here."

She stared at him, her vision being swallowed up by the bruise. By the cold expanding in her chest.

"We could talk about it—the fighting, the emotional masochism—but you'd have to actually want to listen." She shook her head again, taking a step back. "I can't. I can't do this, Mick. I just . . . can't."

She turned and hurried away, pushed her way through the big doors—and ran into Jamie. The paper cup of coffee he'd been carrying splashed to the floor.

"Fuck. Jamie, I'm sorry."

"Where are you going? You okay?"

"No. I'm not okay. I have to go."

"Allie, wait."

But she was already moving past him, walking as fast as she dared until she got out to the parking lot. She ran the rest of the way to her car, dug in her purse for her keys.

"Come on, damn it," she muttered.

She finally found them, unlocked the car, yanked open the door and got in. She started the engine and put it in reverse just as a sob surged into her throat, choking her on its way out.

She clamped a hand over her mouth, but another one came, then another. Blindly, she put the car back into park, leaned her head on the wheel and gave herself over to the tears.

There was no conscious thought in her mind as she cried—just emotions too big to name. Too long held to make sense any longer. Tears she'd been holding since she was ten years old. Since she was sixteen. Since she was twenty. All the old pain, the tears she'd refused to cry since then, thinking she'd just get over it—all the events that had left her feeling devastated. But she never had. She never had.

She knew she never could if something happened to Mick. Better to stay away from him, the way she had for most of her life. If he wasn't right in front of her, he couldn't hurt her. If she didn't love him . . .

Except she did.

God, she loved him.

Another sob broke through but she caught it halfway, swallowed it down, the hard edge of the steering wheel digging into her hands.

"No. No more."

She pulled in a deep breath, blew it out. Shifted the car and drove away, hoping to leave some of the pain behind in the white, white hospital that spoke to her of death.

"Jamie, what the fuck?"

Mick was trying to sit up, but his friend held him down on the bed.

"You have to stay put until they release you."

"The fuck I do! You're as bad as Allie."

"What did you say to her? She ran out of here like a bat out of hell."

"I didn't say anything. She just freaked out."

And told me I was stupid. And a masochist.

Apparently I fucking am.

He stopped struggling. Jamie backed off.

"Whatever's going on with you two, you need to sit tight for a while," Jamie told him.

Mick put a hand to his head, winced when his fingers smoothed over the bruise there. "Yeah, fine. Maybe I don't need to talk to her right now, anyway."

"That sounds cryptic."

"Don't want to talk about it," he muttered.

"You have a head injury so I'll ignore that grumpy-ass tone."

"Go ask the nurse when they're letting me the hell out of here, will you?"

"Yeah, okay. Don't go anywhere or I'll hunt you down, Reid."

"I won't. Just go find out."

His head was pounding. From the knockout. From the hard lump in his gut that told him what Allie really thought about him. Hell, he should have suspected. It was what he'd always thought himself. But to have to hear it from the woman he loved . . .

Maybe he'd been right all along. They should never be together. He was poison to her—that had been obvious tonight. He'd never forget the look of misery and pure terror on her face. His damn fault. And still he'd argued with her like an ass.

But he couldn't give up the fighting.

The fighting? Or the rest?

Fuck, his head was spinning, his stomach churning.

He closed his eyes and leaned back on the pillows.

He'd have to let Allie go. Again.

For the last time.

CHAPTER

Fifteen

MICK WOKE AT six out of habit, his limbs itching to go for a run, but the ER doctor—and Jamie—had made him promise he wouldn't work out for a week. It had only been five days. Maybe he could push things a little?

He felt okay. The bruise was already clearing up, and he hadn't had any nausea or dizziness since that first night. Physically, he was fine. The rest of him was pretty well fucked up.

He got out of bed and pulled on a pair of sweats and a tank top.

"Fuck it," he muttered as he put on his running shoes. He was going to lose his shit if he had to hold still any longer.

The sky was dark and heavy with clouds when he stepped outside, and he could feel the damp air cool on his skin. Didn't matter. He'd warm up fast enough.

He did a few quick leg stretches on the sidewalk in front of his house, then he took off at a slow jog to get his muscles warmed up.

He went down Dauphine to Canal Street, turned toward the water and let himself speed up, his legs and his lungs pumping. It felt good, even if the bad leg hurt. He didn't care. It was good to be *out*, to be moving.

The last few days had been pure torture—constant thoughts of Allie with not enough to distract him, going back and forth with himself about whether to call her or to stay away. He had a great argument for keeping his distance. Logical reasons. But emotion was telling him something else.

He loved the girl.

There was no getting around it. And she loved him back. Despite her walking away from him at the hospital, despite their history. Despite everything. And maybe—just maybe—there was something to it, some reason.

She was scared, which he understood when he could get out of his own head long enough to let his own shit go—all the shit that had been holding him back his entire life. The shit that had been stirred up once more by the angry words she'd hurled at him in the emergency room. He'd let it get to him, he realized now, in a way that was . . . every bit as stupid as she'd accused him of being.

And he was if he couldn't give up the Goddamn fighting to be with her. She was worth it. If he could have Allie, why would he need it anymore? What did he even have to be so pissed off about? Hell, weren't there other reasons why he shouldn't need to fight anymore? Wasn't he stronger than that? Better than that?

It was time to fucking get over himself.

Heat flooded his body, a kind of release as years of tension and stubbornness drained from him.

Amazing what a good knock on the head could shake loose. That and the love of the most incredible woman he'd ever met.

He really was stubborn to have hung on to this image of himself all these years—even now, knowing she loved him. Was he really so in love with the idea of him being the bad seed that he hadn't been able to let it go? Had he really been so damn stuck in that awful place inside his head where all the good things he'd done with his life counted for nothing?

His legs pumped, taking him down one block, then the next, past houses and stores, bars and restaurants, all of it a blur.

He'd been standing in his own way for most of his damn life. He hadn't been able to stop until she'd come back into his life and made him feel worthwhile again.

They'd wasted so many years . . . *he'd* wasted so many years.

He had to tell Allie. *Had* to. He had to tell her what he'd just figured out. And he had to get her back.

"Fuck," he puffed out, increasing his stride until he reached Magazine Street and made the turn to head toward Allie's neighborhood just as the sky opened up and it started to rain, a light spring shower that felt good on his heated skin.

She made him feel amazing. No more letting this twisted shit inside his head talk him out of that. With her, he could believe it. Now it was time to learn to believe it on his own. Because if he didn't, then he really didn't deserve her.

He did, damn it. He was going to make her see that.

He concentrated on keeping his legs moving, breathing in, breathing out, until he turned the corner at Orange Street and ran toward her house.

The sun was beginning to break through the rain, lighting up the sky in shades of pale silver, bathing the old cottage in a watercolor wash. He had to stop on the sidewalk, bent over, hands braced on his knees while he tried to catch his breath.

The leg throbbed, but he didn't care. Allie was the only thing that mattered now.

He straightened up and went to her door.

ALLIE SKIPPED TOWARD *the French doors that led into her father's study.*

"Papa! I have to go to school soon. Play something for me."

She stopped in her tracks when she saw him. So still. Slumped over the piano keys.

"Papa? What are you doing? Does your head hurt?"

The house was more silent than she'd ever heard it. She knew something was terribly, terribly wrong.

"Papa, why won't you answer me?"

She stepped closer, put a hand on his arm, running her fingers over the crisp blue cotton of his shirt.

"Papa?" she whispered, her heart twisting in her chest.

She took a step back, terrified. Guilty for being scared of her own papa. Tears slipped down her cheek.

She woke to a loud pounding, clutching the sheet—and wiped the tears away.

The pounding continued.

She glanced at the clock. It wasn't even quite seven—who would be there so early? Allister wasn't due to work on the kitchen until Monday.

She got up and padded barefoot down the hall in her pink cotton nightgown as the pounding came again, more insistent this time.

"Okay, I'm coming!"

She unlocked the door and pulled it open. And froze when she saw Mick standing on her porch.

His hair and his skin were wet, and it was only then she realized it was raining. He was panting hard, his expression grim.

He was so damn beautiful it made her heart ache.

"Allie, you're crying."

"What?" She swiped at her eyes with the back of her hand. "It was . . . just a bad dream."

The same one she'd had every night since she'd last seen Mick.

"I had to come," he said.

"Why?" She couldn't think of anything else to say, her brain still half asleep yet churning a hundred miles an hour.

"Come on, baby. We have a lot to talk about."

She bit her lip, trying to stay strong in her resolve even though every cell in her body wanted nothing more than to reach out for him. To feel the texture of his skin. The crush of his arms around her.

No.

"Can I at least have some water before you decide you won't talk to me? I ran all the way here from my place. I'm a little dehydrated even with the rain."

"Oh. I . . . yes, come on in, I guess."

She turned and walked into the kitchen without looking at him, her pulse racing. She needed a moment to gather herself. She pulled a bottle of water from the refrigerator and took a breath before turning to hand it to him, along with a dish towel.

"Thanks."

He popped open the bottle and drank, ran the towel over his face, his hair.

He seemed to fill up her small kitchen, and it was as much his presence as his height, his broad, muscular shoulders. His skin was slick with sweat and the New Orleans rain. There was rain caught on the tips of his dark lashes.

He wiped his mouth, looked at her. And as was his habit, it seemed as if he could see right through her. How the hell did he do that?

She put a hand on the back of a kitchen chair to steady herself. "So," she started, looking at the floor. Anything to avoid that searching gray gaze. "What is it you think we have to say to each other?"

She looked up then, feeling the challenge of her own words.

"Plenty. At least, I have plenty to tell you. I need you to hear me out, Allie."

"I—"

"Just do it," he interrupted, his voice low. "Give me five minutes. If I can't convince you I have a point, you're free to ask me to go. And if you do, I won't bother you ever again."

There was an edge of command in his voice. And pain. That much was plain to see.

She chewed on her lip. This felt dangerous. *Mick* was dangerous. She'd always known that. But hadn't that always been part of the allure? That and his purely masculine face, the features a little raw, yet beautiful to her all the same.

So beautiful his face alone broke her heart.

Stop it.

"Allie? Come on. Hear me out."

She nodded and sat down slowly in the chair. Mick stayed on his feet.

"Okay." He ran a hand over his damp hair. "I'm sorry. For every rotten asshole thing I've ever done to you. For every stupid thing I've done—and you were right back in the ER—I've been an idiot. I was punishing myself. I think you already know that much. You said as much."

"Yes," she said quietly, her hands twisting in her lap. This was exactly what she wanted to hear from him. And everything she didn't dare believe. "I think it's what you've always done. You told me you'd stopped running, but that's not true. It's as if it's almost habit for you. You create this self-fulfilling prophecy, Mick. Which one of us did you think you were punishing? Because frankly, I'm tired of it being me. And I don't know why I convinced myself that it had just gone away. That's what's kept me in this with you, but I don't have any reason to exist on blind faith anymore. There's just been . . . too much has happened. I can't take any more apologies. I can't take any more worry that something horrible will happen to you because you invited it to."

God, it hurt her to say it.

"I understand you feeling that way. I do. I'm not going to argue a single point. But we've *built* something together, Allie. Something important. And I refuse to walk away from it."

"You don't have to add yet another thing for you to feel responsible for destroying, Mick. You don't have to walk away, because I already did. I did it because I had to. Why can't you understand?"

"Because my life without you in it doesn't make any sense. It never has. Don't you see? It's always been *us*. Mick and Allie. No matter how many years we spent apart. The ones who have to end up together if life is fair. Hell, even if it's not. You were right about that, Allie."

When all she could do was blink at him, he went on. "We were meant to be together. We both know it. You always have. I ran from it for years because I didn't think I was good enough for you. I covered that up in excuses about you being so pure— and I don't mean this as any kind of insult, but I knew damn well you weren't some innocent virgin. I recognized your desires back when we were in high school, when you *were* a virgin. I saw a little of the darkness in you and I blamed myself for it. And the kink . . . back then I thought there was something wrong with me. But even now, knowing what I know about kink, what I know about you, the kink seems more pure for you."

He started to pace then. She still had no idea what to say or where he was going with all this. All she knew was the staggering pain she felt at seeing him there, hearing that raw edge to his voice. But she didn't know what she could trust in.

We were meant to be together.

Wasn't that what she'd always believed?

He stopped and stared at her for several long moments.

"Are you letting me stay?" he asked.

"Yes," she said. "You have my attention."

He leaned against the counter behind him. "It's all fucked up, and I'm just now getting it. What played into the way I viewed myself, and the way I viewed you through those lenses that saw me as . . . defective." She saw his hands clench into fists at his sides. "It wasn't about you at all. Except for the part where I love you. I always have. I always will. That much was true from the start." His tone lowered, his brows drawing together. "Do you love me at all, Allie girl?"

Her breath caught on a strangled sob. "Of course I do!"

He was at her side in an instant, but when he tried to take her in his arms, she pushed him away.

"Mick, I don't know how to feel right now. So, you've had this epiphany. Now what?"

"Now I stop the fighting—the kind that's anything more than a workout. The kind that comes from anger and frustration. The kind with that edge of *need* that bites into me. I don't need it anymore. I thought I did. But Allie, if I have you . . ."

"I don't understand, Mick." Her head was spinning. "I don't know how this all comes together."

"I know I'm not making much sense. I'm trying." He stopped,

scrubbed at his goatee. "Okay. Let me try this again. I started having these thoughts about kink back in high school and I felt like they were wrong. Crazy, maybe. I didn't want to pollute you with the dirt going on in my head. Those urges got stronger as I grew older. By the time I was getting ready to leave for college, I was convinced I would ruin you somehow. I was barely eighteen—what did I know? I didn't understand myself what was happening to me."

"But we were together that one time when we were in college. And after that night I never heard from you again." She couldn't keep the anger out of her voice. "That tortured me, Mick! Because that night was . . . transcendent for me. I knew exactly what I wanted—what I'd fantasized about for such a long time. Things I could barely comprehend. I cried because it was so beautiful to me. Beautiful because it was with *you*. And then you took it all away from me."

"I know. It wasn't that I didn't trust you. I didn't trust myself. And after that, I knew how much I'd hurt you by disappearing, and I felt even more like an asshole who could never deserve you. But things got even worse."

"The accident," she said, her chest going tight.

"Yeah. The accident. That pretty much ruined me. I've known it this whole time, when I've allowed myself to consciously think about it at all, which hasn't been too often. And . . . well, I'm a guy, and I admit we're not always the most enlightened of the species."

"Agreed. Go on."

She knew she wasn't being very nice, with Mick laying his soul out on the table. But she was still as pissed off as she was hurt. Almost, anyway. The anger was helping her to keep a lid on her emotions. To keep her from throwing her arms around him and simply forgiving him everything because it damn well hurt to see that Mick having to say these things out loud—to say them to her—was tearing him apart.

"So," he went on, "I need to talk to you about the accident, Allie. In a way I've never talked to anyone about it. Maybe not even to myself—and I swear I'm not saying this because I want pity or to scare you. I almost died that day. They told me I should have, given the speed of the impact and what happened to the bike. You asked me about my Latin tattoo? *Non Timebo Mala*—'I will fear no evil.' It's about that. About having faced death. My own stupidity. And over the years it's come to mean all kinds of things. Facing the dark place inside me that drives the kink. Trying to learn not to fear . . . anything. It's a process. Life is a process. I didn't know until you came back into my life that you—us being together—was a part of it. Not that we're evil, of course, but that I perceived being close to you as an evil because I was afraid to do it. I don't know, it doesn't translate directly. Am I making any sense?"

"Yes. I think so."

He went back to lean against the tile counter and closed his eyes for a moment. "Okay. Back to the accident. I don't know if you understand what it's like to have the reputation of generations before you to live up to. It's not a conscious expectation, but it's there all the same. It's almost genetic in my family. We always knew exactly what we'd do with our lives, my brothers and I. There was no question. We were all a little bad, the Reid kids, but everyone fell into line when it was time to get serious about becoming a firefighter. Except me. I took it too far. Far enough that there was no coming back. And that ended everything for me.

"I was nothing but a walking—barely—black mood for a good year after. Jamie helped me with that. I think he was just glad not to have lost another friend. He was still pretty fucked up about Brandon when I went and wrapped my fucking motorcycle around that tree. It was a shitty thing to do to him. To my mother . . . Christ." He shook his head, his gray eyes going dark. "I remember thinking I was glad you weren't around to see it. By the time I saw you again, I'd convinced myself I was over it. Which really means I'd stuffed it way down deep. But it was always lurking under the surface, waiting to come out in some ugly way."

She knew she should say something, murmur some words of encouragement, but all she could do was nod for him to continue. It hurt like hell to hear it all. To hear in detail what he'd gone through. Hadn't she been asking him to tell her this? But it was almost too hard now, when it felt as if an ocean lay between them—a distance she felt she had to maintain. Her fingers flexed in her lap.

He ran a hand over his hair. "That's when the fighting started. Just the sparring at the gym at first, but it wasn't long before I found the underground fight circuit. Easy enough to find if you're really looking for it, especially in a city like New Orleans. You came back to town after I'd had my first few fights, which is the only reason I even dared to be with you—because the fighting was there to help me burn off some of the anger and the guilt. The only reason I had to believe I could keep my shit together around you. But I couldn't. Not with you. And I've always regretted it."

"Mick, I wanted you so badly that night. I thought we might . . . I thought it could be a new start for us."

"So did I."

"But . . ." She was flabbergasted.

"I couldn't control myself, Allie. I thought you were crying because I'd fucking *hurt* you. Because you thought I was some kind of monster. I couldn't face you. I was a Goddamn coward. It's taken me all these years to forgive myself for that. And the only way I could even begin to was the first time I had you under my hands when you came back to New Orleans. When you forced me to begin to see you as you were—the kink and the purity all wrapped up together. It's slowly been forcing me to see these things we do as they should be seen. As I should have seen it all along—as something beautiful in itself. As something that's only warped by our own motivation. Mine hasn't been clean because I've been bringing in all this wreckage from my past. I haven't come to it from the right place—from a clean place—until I came from a place of love. Don't you see? *You're* my redemption."

"God, Mick, please don't say that." The tears welled again. One slipped down her cheek.

"Why not? It's the truth."

"It's not. I manipulated you. I had no right—"

"You did. But you did it because you loved me."

"Is love supposed to excuse anything?"

"Not anything, maybe. But sometimes. It was sure as hell the right reason to bulldog me into being with you."

She had to smile a little through the tears then. "I did bulldog you, didn't I?"

"You are not a woman to be messed with," he told her, moving closer, one corner of his mouth quirking for a moment before sobering once more. "I'm sorry I ever did, Allie. I'm sorry I couldn't just love you. But I do now. I love you so damn much I don't know how to exist without you. These last few days have been hell."

"For me, too, Mick. I was arguing with myself the whole time. Trying to stay away because I felt I had to. But knowing you were hurt . . ." She had to stop, a sob catching in her throat.

"Baby, don't cry."

His arms went around her, and he lifted her to her feet so he could hold her close. Nothing had ever felt better to her in her life. But she couldn't stop the tears.

"Hey," he said again, his voice gentle. "I'm right here, baby girl. I'm not going anywhere unless you tell me to. Is that why you're crying? Because you want this over?"

Her heart was going to break. "Stop it, Mick. Don't say that to me. I can't take it."

"Then tell me what this means," he said quietly. "Tell me."

She slipped her arms around his neck and looked up into his beautiful gray eyes—the eyes of the man she'd loved her whole life.

"It means I want to be with you. It means I love you so damn much I don't even know where to begin. It means you can be an idiot sometimes, and I'm damn glad you see it, but if you ever end up in the hospital again I'm going to kill you, Mick Reid!"

He laughed as his arms tightened around her until she could barely breathe. "Remind me never to fuck with you."

"Oh, I will."

His face went still as he looked at her, as they both let love tremble through them, between them. He inched closer until she could feel his breath on her lips. She tilted her chin.

"I'm gonna kiss you, Allie," he whispered against her mouth.

She nodded. "Yes you are."

He pulled her up on her toes as he lowered his mouth to hers. Just a sweet press of his lush lips, then harder until she felt that familiar sense of command that was the Dom in him. She gave herself over to it, to him. She couldn't help herself. Any remaining argument she might have had emptied from her mind. All that was left was what was in her heart, and the heat blazing between them.

Her hands smoothed over his shoulders, and she loved the hard muscle there. Then down his strong arms to where they were clasped behind her back.

He kept kissing her as their bodies went hot, then hotter, desire and emotion blending together. It was all one thing—it was all just *need* for him.

He pulled free and kissed her neck, working his way up until he kissed that tender spot just below her ear.

"I need you, baby," he murmured. "I need to feel you. To taste you. To own you."

"Yes, Mick. Please."

He stroked her hair, kissed her cheek, her jaw, before pulling her nightgown over her head, leaving her naked before him.

"So beautiful," he said, awe in his voice as his hands swept over her breasts. "The most beautiful woman I've ever seen."

She moaned when he bent to kiss her breasts, his lips brushing across her nipples. Desire heated her blood, her nipples going hard beneath his touch, her sex going wet. He filled his big hands with her breasts, kneading them, then slipping down over her ribs, her stomach.

"Mick . . . God, I need you."

"You have me, my baby," he told her softly. "You have me."

He went down on his knees and her hands went into his hair. His breath was hot against her belly, then lower.

"Oh . . ."

He kissed her over and over at that sweet juncture of hip and thigh, then moved in until his mouth feathered over the tip of her clitoris. Using his fingers, he parted the swollen folds and kissed her there, quick, tender kisses. Slowly they became more lingering—just his soft mouth until she thought she'd go mad as need built inside her.

"Mick."

"Shh."

He bent once more and used his hot, wet tongue on her, licking at the lips of her sex, still holding her open with his fingers. Her fingers dug into his scalp as her legs went weak.

Oh, his mouth was good. He licked her, finally, and she arched her hips. He licked her again, one long, slow stroke from the top of her hood and all the way down. She parted her thighs and he slipped his thumbs inside her.

"Ah . . ."

He began a slow stroking cadence, his thumbs pushing in, sliding out, his tongue gliding over her flesh, making her crazy with the need to come. She bit her lip, held it back, knowing it would be all the better if she did.

Then suddenly he shifted, three fingers plunging into her soaking-wet sex as he sucked her hard clit into his mouth.

"Oh!"

She came all at once, pleasure surging into her. Lips and teeth and tongue and plunging fingers filling her, and God, she'd never come so hard in her life. Stars flashed behind her closed eyes, bursting into flame, dazzling her with their brilliance—with the brilliance of the sensation pouring into her body like white lightning.

Before she was done he was on his feet, kissing her again, pulling her into his arms, then lifting her and carrying her into her bedroom.

He set her on the bed and was on top of her in an instant, his big body pressing her into the mattress. She could feel his hard cock through his damp clothes. She scrabbled at the hem of his shirt with blind fingers until he pushed off her long enough to pull it over his head.

Her hands went to his tight abs, smoothed up to his chest— she *had* to touch him, to know he was real.

Her heart surged when she looked up to find him watching her, his eyes filled with love and desire so intense it made her squirm.

"So damn beautiful," he told her.

"Mick, I need you. Now. Please."

He slipped out of his sweats and laid his body over hers once more. He slid a hand down her thigh, paused to tickle at the back of her knee before moving down her calf.

"I love this body," he said. "I've loved it all my life. I've loved *you* all my life. I'll love you for the rest of it, Allie girl."

"I love you, Mick. So much."

His hands went to her hips and he lifted them. She spread her thighs wider and wrapped her legs around his back, needing him.

He paused at the entrance to her body, his gaze locking with hers, and she felt his love in that steady gaze. Felt it course through her, making her shiver. With love. With need. She reached for his hands and his fingers clasped hers, holding on tight, lifting her arms over her head as he slid into her.

"Ah, Allie . . . baby . . ."

She watched as his face went loose with pleasure, as the same pleasure coursed through her. He began to move and she moved with him, every lovely motion liquid, sinuous, as though they moved with one body. One desire.

He turned them both until she lay on top of him, their hands still clasped above their heads. He surged up into her, his cock instantly hitting her G-spot. Pleasure blazed, searing her as the need to come took her over once more. She paused at that keen, lovely edge.

"I can feel you, baby girl. So hot inside. I can feel you . . . clench around me. Come for me, baby. Come with me."

"Yes . . ."

She let it happen as he bucked into her over and over, her climax flooding her until she was drunk with pleasure, drunk with him. And she felt the stinging current of his own climax inside her as he called her name.

"Allie . . . my baby . . . my girl."

He let her hands free and wrapped her in his arms, holding her tight. He kissed her hair, his breath rough against her cheek, then he took her face in his palms and kissed her hard. His sweet tongue slid into her mouth, and they were making out as they'd done in high school—everything that hot, that desperate even now, after they'd both come. But the need was more about the pure need to be together. To love each other.

Finally they slowed down, until it was simply one soft kiss after another. A press of lips, a slow delicious glide of tongues. Finally he held her head to his chest. His heart was a hammering beat against her cheek. Everything about the moment was exactly what she needed.

They lay together while the rain fell outside—she could hear the soft patter against the leaves in her garden. Could almost feel the rain and the clouds like a soft blanket holding them in the city's arms. And knew, finally, she was home.

THEY'D HAD A glorious week together—or almost. Mick had been called away for work on Thursday night. It was Saturday night and Allie couldn't wait to see him. But the anticipation of seeing him again wasn't the only cause of the butterflies in her stomach, the breathlessness that was making her dizzy as she knelt on the floor at the foot of the big four-poster bed behind her.

He had told her he'd arrive at The Bastille at nine o'clock, and she knew it must be nearly nine. She glanced around the Victorian-themed room, where he'd instructed her to wait for him—the damask wallpaper, the carved furnishings, then down at the ornate red-and-gold Persian rug. She knew she'd done exactly as he'd asked—dressed in the ivory silk waist-cincher corset that had arrived at her house that morning, and nothing else. But in her hand she held the one surprise she had for him.

Her fingers stroked over the leather, and she inhaled, taking in the earthy scent.

If only he would hurry. But it was Mick, and she knew he wouldn't.

She closed her eyes and took in a slow breath, exhaled the way she'd been taught, trying to center herself. And had barely managed to get her pounding heart to calm when she heard the door open.

Mick.

"Good girl."

Ah, the words that always made her melt, and he knew it. She felt her body yielding, her mind following. Her heart was already there.

She looked up and smiled at him as he drew her to her feet. He was so handsome in his dark jeans, his black shirt rolled up at the cuffs, revealing the strong muscles of his forearms. Then those arms were around her, and she was being crushed against the hard planes of his chest as his mouth came down on hers. He kissed her hard, bit her lip, drew it out between his teeth before letting it go to bury his head in her neck. He kissed the tender skin, bit her there, letting his teeth sink in just until she gasped.

He pulled back, smiling at her. "I missed you, baby girl."

"I missed you."

He stroked her hair. "Are you ready for tonight?"

"Yes. I'm ready."

"I can tell you're sinking down already, Allie. I hear it in your voice. I see it in your eyes. In the flush of your pretty skin."

"Yes, Mick."

He ran his hands over her arms. "Hey. What have we here?" he asked as he found the leather blindfold.

"It's my gift to you."

His brows drew together, emotion in his intense gray gaze. "Allie, are you certain you want this?"

"I trust you, Mick. I needed to show you. This was the only way I could think of."

"Baby, you know we don't renegotiate once we're in scene, once you're subspaced."

"I bought this the other day, a few hours after you left. I made the decision then. I love you so much. And I can't really love you without the trust, can I? I have to believe we're working together on whatever our future will become. I have to believe in you. And because I do, I don't have anything to be afraid of, do I?"

"Not from me. I promise you that. Never again."

"I know it. So please, Mick. Cover my eyes and let tonight be a mystery of sensation for me. I want to let go of this last boundary. With you. Only with you."

He stroked a hand along her jaw, his gaze holding hers. "My baby."

"Yes," she said softly, her heart filled with love.

He led her to the high bed and sat her on the edge of it while he went to get his rope bag that she'd brought with her. Her body was softening all over, waiting for the night to begin. To feel the embrace of the ropes. *His* ropes.

Mick.

He laid the different lengths of well-washed jute on the bed in their bundles while she waited, then he turned to her. He leaned in and kissed her eyes closed, then he slipped the leather over them and tied the blindfold at the back of her head. There was no panic for her—only a sensation of lightness, then focus as she became aware of her individual senses. She smelled the citrusy scent of the soap he used, took in the distant beat of the trance music playing in the club somewhere, the quiet cadence of his breathing. Felt the soft cotton sheets on the bed beneath her thighs. The corset tight around her waist, forcing her to sit up straighter, to breathe into the upper portion of her lungs. And her body was responding in some unexpected way—her nipples going hard, her sex damp.

No panic. Only utter trust and exquisite desire.

She gasped softly as Mick kissed her shoulders, her bare breasts, before she felt the mattress give as he got onto the bed behind her.

He drew her arms behind her, crossed behind the small of her back, and the first loop of rope slid around her wrists. With her eyes covered she felt the silky slip and pull of the rope even more keenly. Felt Mick's command more acutely. Knew in a new way that she was his.

He pulled the rope through her arms, binding them together from wrist to elbow. And with each moment her body let loose a little more, sank into the giving of herself to his command.

When her arms were secure, he slid more rope beneath her breasts, making a chest harness, binding her breasts, the rope winding over and under and ending in a series of knots between them. She felt the bed shifting as he got off it, then his hand gripping the rope between her breasts. All at once his knuckles dug into her flesh as he pulled her to her feet.

"Oh!"

But she was melting, loving being handled this way, his hands rough on her. He yanked her in close to his body, his knuckles biting into her flesh. The pain released a lovely rush of endorphins, and even though she was already in subspace, she was aware of her head growing lighter in a way she never had been before. The blindfold made it all the more intense. Lovely.

"You good, baby girl? Tell me," he demanded.

"Yes. So good, Mick."

"Excellent."

He pulled hard on the chest harness again, and she stumbled, but he caught her. He did it again, and again, his knuckles digging in hard as she lost her footing, as he righted her against his solid frame. And she came to realize distantly that it was all working to gain her trust even more—the way he caught her each time. She knew he would never let her fall. She smiled to herself.

A small chuckle from him. "This making you happy, my girl?"

"Yes, Mick."

"Very good. Hold still for me now."

Leaving one hand on her body, she felt a cooling of the air as he leaned away from her. Then the soft kiss of the rope being swept over her shoulders and between her thighs.

She moaned softly, went soaking wet.

He slid the ropes over the lips of her sex, and she groaned aloud. He pulled the rope tight as he wound it through her chest harness, making it press tight against the hard nub of her clit, and she gasped. And went dizzy when he picked her up and laid her on her back on the bed.

"Spread," he commanded, and she obeyed.

She heard a buzz . . . and before she could even grasp what he was doing, he touched a vibrator to the rope between her breasts. The buzz reverberated, seeming to spread all over her body, to shiver in the rope between her thighs.

It felt so good, was so unexpected, she tried to draw her thighs closed, but he forced them apart with one hand.

"Just take it, baby girl. Take it and hang on to it until I say you can come."

She bit her lip as he turned up the speed on the vibrator.

"You look so damn gorgeous like this," Mick said, his voice heavy with desire. "I'm so hard for you, my baby. And I can see how wet you are. You know I love that."

He reached down and swiped at her sex, pressed the swollen lips together around the doubled length of rope between them, making the vibration even more intense.

"Oh!"

"Not yet," he ordered her.

She had to fight hard not to squirm. Not to come. But she would do it. For him.

Mick.

"I'm going to tie the vibrator to you now."

"Oh, God."

"Shh. Quiet."

She was struggling not to writhe on the bed as he did exactly as he'd said—used a length of rope around her hips to anchor the shivering vibe to her body. Pleasure sang through every nerve.

"Be still. I'm right here."

He lost contact with her for several moments, then she felt him press the vibrator harder against the ropes.

"Come, baby girl. Now!"

Her body let loose, her climax crashing down on her, a wave of pure pleasure so strong it made her scream. And even as her throat grew sore with her screams, the ropes between her thighs were cut away and she was impaled by Mick's thick shaft.

She started coming all over again as he sank into her, as he bit into the soft skin of her neck.

"Oh! Oh . . ."

He pulled her blindfold away, and she blinked as she came, pleasure spiraling, a fever that wouldn't stop burning through her.

"Baby," Mick muttered, his face above her a torn mask of desire. "I need you. You're mine. Mine, baby girl."

He kept his gaze on hers as he came, his eyes glittering, a bottomless silver pool. And when they were both done, their bodies stilled, he kept watching her, gazes locked, the towering heights of desire calming into something more solid. Into the steady beat of their hearts. The steady beat of the love between them.

"Love you, my baby."

"Love you, Mick."

And it was true—the only truth that mattered.

The past was behind them, finally. Exactly as it should be. All that mattered was right now. The way they felt about each other. And the future they would share.

DON'T MISS THE NEXT DANGEROUS ROMANCE
FROM EDEN BRADLEY

Dangerously Broken

Coming in 2015 from Berkley Books